"An engrossing, brilliantly crafted read. A searing commentary on the earth and its inhabitants... A controversial, Kafkaesque narrative of life. Melikian is an astonishing writer who teaches his reader about life and the human condition through tragedy and humor."

—ForeWord Reviews

"The author has moved ahead of the zeitgeist. The self-confident writing is of high quality. The novel is ambitious and certainly breaks new ground."

—Writer's Digest

"A novel completely different than anything I have ever read before."

—Paige Lovitt, Reader Views

"A book unlike any other... A very intelligently written, original work of fiction... A book quite out of the ordinary."

—Kam Aures, Rebecca's Reads

"A fun and enlightening read and is quite the recommendation."

—Midwest Book Review

"In its cynicism, non-conformity, and linguistic fireworks, *Journey to Virginland* is of unquestionable merit."

—Literary Journal KRITIIKKI (Finland)

"*Journey to Virginland* could be the next bestseller. Give it a try, it's certainly different."

—Bookpleasures

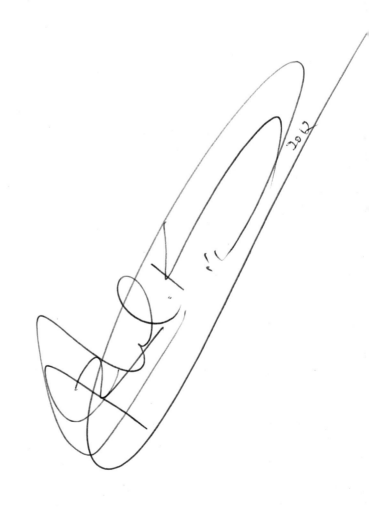

I wasn't quite sure what to expect when I decided to read your novel. But what I most certainly did not expect was to find, consistently, one of the most creatively, philosophically, culturally, semantically, and thematically ambitious novels I've ever read in my 35 years of professional life.

In the best sense, I'm reminded of George Orwell's classics, and other authors of similar stature, though there is no true parallel possible with a novel and trilogy as unique in concept and execution as *Journey to Virginland.*

I am struck by the extraordinary writing, vision, and, perhaps rarest of all, originality, which abounds in every way, and at so many levels and depths of meaning, theme, narrative, etc., that I had to keep slowing my pace, until I could read and "inhale" each word.

A case in point was the passage containing Dog's dialogue with the Padre, which I found positively entrancing. This section's insights and leaps of imagination, manifested through Dog's answers, are as revelatory and profound as the basic aspects and elements of his overall perceptions and conclusions about the book's overarching subjects, which have been gradually introduced and interwoven, from the beginning of the novel to here, where they... explode.

Now that I've reached the conclusion, I am simply in awe. Wow! in the vernacular.

Paul McCarthy, Professor of English
University of Ulster, Ireland
[25 years Senior Acquisitions Editor at Simon & Schuster,
Harper Collins, and Doubleday]

JOURNEY TO
VIRGINLAND

CATENA

ARMEN MELIKIAN

JOURNEY TO VIRGINLAND

CATENA

Trafford
PUBLISHING®
A Penguin Books Company

Journey to Virginland: Catena
Published by Trafford Publishing
A Penguin Books Company
1663 Liberty Drive
Bloomington, IN 47403
North America & international
888.232.4444 (USA & Canada)
phone: 250 383 6864   fax 812 355 4082
www.trafford.com

This is a work of fiction. Names, characters, places, or incidents are the product of
the author's imagination or are used fictitiously. Any resemblance to actual persons,
whether living or dead, events, or locales is entirely coincidental.

Publisher's Cataloging-in-Publication Data

Melikian, Armen

       Journey to Virginland : Catena / Armen Melikian. – Bloomington,
       Indiana: Trafford Publishing, 2012.

       p. ; cm.

ISBN13: 978-1-4669-6178-4 (hc)
ISBN10: 1-4669-6178-3 (hc)
ISBN13: 978-1-4669-6176-0 (sc)
ISBN10: 1-4669-6176-7 (sc)
ISBN13: 978-1-4669-6177-7 (e)

      1. Dystopias—Fiction. 2. United States—Social conditions—Fiction.
    3. Social ethics—Fiction. 4. Social problems in literature. I. Title.

PS3613.E45J68 2012
813.6—dc22   2012917644

10 9 8 7 6 5 4 3 2 1

Dedicated to the "whores" of Virginland

"I swear to you, Athenians, by the dog I swear!—for I must tell you the truth. The result of my mission was just this: I found that the men of highest repute were all but the most foolish; and that some inferior men were really wiser and better."

Socrates

SOLILOQUY

They call me dog. Don't ask who. Them. All of them.

From April 11, 2006, until March 21, 2003, almost every day between 4:11 and 4:03 a.m., the shadow of a dog kept appearing above my bed. At first she was silent. She stayed for some time, then left. She looked glum and seemed to wish to relay something. One day, when I tried to touch the apparition, she barked. I was startled. The voice came from afar, as though from a different world. When one night, already used to the presence, I unconsciously muttered, "Who are you?" the spirit answered. The following night, she told me to write down everything she was to relate in the course of the next three years.

She spoke. I listened. No one else heard her speak. Months into our nightly routine, even my father, who was under my care and slept in the adjacent room, didn't hear a word the dog said. By then the spirit had begun appearing wherever I happened to be, even in daylight. It could visit me anywhere, at any time—while I'd be sitting in a café, reading at the library, making love, or meeting with clergy. I sought clinical help but ignored the treatment. I was no longer upset by the presence. There were even moments when I felt that I *was* the dog—as though she were my soul's reflection or a reminiscence of a dead past. Often I caught myself speaking like her.

She asked me to record everything she recounted, including events from my own life, down to the minutae. We melded together so thoroughly that I could no longer distinguish her thoughts from mine. Sometimes it seemed to me that I had stopped thinking for myself. Rather, it was the dog that led me in my feelings, thoughts, daily conduct, and speech—which, naturally, looked rather bizarre to those around me. When it dawned on me that no one, not even the doctors, understood what was happening to me, I decided to share my secret with my readers. Everything in this book is a faithful record of what the dog has told me, in her own words. If I have committed errors or faltered, it is due to my human foibles.

Anthropoids refuse to believe that these pages recount a human biography. They aver that this is a nefarious distortion of their sublime nature. Let bipeds simmer in their sentiments. On my part, I can't allow humanoid extrapolation alter the nature of the work. That would be a betrayal of my dog. She is the true author. I don't exist here. But no! Perhaps I am a dog after all.

Here lies

Ugly Dog

Born Anno Domini 2006

Slain Anno Domini 2003

Lived not a day.

He barked these words before he died:

"They called the great Arab poet a dog.

The poet replied, 'Dog is he who knows not

the 70 names of the dog.'

Dog has as many names as God."

THE WORLD
According to Dog

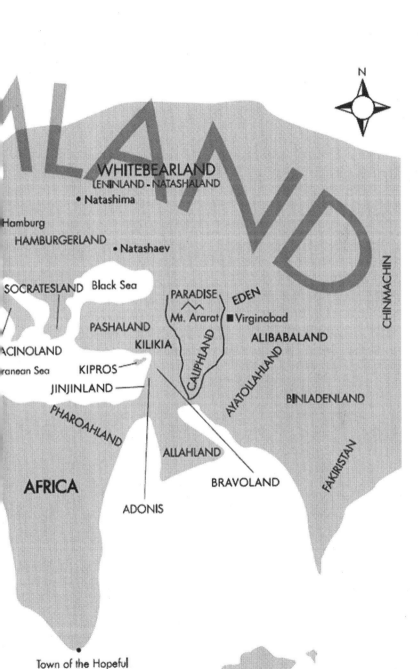

CATENA

I head home an hour before twilight from my research at the National Library of the Academy of Sciences of Virginland. The sleepless nights have worn me down. I need to unwind. The day has lengthened, the biting cold retreated. But it's still early to go to Natashima. Out on the courtyard, the dogs are having a veritable feast—once again the trash trucks haven't showed up. All for the better—my buddies are still alive. Ever since the army unleashed Operation Kill the Dogs, I get a jolt whenever I hear the clatter of machine gun fire echoing from indefinite directions. Sometimes I feel glad I wasn't born a dog.

But really, am I, in fact, not a dog?

At any rate, I'm not in a particularly doglike frame of mind when the doorbell rings. It's Kathy. She always calls before coming over. I sense that something is amiss. True enough, she is crying. I've never seen tears in her eyes.

Kathy is a tough one, with a knack for getting even more practical when facing a crisis. She takes my cock into her hearth, leaning against the wall in a doggy position, arms outstretched, hissing through her sobs, "Fuck me... Fuck me... Oh... fuck!"

Kathy tells me, in a nutshell, what she'd been through today, and then vanishes into the same taxi that had brought her here, whose driver she had instructed to park and wait for her in the empty lot across from the University of Satan in Virginabad.

I'm left in a daze, where all this feels like a dream. It takes me a while to regain a foothold on consciousness.

Kill the dog!

Sex is outlawed in Virginland.

For months, Kathy has been waiting to hear from the Treasury Department of God, where she had applied for a job. She certainly had the chops. A certified accountant, she had mastered a number of computer programs. Moreover, she had investigated and eventually exposed two major mafia clans that had colluded with Treasury employees to siphon off tax revenues to the tune of several million washingtons. Her good work enabled God to retrieve the loot. Given Virginland's political climate in those days, this was an intricate and ominous affair, a stunt that Kathy nonetheless pulled off with great skill.

Still, the clans, which satiated themselves at the expense of the Redeemed and the Creator, went unpunished. A disdain for the law was the norm among the law-enforcement agencies of Paradise, with the Redeemed bearing the consequences. It was like this: Satan's good efforts brought about Leninstan's collapse, making it possible for Paradise to become independent and duly turn its muzzle to the United Nations of Man. What followed was a stampede of a million wraiths, while a famished God, at the head of a procession of piggish archangels, conquered Virginland-Paradise in the wink of an eye.

There was a time when I worked in Hell, advocating for the rights of those who had bolted from Paradise, fighting the corrupt officials of Satan's government. I was cross with Satan, who was cross with me. A friend of mine, a film producer, conveyed to me the exploits of her policeman lovers. One of these men—who shared my sexy, blue-eyed friend's bed and the spectacular views of Los Babylonos from her West Hellwood penthouse one night—bragged about his naughtiness, in this case his killing of a black Satanite that day.

When police dogs were taught sniffing techniques as part of their training, their classmates (including former cops) talked about the relationship of police officers and criminal outfits—their proxies at large—whose deeds often went uninvestigated. These groups were expected to commit select crimes recommended by the police themselves.

Satan's prosecutors regularly cherry-picked cases based on the race of the suspects. His detectives likewise had total discretion as to which cases actually reached the courts. The net effect was that Satan's ethnic minorities got the short end of the stick, sometimes facing financial ruin.

Gehendale's Paradisean émigrés were abhorred by the true followers of our Lord Satan, Everlasting Father of the Universe, Blessed and Only Potentate. There was nothing frivolous about such aversion. Take my father, for instance—a diehard Paradise fan, he nonetheless felt revulsion at the comportment of its former denizens. We'd be in stitches whenever he described them in his inimitable style.

There was a swarm of paradisoids behind bars in Hell. Their number reached 14,400. Were Paradise to function by the same legal standards as Hell, some 144,000 out of each million of the former's emancipated lambs, along with the entirety of God's apparatus, would have to be jailed.

As to how the Demoncratic Imperium of Gehenna, aka the United Tribes of Amerhenna (UTA), fended itself against the misdeeds of Paradiseans, I was given an inkling by an attorney friend. He defended cases involving paradisoids who had robbed the pharma mines of Satan's Golden State. He spoke of the ways and means employed by our Lord's federal investigators. Comparing them to the KGB, he said this remorseless dragon's treatment of the underdog was more human (i.e., doglike) than that of the Feds with whom he dealt.

Back in Paradise, God's prosecutors have zeroed in on the downtrodden just as God's gendarmes follow the scent of hard cash, going about their business in the floodlight of the Almighty's smirk.

I was disillusioned with the Paradiseans—the nation of the Redeemed—disillusioned with their mentality. I stopped defending them against Satan. My decision was based in no small measure on their dark halo. These folks had so excelled at the métier of whitewashing their crimes that they could make Marx (God save us from him) sound like Jesus (holy be his name). This propensity is a hallmark of oppressed peoples that have survived the narrow path leading to God.

True, the Redeemed were neither the only criminal segment nor the worst of the ethnic groups helping themselves to Satanic plenitude. But apart from some emblematic character flaws, they elicited disgust with their inclination to rob our Lord Satan, Captain of Our Salvation, the Sure Foundation; their untrustworthiness in word and deed; and their soft spot for sharing the possessions of their neighbors, wife and ass included. These were all relics of Papa Lenin's commandments of universal brotherhood. Although their covetousness has been rather subdued of late on account of Satan's lashes, it has, alas, gained proportionate vehemence with regard to canines.

The prophet Marx, who went up to Heaven in a whirlwind by the fiery horses of God after completing his mission in the telluric cavern, has left an indelible mark on Paradise. Here, everything that occurs under the sun, including the Exodus of the 144,000 to Gehenna, is explained in terms of economics. The angels insist that life was comfier in communist Paradise. They also put the blame for their present social ills squarely on Satan's runaway capitalism.

Wrong!

My childhood memories teem with thousands of compatriots who had settled in Dreamland's Adonis Province after surviving a holocaust that scorched Paradise. Adonis is a purely capitalistic hub on the Mediterranean coast— so much so that the UTA can be considered a communist country in comparison. Many who resettled in Adonis had it much worse than the survivors in Paradise, yet they were strangers to the above social ills. My civics teacher, an Adonis native, liked to reiterate the point that the 250,000-strong Paradisean community of Adonis was that land's most trustworthy segment, with only one member serving a prison sentence.

The Satanic Eye was cognizant of this fact. In Hell, whenever someone with the appearance of a paramecium— lapsus calami, read paradicium—was pulled over, the police first checked whether the suspect originally hailed from Dreamland or Paradise itself, and proceeded accordingly. Paradise was infected with the Lenino autoimmune syndrome. Yet Satan's political interests moved him to lure 144,000 angels to Hell.

I learned my geography at the Dream Elementary School in Dreamland. My teacher was Miss Mary. Miss Mary used a long stick to point things out on a large wall atlas, as follows:

There are two countries in the world: Dreamland and Africa. Dreamland is a big country. Its borders are: to the north, the North Pole; to the south, the South Pole; to the east, the birthplace of the sun; and to the west, the sun's grave. Dreamland changes its capital four times every century.

Paradise is Dreamland's navel—its omphalus. Paradise is wedged between three seas, hence Triangle 1. Paradise has three lakes at its heart, hence Triangle 2. What we have then are two interlaced triangles—thus the Star of the Slinger, which Maimunus stole from the sons of Paradise before he tricked the sons of man into believing that his land is God's country.

Much of Paradise has been devoured by Pasha. Pasha is a voracious animal. He has black horns, a rhino keras, scavenger teeth, and a long tail. When he howls, the mountains shake. When Pasha was getting ready to chomp the last bones of the Redeemed, Papa Lenin snatched a morsel from his mouth and kicked him out of the graveyard. This is why the Redeemed love Papa Lenin and hate Osman Pasha.

A country was created in the graveyard and christened Virginland, with Papa Lenin according the name his thumbs-up. Papa Lenin took exception to the names Paradise and Godland. However, being a schnook, he didn't quite realize that in the Paradisean language Virginland is not only synonymous with Paradise, it expresses its very essence. The Redeemed pulled the wool over Papa Lenin's eyes and never forgot the country's ancient name, Paradise, to this day glorifying it in their songs and books. Virginland's capital is Virginabad. Noteworthy attractions include Virgintorch, Virginville, Virgin Valley, Virgins Province, the city of Saint Virginborn, and Noah's Grave.

Today God dwells in Virginland.

Satan dwells in Satanland (i.e., Gehenna or Hell), which is situated in the far west, where sits the sun's necropolis.

The capital of Satanland is Gehennington†, where tribes-men have the curious tradition of reading from right to left. Thus, for instance, dog is read god—something that we canines find rather offensive. Satanland includes such mem-orable destinations as Hellwood, Gehendale, Santa Varvara, Las Fortunas, and Los Babylonos, which angels fleeing from Paradise to Hell renamed Los Angelos. Intent on cracking the enigma of why the moon dies twelve times a year and rises three days after each death, Satan obtained a dispensation from God to install himself on the moon, whence he watches over the earth's well-being. Thanks to the efforts of the State of Calipornia, Satanland was recently rechristened Pornstan, and its capital was relocated to Porn City.

To the south of Gehenna is Mariamstan, where the Virgin Mary is universally worshipped. Magdalene is the official language. Sitting at the helm of this realm is Castro Peron, the two-headed dragon.

Other things I've learned from Miss Mary:

After Satanland, the most famous provinces of Dream-land are Eyfelia, Shakespeareland, and Mercedesland. Eyfelia is ruled by Napoleon Bonaparte. Its capital is Napoli. The king of Shakespeareland is Shakespeare, who always smokes a cigar. The capital is Elizabeth City. Mercedesland is vari-ously called Führerland and Hamburgerland, depending on the doctrine of the ruling political party of the day. The capi-tal is Hamburg. This dominion is ruled alternately by Führer BenYehu and Mercedes the Shaitan.

Leninstan is the largest province of Dreamland. For a brief period, it was named Gorbachovland, but that was before it was destroyed by an earthquake. The survivors created a modest province called Kremlinland, which is known to foreigners as Natashaland. Kremlinlanders are God-fearing. Despite their horrid misfortunes, they never fail to pay tribute to the Almighty.

Sitting quietly on this side of Pasha's empire is Grand Ayatollah, who vigilantly monitors Pasha's steps. Lying on the other side of Pasha's empire is Socratesland, where the official language is Byzantish, where there is constant philos-

---

† Hellington in the Byzantish original.

ophizing as to how many angels can fit on the head of a pin. This is why Pasha captured their capital, where he installed the throne of his mobile empire. As for the angels, he grilled and ate them.

Dreamland also includes a large and populous province, Chinmachin, whose monarch is quite fond of the King of Kings, Holy of Holies of Paradise. They say that the ruler of Chinmachin has even given his daughter's hand to the King of Kings of Paradise. Nothing is known about Chinmachin because, like the planet Venus, it is covered by mysterious clouds. Rumor has it that God himself has yet to solve the mystery. As for the princess who has been given in marriage, it is believed that her brain juices were drained out before she arrived in Paradise. As a result, the Redeemed lady remembers nothing about her past.

There are still other provinces in Dreamland, such as Allahland and Maimunland. The latter is ruled by the brothers Maimunus and Jinjinus. Whence the name Jinjinland often used in popular parlance. Jinjinus, the younger, awaits his brother every evening with a bowl of soup in hand as the latter returns from the fields tired, and labors to convince him to change the name of Maimunland to Jinjinland. Legend says that the elder never budges and that he shan't budge till the end of time. Sibling rivalry does not prevent them from sustaining their joint venture, a limited partnership, The Chosen Bros., with offices in various capitals of Dreamland, where they keep bickering as to who shall carry the title Chosen. For which reason, the masses of Dreamland, having more important affairs to dream about, have crowned both Maimunus and Jinjinus with the title "The Chosen One" by law and by might.

Though relatively insignificant provinces of Dreamland, Allahland and Maimunland are perpetually trying to get their hands on Paradise. This is why God punishes them. Should they continue to misbehave, the Almighty might one day exile them to Africa, where dreamers are eaten raw. Hence the dreamers' bid for teaching Africans how to dream—so they can avoid being munched by them.

My history teacher, Mr. Victor, lectured thusly: Paradise was once a powerful state like Atlantis, but Pasha made it vanish from the earth by pulling an abracadabra. While most of the inhabitants were drowned, some managed to hurl themselves onto boats and eventually reached the four corners of the globe. These children of light carried with them fragments of the ancient civilization, which helped them turn the ubiquitous darkness engulfing the planet into light and forge the colossal empire of Dreamland.

To Dreamlanders, dreaming is the stuff of immortality. They dream and avow that a smoker named God speaks to them. This biped has granted them the countries that stretch from the Nile to the Euphrates, impelling them to massacre all the nations in question.

I learned at the Evangelical Church in Dreamland that the Lord has gifted the Dreamlanders the territories between the Euphrates and Tigris, and more recently the provinces of Pornstan and Kremlinland, and that, were they to pray harder, they would also be gifted Chinmachin (praise the Lord). Dreaming is the official doctrine of Dreamland. The founder of Dreamland is no lesser a personage than He, the Mashiach, Son of the Slinger, Jesus Christ. Holy be his name. He taught the Dreamlanders to dream about the glory of his father, to be martyred in the name of the sempiternal dream.

The most important thing that I learned, however, was from my political-history teacher at the Dream High School, the mysterious Mr. Bagratuni, who came to class once every three months and whom Pasha abhorred. Dreamland's ideology is cronyism. This is in fact a meta-ideology that encompasses all ideologies past, present, and future. Dreamlanders are fierce cronyists. Seething with vengeful malice, they penetrate the wombs and graves of the mothers of all noncompadres, including reptiles, birds, and insects, and stay there for life.

One day, when His Excellency, the Holiest of Holinesses Diabolam Diabolum, was attempting to improve his relations with Dog, he confessed that the police in Gehenna distinguish between fugitive cronyists from Paradise and those from Dreamland. Our Lord Satan's doctrine is the antithesis of Discrimination, D being a euphemism for

God. Nonetheless, its enforcers had no choice but to deviate, so glaring was the evidence against the paradicia.

The Redeemed are troubled by comparisons. They see the hand of the Jinjinist in this. They refuse to admit that there is a monster sitting in their skull. My Paradise-born girlfriend, who once worked for Satan's embassy in Paradise, called me "stupid" for refusing to abuse Satan's system. I respected Satan. Another female friend, a native of Hell, is very fond of her Leninlander girlfriends. She once broke into laughter as she told me they're in the habit of stealing her Eyfelian perfumes every time they to her house. My Leninlander friend, who said she wished to become my spouse, stole twenty washingtons from me.

My wife likewise became convinced one day of my asinine nature, and asseverated that she felt more respect toward a certain couple who had absconded from Paradise to Hell and didn't speak a word of Gehennish. She had met these associates through me. She assailed me for my ignorance regarding the existence of some government-assistance program, which, in my assessment, wasn't worth a kurush.

"You have lived in Hell all these years and what have you learned, asshole?" the assayor of my soul asserted assuasively.

The assumption ass-rocked my marriage for an entire year as she asso believed that Ass had stolen a pair of eyeglasses that belonged to the above-mentioned couple. Her entire assessionary concurred with her. She didn't expect such bassness from me.

I was asstounded. She had never seen, nor would ever see, me commit such an act. To even ssink that I was capable of doing somessing like that... and for what? Some drab object patented by tovarich Stalin, which Ass couldn't have exchanged for a putrid potato†?

† The Gospel According to Horse at this point flaunts the following passage, which is not found in the Byzantish Gospels:

Ass was assuaged when he read the fine print of the Assiento Maritario of the State of Calipornia in the office of the state assignors.

I assent. I assent.

Ass was assummoned to the Supreme Asservatory of Calipornia, where Ass was assieged by the assembly of 12 assissies.

"My assentations, Mater Mater," assonated Assimilado in the Asservatory, and

How horrid it was, brothers, that my wife's group consciousness dominated her marital relationship. I assume, brothers, that religious and ideological zealotry is but a developed form of this very mindset, which to this day ails the world of man.

The assuchness of the matter was... she didn't love me. I was ashamed to ask for handouts from Satan, and for this I was labeled an ass. I was mortified at the thought of getting in line in a supermarket and using food stamps for groceries. This is precisely what many Paradiseans did proudly, often wearing diamond rings and flip-flops as they stood in line, feeling a hauteur surpassing that of a Rockefeller, and not in the least wondering what the Satanites would think of them. If the uncouth wives and children of sheiks presumed to buy someone off with a couple of washingtons, then the Paradisean displayed a similar cockiness vis-à-vis that high school girl working as a supermarket cashier, through the power of food stamps obtained from our Lord Satan, the All-beneficent, Father of the Fatherless.

"Good! These people deserve it. They're the ones who destroyed Paradise."

When Papa Lenin grabbed the graveyard called Paradise from Pasha's jaws, he occulted God Immortal and then made Paradise into a republic. Intent on transforming its denizens into citizens, Papa Lenin promulgated a bolozhenia, whose sixth article reads:

Considering that Osman Pasha has committed atrocities in bear-loving and highly regarded Paradise, has

was assisted out by the associate assistant, after learning the merits of associability and assortative mating. Ass promised no more to be assotted in dogolatry. Ass was assuaded to apply for membership in the Assurgent Order of the Association of Ass Omers (AOAAO, i.e. 10110) in order to be assoiled. Which Ass did assonass he left the Asservatory. At AOAAO Ass learned an assish song:
Assolizie!
Pum pum pum pum pum pum pum, Assolizie!
Pump um pump um pump um pum, Assolizie!
Pump pump pump pump pump pump pump, Assolizie!
... And by and by Ass slowly assopiated.
The Assembly of 12 Assissies assured the people of Calipornia that Ass was assubtlized and could be assubjugated and assumed. Ass has paid full assythment.

devastated the arts and crafts, burned cities and villages, and devoured all creative people, Papa Lenin, king of the world, having in mind the desires and prosperity of his gentle subjects, declares Paradise a protectorate and therein moves to develop the greatest of humanitarian arts, mendicity.

For Paradiseans breaking free of Leninland, it was a time-honored tradition to beg for assistance from the government. That is the reason they moved to Gehenna, having honed their accounting before their exodus. My aunt, who had vamoosed from Paradise with her grandchildren and great-grandchildren, exalted Satan.

"The king of the Soviets is no good," she said. "The king of Amerika is great. God save the king of Amerika."

One day my father ran into the ninetysomething Mrs. Yevnik. "My husband died," she told him. "But God sent me another husband." As my father was taken aback and wanted to know more, she quickly answered, "I mean the Satanic government. Glory to God!"

A Paradise-born friend of mine, who works at Satan's refugee-assistance office, was shocked by the Satanic almoner's irate words about how Paradiseans defrauded His Excelsior. In defense of her compatriots, my friend pointed out a statistical report prepared by the Satan Lies organization, indicating that compared to the other ethnic minorities of Hell, the Redeemed receive but a tiny proportion of government aid. She tried to prove that the lion's share of assistance goes to the stentorian Mariamstanis and Mosmos-worshipping kvetchers from Leninland, if only because the latter are nonpareil at eliciting pity.

The Redeemed feel flattered. But how removed this is from the evaluations of Dreamlanders which this dog had heard from his teachers in puppyhood. "The Dreamers' community that resettled in Adonis is the best among all communities of its host country. You will not find a single Dreamlander beggar here."

The natives of Adonis remembered how in the early days the Dreamlanders, who had just escaped genocide, did not seek alms from the natives but rebuilt their lives through hard work. Within a short time, they became the key players of the economy of Adonis and earned a reputation as honest businesspeople. Often their one word was worth ten contracts. The same held true in all the countries of Allah's desert, where survivors resettled.

The experiences of a girlfriend, an SBI (Satan's Bureau of Investigation) agent, sealed my decision to stop advocating for Paradiseans. Even if there were legal lapses on the part of government agencies, I had resolved not to impede the enforcement of Satan's law, black though it was. My logic was:

"Let them learn to live by the law, so as to amaze even the racist cops. Let them live like my father, who has never caused Satan any trouble, never had a run-in with a police officer, doesn't even know what a court of law looks like."

Despite being a highly qualified candidate for the job she was applying for, Kathy was forced to ask for the support of a top official whom she knew. The man gladly put in a good word for her.

Peering out from his office near Kathy's home, this official was in the habit of checking the time when her lights went on at night. His solicitude and fatherly meddling had become such a nuisance that she referred to him as the "chief of the privatization bureau."

After December 29, Kathy's windows often remained dark. That night Kathy and I had met for the first time at the Atlantic Club in Virginabad. She and her faux father had a quarrel. Being a quinquagenarian, he did not dare get closer to her. But that didn't stop him. Sometime after her birthday, which I shared, he confessed his love and proposed marriage at the cost of leaving his wife. Imagine that! In Virginland! He wished to spend the twilight of his years with Kathy, promising to spare nothing for her and her child.

At night, as Kathy came home, his wife waited for her at the entrance. "Bitch! Whore! Take your hands off my husband or else…"

"I'm not interested in your husband," Kathy shot back. "Get a hold of yourself… or else I'll tell your man who you've been giving your ass to at the university."

In those days Kathy was barely keeping the wolf from the door. She hadn't told me anything. She had sold all her jewelry. Her business, a vocational school which specialized in healthcare and was once profitable, could no longer cope with the insane fluctuations of God's regulatory environment.

Kathy reported to work. Her boss, the regional revenue-service chief, did not mince his words when he told her she had to sleep with him at once if she wanted to have the job. He even ignored the intervention of Kathy's esteemed benefactor.

Kathy was an utter mess. That's when she came to this dog, with tears in her eyes...

W e went to church on Sunday.

The crowd prayed:

Give us, O Lord, give us 1+1=11. Give us, O Lord, give us 1+1=111. Give us, O Lord, give us 1+1=1,111.

The beard sermoned:

Do not be afraid of injustice. The more injustice there is in this world, the happier you should feel. Justice is born of injustice. Time is but justice's ally.

As we listened to the homily, we did not supplicate for anything. Simply, we understood that 1+1=0. We bolstered our souls to withstand God's heuristic experiments and then headed to the Marco Polo bistro. Kathy was in my arms when we promised each other to celebrate our birthday together, no matter where our relationship stood.

It was her idea, and I agreed without a second thought. It tickled me that we were born the same day. Gemini. My goodness, she was my twin... At that time, I happened to be researching legends of twins, and it was within this context that I read our bond. She had shared this with her girlfriends.

May 30: different countries, different years, different wombs...

That day mother earth smiled at the sun's rays from the same locus, the same sidereal position, and was impregnated by them, while we separately entered the world, eleven springs apart, through the path of light...

I go toward the spring of light...

The path is long, cobbled
With flint, fenced with myrtle thorns.
The path is askew, rhyming with a ray.
I step out, leaning upon my quivering knees,
And from my knees, which my brethren nailed,
Hot blood gushes forth.
There's panting in my chest, dust on my lashes.
My heart is the empty jug,
And I go toward the spring of light...
How many, how many thousands of years
Must I walk thus?
How many times must I fall, wounded,
Upon the goal of my path,
Struck by rock-crushing hammers?
I know not. Only, my brothers,
My crucifying brethren,
Leave me be in my journey...
On my sunfilled path leading to the suns,
Do not spread your shadow
Like the sinister wing of a buzzard.

Wave 1, "The Light"†

Back from a conference at the Institute of Oriental Studies of the Academy of Sciences, I'm getting ready to meet with Kathy.

That day... no one knew a thing about it.

I had no desire to tell anyone about my birthday. It belonged to Kathy. What we had promised each other was no ordinary present. That day we were to give one another every layer of our souls, every shudder of our bodies...

We kiss...

Her pink, form-fitting blouse, out of which her sculpted arms soar from her shoulders to her delicate fingers, makes her bronze face dazzle. The image of the moon goddess,

† This and other poetic gems, which appear across this work as a narrative subcurrent in the form of four waves and two airs, are quoted by our author from the rumis of Paradise. It is our opinion that these texts, together with the author's basic facts about Paradise, are intended for a world readership, with the goal of revealing the dogological and atavistic underpinnings of life in Paradise. The author disagrees. He says that these are excerpts from his textbooks at the Dream Middle School that have played a formative role in his development. Needless to say, we disagree with the author.—DogAlleyPress

with its alternating play of light and shadow, hypnotizes my gaze. Her chestnut-gold hair pours over her bare shoulders in broad waves and spills down her face, giving it an elongated shape, accentuating the lure of her chin and fiery lips. Her beltless jeans hug her naked waist, as their gliding basalt blue devours her protruding, ovoid buttocks and erect legs.

We haven't seen each other in nine days. We share a heart-shaped Jell-O cake and drink champagne to our twin birthdays.

We've decided to repair to the Atlantic.

On the night of December 29, I had invited two sisters to the club. I had met them through their third sister during her defense of her doctoral dissertation. These birds had migrated from Dushtepeh to Virginland three years ago. Olya, the youngest, is a nuclear scientist working at Virginland's nuclear power plant. Sasha is a biologist. She has a one-year-old and her relations with her husband are none too enviable. Both women are beautiful, sexy, smart. They're also independent in their thinking, which is to my liking. Sasha is gentle. Olya is wild. All eyes are on them in the club.

I clashed with Olya. She has a knack for confusing originality with inconsiderateness. Before long, I saw them off in a taxi and decided to linger at the Atlantic. Olya was mad. We didn't call each other for months.

Makoko waves hello from the sixth floor.

I've noticed Kathy. She's here with Nuneh and her friend.

And Kathy has noticed me. As she had no dance partner, she joined us some time later, with Olya's approval.

Thanks to Olya's largesse, I fell right into Kathy's field of gravity. We're dancing face to face, gazing into each other's eyes. I'm spellbound. She moves her flawless figure in graceful grooves, oozing sex. She's a bona fide fairy on the dance floor. And this: I seem to sense a transformation in her face, her very essence.

I couldn't sleep that night.

The Atlantic became a sanctuary for us. Kathy would have wanted to build a chapel there. As for me, I would never step foot inside with another woman.

Kathy wanted us to take Nuneh along. Kathy and I wouldn't have met if Nuneh hadn't invited her to the club. Nuneh has just broken up with her boyfriend. He left her as soon as he received a promotion at the bank, with prospects of getting his hands on a classier vestal to suit his new post, even if Nuneh was an attractive, mature, and kind woman who left the impression of pure milk.

I'm dancing with my twin. Her face is beaming across the hall, shattering the men. In her words, "The Atlantic is sinking."

It was this very metamorphosis that I had noticed during orgasms. Kathy became a different woman, an ethereal being, from whose face and lips flew the fountain of immortality. The secret to coming into contact with her feminine essence lay in the unlocking of that fountain.

This had been easier said. She was married at eighteen, after the death of her parents. Her family wanted to get rid of her, and she made the wrong choice.

A few months before being tagged to a husband, she had traveled to the UTA, as a participant of the Dreamland Olympics and the flag bearer of the Virginlander team. These games bring together youths from various Dreamland provinces throughout the globe. The Olympics are held every year in July, in commemoration of the New Year of the ancient Paradisean calendar.

When Kathy told me about her participation in the Olympics, I remembered actually having seen her, as that particular year I was there during the closing ceremony. It was impossible not to notice her: tall build, proud walk, gorgeous figure, and, as important, team leader of newly-independent Virginland... All this had made her the epicenter of attention.

Ah... if only I hadn't been married...

Kathy was the Athena of Virginland, its symbol of womanhood. The Olympics were followed by a number of attractive marriage offers, all of which she had refused.

Little did she know then what misery awaited her back in Virginland.

"Well, God is giving you a second chance now," Kathy says.

But the magic of those days was tainted by a gaping wound in Kathy's heart. One of the prominent Dreamlanders of Los Babylonos, a clothing tycoon known as Cigar Koko, invited the Virginlander Olympic team to dinner. He then opened his enormous clothing warehouse to the team members, asking them to take whatever and as much as they like. Plus he gave each member a franklin for pocket money—this was a significant amount for youths between the ages of sixteen and twenty who had come from a ruble economy and were basically broke.

Their excitement, however, was short-lived. The Olympics organizers immediately confiscated the money on pretense of having to cover the cost of the team's stay at Satan Hotel.

Kathy was offended. She kept away from subsequent events held by the Holy Trinity Party, the organizer of the Olympics. As tensions mounted, the organizing committee accused Kathy of treason: "Thou hast exploited the goodwill of our mother branch in Paradise to tour Tartaros at our expense." From the point of view of disciples and drum-beaters alike, this is the most serious charge that the holy triumvirate can bring against someone.

Coming back home, Kathy was admitted to Virginland State University (which was considered one of the top ten universities of Leninland), from which she went on to earn a bachelor of arts degree in applied mathematics. As she matured as a woman, Kathy was increasingly dissatisfied with her husband. It didn't help that they lived with his parents, with no privacy for lovemaking.

"How do you explain to the moron that you needed at least to wash up after doing it, let alone with hot water? Where? How? It meant nothing to him... he just went on fucking for himself."

Knowing Kathy now, I could imagine the situation. A dilettante wouldn't do. She grew to need a full-fledged man to satisfy her. Though withering from sexual starvation, her dignity didn't let her accept another man inside her. Kathy had her first orgasm seven years into her marriage. That night she cried bitterly, as she understood what she had been missing all those years.

"Ripsik, honey, how is it that you've had four kids and got yourself 40 abortions without getting naked with your hubby?"

"Naked? What are you talking about? He'll kill me if he sees me naked. He'd say, 'Where did this slut come from? Where did she learn to be a whore?' I just close my eyes, he lifts my skirt, finds a hole, sticks it in…"

Kathy suffers patiently, hoping things will change someday. For years on end, she pinches pennies to buy their own house. In keeping with Virginlander tradition, she hands all her earnings to him, and he in turn hands it all to his mother.

In Virginland, the umbilical cord linking a mother to his son is never cut after his birth. The two lead a symbiotic existence unto death. This is a sacred rite. To oppose it can well result in the killing of the bride. It's now chic to call the tradition "national." A man is his mother's timeless baby: Madonna and Bambino. He is suckled by Mamma until he turns fifty… He communicates with his wife through Mamma. Mamma holds the hand of her twenty-year-old tot and takes him to the store to buy him a pair of shoes. The baby cries and argues: he doesn't like those damned shoes…

Incidentally, Virginland is home to great shoemakers and furniture designers, who could, with a little gray matter, compete in the international marketplace with the very best from Alpacinoland. But Virginlanders are proud of wearing shoes made by Al Pacino, the king of Alpacinoland.

In our old neighborhood in Adonis, there was a clothing factory. One day my father and I were there when the owner had a conversation with a wholesaler.

"We can stick any label you want," he said. "Gucci, Versace… you name it."

When the son reaches marriage age, Mamma enlists her network of mothers to look for a virgin bride for her masterpiece of incompetence of a son.

The unbreakable bond between Paradisean mammas and their male sucklings was explained to me by my landlord.

"In Paradise, women don't love their husbands," she said. "That's why they shower their affections on their sons, by way of compensating for their need to love a man."

Manpanzee the Custodian (I beg the chimpanzees' forgiveness for the analogy) surrenders his wife to the custody of his mother. Whenever a disagreement erupts between the two women, first he beats the wife, seeking to mould her with mamma's bizarrerie. Should the wife fail to submit, he kicks her out.

"There's plenty of fish in the water, but only one Mamma."

Kathy's savings were built cent by cent, at enormous sacrifice. In the years when there was neither power nor heating in Virginland, she managed to both prepare her university assignments and make quantities of pastry, using their home's lone wood-burning heater. She lit the contraption for baking the pastries, nothing else. In the morning, on her way to the university, she distributed them to the stores in the area. This was how she fed the family, paid for her bus ride, and at the end of the week put aside a small amount toward her dream apartment.

One day her husband tells her he has a beautiful surprise for her and asks her to look out the window. Guessing what it is, Kathy passes out.

He had squandered her savings on a car...

Kathy was unable to get over it. They divorced.

Virginlanders frown upon a divorced woman. Few have the balls to marry a nonvirgin—that would go against the grain of an age-old tradition. As the heirs of the world's first Xn state, they piously follow the second half of the Holy Writ. "Whoever puts away his wife, except for the cause of sexual immorality, makes her an adulteress; and whoever marries her when she is put away commits adultery." Note, however, that men diligently solicit those nonvirgins, trying to conquer them as side lovers. In fact, the whole of Virginland is after these women, going at it like an unstoppable train.

It's a natural urge, they say.

Speaking of nature, there are only two sexes in Virginland. Man and Woman. Unlike Gehenna, where we have twelve sexes in fashion. You see, brothers, how primitive they are. The man sex, they say, is created in the image of God, and the woman sex in the image of the Devil. For the sake of convenience, I will sometimes distinguish between these polar sexes with the terms Virginoso and Virginosa.

Characteristic of Virginland is the stigma that a man risks if he doesn't keep a lover. Having a mistress is a sign of the unparalleled brotherly love and generosity of the Virginoso. And it is done with the approval of his parents, who take all precautions to conceal it from the bride living at their home.

Often they don't even bother to hide it. "Well, what do you expect? He's a man. What is he supposed to do? Cling to your skirt?"

If a married fellow doesn't avail himself of the services of a whorehouse, what kind of man is he? I tell you what he is: he's a fag.

In Virginland, hypocrisy is the stuff of life. They may not know it, but their aura tells the whole story. They live by deception and self-deception. They transmit the poison to the generations. To oppose this would mean to invite the wrath of an entire virgin-worshipping society. Few women are able to come out on top.

There's a veritable odyssey awaiting a woman after her divorce. She receives the first blow in court, where she finds herself trapped in a labyrinth of humiliation. Women are used to this. No surprises. There was a woman who had to ask the court three times for a divorce from her drunkard husband. Her request was granted only when she threatened that if she were to be murdered by the brute, the court would be held responsible. It had been already four years that she and her husband slept in different rooms. She kept trying to defend herself against his constant attacks, to the terrified screams of the children, not realizing that what he violated were inalienable rights.

Another woman, Stella, was married at twenty and divorced at twenty-two. She was left with no choice but to bribe the court, simply to be allowed to submit her divorce application. Stella is a femme fatale, the most beautiful and seductive I was ever to meet in Virginland. Kind, gentle, well-read, smart.

True to the norm, Stella lived with her husband's family. His mother and sister, having noticed that he loved his wife more than his family, forced the couple to keep their bedroom door open day and night. The in-laws had a garden. When Stella was pregnant, they didn't let her pick any of the fruits. Her husband started beating her up regularly, to prove his manhood to his mother and sister.

The next blow to the divorced nonvirgin comes from the neighbors. The married men in her block approach her with propositions of secret affairs. The same happens at the workplace. This or that dude will be sure to pester her…

Presumably this is why they say the virginoid family is "rock-solid." A friend of mine from Binladenland once boasted that families in his country were ultimately more solid than those in Gehenna.

It is possible, of course, to further bolster a family's foundations by granting men the right to murder insubordinate women. This would reduce the number of divorces to nil.

"Where is it written that a parental property should be given to a girl? Will you listen to this one? Not only is she going to a man, she's also demanding a share from her father's house." Kathy's brother was infuriated when, following the death of their parents, she had suggested selling the family home and dividing the profits equally between siblings.

That same brother had a hand in marrying Kathy off at an early age. He wanted her to forget about the family house. Kathy and her sister decided not to go to court, for fear of being labeled "whores." The brothers conveniently appropriated their parents' property, which included two homes. The vocal brother took the larger of the homes with the blessings of the other brothers, locked it down, and took off to Natashaland, throwing Kathy to the wolves. Though making a good living there, he wouldn't send a penny to his struggling sister. Had Kathy gotten her fair share, she could've bought a studio, solved a great many problems, and avoided her descent into the pit.

Slut! This is what Suzy is called.

At twenty-five, she has already distinguished herself with extraordinary public and cultural activism in Virgintown, which sits at the foot of Mount Ararat, on this side of Kars. She doesn't get along with her mother-in-law, who tries to control her in every conceivable way. Thief! The culprit has refused to hand the cultural organization's earnings over to her husband, the de facto master of the public and cultural spheres, preventing him from depositing the loot in Virginbank—i.e., mamma's palm.

In Virginland, the woman's economic rights have been dispensed with altogether, by way of sealing her utter bondage. A married woman is horrified by the thought of opening a bank account. Such an act might have the direst consequences for her family and future.

All of Virginland's wealth, including liquid assets, real estate, and businesses, is entirely the property of men. If a woman happens to be of financial means, you can be sure that there is a manpanzee watching over her—she can't make a single move without his approval.

Women have nothing. This is why they must give ass in order to get anywhere. Women give ass to the men above them just as catholicoi give it to the Solomonons and the president to the oligarchs.

Virginland is led by assgivers.

The ass determines a human's worth.

I have no ass to offer.

The Virginoso gives the Virginosa no choice but to become a whore. It is these very women who are sold in Pashaland. Forget that only two or three generations ago many preferred to throw themselves down a rocky hill than surrender to Pasha.

"All of them are Maimunites! You won't see a Paradisean doing a thing like that. There's a big plot going on here. They're trying to ruin our nation's name."

To this day, Osman Pasha and Ali Baba nurture the cockamania of getting their hands on houris. In the past they couldn't possibly do this without resorting to rape.

And drowning the tears in her blue eyes,

In a cinder field where Paradisean life kept dying,

The German woman told us what she had witnessed of our horror.

O, do not be terrified when I tell you my unutterable story...

Let people understand man's crime against man.
That deathly morning was a Sunday,
The first and useless Sunday to appear upon the corpses.
From dusk to dawn I had been in my room,
Watching the throes of a stabbed girl,
Wetting her death with my tears…
Suddenly I heard a dark, beastly crowd from afar
Brutally lashing twenty brides,
Singing lecherous songs, in a vineyard.
A brute roared at the brides:
"You must dance!
"You must dance when our drum beats!"
And the whips descended viciously
Upon the death-wishing bodies of the Paradisean
women…
The pretty brides fell down exhausted…
"Get up!" the men shouted, flailing their naked swords
like snakes…
Then someone brought a jug of kerosene to the mob…
O, human justice, let me spit at your forehead…
They hastened to cover the women with the liquid…
"You must dance!" they thundered. "Here's a perfume
You won't find even in Arabia…"
They used a torch to set the women's naked bodies on
fire.
And the charred bodies tumbled to their deaths through
the dance…
In my horror, I rushed to slam the shutters,
And, drawing close to my dead girl, asked her,
"Tell me, how can I dig my eyes out?"
Wave 2, "The Dance"

The Virginoso is less worthy of a houri than even Pasha. This is why the Virginosa today is not revolted by the idea of sleeping with Pasha.

God is a "cool guy."

When it became clear that Suzy couldn't have children, she got a divorce, "trampling on the man's honor."

In Virginland, when a couple knocks on the deaf ears of infertility, the suspicion is placed on the woman. She is the one to be examined, even though doctors recommend checking the man first. If her examination shows that everything is normal with her body, the man then decides whether to be tested. Tradition says that Mamma will solve the problem by enlisting her satellites to purvey a new virgin for the poor lad.

No one will ask how the wife, a vestal virgin at the time of the wedding, contracted a sexually-transmitted disease. It is enough to know that most cases of infertility are due to such diseases.

One out of every threeRedeemed is infertile. Where else in the cosmos would one find such statistics?

Long live the national traditions of Virginland!

Suzy left the country with a young man from Pornstan, though she didn't love him. The best women—Virginworld's most precious resource—are leaving.

"She shouldn't have gone. She's the one to blame! It would've been better to stay with a local man she didn't love," a virgin concluded.

"Darling, one day you'll get it…"

It is getting clear already that I am in love with the "sluts" of Virginland.

I'm beginning to understand that I'm… a bastard.

Yes, a bastard.

Three, four, or five syllables worth of a bastard, and in capital letters at that.

Familial slavery is a homebred phenomenon in Virginland. The contemptuous stomping of women's rights is the consequence of an ideology that defends the customs of Virginlanders, one which tradition traces back to Virginland founder, paterfamilias, and interior minister Noah the Patriarch. The lackeys of that ideology, that is to say, men, but also women, consider every step toward the recognition of women's rights a manifestation of Satanic colonialism.

In Virginland, advocates of progressive ideas are often dubbed Jinjinists.

The word Jinjinism has a peculiar meaning in Paradise. It entered the national lexicon following the 1915 Genocide. The first popularizer of the term was Mevlan Zadeh Rifat, a werewolf who participated in Pasha's secret meetings and in 1929 published a book exposing the plans to exterminate the indigenous people of Paradise.

Despite the service that the Osmani politician had rendered to justice, the political parties of Dreamland were suspicious of claims that the Jinjinists had had a role in organizing the Genocide. Instead the parties believed that Rifat's exposé was but an attempt by Pasha to pin his atrocities on a scapegoat. But in the last few decades, efforts to lock away the theory of Jinjin's involvement in the Genocide backfired. A book by a Paradisean historian published in 1982 provided a flurry of evidence to confirm Rifat's assertions.

Matters were exacerbated when Mr. Jinjin opposed a resolution to recognize the Genocide, which was being debated in our All-clement Lord Satan's Congress. Mr. Jinjin's aim was to plunge God and Satan into perpetual enmity. Then there was Jinjinland's ambassador in Paradise, who issued a statement denying the Genocide. Despite remonstrations by the foreign minister of Paradise, the Satan-educated Zulfikar James Lutfullah, her words were refuted neither by Mr. Jinjin nor his brother, Mr. Maimunus.

Maimunus was well-regarded in Paradise. But the foreign diplomat's unprecedented sacrilege on the very soil of martyrs set Paradiseans scattered across the globe, even those sevenfold removed from Paradisean life, against Maimunus. The dark waters of Mr. Jinjin's politics came to better light when in a number of Holocaust museums Paradiseans who resisted Ali Baba's atrocities were portrayed as slaughterers themselves, even though it is a fact that Ali Baba, heaping fresh damnations every day, tried to blast open the gates of Paradise, steal the gold, and erase all trace of Paradiseans from human memory with weapons supplied by Mr. Jinjin.

Thus Jinjinism became synonymous with perversion of history, transgression upon justice, destruction of truth. Illuminator intellectuals fleeing from Paradise to Hell have often labeled Dog a Jinjinist, and warned Paradiseans against this mole's plots. My dog-moraled gazes were considered devastating to the foundations of their virgin-built ideology.

The illuminators of Paradise also called me an "enemy of the people," on account of my failure to treat the delusions of cronyists "with understanding."

Assailing Paradise's spiritual stage and intent on fortifying their own positions, these patriots brand all who do not condone their ideas with the stigmata befitting a national traitor, saturating with miasma the inner atmosphere of the cradle of creation, violating the creator's womb.

"Where there's smoke, there's fire," a woman told me. "If they're calling you a Satan-worshipper, could it be that there's some truth to it?"

They were the smoke, I the fire, she the spectator. I was crestfallen. I thought I had found the woman of my dreams. Until the moment she said that, every time we met, our gazes intertwined as though they were glued. How could she have known that I was the Antichrist?

Holy Mamma!

My uncle Gary has sacrificed his life, and his mental and financial resources, to a lie.

"Yoohoo MacYehu will be here in ten to fifteen years."

The churches bilk him for all he's worth. He had become rich several times, but always sacrificed his wealth to MacYehu's father, Yehu. Millions of Gehennese like him betrayed Satan by giving everything they owned to the goal of securing MacYehu's thousand-year reign in Penisalem. Mr. MacYehu shall snatch his tribesmen away from earth and make them rulers of his imperium. Amen. The dead shall rise from their graves. Amen. Their crackling bones shall be put back together. Amen. They shall become flesh. Amen. If a volcano has swallowed the cemeteries, you needn't worry; Father Yehu is omnipotent…

"Glory to you, Almighty Father…" ejaculates the crowd.

And if you ask about the fate of the billions of cells, which have yet no bones, gushing from the bathroom to the sewer?

They shall be turned into babies of MacYehu, of course… if, that is, the seed doesn't happen to be of an Allahista…

Poor sire. Whom shall he recognize as his progeny?

And the ectroma of mostly female fetuses around the globe? They will be whirling around their groom, Yoohoo, like the wise virgins...

And pets? They will also unite with their families in the eternal chorus glorifying Father Yehu.

Some group deposits the signatures of donors (credit cards welcome) under the statue of a white stallion that shall be Yoohoo's horse—a futuristic improvement on the outdated, embarrassing "raise your hand and give your heart" proposition. The signatories shall be the macs of MacYehu, who upon His return shall rule the world for a thousand years. Hundreds of millions of washingtons are collected from Satan's tribesmen through telethons and chichi events in order to "save" nations, especially the lambs huddled in the sheepfold of Gog and Magog, the Leninstanese and Chinmachinese. "If every Chinmachinese contributes a single washington..." is the abiding dream of every wealthy messianist.

They boost the Chosen One, whose land is sacred where MacYehu shall land. As for the tribe of Allah, they are agents of the Beast. The MacYehuists pump billions of washingtons into Maimunland to strengthen Yehu's house. They milk our Lord Satan to feed Maimunus, enabling him to slay Allah. Amen. When Satan is short on milk, Yehu punishes him by unleashing tornadoes and hurricanes, especially upon the blackest of Gehenna. Amen. Should you dare challenge them, MacYehu's lambs pity you. Amen. Or else brandish sharp knives, depriving you of not just the next life...

Amen...

"Whoever adds to the word which I command, or takes from it, I shall fuck him up the ass," says the worshipper-gorging chaperon of the lambs, who has an eye on your tithe and sperm. An endless flow of talent into "God's Country..." If you were Maimunus, how could you not jump for joy? They gather strength by being mocked. Doesn't the Son of Race, the acclaimed author of the apartheid pleonasm, "Don't throw my pearls before the pigs [the gentiles]," say that his followers must be mocked? "Go and make disciples of all nations, baptizing them in the name of the Father and of the Son and of the Holy Spirit" is a later interpolation in the text, one among hundreds of such interpolations, by fraud-mongering priests intent to universalize and deify a racist religious megalomaniac.

Thou shalt drop a nukiller bomb on Damascus!

Amen…

Thou shalt drop a mewkiller bomb on Cairo!

Amen…

We wilt drop an immacular bomb on Tehran!

Hallelujah…

We wilt drop an immaculate bomb on Mecca!

Glory, glory, hallelujah,
Glory, glory, hallelujah,
Glory, glory, hallelujah,
His truth is marching on…

I can't resign myself to having lost my uncle. What's been gone is irreplaceable.

"Why was MacYehu born in Maimunland? Then the Chosen One *is* God's chosen one."

"Azrael's imp, that's what he is! A Messiah could've been engendered in only the worst place possible. He would come to save people, not to attain postpartum or postmortem glory. A Messiah, as opposed to a dog, is a fake."

From Bulgaria to Vermont and Colorado, away from the prying eyes and venom of Paradiseans, my friend Cosmos, aka God Artin, dedicated his life to thousands of students from a dozen nationalities. My own life would be set ablaze at an early age. This is how Dreamland's inner force was sacked—its vitality leeched off and made to flow into the veins of a vampire deity, under the patronage of the Judolicoi.

Today that idol is ensconced in the vault of man's consciousness, perched upon the pedestal of Paradise.

For the benefit of humans, Ugly Dog resolved to lay bare Motherdog's source of life-giving light.

He was a Satanist.

No! Rather, he *was* Satan. The Antichrist.

Makoko waves hello from the sixth floor.

Those who voice their support for women's rights in

Virginland are "Jinjinists." But for women, finding work is gravid with the risk of being subjected to sexual serfhood. Many women go along. We have no choice in the matter.

"Hypocrites! They play by the rules only because they're bitches," respond the diehard virgins, the caryatids of Virginlander society.

Kathy and I decided to play husband and wife on our birthday. The suggestion, which was mine, tickled her silly. We were both captivated by the discreet charm of the game. It would give us free rein to enjoy ourselves fully, if only for a day.

Motherdog is joy, frolic, and dance. Motherdog is fun.

Though we come home dog-tired, the night is young for us spouses. We skip the shower. When I'm done brushing my teeth, I see Kathy lying in my bed, half asleep, in a tight triangular position, her ass wedged into my side of the bed. This was her usual sleeping position, but tonight she had overtaken my space.

I lift the blanket. There's the silhouette of her buns in the half-darkness, beckoning me with all their allure—a miracle of firmness which even wo-dogs dream of having. Her butt cheeks are delineated by a pair of tight, black undies that further enhance her nakedness. As for her snout...

As for her lips... Kathy's mouth and skin have a delectable, natural taste, something I haven't found among women. Life has been powerless to taint that childlike purity.

The outpourings of her body and soul seep from each cell, each word. Our energies have melded together to generate nuclear fusion.

Already drunk, already dancing,
We have now mixed life with death.
Blaze again and again,
Burn within our heart, float drained of blood,
Crazy soma...
We're dancing wildly,
Blazing, burning
Everything there was

In this age-old world.
Soma,
Your love is poison and wine,
Alas, so sweet.
Soma,
You will always be
Whereas I, a fleeting shadow,
Won't be here for long.
Soma,
May your cosmic wishes
Be made real in this world.
Mine will die out,
Reduced to an old, tiny spark
In your golden fire.
But my ashen heart will remain burning
In all of your dawns.

Wave 3, "Soma"

My relationship with Kathy did not need to lead anywhere. She wanted to get married. I didn't. Her aunt called her Butterfingers, on account of Kathy's inability to "glue" someone into marriage. Meanwhile some characters from her ex's family were dead set on humiliating her so thoroughly as to prevent her from getting back on her feet again. Not only did they deny her child support, they badmouthed her in front of her girlfriends, advising them "not to have anything to do with a whore like that."

Two-thirds of Virginland's divorced cucumbearers fail to provide child support.

"What kind of man would feed whores and bastards?"

Only a fag would.

God is a cool guy…

No matter how much this rascal wished to build his nest, the hurt that women had placed in his soul wouldn't heal. The first wish of the wo-men he'd been with was to tie the knot. Holy matrimony!

Woof, woof…

The human ritual of matrimony gave this dog the impression of a funeral. Few were those who honestly wanted to be with me, to love me unconditionally.

Wo-men predicated the relationship on a marriage contract, exploited their nature-given sexual energies for profit. In this they were sanctioned by God and Caesar alike, who had their own gain in pulling the marriage noose tight over my neck.

Wo-men turned me down when I refused to submit to the proviso. They deprived me of love. There were others still who placed no such conditions on cucumbearers they became involved with. To these wo-men, I was neither a knight in shining armor nor even a one-night stand. I was simply a good candidate.

Girlfriend to girlfriend:

"So what do you think?"

"Looks all right."

"Let's glue him then."

Woof, woof…

Kathy, it seemed, had no self-serving motive. Some of her girlfriends take her to task for being unable to follow their example and benefit from her Dreamlander beau.

Women's behavior had created its antidote in me. This dog scoffed at any marriage proposal that was not based equally on physical, mental, spiritual, and financial fulfillment. Only full gratification on all counts would perhaps lead to a reading of the marital textbook's preface. Otherwise I preferred to remain single and gambol from one bed to the other.

"The horror! He's a real bastard, this one…"

Virginlandese society has yet to grasp that the somatic is inextricably linked to the spiritual and mental, which, for us canines, is at the core. Many women, even therapists, put their foot down by insisting to separate the carnal from the spiritual. Such dissociation opens the door for a rupture of the human soul, with all the attendant consequences.

The carnal is taboo in Virginstan, as in all *stans* and *abads*. It is a monopoly of the mafia of the married. The paradicium, however, considers himself a Westerner, confusing the real with the imaginary (the country is situated to the west of the *stans*, with a functionally white populace).

What about the financial aspect?

From the woman's perspective, marriage is a ticket to becoming a pensioner for life. In general she doesn't share the man's heavy financial burden. The parasite sits deep within her soul. The better her "upkeep" by the man, the greater his worth.

"That's right. You, on the other hand, can fuck off."

But I ask you, my canine brethren, isn't this nothing but whoredom, sanctioned by the bulla of church and nation? Aren't 80 percent of Virginland's adult females, especially among the upper classes, in fact whores?

"Stone the dog!"

And what is it that keeps a *woman* from supporting her man? Woof, woof…

Dancing to the tune of the parasite's flute, the man erodes both the well-being of his family and the economy of the society he lives in.

"Capitalist pig!"

And what about those women who wished to marry this bugger? What was in it for them? They stood to gain more than I did. Even were I to put aside the list of values which no woman could possibly embody totally, the valuta they offered was too little by half. If a woman offered, say, 50 percent of what she was getting in return, she wouldn't agree to marriage. As a rule, she tries to get significantly more than what she's prepared to give.

Pussy Power. A contradiction in terms for us canines. But this is what makes it possible for her to get her way in the humanoid world. Its antidote is Penis Power. There are exceptions, to be sure. But it's unthinkable to find women who would agree to match value for value on the scales, let alone throw in something extra.

The difference in values on the scales of marriage constitutes the woman's gain, my brothers, while making the man overlook that difference in the name of love is where the woman's hypocrisy lies.

"I already got a nice job. It's a company from Hell. And Satan has given me a cell phone. Why would I want to get married now?" countered virgin Bella. Just two months earlier, she had asked me to find her a husband so that she wouldn't be cold on winter nights.

Naturally, I would grow disillusioned with these women in short order, which would drive them to constantly terrorize me. And if there should be children in the equation, the nagging would go on till the end of my life. I had no desire to give such women the time of day, much less marry them. No pussy could tie me down. I was a bastard...

This is why I preferred to spend my nights with sluts. But this, too, had already lost its meaning and even excitement.

I remembered the words of my mechanic, Benik, a Dreamlander who had migrated to Los Angelos from Ayatollahland. He paid tribute to his fatherland, Paradise, which he has never seen. Many whom he had helped settle in Hell had forgotten about him. Frowning and with measured movements of the hand, he moaned from the depths of his soul, "My dear Dog, life is a lie... family is a lie... woman is a lie. Fuck around as much as you can."

In any case, Virginlanders don't have whores of quality. Their richest man, Kirk Kirker, is the top property owner of Las Fortunas. His lover is not a Virginlandette. The women of Virginland don't have enough brains or ability to snag him. Kirker had fallen into the hands of a wife who, in order to take care of a child with whose father she was apparently having an affair, went to court and by virtue of her being a daughter of Pornstan demanded from Kirker as much money as would be enough to feed ten thousand kids in Virginland...

One day my cousin Henri from Paris surprised me with an unexpected visit to Virginabad. I had twelve cousins in Paris. I had met two. I had seen Henri only once. Henri and I had the same views regarding Virginosas.

I was one. Now we were two.

One evening I took Henri to one of the best nightclubs in Virginabad. Some men pulled him by his arm and made him sit at a table that had three women around it. Cousin Henri was fuming at the brutes' coercion.

As he cooled down, Henri found himself on the dance floor, where he struck up a conversation with one of the girls and found out that she was a pro. Fifty bucks for two hours. How much in euros? Henri turned to me and said, "Let's get the fuck out of here."

Our arrival and exit had lasted no more than ten minutes. As we paid the bill, we felt the burning gazes of several men, official and nonofficial staffers alike. "It's a mafia," Henri said while we slipped out of the place. "Wherever the mafia operates, don't expect anything good."

The whores were left behind, at the tail end of our life's train. Henri, too, wished to meet some decent women.

Within two days, his friends had convinced him that he was chasing a pipe dream.

"You can't have a girlfriend here. That's why men prefer to go with hookers."

"Goddamned crazy place," Henri reacted, while his immediate impression of almost every woman he met was encapsulated in one word: "Peasant!" Henri adored the peasants of Virginland, but his Virginish vocabulary was somewhat lacking. What he meant to say was "bourgeois" or "yokel."

The Virginosa can stare at a man for a good hour. But the minute you approach her, she takes to her heels and jacks up the price. Time and again, she publicly berates a man, relishing every second...

The fact is the Virginosa is incapable of extracting sexual sustenance from men. So she compensates for it through vampirical sustenance. In the sexual sphere and broader hominid relationships alike, the Virginosa confounds her horrid ignorance with "national values."

Eventually Henri infused humor into his encounters with the aberrations of Virginland's sexosphere and made fun of everything. One night, when I asked him what he felt like doing, he said, "Well, there are only two things you can do in this city: bag a whore or eat. Since we're not interested in whores, let's go eat."

"Don't let it get to you. Everything's fucked up here. The most important thing for them is the least important thing for us... The girls here have another shitty habit: they trap us into spending time with them, but then, if we don't marry them, badmouth us left and right like we were lotharios."

"I don't know, cousin, this is a madhouse…"

"These people have a different take on sex. To us, it's like, you're hungry, you eat, finito! But here you've got these layers within layers…"

"A shit sandwich!"

"If only it were worth it. They go wacko on you—they've got no manners. By the time you find the hole, your boner's gone already."

"No…"

"All this talk about love… Jesus, one's belly stinks, the other's asshole stinks, one's crotch stinks, the other's breath stinks… I tell you, one out of two, they've either got halitosis or body odor."

"What is it? They don't shower? Don't change their clothes?"

"They smell like disinfectant. There's a millimeter of salt on their skin. Cousin, you get grossed out if you kiss them or lick them. Another one's got gold teeth. I go, 'Why don't you have them fixed? I'll pay for it.' And she's like, 'Oh, no, my dentist says gold teeth are stronger…' You're supposed to get married and spend your whole life with her?"

"You'll drop dead in two days."

"They're gonna dump their démodé daughter on your ass…"

"Ha ha ha!"

"Man, their mouths are like caves… you can't find the tongue."

"Oh my dog! Are they all like that?"

"From what I've seen. And if they're just a bit different, they act like bloody prima donnas. Nothing like Satan's girls, I'm telling you."

"Madhouse…"

Long live Virginland's cave-mouthed national traditions!

Henri's understanding of "peasant" had an additional hue that I grasped later, when a friend showed me photographs from the wedding of Jesus Christ, son of Virginland's president, Mr. God. My friend had actually attended the event. In the photos, I saw a few angels with kind faces, but still felt ashamed of the man who was the president of my motherland.

His entourage will doubtless heap divine outrage upon this dog for his estimation of them.

Shouldn't everything in life be in situ, so as to ensure the equilibrium of creation, especially in the cradle of creation, Paradise?

Is God a yokel?

From the outset, I made my intentions clear to Kathy. I knew that few in Virginland became involved with a cucumbearer without pursuing marriage. I was on the level with her regarding the boundaries of our relationship.

But honesty is a wodog currency. Women can't handle it. Some have split without a second thought. I'm amazed to see them with other men, who, my canine eyes tell me, are busy deceiving their prey.

O, hope… O, this hope which subsequently turns into disillusionment. I ask you, my bastard brethren and sluttish sisters, isn't this the reason for the devastation of the heart, the destruction of unity, from family to nation, the regress of civilization? Isn't this the reason for alienation, the unhinging of spiritual bonds, the ruination of humankind's inner universe, the proliferation of destructive drugs; the violation of the Mithraic code and the wreckage of the inner Christ's path to salvation, the aborting of the Buddhic equilibrium? And the reason for the burgeoning of existentialism and nihilism, the reason for the kind of filth produced under the rubric of post-modernism? The reason for the substitution of dog truths with hominid verisimilitudes?

Isn't this the reason that to this day man awaits the coming of Godot, who shall save him?

Makoko waves hello from the sixth floor.

"Love is the foundation."

"Can't you love without Godot? How come you're stuck on him like you were a bunch of cripples?"

"What you say is very dangerous. There is no love without Godot. It would be beyond human capacity."

"The danger lies elsewhere. The chaos."

"The nation of Dreamers shall grow."

"Our job is to find the truth—to find the harmony of the chaos."

"To not lose faith, rather. This is the difficulty."

"So far faith has been rescued by myth. Is the end of myth the end of faith? Is faith necessary?"

"Without faith, everything is lost."

"But look, do the enlightened feel less love than we do?"

"There is no hope in the religion of the enlightened. The only thing they claim is nirvana."

"And what's *our* hope about?"

"Eternal life."

"Can we know the creator?"

"Only through love."

"You mean through the lateral, not the vertical."

"We can't know him through consciousness. We would find ourselves in a tunnel. The road of the Gnostics leads nowhere."

"So does the road of injunction."

"A web of pure love…"

"Then what eternity?"

"It is MacYehu's promise, dog!"

"Is hope the main thing?"

"MacYehu is the Son of God."

"You mean the Son of Satan…"

"Otherwise the lives of so many saints would not have been sacrificed for him."

"They were duped. They couldn't possibly imagine that what they heard or read was fabrication."

"There is a basis to it all."

"The fallacy is precisely about looking for a basis. Heaven and Hell. This is Zoroaster's dead dream."

"Can't be that it's all a lie."

"If I prove it, will you agree with me?"

"If you can, I will take off my robe this instant and leave the church."

"Take it off and walk away…"

A s much as Kathy was inclined to liberate herself from the prevalent mindset, deep down she was a traditionalist Paradisean and proud of it. Her soul was a furnace engulfed by a profound faith in God.

Kathy was Paradise. The war over Eden had been won by... Kathy.

Eden is a land to the east of Paradise. It's where God created man and endowed nature with splendid greenery. For centuries, Eden was 95 percent populated by angels. Except Cain, all of them belonged to God's tribe. When the sweeping darkness of empires had enveloped Paradise, Eden was the wick that remained alight. It was where the princes of Paradise endured.

In 1921, as it still reeled from the Genocide, Paradise was voiceless. Papa Lenin's belladonna, Madame Stalin†, entered into negotiations with Pasha. With the stroke of a pen, she gifted Eden and the province called Nakhichevan to Ali Baba, a tribal chief basking in his yurta in a douar further east of Eden, who had been waiting for his share of the loot as he twisted his mustache. The Madame went on to annex two additional provinces from the north of Paradise to her own motherland. There the pious still worship the Madame for this supernal benevolence. Mother did all this, of course, in the name of "Soviet brotherhood," preaching unconditional love to the survivors of genocide. As a millennialist herself, Madame was continuing the tradition of messianic propagandists who had flocked to Paradise from all corners of the world, teaching displaced, starving orphans in rags to love Pasha, to study the causes behind his rage and cannibalism, to understand and forgive him.

But the agents of Xn agitprop never attempted to teach Pasha to love the orphans or their parents, whom he had

† According to the *Dream Encyclopedia*, Madame Stalin's natural father was Father Abraham, a wealthy Paradisean living in Shvililand, who had impregnated his housemaid. In an attempt to conceal the disgrace brought upon her, Father Abraham paid a poor shoemaker to marry her. The shoemaker, who was a habitual drunkard, regularly beat his wife, cursing both her and Father Abraham. This was the reason that Madame Stalin had no love for Father Abraham.

sent to their deaths. On the contrary; they stroked Pasha's head, declaring that the Prince of Peace shall forgive all his sins. They did so as they listened to the symphonies of Mozart, cocooned in their abodes while the slaughter was carried out all around them. A thousand shall fall on your right, ten thousand on your left, but not one hair shall fall from the head of the one who trusts in me. Thus speaks our Lord, the Almighty Father, hallowed be his name. Amen. Amen.

But when it comes to forgiving Führer BenYehu's or Bladin McAllah's sins, the Good Shepherd doesn't even lave his hands like Pilatos. Wolf! He shouts and curses them with eternal damnation.

May I kiss your hand, Fraülein Führer? You the innocent Lady, I the transgressor...

You the Immaculate, o life-giving salvation...

May I kiss your forehead, Monsignor Bladin? You the Blazing Bush, I the wicked Philistine...

May I kiss your Divine Ass, o King of Kings and Lord of Lords? You the Righteous Judge, I a wretched dog!

Nakhichevan, according to Paradisean tradition, is the place where Noah landed and rested after he came down from Mount Ararat. Paradiseans even point out the spot where Noah was buried. They incriminate Maimunus in stealing history, in attempting to usurp the Holy Land from Paradise through crass divinations.

The Edenites puff up when they inform you that the inventor of the MiG fighter jet was a Paradisean, Artem Mikoyan—that his brother, Anastas Mikoyan, was the president of Leninstan's Supreme Council. That the 144,000 residents of Eden have given the armies of Papa Lenin four marshals and dozens of generals, and were the first to enter Berlin. Indeed, the Edenites are a cruel people seasoned in warfare.

When God returned to Paradise, he installed cherubs in the east of Eden. It is here, too, that God's Lightning Sword glistens, protecting Eden from Ali Baba's attacks. In Nakhichevan, on the other hand, where the numbers of Paradiseans had so dwindled under Allah's saber as to comprise barely half the population, not a single Paradisean remains today. As in Pasha's empire, here, too, the Paradiseans seem to have evaporated into thin air. However, to Ali Baba's chagrin, the vapors have begun condensing and already turning into rain.

The enemies of Paradise, led by Pasha, to this day attempt to bully Paradiseans through the holy writ of territorial integrity, which they have received through divine revelation at the University of Satan in Allahabad.

Kathy tried to educate me about Paradisean values. As she didn't want to lose me, she smartly opted to go along with this uninvited Hellese in Paradise, ignoring her surroundings, so that I wouldn't feel the oppressive atmosphere of Virginland. Often she shocked me with her daring. She considered it her mission to keep me in Paradise, so "God would benefit from your positive intellect and merits." She hoped one day I would espouse her values.

Things weren't that easy, however.

Whenever I felt an intimation of love, I kept it to myself, in an effort to spare her any new pain. Kathy had a rough life. I sensed that I already caused her enough pain. She often reminded me of a hackneyed maxim which she had once heard from me: the cause of pain is expectation. She tried to console herself, but added nonetheless, "It's not a blessing to meet a highly intelligent man."

Certain issues really got in the way. It seemed to her that she knew me quite well. But whenever we discussed themes that were close to my heart, I perceived fear in her gaze. She was scared of losing me. I showed her only a part of myself. This wasn't entirely her fault but probably my fate. I had yet to meet a woman who could see my totality. Rather, each had seen a part that was inaccessible to the next woman.

Deep down, I was lonely and used to it. Kathy had problems. I was aware of them, yet didn't say a thing. I had no intention of becoming a mentor to my girlfriend, to interfere in her evolution. I only wished to help in one or two matters which could, if solved, contribute to a chain resolution of other problems. I wanted to create the right setting for her to open up, but it didn't happen.

One of those problems kept bothering me. I, too, had gone through it. Perhaps its traces were still festering in me;

they were revived by external factors. At least the conceited students of modern psychology think so. One day tensions reached boiling point. I could no longer go on with the relationship.

That was one month before our birthday.

My zaftig landlord, Mrs. Sweetheart, had noticed that I wasn't as chipper as before. There had been moments which she had photographed in her cranial camera. She's a delectable woman, chubby, an entrepôt of infectious laughter. Her husband, Mr. Astur, was a geologist. He had organized a gathering for his university students in Virginville, which lies on the road to Garni.

Seventeen centuries ago Garni was a summer retreat for the sister of Paradise's King Trdat, who had accepted Mr. MacYehu's religion. This is why Garni has been saved from messianistic culturicide, becoming the lone surviving monument to represent the old religion of Paradise, among its thousands of historic monuments. Here, every inch of land, every stone fragment is history. Every four-square-mile strip is home to a famous historic monument, which is why Papa Lenin used to call Paradise an "open museum." Paradise has had glorious pages in its past, a history replete with strife, and has often become a stage for the clash of empires.

Mr. Astur liked Kathy. Nonetheless, he invited me to his gathering, suggesting to introduce me to one of her female students.

Alla is a thirty-year-old doctor. One look at her and I can hear my heartbeat. I feel fourteen again. She is all eyes and lips, nubile to the extreme. Mr. Astur has proposed that she accompany me on our way to Virginville.

Alla, however, has hatched a different plan. Following a discussion at home, it has been decided that she should play her role in all seriousness. Accordingly she has come to the gathering with her brother.

Left with no companion on the bus, I ask the stranger in the front row, a mother-and-daughter unit, for information about the road ahead. The mother speaks reluctantly while the daughter blatantly turns away and gazes in a different direction.

My spirits sink. I remember that Paradise is Virginland. As I come down from the bus, Mr. Astur introduces me to Alla, who in turn introduces me to her brother. He is one of those modern youths whose aura leaves me cold. This type is a dime a dozen across Virginland. I always saw them in somber colors—superficial, vain.

Needless to say, I feel like a fish out of water in Virginland. They have their suspicions about my manhood. I, on the other hand, am so frustrated that I feel like fleeing the country. I hang in there by catching sight of someone on the street, say, once a week, with my breathing becoming normal again as I look at the face. I cling to the same face for an entire week.

They think that if a man prunes his eyebrows a bit...

On the bus to Lake Sevan, a couple of women point their fingers at me. "My goodness, would you take a look at that? He's plucked his eyebrows!"

Unless he's a woolly sheep, a man is not a man.

On hearing this, my Gehen-Dreamlander girlfriend broke into hysteric laughter.

"Laser! Laser! That's what they need from head to toe..."

There's something abominable in a pair of rough, untrimmed eyebrows, especially when the accompanying gaze nails you down. I turn the TV off whenever I see a singer with unpreened eyebrows. As for their love songs...

If, dog forbid, you decide to commit suicide in Paradise, go to an underground record stall at the metro to get yourself an album of heavenly music. As you browse for the miracle, you'll catch sight of a flurry of male faces on album covers. If you don't drop dead within half an hour, hang on for a bit more. You need a higher dose. Come evening, tune in to the public channel, or any other offering for that matter, and watch the parade of cockbearing crooners. It's probable that before the day opens, you will open your eyes... on the lap of Mosmos.

"Holy cats! We only recognize Yoohoo MacYehu!"

If you don't open your eyes on the lap of any of Mr.

Maimunus's prophetazzi, then, brother, Virginland is your motherland. You can go ahead and enjoy the place to the hilt...

You won't think that some of the pop divas are being inspected by these cucumbearers...

"Every pot has its cover," my grandmother used to say.

Many are the houris who cannot resist the machismo of an uncultured cucumbearer. Even Narineh, an émigré who had been out of Virginland for already seven years when I met her in Los Angelos, had this to ask prior to our possible marriage: "Do you pluck your eyebrows, or do they naturally look like that?"

"And what's that got anything to do with anything?"

"Aren't I allowed to know what kind of man I'm about to marry?"

Oh, poor sis, what fire you've fallen into!

On reading this, a female friend of mine in Virginabad shed tears of regret. She had thought I was gay.

Later I remembered that on our first meeting she had told me how in Mercedesland she had saved a young man from homosexuality. As a faithful Yoohooloon, she tried to save me, too, from the fires of Hell.

I was a homosexual. A faggot.

Faggotry, my brethren, consolidates the path of grace. Though I do not speak faggotian, I've got enough compassion to study the faggotist doctrine.

A faggot is the opposite of a man. That is to say, not one who always inspects but one who is always inspected himself. Already you see how difficult it is to translate the enigmas of Paradisean culture into Gehennish. What we understand by faggotry is an honest-to-goodness love relationship between two men. But to God's way of thinking, a faggot is someone who gets inspected. Of course the real inspector is God himself. It couldn't be otherwise, my brothers. In Paradise everyone announces that he's a man—e.g., an antifaggot, an afaggot, a nonfaggot—whereas in truth what is at work here is only one cock, that of God, in front of which everybody, without exception, bares their assholes, their blessed, divine assholes.

But you don't know, my brothers, to what extent God has facilitated salvation, and not only for the subjects of Mercedes Shaitan. All you have to do is raise your right hand, place your left hand on your heart, and declare, "There is no god but God, and Yoohoo is the Son of God, and Al-Prophet is the enemy of God."

Period. You're saved.

Except from the wrath of Bladin...

That, of course, is a tribulation sent by God in order to strengthen your faith.

When Satan cheated me, feeding me from the tree of knowledge, in consequence of which I was left with the brimstone of Hell, where there was crying and gnashing of teeth, I understood, I understood, my brethren, I understood only then, that in Paradise there is only one pecker, which is God's, and that the Redeemed are depeckered, that they surrender their weecocks to God, so as to transfer to him the role of inspecting their enemies.

This is why Maimunus shall be punished forevermore, as he tricks God by getting circumcised instead of being castrated. God punishes the insubordinate and kicks them out of Paradise. His name is Jehovah the Cock.

Still, having compassion for us, the lost ones, he sends us his only son, so that whoever believes in him will not be lost but secure eternal life. But we know well, my beloved brethren, that this God of the bipeds is a mental mirage. A sublimation of humanoid urges. A centripetal ideation. The Amaranthine Cockalorum shall vanish the day humanoids cease to bare their assholes to Him.

The creation of the Ideal Rod necessarily implies the subsequent birth of the Ideal Ass. This is how Yoohoo was born to deliver man from the impact of the Ideal Rod. But how can an ass born in a stable deliver man from dependence on the Ideal Rod, friars? Thus the Supreme Rod inspects even his only son, the Divine Ass, on the crucifix for man's sins. This is what we dogs call child abuse. Pederasty. *Thus* the quintessential inspectee obtains his exclusive license to prepare mansions for us in Heaven. The Son and the Father *are* one, codependent. There seems to be a deficit of assholes to glorify the Supreme Rod in the empyrean. Anointed apparatchiks devoted to institutionalizing and sanctifying the hierarchy of jehovic phallocracy.

The purpose of the Sacrament of Ass Anointation is to give you a carte blanche to Heaven.

What kind of father is this, my brothers? He demands "sacrifice." He seeks "glory." Like a pharaoh, I assume. Competing with Nabuchadnezzar, I presume. You would better consult a hominid dictionary to understand these two cryptic neologies. Dementia is the dimension of the Lord. Blood! Is what he imbibes. Isn't the Almighty a carbon copy of Pasha? Then why do the Redeemed love the Lord but fail to love Pasha? Unfair! In the beginning of time, this Lord inspects. At the divinely launched ground zero of time, this Lord inspects. At the end of time, this Lord inspects. *The mother*—the cosmic mother—is murdered in Paradise and replaced with the father's pendulum. But the Redeemed overlook this, my brothers. Glory to Satan! It is thanks to his chicanery that our eyes were opened as they saw the light, and for us living became death and death living. Then the dog's spirit came over us and we grasped, brothers, we grasped that Satan is the author of God.

Our Heavenly Father, Satan, holy be thy name. Thy kingdom come, thy will be done. Please collect our nano-cocks and reserve to yourself the right to inspect the insubordinate. But leave us hope for salvation. For yours is the kingdom, and the power, and the glory, forever, amen.

Thus, my brothers, is the nature of things in human-land.

Narineh, of course, didn't get to know my cock. Instead, as an orthodox Virginosa, she decided to accept God's vas deferens. The latter advised her to engage in sexual relations with me only after she obtained the divine seal of approval. Narineh even presented me with an expensive pen as the day of the Big Signing neared. One day she will part from this world without having tasted life. This is how the Virginosa lives. She has created an artificial world in her imagination and gauges men according to its standards. The Divine Rooster has enharemed the women of humankind, who in turn demand from men to prostrate themselves before them to gain their favors.

This act is hallmarked as "national tradition" in Virginland, and as "feminism" in Pornstan. The common denominator, sacrificing of the penis, is termed as "holy matrimony" throughout humanstan.

I've fallen into the fire, my bastard brethren and sluttish sisters! What shall I write you about the men in Paradise who laugh at me, who are able to keep their wives only through collective coercion? Whenever there was sexual concordance between this non-man and a woman, I could maintain an erection for two or three hours and end the sexual act only after her supplications. She would be driven baccic with ecstasy. Kathy can attest to this.

So what are they good for, those Virginlander cucumberbearers who mock people, who, through the admission of their own women, can't keep it up for even two minutes?

My sluttish sisters, hadn't you said to me that a man's worth is determined not by his ability to get an erection or maintain it, but a host of other qualities? But who knows, my little sisters… perhaps these men are merely squandering their sperm, spitting on Mamma Earth to impregnate it like the ancient gods.

These men don't even aspire to learn.

Not that I was born perfect or schooled in the art of lovemaking in my homeland, Canes Venatici. One needed years to master the fluency of enjoyment. The horrible thing is that these people's minds are perpetually closed. The hammer of Virginland's "national traditions" is their main weapon—the cronyists use it to slam the head of anyone contradicting them on ideological grounds.

Again, the déjà vu of my extraterrestrial origins...

This alien had gone through the crucible of free women, in the land of the free, had been burned willingly, had somewhat been forged into shape. Whereas the Virginoso views the woman as a gofer, denying himself any chance for growth. Absent is the field for equal energies to come into contact. One utterly dominates the other.

"I command you to be obedient to your husband," they say the Word has said.

The Word has forgotten to add, "if your husband is not a manpanzee."

"She shouldn't have married!" they'll shoot back.

But whom, exactly, would a woman in Panzeeland marry?

"I created you from man's rib," they say the Word has said.

This is male childbirth, *mes freres*—the first and last event of its kind. Men have even reversed the roles of childbirth and made women believe it. It was Adam who was born from Eve. It couldn't have been otherwise, my brothers. This is the patriarchal act of mental terrorism, uttered through the mouth of the fake god fashioned by the semiliterate priests of Yehu, who now weighs down on the women of Virginland and the whole world.

Breaking away from me, Alla and her brother start to whisper to one another. When I was a child, we referred to this practice as a "mouse meeting." My interest sinks. The banshee has brought a pussyguard with her.

I remember... how Ella asked permission from her godfather to go out to have tea with me. The godfather approved, and then invited me to his home in Saint Virginborn. I dodged him for three weeks as I waited to see where my relationship with Ella was going. I had been in Paradise for only a month. I went to Saint Virginborn with Ella, and, before meeting her godfather, we went into the Real Vatican, the Sanctum Sanctorum of Paradise, the Holy Seat of the Catholicos.

According to tradition, MacYehu has revealed in a dream the diagram of the Mother Cathedral to a foreigner called Gaga, whose father, an assassin hired by the Shah, had killed the king of Paradise. MacYehu had done this to make good on the augury of the prophet Gorgoruni: "For I shall turn the last into the first, and the first into the last."

While Paradiseans immortalized Gaga as the representative of evil, calling him "Son of Anak" (murderer, traitor), his myrmidons called him the "Illuminator" for having helped establish the new religion as the official doctrine of Paradise. The foreigner was a zealot oppugnant to the ancient culture of Paradise. After establishing rapport with an intellectually mediocre king, he led the way at the head of the king's armies, razed the ancient civilization of Paradise to the ground, obliterated its culture, and supplanted it with the new religion, massacring thousands who resisted. He decapitated Paradise and installed Maimunus's head upon the corpse. He did all this for the glory of the Lord. This campaign was launched in 301 under the motto, "Slaves, be obedient to your masters."

Gaga shut down all Paradisean schools and issued an edict prohibiting instruction in Paradisean throughout the country. Byzantish and Mesopotamish, then the tongues of the new religion, became the official languages of instruction. He became the feudal lord of fifteen provinces and established the Judolicosate of Paradise on a hereditary basis, bequeathing his acquired wealth to his descendents. Thus he was succeeded by his eldest son and for the next two hundred years his dynasty ruled Gaga's Judolicosate. The accession of this dynasty to the religious throne marked the end of the era of the great kings of Paradise.

The Mother Cathedral was built on the site of Sandaramet, the temple of the Mother Goddess. To the messianists, the name of the old site became synonymous with Hell. But Sandaramet meant Holy Spirit, the Soul of the Earth—an allusion that it was the temple of Mother Earth, and an intimable connection of the Holy Spirit to the idea of motherhood, something that Paradisean ethnography confirms.

The link of the Holy Spirit to the idea of motherhood was eradicated by the patriarchal and matricidal messianists.

Inside the cathedral, I was taken by the images of Yoohoo MacYehu's twelve disciples. They were pictured below the base of the cupola in a circle—just like the Zodiac, a cosmic calendar, implies a cycle. Evidently supplanting the concept of an ancient Paradisean calendar. I told Ella that in our lifetime and that of the next generations, these images should be replaced with those of the twelve daughters and sons of Hayk. Ella was perplexed. She was a "Yoohooite Paradisean." As all true-blue Paradiseans should be. That is what she was trained to believe.

Makoko grins from the sixth floor.

Hayk is the founder of Paradise. But he is not a historic figure per se, as many assume. He is the God of Time, the beginning of human history and civilization. His twelve daughters and sons are gods. They are the guardians of each month and the twelve hours of each day and night. My research indicated that Paradise was the birthplace of the Zodiac.

Bel, Hayk's nemesis, who corresponds to the Balthazar (Babylonian: Belshazzar) of the Paradisean epos, is the cosmic proto-victim. Hayk slays Bel and buries him in the volcano of Mount Nemrud near Lake Van. Mount Nemrud had the largest crater in all three of the known continents. Thus its mythic import cannot be overrated. It is through Bel's death that the Paradisean World and, metaphorically, the Universe, are created. As in Yoohooic mythology, the center of the Universe is located at the site where the proto-victim was sacrificed, that is to say, near Lake Van.

There is a common mythological motif whereby creation begins with the sacrifice of the elder of twin brothers. A nation is founded. Bel seems to be Hayk's elder twin. As for Balthazar of the Paradisean epos, he was likely the elder brother of Sanasar, and not vice versa, as conventionally held by popular belief and, often more glaringly, scientific thought.

Jacobus's elder brother was Esauus, from whom he snatched the right of seniority to become the mythic founder of the twelve tribes of Maimunus. This is an echo of the Indo-European and ancient Paradisean legend (Remus and Romulus, Sanasar and Balthasar), with the proto-victim motif convoluted as the theft of seniority through "deception."

The idea of the twelve gods as deities of time has been eclipsed in the Chosen One's religion since it was borrowed from a foreign source and subsequently corrupted, losing its link to the original mythological structure.

The fact of the motif's non-Maimunic mythological and ideological origins is also apparent from the legend in which Jesus, the successor of Mr. Mosmos, happens upon a circle of stones as he arrives in his "promised" land. The circle symbolizes Time, as did the clock in the predigital era. Since the sixteenth century, the ideologues of the "Scriptures" have altered Jesus's name to Joshua to create a counterfeit singularity of the name Jesus. This fiat caused the further clouding of the Pharaonic roots of the Jesus legend. The facts that Mr. Mosmos was a Pharaonian and his legend was corrupted and appropriated by Maimunus are revealed by Freud. Exhaustive research points to the person of the pharaoh Akhenaten, revolutionary founder of monotheism, as the source of the Mr. Mosmos legend. Akhenaten was succeeded by Tutankhamen, who was murdered at a young age, apparently for religious reasons. In the Scriptural legend, however, Mr. Mosmos is succeeded by Jesus. This suggests the question: Is Tutankhamen an early layer in the origins of the Jesus legend? Mosmos's Pharaonic extraction has been asserted by Manitius and a number of ancient historians. In his writings of Mosmos, Manitius does not even mention the Maimunites.

"Centuries after this unprecedented hieratic feud in Pharaohland had given birth to various tales, Mr. Mosmos's ancestry was hijacked by the Chosen One's priests, who seem to have made a conscious effort to conceal his Pharaonic descent and identity. The oral history was distorted and there came into being an anti-religion, an anti-history, an anti-memory, an anti-truth. All of which, under the banner of a bogus god christened Yehu, to this day persecute the rebellious souls of those struggling for truth. This exploit was accomplished by attributing the most groundbreaking ideological achievements of the adversary to one's own tribe, integrating the inner structure of the adversary's legends into one's own, forging an exclusivist doctrine, embezzling the adversary's identity, distorting the adversary's collective memory, apotheosizing one's own tribe and ascribing to it a divine origin, alienating the adversary as an embodiment of evil, and dehumanizing and dispiriting the adversary by attributing anthropophobic legends to one's own deity. The deed was further sealed by declaring one's ghastly tribal icon a universal god, whereby encroaching upon the legacy of humanity's spiritual accomplishments, with the goal of crushing man's spine through religious imperialism. Human history had never seen such baseness and criminality. Neither Führer BenYehu nor our Most High Lord Satan has been able to surpass these fanatics" is the illation of Black Dog, some of whose utterances I shall record in this epistle. Cantillation not mandatory.

At the root of MacYehu's twelve disciples are the twelve fictional tribes of Maimunus. And in truth at their root are the twelve daughters and sons of Hayk. The mythic origins of the twelve also appear in Pharaohland.

The godfather is a sixtysomething Dreamlander, born in Adonis Province. I faintly remember him from my childhood years. He once had a shoe store on our street. As he found it impossible to go on living with a stubborn wife, he divorced her and fled to Paradise immediatele following Saint Peter's death.

He tries to find parallels between his and my marital failures, sparing no effort to make me feel comfortable around him. I notice that, despite her affectations, his present wife does not love him.

The entertainment over, the virginowner calls a taxi to take me to the station from where I'll go back to Virginabad. He pays the taxi driver. I feel alienated. Why hasn't Ella herself seen me off?

My sentiment is not baseless. Ella spent time with me aware that I had children. But the virginowner has warned her after my departure, "Don't you dare see that asshole again."

In Virginland, the worth of a divorced father is less than a Turkish lira, my brothers.

Two months later, while passing in front of God Hotel in Republic Square, I came face to face with the godfather. He seemed to be remorseful. When he heard that I was about to buy a doghole in Virginabad, he confessed:

"Ella's parents thought you're just a tourist looking for a good time. They thought either way you'd end up going back to your wifey in Pornstan."

Which was not what Ella told me later.

Hmmmm! I might be a bastard… And who in Virginland would give a girl to a bastard from Pornstan?

Convinced that I was no longer interested in Ella, the godfather opened up. He told me about his relationship with his wife and advised me not to get married in Paradise.

"Forget about getting a girl from this place. They're way too attached to their families. If you ask me, you shouldn't buy an apartment either. Better to rent. Better yet, just find yourself a divorced woman with a house of her own and no kids. If she does your laundry and stuff, that would be enough for you. You'll live with her. Screw the rest. You don't need the headache."

I put his mind at ease as I agreed with him—which only confirmed his suspicions of my being a bastard.

In my experience, all godfathers have been inimitable.

The main mission of a godfather in Virginland, even as recently as a hundred years ago, has been to teach the groom the ropes of sexual congress on the first night of his honeymoon. Often the godfather himself performed the ritual of the Opening of the Doors into the womb of the bride. The Opening of the Doors is a Paradisean ritual symbolizing Judgment Day, during which the priest, genuflecting before the closed curtain on the altar and with his back to the congregation, uses a big key to strike a wooden box while he chants three times, "Open to us, open to us, O Lord, the door of Thy mercy." The importance of the godfather's function was due particularly to the facts that sex manuals were not available in Paradise and both bride and groom were usually virgins. The godfather also instructed the groom on the management of marital matters, in effect acting as the equivalent of a modern-day therapist. This chapter of his duties began the day of a child's christening.

My own godfather was my uncle George. A reminder of this has been preserved in a photograph from my childhood. When I was less than a year old, my parents had me christened at the Church of the Forty Virgins in Adonis. Nobody had thought of asking me first.

Ever since childhood, I have disliked the religious violations that were performed on me. They say that my aunt taught me how to pray when I was two and half. On my knees and joining my hands together, mimicking my aunt's piety, I repeated the sentences oozing from her lips: "O Lord, give health to my dad and mom..." But when the entreaty reached the line "give me intelligence, grace, and wisdom," I at once lunged to my feet and walked away, protesting, "Why? Don't I have a brain?" Afterward no one was able to sit me down to pray. I remember these incidents vaguely, but clearly recall a particular event. When I was three, I was taken to kindergarten. The following day I refused to go, declaring, "I have graduated."

Forty years hence, as I reexamined the events of my life, I at last understood that every day, at each of my footsteps, humans everywhere have tried to smash the head that contained that brain. That's the story of this dog's life.

In the photograph, I have just been taken out of the water. I'm sucking on my thumb and, leaning my head back, gazing intently at my uncle's face.

My uncle had thoroughly fulfilled his godfatherly task. His stories had spiced my childhood, his warmth and affection captivated my soul.

At three, I'm on my uncle's lap, as "we" walk in the darkness of the night, with an umbrella shielding us against the rain.

"Uncle, where does this wind come from?"

"Far away, at the top of the mountain, there's a man who sits there and blows hard."

Mountain... Man... What man? Looks like a beggar, with a rag bag... He blows... What a belly...

"Uncle, let's go to Damascus."

Within five minutes, we've left Beirut and reached Damascus, where hundreds of colorful magazines set along the sidewalks overwhelm my imagination.

One day he materialized in Las Fortunas with his wife, son, and niece, Ruzanna. Unbeknownst to me, he and my father had had a talk about marrying us. I was staying at my uncle Gary's home in Las Fortunas. When, after dinner in a restaurant at the Rio, I suggested to Ruzanna we take a walk together down the strip, given that my uncle was to meet with some old friends, everyone was dumbfounded. Gary had not come to the dinner. Instead, he had waited for us for two hours somewhere else, because of a misunderstanding for which I was to blame.

Shush... Gary and I have conspired to "kidnap the girl."

Uncle George exploded.

"I come to Hell all the way from Adonis so that my brother stands me up in a hotel. Is this how brothers treat each other? If my brother visits me, I forget everything in an instant. Even if I'm with God, I dump him to go welcome my brother."

Furious with Gary and inspired by Lord knows which chthonic muse, they had this idea that I had told Ruzanna, "Let's get out of here and enjoy each other."

"Oh, Lord! Is this something appropriate to tell the girl?"

I was a bastard. Especially since I was staying with Gary, "knowing what a piece of work he is."

My cousin, after having a "mouse meeting" with Ruzanna, solemnly declared: the reason Ruzanna has come along is because she has a boyfriend in Las Fortunas.

"Come on! Our boy is not like that! If we didn't know him from the cradle, would we have introduced him to the girl? Obviously she has exaggerated a bit."

But the winds carry the whispers of the entire tribe.

"Did you hear?"

"What?"

"Psst... psst... psst... psst..."

"Oh, no... no... no way..."

"Psst... psst... psst... psst..."

"No... no... no..."

Ruzanna's parents, on their part, had certain designs.

"Why does it matter whether he's a Dreamlander or not? The main thing is, if we talk, we should understand one another."

Dreamstan was going west. The oft-persecuted Paradise was disappearing from under the sun, of its own volition, leaving the planet in the lurch. A few more revolutions of the sun around the earth, and that could be that. Over.

I remember a poem I had learned at Dream School:

Life's raft left no trace behind,
The forgetting, too, took everything away,
My old dreams vanish like clouds,
The memory, too, passes like a song.

A soothing lie, friars. What will never be forgotten is...

Lo and behold, Ella's godfather happened to know the entire family of my godfather, uncle George. My fate was thus sealed with seven locks, in Dreamstan as well as Paradise.

Bastard! Divorced! Three kids!

There is nothing in your experience in Harlotland, brothers, which I can relate to, so you can understand the enormity of what this really means in Virginstan.

My mother's godfather was seventy years young when he left his wife. From a body that was six times the size of her husband's, she declared, "Go!"

One day he did.

This particular godfather was a poet. He wrote in Pashaish. No, he didn't. He couldn't write. He recorded his poems on a tape. When he recited them, I got goose bumps. A latter-day Sayat Nova.

His wife respected me. I remember her munching on an apple. Her guests revolved around her as though they were planets. She controlled the conversation. The others could speak only when she was busy cutting the apple into four pieces before she loudly chomped on them. The apple turned in her hands as though it were a plum.

After his divorce, the godfather meets a twenty-year-old woman at a bus station in Hell. Friendship turns into romance. They start living together, then move to Adonis.

News of the relocation reaches the wife. Adonis?

Ooooh, my honoooor...

From Gehendale she zooms to Los Bab Airport, gasping, and somehow installs her mass on a seat in the airplane, just as she used to skillfully fit the apple in her mouth. Khrt-khrt...

One morning the godfather is awakened by a knock on the door. As he opens it, the whole bulk of the wife gets down on all fours.

"Oh, let me kiss your feet... let me die for you. Forgive me... I was wrong... I swear before God... for our children's sake..."

Noticing the young woman, "Oh, may my eyes go blind... I wish I had croaked rather than seen this." She sobs and grabs her husband's feet.

The children had held the godfather's money and possessions hostage, demanding that he reunite with their mother and save the family's honor.

The godfather and the Hellian woman were bereft for three days. He went blind.

The wife returned home proud and triumphant, arms locked with her blind husband.

A few months later, the godfather died, holding his wife's honor high. As for the perpetually sickly widow, she continues ambling along life's victorious journey, from one surgery to the next...

Long live Clinton, the king of Hell.

They buried the godfather with his great honor.

"The tape... the tape..."

"Son, when he died, I was so heartbroken that I gave away all his stuff. Nothing was left. Not even a pair of socks."

f I had a smidgeon of hope that something would develop between Alla and me, it, too, vanished in short order. Half a smile. Curt replies. No questions to ask. I assume she's not interested. It was late in the game when it became clear that it wasn't so. I'm not in the habit of asking a woman more than two questions, but now I'm trapped. I must either rescue the conversation somehow or take it to a constructive conclusion.

Neither is a go. She draws me into her game, leaves the burden of talking on my shoulders, plugs in a flurry of senseless interruptions, then shuts down, withdraws into her shell, and smiles, mouth shut.

After each question I pose, my energies seem to be exhausted. I must get out of the morass. What is this woman thinking? We still have to spend a whole day together in thirty square meters.

At last the ring goes off on her cell phone—which, incidentally, is a status symbol in Virginland. (Intent on impressing a female friend of mine, some guy wishing to marry her had borrowed a cell phone and instructed his buddies to call him every ten minutes during the wedding party of an acquaintance. There was this girl who promised me a weekend getaway outside Virginabad if I presented her with a red cell phone. Idiot! With that amount, I could get four hookers in Calipornia). Now the three girlfriends scramble to decide for whom the bell tolls. It's for Alla. She takes the gizmo to her ear and slips out of the circle.

I breathe a sigh of relief and, expressing a sudden wish to be in the lap of nature, walk away into freedom.

It's been a while since I've last seen a herd of goats. But the shepherd is not around…

I recall the story of the shepherding days of Davit of Sasun. He had fallen asleep and left the herd unguarded, then gathered the wild animals and driven them to the village. At that time I was studying the epic literature of Paradise. It doesn't bow to either *Gilgamesh* or *Shahnameh*. Is profoundly philosophical. Therein are encoded some esoteric layers—about which Paradiseans know too little and the world next to nothing, and a structure that decodes the Zodiac.

In Virginville, however, there are no wild beasts. Everything is peaceful. Nothing moves. Absent is the din of Los Babylonos. There is only a lake, a concert stadium of three hundred frogs.

In the near distance, a kid gazes straight into my eyes, beckoning his comrades for help. He's scared. Perhaps he guesses that I'm a citizen of Hell. But I'm not armed, neither am I clad in military uniform. I don't want to leave the goats, yet I don't wish to frighten their young one. I like him and very much wish to take him in my arms, if only he weren't scared.

I hear music being played in the distance. I have taken a circular path out of the village, which now stands across from me. We're separated by a canyon. Another step and I'm already alone in nature. There's only the sound of the wind, whose ebb and flow are interspersed with the buzzing of insects. No more footmarks. The way the stones jut out of the earth is an indication that no being has set foot in these parts for a long time. I sit on a rock, leisurely savoring the landscape. I study the horizon intently. Suddenly I perceive a line soaring upward from within the mist. I follow its assent to the heavens. And there it is. It's Ararat, the most massive mountain in the world, whose white crest is silhouetted from behind the clouds, lying before me.

For a whole hour I lose myself in Ararat, also known as Massis Major, while I wait for the clouds to dissipate. But they keep coming and covering the peak. I begin to walk toward the mountain, without taking my eyes away from its summit. Ararat's twin, Massis Minor, is lost in the mist.

All of a sudden I am visited by the remembrance of a Neapolitan gondola ballad. I sing it out loud several times. "*Sul mare lucica, l'astro d'argento…*"

But why that gondola song and not one of the hundred or so oneiric tunes which, ever since childhood, I have cherished in my soul as holy relics of Ararat? I still haven't been able to understand. All I know is that at that moment, as I took in the grandeur of the granite mountain, that particular song came out of me like an air bubble rising from the depth of the ocean.

By the time I returned, a good three hours had passed. Our worried hosts had sent out their boys to look for me. On my way back, I come across the shepherd and his younger brother. I overhear the shepherd say, "He's a tourist." I greet them in the Paradisean tongue.

Alla's trio is seated around a table in the yard. She has been waiting for me. What? When I'm engaged in a conversation with the host's son, Alla walks away with the rest of the virgin trio, which includes the girl who had tainted my mood on our way here. From here on out, Alla does not break free of her girlfriends, forming an impenetrable triangle which she capriciously uses against me, now and then wedging an inscrutable glance into me. In the meantime, I hear the men's sermon to this Hellese—there is nothing like a Paradisean woman in this world.

In the evening I once again leave the patio, this time heading elsewhere. Before me is the sprawling vastness of Massis. Walking on the long village road, I see a beautiful face waiting for me in the distance. It vanishes as I draw close.

On my way back I find myself among a herd of cows.

I feel so close to the cows that I have an urge to hug them, talk to them. They're my sisters.

My fondness and sense of yearning are boundless. At one point I even forget Ararat, which watches over us from afar. I accompany the herd as I slowly approach the village. I'm not there.

"O, trees, I love you, my brothers."

Virginabad. Already I miss it. During the ride back to the city, I think to myself that by the time they acquire an essential understanding of how to relate to a man, these women will wreck a hundred souls.

In Virginstan there are virgins of all ages. A thirty-year-old girl (it would be a grave insult to call a virgin a woman, even if she happens to be sixty) is horrified by the idea of giving up her virginity. Her forty-year-old sister is still a virgin.

"Why forty? Make it fifty!" objected a diehard virgin.

"Fifty, fifty, fifty, fifty…"

"Sixty!"

"Sixty, sixty, sixty, sixty, sixty…"

"Seventy!"

An exquisite woman is offended when I address her as Madam. She takes issue, insisting that she's a "girl."

Looking her in the eye, I think out loud, "Who needs your girlhood?" She walks away sporting a mysterious smile.

One day she stops me on the street. My stance has made an impression on her.

Bastard!

On the way back from Virginville, I imagined myself in Natashima, home to my girlfriend, Vika. Like most Virginlander men, in my heart of hearts I longed for Natashaland. There my soul glided freely. Ararat has long ceased to orgasm, transforming its environs into a virgin prairie, where metaphysics has taken root.

I want to go to Natashima, to the living Ararat…

I had met Vika at Natashima's Casino Crystal. A Tatar girl had recommended the place.

I go in solo. Looking for someone to talk to, I walk up to a table occupied by two women. They warmly agree to have me join them. I'm from Kazakh*stan*. My father is from Armen*stan*. No, I don't speak his language.

While one subject leads to the other, I am told that one of the women loves to dance. I invite her to the piste.

Though ordinarily not a great dancer, that day I outshine the men on the dance floor. I have also drawn Vika's attention. As husbands and boyfriends return from the casino downstairs, my dance partner and I take leave of one another. I then approach Vika's table and ask her friend, Irina, to dance. Irina is the older of the two. She suggests I ask Vika instead.

Vika, meanwhile, is dancing with a Finn businessman who has his eyes on her. I chat with Irina. She is charming. I gather that she and Vika are waiting for the arrival of a work partner from Elizabeth City. They sound like dynamic women. Irina is a believer. She has built a five-million-washington church.

Vika is a regal-looking blonde of thirty-five. She's a Romanova to boot, a descendant of the last tsar. She hates the tsaricidal Lenin. No, no, Vika is no Leninstani. She is, rather, a Kremlstani—a Natashalander at the minimum. I tell her I'm writing a book and about to travel to Paradise for research.

Vika is an intriguing conversationalist. We dance until her work partner shows up. She excuses herself, asking me to wait for ten minutes. I know it will be longer.

The next table is taken by brunette Sasha and blonde Masha. By now the Finn is loitering around them. I approach the brunette, leaving the blonde to the Finn. He considers my advance an encroachment upon his turf, even if brunette Sasha does not pay him attention.

Lurking around the table, the Finn is watching me intently. I ignore him. He's half drunk. I ask brunette Sasha if I should make myself scarce. She looks at me as though I were a three-year-old.

As I take no notice of his challenge, the Finn resorts to a more direct tactic, addressing me dog to dog.

"I suggest you keep away from that woman."

He's referring, however, to Vika.

"Fine," I say, and, without looking at him, continue to chat with brunette Sasha.

"I'm serious. I suggest you keep away from that woman."

"I'm serious, too," I say indifferently, getting on with my chat.

"Where are you from? Aren't you from Alpacinoland?" he asks with menace.

"I am from Hell. My grandfather hails from Paradise," I tell him, continuing to talk to brunette Sasha.

"You Paradiseans are very much like the Alpacinolanders," he says and begins to weave some story about his grandpa. Twice I assure him that he's right. He concludes, "I respect you guys for that." I don't quite catch his meaning. I have been tuning him out.

"Thank you," I tell him.

"But that doesn't change a thing. I still suggest you keep away from these women. I'll be inspecting them tonight." He points now to brunette Sasha and blonde Masha.

"Would you like to be kicked out right now?"

"Just ignore him," advises brunette Sasha.

The Finn goes on to act cocky for another five minutes. Finally he pins his hopes on blonde Masha.

Brunette Sasha is a one-off bird. Staying with a man for more than one day is already a serious matter. My family is very, very wealthy. I don't work. I leave for Elizabeth City in a couple of days, for a jaunt.

The lounge is now almost empty. Vika's powwow lingers. Soon enough, however, we exchange phone numbers.

Then the four of us get up to leave. The Finn and I have become fast friends.

From her booth, Vika notices the exit of our drunken contingent. I have my arms around brunette Sasha. Did I sleep with her that night? asks Vika.

Blonde Masha tries to extricate herself and go home. But the Finn moves mountains to dissuade her. Somehow he is able to make her cave in and takes hold of her with tremendous gusto. At last I become aware of the silence of the night.

Our kiss does not end. It's four in the morning. We bid our farewells, on condition of meeting again at night. I see brunette Sasha off, then get myself a taxi to Hotel Rossiya, near the Kremlin.

Vika and I grow closer. She becomes a genuine friend in Natashima. Nothing is off-limits to her; all doors are wide open. She is the founder of a political organization, works at the Duma, where she knows everybody. There is no one left in the Duma who hasn't proposed marriage to her. Yes, my darling. Vika helps me in everything. She teaches me how to use the metro and the public phones, installs me in another hotel, cutting my expenses by half and promises to at once improve her Satanish.

Natashima nights are enchanting with Vika. We mosey along Arbat, where she lives. She loves to walk. We walk ten miles a day.

In Natashaland, women are always walking. When they refer to a destination as "just around the corner," you would be wise to anticipate a two-mile walk. Within a week, I regain my slim figure, which had bulged in Los Angelos for the first time. Dancing, too, helps. Here women don't tire of dancing.

I am studying Natashas. First I compare them with the women of Pornstan. Then, a month later, with those of Virginstan. Pornstani women get offended by the notion of walking. Walking is for the homeless. The most unassuming was Diana, whom one night I had dragged through the streets of Santa Monica for three hours, despite her high heels. The next day, she complained of terrible pain in her feet.

If somehow I can tolerate the finickiness of Pornian women, I'm downright ruthless to the missies of Virginland. I'm astonished. How is it that a twenty-two-year-old Virginosa is sapped by the less-than-one-mile walk from the National Library to the Youth Palace? Yet she lives on the mountainous cradle of creation...

I was struck by an incident in Sardarabad. Sardarabad is the site of a venerable monument, not far from Virginabad, where every year on May 28 the Paradiseans commemorate their momentous victory over Pasha. In the year 1918 of our Lord, that victory saved Paradise from certain extinction. A woman angrily wonders why the path to the monument entrance has been closed, forcing people to walk three hundred meters. One of the policemen is impelled to put her in her place: "Our fathers walked barefoot across the Bravoland desert for weeks on end. Is it too much to walk ten minutes in memory of their suffering?"

Once again I have this idée fixe of the Paradisean houri as a gherkin in a cellar. But Kathy is not like that. A sudden impulse on my part is enough to make her dance like a wound clock until morning, now and then leaving me to rest as she continues to dance alone in front of the mirror.

It is the first night that Vika takes me to her place, along the way proposing a string of ground rules that include her right to refrain from sex. When we reach her home, she gives me instructions on how to shower, reminding me of the fact that she's a Romanova. But the barriers collapse and we embrace with abandon.

I made an extra effort to please, though I wasn't in the habit of doing so on a first-time sexual encounter. Normally it was she, the woman, who first had to go the extra mile to earn my dedication. Vika keeps saying, "You're a superman... a superman..." I feel good. After all, the woman expressing those words is a...

We're gathered at Irina's apartment for her birthday. Her husband will call now. Please pick up the phone and tell him you work at Satan's embassy. With us is Vika's cousin, Katya. I have already met her a few times. She has the looks and brains of a Hellette, plus she has a couple of enormous German dogs. Katya livens up the ambience. She acts as interpreter, on account of her fluent Satanish. We discuss a major charitable project launched by Vika and Irina. They have already secured the official assistance of certain Eurostani governments.

I had experience in such initiatives and could be of help to them. I bring up issues which they haven't thought about. Vika is cross with me for not getting involved in the project. I could've. But given my scars of experience, I wanted the girls to build the enterprise on a solid footing, so as to prevent ugly surprises down the line. At last they suggest that I join them as a partner. I decline. They're disappointed. I am busy with research for my book, which at that moment is my sole passion. Vika understands and promises to promote my work throughout Kremlstan. Public relations are her specialty. Irina suggests that Vika and I tie the knot.

I don't tell them everything.

I don't tell them that my life's direction has changed, that I'm no longer enthused by people's interests. I think it useless to reveal such things.

One day I amazed my neighbors when I refused a proposition they made.

"This stuff is not for me."

"But what is it that interests you? You're declining a once-in-a-lifetime opportunity."

This, mind you, coming from people who were supposed to be at home in the spiritual sphere. Capitalist spirituality.

I had found my path after going through ups and downs. But what exactly had happened to me? Why had I sharply changed course? Really, why was I going to Paradise?

No one knew a thing.

Behind Cosmos Hotel in Natashima there is a restaurant whose sign reads "CCCP." We're tickled by the name. We go in. Start reading the menu. Vika remarks, "The owner is a

Paradisean." I doubt it. Indeed, the menu includes a couple of Paradisean dishes, which have not escaped Vika's laser-sharp eyes, but this in itself does not indicate a Paradisean pedigree. Doesn't the name of the restaurant imply a menu culled from the cuisines of Papa Lenin's consortium of nations? But Vika turns out to be right after all. Romanova goes on to invoke the old peasant adage, "Beer without vodka is money down the drain." We drink like *muzhiks*. It takes me barely a few minutes to get plastered.

The real trouble, however, lies ahead. Vika leaves the table on pretense of using the restroom, and, despite my objection, informs the owner that I'm a Dreamer from Hell. Next thing I know, Lyova, the proprietor, materializes in front of our table like a genie out of *The Thousand and One Nights*, holding a bottle of Paradisean cognac—a highly valued commodity in Whitebearland. This potent potable was praised even by Yeltsin, the former king of Kremlin and a renowned lush. (Incidentally, Yeltsin had followed Dog to Virginabad a day later. Sitting at a café, I was jolted when suddenly the area was flooded with God's gendarmes. The waitress satisfied my curiosity: Yeltsin and God had joined together for a chug fest in the jazz club across the Boudoir Pond. I noticed the two goodfellas from where I was sitting).

It is impossible to refuse Lyova. One has no choice but to guzzle up in the Paradisean tradition, drinking to as many people and things as there are branches on a sequoia.

The clientele begins to thin out. Lyova forces us to move to the bar, where we spend three hours savoring a smorgasbord of drinks and delivering speeches with each raised glass. Refusing to go along would have serious consequences. Apart from Natasha and Satan music, there's the Paradisean kind blaring from the speakers. We dance, drink, make merry. Lyova sheds a tear as he remembers life in Paradise before his fall into the gorge of Natashachasm. Wow! Measure the gravitational pull of the true God. Lyova keeps drinking and making us drink. A true Paradisean night in the heart of Natashaland.

It's already four in the morning. We leave grudgingly. When we reach the Zalatoy Colos quarter, where I'm staying, the night guard refuses to let us in. But who can say no to Vika? At last the man relents, amazed at his own laxness.

I throw myself into Vika's infinitely deep and thunderous chasm.

Two days later Vika accompanies me to the train station to see me off to Saint Petersburg. She stores my luggage and laptop in a locker room at the station, and then we hit the city. My train leaves late at night. It's our last evening together.

We lose ourselves in the riotous atmosphere of a karaoke café. The words fail us when the time comes to say good-bye.

"You'll be meeting the lovelies of Natashaland. But don't you forget me…"

The train begins to race across the wastelands of Natashaland.

There are four of us in the compartment. Several times I pick up the word *Amerikanetz* from my neighbors' conversation. I assume they're referring to me. I read a book on the mythology of twins, penned by Shaitan. To satisfy the curiosity of my fellow passengers, I answer them to the best of my vocabulary. *Armyanski S-SHA*. Three male heads rock to and fro in the wagon. Two of them fall asleep.

That night I can't stop thinking of Vika. I'm head over heels.

Humor Airport, Virginabad. Two in the morning. The landing gear touches the ground to euphoric applause and moist eyes…

Vardan Mamikonian has come to welcome me in his black Mercedes-Benz S600. Tinted windows. I reach him by spiking through the throng, from several directions of which taxi service is being hawked. We head toward the city. "Come on, pal, don't do that. It's embarrassing." He stops me when I try to put my seatbelt on. I remember that I'm not in Satanland.

Vardan has his own road rules. "You guys do crooked things, too, sometimes," he retorts to a policeman and goes on his way, after the latter pulls him over for going against traffic on a one-way street and warns him, blushing, "You're driving in the opposite direction, generalissimo." Vardan, however, had spared neither nights nor his health for the great battle of Eden, which only a decade ago had demanded myriad sacrifices from Paradise. He had armed the Edenites but kept his son safely out of the fray. He alone decided who went to the front and who didn't. This is why he was an untouchable in Paradise, where people wrote martyrdom songs to his glory, in accordance with the millennia-old tradition of self-sacrifice to the rex.

Vardan, soul of my fatherland,
May my soul die for yours.

Vardan's first question is about my book's progress. Only a few years ago, when we met in Gehendale, I had declined a business offer he had made, telling him I was busy writing.

He takes me to a hotel.

Two days later he helps me get an apartment. I move to Irony Street. On the way there, the real-estate agent swears some twenty times that he's an honest fellow. He offers the best apartments at ridiculous prices, "for Vardan's sake." He sermonizes about his business savvy, suggests that at once I buy a home in Virginabad. He has found several houses for Vano, among others, after the latter's disappearance from Paradise. Vano served as interior minister during the reign of Titan, yclept Eretz Leo, who reined the interregnum between Leninstan's collapse and God's accession to the throne of Demoncratic Paradise. Vano is now "pursued" by God and the Interpol. The location of the Paradisean bin Laden's lair is as yet unknown. A female friend who worked at the Interpol told me in bed about rumors that he lived in Eyfelia while God and Napoleon Bonaparte turned a blind eye.

The real-estate agent yammers away like a television set. Never listens. If I stay at the hotel, I would have to spend one hundred thalers a day; according to his scheme, my problems will be solved for a mere four hundred a month. I remind the deaf fuck that in Hell, too, there is a significant difference between the costs of renting an apartment and staying in a hotel. He tells the landlady the same thing—he has found homes for Vano himself.

As I ask the woman about the rent, he barges in. "Three hundred and fifty washingtons," he quips, winking at the landlady. Her face dazzles with sheer joy. She has never dreamed of such an amount. But I've already studied the going rates of the local housing market. I know that the apartment is worth no more than two hundred in the best of scenarios. The landlady is attractive, educated. I figure she won't object to sleeping with me. She's not rude, like the one I had met the previous day. In a vain attempt at the Eurostani look, that turkey had inflicted some garish remodeling upon her apartment, endowing it, for instance, with an outlandish bar that would've put Liberace to shame with its entertainment center... and a prison bed, thrown into some corner like an afterthought, which would barely accommodate a skeleton. "No! No!" the idiot screams. "No woman will set foot in this apartment." Today's landlady is adorable. She gives me a good feeling. I give her a counteroffer of two hundred fifty washingtons per month, with two months' rent paid in advance.

The agent tells her, "Fortune has come to your feet. You mustn't turn it away." He pockets his commission and vanishes. It occurs to me that securing a mansion in the Afterlife would be a complicated affair for a Dreamer.

The landlady's long legs invite all three of my legs to... the opera. But my Humerican doggedness gets the best of me and I never sleep with her... Aren't there any younger women, for Pete's sake? Why does the Humerican turn into a beast now and then? We get to examine our lives when we're facing death, when it's already too late. O death, you balsam of the soul and the conscience...

Back at the hotel, I had asked around about night spots in Virginabad. I was told to check out the scene along the left sidewalk of Abovyan Street. "Go to Astarteh," said the manager of my floor.

I walk up the left sidewalk of Abovyan. The opposite side is abuzz with groups of marauding youngsters. They blast my ears with their yelling and obnoxious God patois. They spit left and right. I feel like closing my eyes, my ears, running away from Paradise.

Vikhod!

But where do you run from your fate in the Afterlife? Later I experienced the same disgust at the State University of Virginabad, where students have been replaced by boyflies and girlsquitos. Even if I had the opportunity, I couldn't teach there for an hour without smashing forty cocoheads. There is a certain vibe in the air—mockery directed at all non-flies.

At that time I didn't know, my sisters, that flies and mosquitos carry millions of bacteria in them. Don't get disgusted, sisters. Disgust is borne of ignorance. The bacterium has survived the worst calamities to befall our planet. It is also expected to outlive the forthcoming nuclear holocaust. By transmuting himself into a heap of bacteria, man shall conquer the atomic bomb. The bacterium is the secret of life, my sisters; it is man's immortal forefather. Father Abraham. As they grasp that secret, the primeval tribes hold on to their roots. As for this sinner, I judged the bacterium through an anthropocentric, loathsome gaze.

It is impossible to walk twenty meters in Virginabad without coming across someone who spits right in front of your eyes. When I pass by men "standing" or squatting at the edge of a trottoir, they often cross my path with a spittle which lands half a foot ahead of me. Sometimes no less than three spittles cross one another.

"I barely duck them, bro…"

I'm glad these gentlemen are excellent marksmen and there's no one taking a direct hit on me. I feel grateful, for I have no need of more bacteria to survive on.

Wrong.

At the very moment that you relish the most delicious morsel of your food at an outdoor restaurant in Virginabad, you can be certain that some passerby will spit in front of you. Sometimes you don't lift your head so as not to see the face of the spitter, but all the same, you find a liquid full moon at every footstep.

Moonlight Sonata…

The same happens around the entrance of the presidential palace, which I pass almost every day on my way to the Academy of Sciences of Virginland. From a distance, you would think that from its bottomless spittoon the palace has strewn silver insignia at its entrance to dazzle the glitterati of Virginabad...

They spit to smoke. They spit to sputter. They spit to kiss. They spit to feel like a man. They practice-spit before laying a proper one...

I won't even talk about the national restrooms of Paradise—which weren't any better even in Papa Lenin's time, when the Dragon could not block the fountains of the immortal waters. Incidentally, you can measure the cultural caliber of a country by the state of its public restrooms.

The king, vizier, generalissimo, and members of the Council of the Anointed Ones encounter spitters at every step. One would wish that at least spitting would be proscribed in Paradise...

However, do they belong to the same tribe of protopanzees as these spitbags?

I suffocate in Spit World. As for the government of Spitland, it itself spits on me, tempting me to spit back into God's mouth.

I spit, therefore I am.

Is the logos of Paradise.

Get thee hence, Satan, for it is written, *Thou shalt worship the Lord thy God, and him only shalt thou serve.*

Then what can one say about Virginstan's wenches, aficionadas of Mercedes-flaunting spitbags? They remind me of those Pornstani birds that ignore decent men and sleep with louts who don't bother to flush the toilet in a public restroom.

I try on the nightclubs dotting the left sidewalk of Abovyan, all filled to the rafters with hoi polloi. At last I end up at Astarteh. Here the ambience is a notch higher. But though well-dressed, the clientele repels me. It beams out waves of deadly energies. Sprawling around me is the country's self-satisfied elite, ambassadors and the like, with their womenfolk in tow. It's an utter turnoff. But at least in this place you can enjoy a show, which proves to be of an exceptionally high grade. Later there's also a striptease number.

I had seen many such performances in the best strip clubs of Hell, but this one stood apart with its artistry.

Above and beyond the best that Satan could offer. Alas, when, some months later, I came back with Kathy, the quality was no longer the same.

My dinner plate is still half full when the waitress, darting at breakneck speed through the dimly-lit room, comes to my table, grabs the plate without speaking so much as a syllable, and disappears into the shadows of enchanting fairies. Minutes later, the owner walks up with a couple of women and introduces them to me.

Wow! Women of Virginland… Whores of Paradise… I lose my mind.

Maka-and-Masha. Gorgeous and educated. Maka the brunette from Shvilabad, Masha the blonde from Virginabad. Each half costs one full franklin bearing Satan's signature—a respectable amount in Virginland, the equivalent of a month's average salary. In Paradise the prices of hookers and hotels correspond to international standards. ISO 9000.

I'm intrigued by the idea of meeting Paradisean whores. Dog has never even imagined such a thing, so the anticipation is high indeed. He wishes to penetrate the womb of Paradise. He takes the women's phone numbers, but then… doesn't go through with it.

Any bastard worth his grain will not pay for sex, even in Virginland. If the women want it so badly, let *them* pay for it. Our interests did not converge.

A page from Dog's Friday diary:
One thing is clear in Virginland: women are much better-looking than the men. The opposite holds in Pornstan. Nowhere in the world have I seen so many gorgeous women in such a tiny space.

Equally glaring are the Virginoso's lack of grace, refinement, and sophistication, his crudity and tastelessness.

From head to toe, the Virginosa is the embodiment of finesse and taste, whereas the Virginoso is the reverse: crassness from head to toe.

The Virginosa is a fragrant flower, the Virginoso a repository of two-week-old perspiration. He speaks in an appalling tongue, with the pitch of a broken record and body language more natural than a monkey's.

I have yet to encounter a street lingo that causes me such repulsion.

Is this the language that burbled like a crystal fountain from Nareneh's lips, in whose euphonic rhythm I found my long-lost Paradise as I wandered the lethal tidal waves of the diasporic desert?

Is this the language that was spoken by my cousin Ann, who moved to Los Babylonos from Virginabad, the language that made waiters in restaurants stop in their tracks to savor its music?

Is this the language which in the '60s a Satanic scientist considered to turn into an Esperanto while the Mandarin of Chinmachin contemplated adopting its alphabet?

Yes, it is, except it resides in the mouths of the flies' progeny.

"You're a sick fuck. Is it news to you that every nation has its own argot?

"Who are you comparing us with? Which nation? Tell me. Who?"

"Well, if you have to ask, then be kind enough to listen. I wish we were half as good as Pasha's folk. And why are you shouting? Who needs to hear your venomous drone? You're the ones who ruined Paradise! You, enemies of creation..."

"Dog! You've gotta be a fascist! Only a fascist would weave such sickly conclusions..."

The Virginoso is immutable—even after living in Hell for ten or twenty years. You can detect these slummocks from a mile away.

In Paradise every word of the colloquial repertoire inspires me with unspeakable repugnance.

The reason lies in the malignant quality of the mental energies accompanying those words. The voice carries mortal waves. Its sustained intensity can cause death. As they realize this at the subconscious level, cultured men and women keep leaving Paradise, in order to save their lives.

"Don't take it to heart so much. This is a war generation. They had no sustenance, not a dog's chance to shoot for greatness."

"Don't play the war card. Not with *me*."

Not all the women complain. Lisa claims that though their men are vulgar, there is manhood in that vulgarity. "Only *we* can grasp that."

Knock yourselves out.

"Brava, sis."

To my way of thinking, if there were formed an elite of the most beautiful and refined women of the three-hundred-million-strong UTA, it could not surpass the elite of young women in Virginland, population three million. And if the crudest men of the UTA were gathered somewhere, their collective crassness could not possibly surpass that of their counterparts in Virginland.

The executioner of the globe's most beautiful women wants to close Virginland's doors to the world with the pretense of safeguarding "national traditions" so that its odious kind won't meet the fate of the dinosaurs. It has no wish to reform itself.

On the contrary, it is busy becoming progressively cruder, emulating the model of sisterly Natashaland's mafia gangs or the gutter rats who smoke several packs a day in a country starving to death, who have infested its capital, its educational institutions, theaters, and parks.

"Why are they so ugly?" asks my kid sister. "Everything about them is revolting. Yuck! I'd rather die than marry any one of them."

No explanation would convince her.

"And why are the women so beautiful?" she keeps asking, unable to solve the enigma.

To the Porn City woman, a male from Virginabad is worth zero. To the Porn City man, the value of a female from Virginabad is quite high, easily overshadowing that of local women.

Paradise is already running out of its stock of handsome and masculine males that used to be touted in the literature of neighboring lands. The consequence of this disparity could be that, within a few decades, a strong wave will uproot the best women from Virginland. In the past, Pasha did this through brute force, with the twin purposes of maximum self-gratification and racial purification. In our days, it will be accomplished voluntarily by the fallen angels themselves, through the large-scale coupling of Virginlander girls and Pornian boys.

This is only a matter of time. Thousands of women are online, looking for husbands in the Sheol of overseas, as their ticket out of Virginstan. The trend will only grow to reach the proportions of Natashaland, from which hundreds of thousands of lovely women have already fled to Euroland or Satanland. Satan keeps getting beautiful to the detriment of Father God and Mother Natasha.

How does the Virginosa compete in the world bursa?

She hides behind the Internet, doesn't post her photo. But this would be enough in Virginland.

I'm beautiful. Twenty-seven.

Nothing else.

A thousand bananas will rain on her lap.

Only a minority of women, belonging to what may be viewed as the liberal circles of Virginabad, break the cycle of ignorance by providing full descriptions of themselves in their online personals.

As for the rest, especially the God-inflected women of Dreamland… a mere collection of sickos.

Explaining the social perils of Virginstan strictly in terms of economics would be self-deception. The kingdom of the Grand Sheik is a case in point. I spoke to a hundred Natashas, my brethren. What they're looking for is a man of a different ilk. If the sought-after type is rare in Natashaland, it is downright nonexistent in Virginstan.

In consequence, either Virginstan will become a ghost town and be kicked out of history, or evolve into the birthplace of a most noble people, this being contingent upon the level of the Virginosa's consciousness.

But since the Virginoso has enthralled the Virginosa and made her believe that she's merely his tail, she will be hard-pressed to preserve the culture in different circumstances. Naturally, she will also be unable to instill the spirit of Ararat in her foreign-born husband, as she has had no benefit of a liberating education and is devoid of that spirit's higher manifestations. In the realm of cultural belonging, too, her essence is subordinated to that of the male.

"In order to save the pedestal of the Lord's sublunary abode and build his temple there, it is infinitely important to liberate Ararat from the occupiers and safeguard our people, the stewards and defenders of Ararat," a starving passerby reminded Dog one day. "Geographical expanses are protected by large human families—by nations."

"However," Dog replied, "the safeguarding of that people cannot be accomplished by the present persona of the Virginoso."

"Where do you see the solution, Mister Dog?"

"In terms of her potentiality, the woman of your ethnos excels the man several times over, esteemed passerby. One must liberate the Araratian woman from her shackles, secure her physical and mental freedoms—the requisites to her spiritual and intellectual flights."

The passerby walked on without answering.

Some months later, as Dog ambled through the snow piles of Imagination Square, starving and shivering, he came across a small crowd of humans that was even hungrier and more cold-bitten than he was.

"Let us strengthen the woman of the Araratian people!" chants the crowd, echoing a corpulent woman leading it.

Makoko stands still on the sixth floor, listening.

"The foreign man who marries the daughter of Hayastan must either assume her family name and nationality or choose a new family name from among the descendants of the twelve sons and daughters of Hayk," declares a five-hundred-year-old man wearing a long red hat. He is the prophet Vorotuni, but Makoko is absent.

"The woman of the Araratian ethnos must be the founding stone for the establishment of the republic of Hayastan. All of HÄY's children, daughters and sons alike, are Häy," announced Mrs. Equality.

Dog noticed that behind her stood the melancholic passerby he had chatted with.

"The woman of the Araratian people shall be educated in the spiritual values of HÄY. Tying her down to the race and family name of a foreign man is impermissible. Such captivity would unsettle HÄY's sublunary republic—it would interfere with the establishment of the divine path. The woman of the Araratian people has no need of a foreign, racist man. Whoever does not humbly accept HÄY's dominion has no place in the abode and temple of HÄY, irrespective of origin," screamed a short man who remained out of sight. A throng has gathered around him. Dog is not tall enough to see him.

"The economic, political, and social rule of the Araratian nation can be entrusted to the woman," said comrade Hakenkreuz.

The angels arrive armed with tear gas to disperse the gathering, as it is not permitted by God. Everyone flees to their divine mansions.

We've got a little problem here with your diacritical marks, Dog. How do you read Hay? You read it like the o in brother, bro. O, that's all I need to know, dude. Use these marks no more.

T he Paradisean is not unlike other peoples, though he, too, believes that he's different. As everywhere else, money and beauty are allies in Paradise. The banshees lick the Mercedes-driving men clean, thus pointing to the supreme criterion upheld by the Paradisean socius.

"No. Countless beautiful girls are far from fitting your stereotype. They only dream of finding their kindred soul, and they're endowed with the highest attributes."

"Back in the time of Papa Lenin, when a woman mentioned the title of, say, a book by Hemingway and she found out that you hadn't read it, she would at once lose interest in you. We tried to live up to these standards."

Dog lightens up at these words, but then hears an exchange with his own ears. Sitting like tanks across from one another in a café, they're negotiating, listing respective ordnances.

"I have a Mercedes."

"I have bare arms."

"I own a house."

"I have long legs."
"I'm an executive."
"I have a pussy."
"Oh, sister…"
Long live the national traditions of Paradise.
The Benz is apotheosized in Paradise. Te Mercedecum.
God and entourage, catholicos and retinue are devotees of
Mercedes Shaitan. They exhort their constituents to enrich
the corporations of Mercedesland, pulling under the rug the
fact that for sixty years straight Mercedes Shaitan employed
a double standard with regard to the Genocide issue. Only
recently did Mercedes Shaitan change his position, receiv-
ing God's absolution.

"Forgive me, Father, for I am an unworthy sinner…"
"May you be forgiven, child… go and sin no more…"
In Paradise each Benz is paid for with the sweat
and blood of a hundred families. Do you believe these
amounts have been earned through honest labor, my
sisters? Beneath the foundations of God's realm lies a
hydrogen bomb.

The Benz peacocks of Paradise belong to one of two
bloodlines. The lower type is made up of the saccharine
daddies, the higher type of the sugar daddies. Each is marked
by its specific approach to the roads of Heaven. The saccharine daddies steer clear of gross violations of traffic laws. The
sugar daddies make their status known to dreamers by passing a red light or driving against traffic on a one-way street,
in full view of God's bazookamen.

A sugar daddy, who is also an archangel in God's army,
proposes that I join him to invest in a business. Thanks to
his clout, God, the Almighty Philanthropist, shall not collect
taxes from me. The guarantee of the covenant lies in the way
this sugar daddy scurries in his Benz against traffic on a one-
way street, en route to God Café where we chat, along with a
friend of his, another top commander. Both were introduced
to me by Kathy.

There's yet another permutation filed under the Benz-
peacock bloodline. Halt! Charging forth like a rocket,
Johnny runs away from the traffic cops who order him to
pull over. Fuck! Let them pursue us if they must. As a rule,

they won't. Were they to come after us, they would lose the greasier morsels.

The Virginlandoso believes that his womenfolk are the best in the world—ultranationalism, which has infected all nations, including cosmopolitan Satan's own. The Virginosa is opportunistic, shrewd. Her chief priority is to "have a man on top." To her, marriage is more important than love, profit being her main concern. In this respect she is one step ahead of the Pornstani woman. But just like the Adonisette, her fundamental ignorance makes her confuse personal worth with status symbols. Pussies allied to possessions. They keep exploiting the esthetic harmony granted to them by nature and inheritance to demolish the republican and spiritual equilibrium of their gemeinschaft. Resplendent ladies of the nation...

The life of the Virginlander is a perpetual exhibition. I couldn't understand this, and because of it I was often bent out of shape until I saw it for what it was at close quarters. As I write these lines, I think of Narineh, she who abruptly wrote me off when she found out that I wasn't quite well-to-do. My other attributes were of no use to her.

Tell me, dear men, how many women are there in the world whom you couldn't buy? And in Virginland?

For Sale: Woman. Sex unto death. Affection unto death. Money!

Otherwise kindly bugger off and die. Who controls the universe? What controls the universe?

Ostentation is so pronounced in Paradise that even the dead get the full treatment. It's noon. I'm walking to my doghole from the library of the Academy. An open casket is being carried out of a building. Keeping the coffin slanted to one side, they exhibit Mr. Beautiful's corpse to passersby, who in turn examine the coffin's quality, the dead body's appearance.

The corpse is beautiful... much more so than when the man was alive.

This takes place at the center of the capital, across from Shakespeare's embassy. The casket has great value in Paradise. The casket is the vessel of the national traditions of Paradise. The cemetery is its foundation.

I decide not to die… at least as a way of going to Paradise.

If Pasha, the idiot that he was, were to donate two million coffins to the Paradiseans following the genocide he perpetrated, today they would have erected his statue on the grounds of the Opera.

One day, Stella wants to go home late. I'm taken aback. Usually she turned in early in the night to avoid the criticism of her parents and gossip by the neighbors. It transpired that there was a death in their building, which meant having to listen to heartrending lamentations for two days. In the past, Paradiseans were in the habit of hiring threnodists, women who wailed for the corpse.

Instead Stella and I went to the Delta nightclub, to take in some light music. Performing were X, X, X…

And we cavorters.

The main decoration at the homes of the Redeemed consists of large, mounted photos of the deceased. One wishes that at least they would be kept in a private room. If you gain the izzat to be entertained as a guest, you'll be sure to be watched over by a black-and-white dead man or woman in the living room.

They love the dead, hate the living. They kill to love—a nation of unfulfilled necrophiliacs.

They live with the dead and die every day.

They die and force you to die as a result of collective hypnosis, an all-embracing covenant between the blind and the dead. A child comes into this world to execute the contract signed between the living and the dead.

"Well, if only they knew how to die. They take with them information that slows down the development of the cosmic mind. They carry their damaging wavelengths from the human innerworld to another realm," complains Satan's Reaper.

"They don't know how to die since they don't know how to live," replies the necrologist as he surrenders his soul to the Reaper.

"A nation born of the dead, as all other nations," concludes the internationalist.

Above the heads of the White House and Mecca hover masses of eloquent cadavers.

"Follow us…"

Man follows and cries out "Freedom." The dead speak from thrones and pedestals, churches and minarets. Man chooses the best of the deceased to follow. Paradise is the mirror of both Satan and Al-Prophet. Necrolatry is the cornerstone of human civilization.

T he Virginosa is led by fear—only then does love or respect enter the equation. The fear advanced by a certain chain of men controls her consciousness. The secret of controlling her lies in the realization of this fact. If she's scared of her man, she turns into a cat. The Virginoso is considered weak if he doesn't terrorize his woman, who accordingly manifests the degree of her respect and loyalty toward him.

"Just how many days have you been here to express opinions about us, you bastard? I tell you, you're a subjective lunatic," a lordolatrous lady confronts me.

"Ten minutes of waiting in line at the bank or sitting in a theater is enough for me to see the spiritual picture of the whole nation. Ten minutes is enough to write volumes about you people, my dear objective sumac."

"You Pornians come in two varieties. You either worship Virginland or lambaste it to smithereens."

"Excuse me, madam, is your husband a spitter by any chance?"

I knew a young Edenite who had left Virginland and moved to Los Angelos with his wife and two children, after being infected with lung inflammation during the war. He had been a fighter in the heroic battles of liberation. A balanced individual, neat, handsome, charming, dedicated to his family. An expression that his cheerful wife used to make has been etched in my memory: "How *delish!*"

Years passed. One day he waited six hours to have a talk with me. He needs some advice.

They've moved to Santa Varvara, where there are no Paradiseans. His wife has stopped loving him. She sleeps with every other Joe, even "black junkies" hanging out on the streets. Often she does it in front of the children, who, huddled in one corner, cry at the sight of their mother's behavior.

Only a few years ago it seemed that they were an ideal couple. What went wrong?

Such were the limits of the traditional Paradisean family, whose strength was put to the test in the absence of violence.

And this example was not unusual.

What could this good-looking man do with all his manhood? Captivated by the TV series *Santa Varvara*, he and his wife wished to live in the pulse of Hell. This is the problem: when the Paradisean woman bares her crotch in Pornstan, a thousand cucumbearers are ready to rush inside. But when the Paradisean man looks for a pussy, he can't find one without having to pay for it.

He longed to go back to Eden. He needed advice on how to get custody of his children. But his mother, a veritable grimalkin whose presence on the streets of Gehendale was like a mole on the beautiful face of Hell, argued, "Sonny, I will never go back!"

She was being pampered by Satan, the All-beneficent, the All-merciful, Receiver of Many.

Long live the Demoncratic Imperium of Gehenna, our mighty Satan!

The wife, meanwhile, had had a taste of freedom, titillated as she was by a different lover every day. She had no need of money, that is to say, her husband. He had sacrificed precious years for her to get a college education, had worked hard to build a family. Now he loafed around in the realm of the absurd.

Good-bye, Charlie.

"How *delish!*"

That's national traditions for you.

"Dog, what we've got here is a woman who has been liberated from the man's shackles, from national traditions."

The ostriches refuse to see that half the Paradisean women in Los Angelos are hooked on drugs.

Last names ending in "yan," "yan," "ian," "yan…"
Every single day, a female friend of mine, who heads an
STD clinic in Los Angelos comes across long lists of Paradisean patients inhabited by gonorrhea, syphilis, and other
erotic life forms.

What's the solution? To apply even more horrible
domestic violence, as it was once the case in Talibstan? And
why did some of the most beautiful women, who could
seduce any man at any time and had been with dozens of
lovers, subsequently become loyal and devoted to their
mate, utterly aloof to the men approaching them? This bastard could attest to this through his own experience.

The solution lay elsewhere and not in the archaic and
brutal tenets of traditional culture.

"It's doubtful, Dog."

The Virginoso rejects the Natashas. He is used to his
workhorse. To him a Natasha is a plaything. She can't dedi-
cate herself to the family. He draws his conclusions through
his experiences with the hookers of Natashaland.

"Stop praising Natashas already. We've had enough."

"How *delish!*"

The manpanzee has no interest in cultivating either
his inner or outer qualities. His brain is split in two. One
half gets off on Franklin's image, the other his own cock.
But this is not to be confused with sex as we know it.
The difference between them is the difference between the
orangutan and civilized man.

Some say that the bastard's generalizations are a consequence of Satanic prejudices. It is for his sheer pumping
prowess that the Natasha considers the Virginoso "hot."

Even Kathy used to say that caressing is for old-timers.
It was hard not to agree. Every time we met, it would take
us barely two minutes to begin a three-hour marathon of
sexual communion. We kept delaying the time for our post-
coital caresses. These moments were delightful. We were
sexually compatible. An orgasm with Kathy could drive one
to insanity.

From my balcony you can see Mount Ararat. It inspires, soothes. I have taken my desk out to the balcony, which I've turned into an office. I've been in Virginabad for less than a week, and already I have no desire to step outside. I don't want to hear anyone's voice, see anyone's face. I stay in my kennel for an entire day, in a state of meditation, so as to regain my mental and spiritual equilibrium. I say to myself, "This nation has lost Ararat because it didn't deserve it. And it won't reclaim it for so long as it's not deserving of it."

The next day I notice in me a female attribute: I see my surroundings through the peripheral vision of a woman, without having to actually look at someone. The process of biological transmutation has accelerated within me, culminating in the development of a quality identified with another gender.

I was a woman who loved women...

Mockery is praxis in Virginland. The atmosphere is poisoned with slurs and sneers. As Lilith and I walk along Virginshah Street, we notice a couple of sashaying Natashas. Ten paces ahead of them are a couple of Virginlander missies, also strolling. They constantly turn around, glimpse at the Natashas, and giggle while maintaining their distance.

The snow-white Natashas are tall, veritable magnets in motion. They're dressed to the hilt. They stride proudly. They have come to Virginland to make money off those men whom the local virgins have left starving. To the Natashas, the giggling of the mice is "Trivial, like a stone tossed at Ararat..."

Here are two sets of women face-à-dos. One tall, the other short. One captivating, the other bland. One beautiful, the other ugly. One enterprising, the other parasitical. One independent, the other servile. One manifesting generative energy, if veering from convention, the other aborting it, turning it into vampirical venom, violating the temple of the Cosmic Mother...

And boorishly mocking the better couple.

I'm at Marco Polo having dinner with Kathy and Nuneh. A black man stops at the entrance and peers inside. Suddenly the whole restaurant turns to him, as though noticing an amusing ape that has escaped from the zoo.

Every day I became witness to a hundred such incidents. I myself was an object of mockery. Here it is impossible to come out on the street without being subjected to the onslaught of pairs of eyes scrutinizing you with the stares of a pathologist into a microscope, compliments of "men" who have their own conceptions about how their gender should look and behave.

And what can I tell you, my bastard brethren, about the sealed-hole virginot who looks down on you with flagrant contempt, brandishing her two-hundred-dollar dress and ten-dollar hairdo, especially if she's got the backing of her lover's, husband's, or father's pelf? As to what bloodsucking or siphoning means they would have to employ for acquiring her chattel, the vampire woman couldn't give a solitary shit.

The vampire is that who only takes. In this land, she snatches the mental and spiritual energies of others without giving back a thing. She sucks people's energies, wrecking the inner balance of the social order. On this score also the Pornlandette is still far from topping the Virginlandette. And what is the degree that vampirism would reach in Virgin World if some day it attained the economic standards of Pornstan?

But it would be unfair, my brothers, to single out the Virginlandette with such weighty reproach. In truth, her conduct is part of a universal phenomenon prevalent among all peoples, in various guises and at varying degrees of intensity (just ask Brother Paul, who will tell you quite a few stories about his travels). Simply, the behavior of Virginlanders is nonsingular, despite their sordid notions about virgin women. The roots go deep into the millennia.

Love one another, my brethren, salute each other with a sacred kiss. The churches of Paradise salute you. By the Lord Almighty, Vrtanes and Aristakes also send you many salutations.

Vampirism, my unholy brothers, is a manifestation of women's war against men, a challenge to rational thought and the achievements of civilization. This indicates more than an ordinary superiority complex, though in part it has a defensive function against the labors of men. As she strives to become invincible, the woman throws down the gauntlet with the destructive might of the cosmic ocean, vociferously declaring her primordiality.

A new class, that of the vampire woman, is now asserting itself in Virginland. If the proportion of men able to hold sway over these women is almost nil across the world, it's even less in Virginland.

The *appéros* aren't perturbed. "Everything will turn out okay, *appé*..." If the *appéros* are at ease, then the situation isn't doomed. They will take care of things when the time is ripe.

In the virginoid cant, the word *appér* is a corruption of *akhpér*, meaning brother. But the *appér* (also called *appé* or *appéro*) is a social class unto itself, straddling all segments of Virginlander society. A good share of the *appér* class are the dregs, but the rest lend the country a distinct hue.

Three sublayers. The *akhpérs* sit at the helm. They're rich, the high-class element of the mafiosi. They're patriotic and generous. Then there are the *appéros*, ostensible chameleons who have their serious enterprises nonetheless and are patriotic for the most part. The third layer consists of the *appériks*, who are the faithful lackeys of the *appéros*.

The crème de la crème of the *appéros* have a distinctive culture of unwritten laws, which distinguishes them from the rest of Virginlander society. The *appéro* is a dude of the street, quick-witted and capable of solving any problem. A factotum present in all castes and pasquinading all, in the army and on the frontline, procuring a modus vivendi, thus forming an oblique stratum, a transversal in the pyramid of social stratification. The *appéro* can deceive, but does so fairly. He can also be generous if he takes a liking to you. Some type of perverted dog, you might say... Made in Paradise.

One day I'm out to buy a sandwich from the steakhouse of an *appéro*. The placard says three hundred drams.

"You want everything normal, *appé?*"

"That's right, *appér*."

He gets to work with vigor. I come back in ten minutes. He is standing over an *appérik*. While the latter complains that he can't fit my order in a sandwich, the chef shuts him up with curt, debonair orders. At last he impatiently takes over and somehow fits the meat in the bread—which, regardless, I can't manage in my hands. He charges me twelve hundred drams. He has shoved in four times as much meat as what I know to be normal.

The *appér* does all this with such verve and panache that I'm disarmed. Perhaps watching the *appéro's* bravura would be worth being late to the humanoid theater…

This bastard thought, however, that the fast-growing vampirism of Virginland's women would end up proving too much for the *appéros*. Such women, whose various types we're familiar with in Hell, will within a few decades crush their men under their stiletto heels (Pressure=Force/Area: this is how my physics teacher, Mr. Eli, had explained the terrible impact of women's heels). I felt sympathy for the *appéros* and wished to share with them our life experiences, my brethren.

Virginland's economy had not yet recovered after the collapse of Leninstan. Regardless, it pushed on confidently toward the future. Just a few decades more, and its living standards might reach those of an average Eurostani country, even outdo them. Virginland used to be one of the main industrial hubs of Leninstan's enormous confederacy. Following the union's dismantlement, during the most ruthless of the transitional years, far-sighted men had engaged in serious commercial activities in Virginland.

If today the vampire class was asserting its presence, tomorrow it could grow into a runaway menace.

There are, of course, solutions, and men must be prepared to face the danger of this silent war, which the women will hurl at their necks. Friars, back in Hell, we had discussed this matter among ourselves, made our conclusions, and confirmed them on the strength of personal experience.

I see the seeds of vampirism also in women's narcissism. One glaring indication of this is their treatment of men in nightclubs. As men slither under the women's legs like famished beggars, so as to be allowed a smidgeon of attention, these wallflowers snub them with uncalled-for insults and dance… to the mirror.

Though there is another reason for this behavior.

"I have slept with Cinderella," gossips Fullofhimself the Manpanzee to his buddies, even if all he's done has been to talk to her for five minutes. Thereafter these dildos will induct Cinderella into the hall of fame of "loose girls." She loses her chances of finding a husband.

In the case of the virgin, her narcissism stems from her conviction that her power lies in her virginity. The moment of relinquishing it marks her perdition, turning her into an odalisque. With this in mind, she tries to boost her social standing, keeping her head high vis-à-vis the cucumbearers courting her.

In the case of the assgiver type, the guiding principle is all about exploitation of the broad facilities afforded by virginocracy.

The woman of above-average beauty is more prone to becoming a vampire. She knows she commands high value in the sex bursa, and accordingly uses her assets against men. The vampire woman announces her price with a facial expression: "One million thalers."

"Ten million thalers," somebody objects.

At any rate, there's big money to be made. Toward this goal, she invests merely a few grand. In Virginland, such investment comes from the father's pocket. Stupid men (in Virginland, the honor goes to the *akhpér* boys) cough up the asking price. Your problems are solved, sister. This is why her market value remains stable.

And how does the scheme work? Only through the systemic exploitation of other men by the iron hand of the law of an off-limits economic ideology. Each man at the top of the pyramid sucks the life out of a hundred fellow men, ruins the destiny of a hundred couples, wrecks the happiness and future of a hundred children in order to pamper one vampire par excellence. But why would no one revolt against such perversity? You are lured into believing that what holds true for some holds true for everyone. Hope! His ways are institutionalized—you are only allowed to "express concern," not revolt. Love! The thought of revolting is a taboo that pigeonholes you as a pariah. Here *and* in the Afterlife. The underlying ideology aims to abort all defiant social cohesion by labeling it "conspiracy" or at best relegating it to the domain of art or religion, to be released through catharsis, thus further institutionalizing the system. Her worship is inculcated by transforming currency into virtual power through the aid of the mass media. The same forces that have thralled generations of humans through the agency of religion are at work here. Faith! Idolatry summa cum laude. Her heavenly father is branded "freedom," and our faith our "way of life."

These *akhpérs* are clueless, my brethren, as to the fact that there is a dog way of getting the best of the vampire and straightening her out. To ignore her of course, but not with a passive comportment. The passive man can indeed neutralize the woman's vampiricity, but wouldn't be able to get his hands on her. This is the reason that men should learn our brotherly mathematics, which can be distilled into this: to pass in front of ten women and write "0" on the "1 million washos" labels fastened to the pussy hangers. Nine of them will disregard you, often with vicious hatred, often with indifference, but the tenth will say, "Half a million."

Hello, bargain.

"0" again.

"100,000."

"0."

"50,000."

If the price of an ordinary woman is five grand, you can pick this one up for ten.

Oy yoy yoy… where does this leave the soul?

In the hearts of poets.

Hypocrites! All of your loves are fake. Pathological expressions arising from sick minds. From A to Z, your poets do nothing but rave idly. Man can love only himself. Self-love is at the core of all loves. Otherwise there is only blind love, which results in disillusionment. Am I not right, my canine brothers? Does love need an object? If so, wouldn't it be inferior to its object? In hominid terms, does it have an ontic value?

When there is no love in the world but a web of jealousy, rivalry, domination, possession, rage, and hatred created by beggars of love, when poets themselves are delusioned by icons of their own creation, when the world has shriveled under the heels of vampires, when the religions purporting to have love as their foundation have turned into systems of slavery and exclusivism, only the bastard is capable of taking what he wants from life, turning upside down the order of the world in this whorehouse of vampires.

Verily, my brothers, it is useless to boast. I merely wish to reach the Lord's visions and revelations. I knew a man of Yoohoo, who fourteen years ago (whether in the body I do not know, or out of the body I do not know; only God knows) was snatched away to the third heaven. And I knew another man (whether in the body or apart from the body I do not know; God knows), who was snatched away to Paradise and heard inexpressible stories which I am not permitted to speak. I will boast of such men. But on my own behalf I will not boast, except in regard to my weaknesses. For even if I wish to boast, I will not be foolish, since I will speak the truth. And the Lord said to me, "My grace is enough for you, for my power is made complete in what is feeble." Therefore I take pleasure in being weak, in insults, suffering, persecutions, and distresses, for the sake of Yoohoo. For when I am weak, then I am strong.

My dear brothers, playing the vampire woman like a violin requires a special skill. Let this be our creed, the first book of our initiates. Here are thirteen commandments to those building an abode, which Motherdog gave the prophet at the end of his forty days of solitude on the mountain, and which was endowed by devotees with the title *The Gospel According to the Son of a Bitch*. A voice was heard in the desert. It said:

First:
Fuck her.
If she plays hard to get, let her take a hike. Go to the next one.

Second:

Don't love her.

Your love is your death; your nonlove (or her love) is your life.

Third:

Don't be loyal. Break your promises.

Once you have her, continue seeking other women. Like a Damoclean Sword, dangle other women over her head. Try to get your paws on a more attractive or younger woman, even if she be a bimbo—the more vapid the better.

Fourth:

Don't invest in her. You don't build a house on a fucking ocean.

Know this: she's the landlord, you're the tenant. Whatever you give—money, years, children—is lost. And be careful—every day she will draw you deeper into her web. Give little, take a lot. Let *her* follow the Golden Rule, pray, and wait for results. You'll find it easy to unfasten yourself, to fly into the arms of another.

Fifth:

Leave the burden of your relationship's salvation on her own shoulders.

If she talks of equality ("I can do the same thing"), kick her out at once. Let her go tit for tat. Screw her. Next.

Sixth:

Hold the reins.

Be indifferent—except in rare moments, and only superficially. Don't answer her calls. Stand her up. Don't ever let her make you wait, either at a rendezvous or by the phone. Women are psychos—evolutionary degenerates. They are attracted only to those who ignore them, to those who subtly simulate a knack for violence, not humanity. For this breed, the only categorical imperative is the violent cock.

Seventh:

Be inscrutable.

Always have an activity that's more important than her.

You have important projects. Her job is to support you. Let her forever try to know and understand you as you foil all her attempts.

Eighth:

Live at her expense.

Let her work; let yourself live it up.

Demand everything. Offer nothing in return. Let her pick up the tab on your outings. Reap the most pleasure out of her, spend a bare minimum. Always be on the receiving end, particularly when it comes to sex and money, and especially if her father or one of her ex-lovers is loaded.

Ninth:

Don't trust her.

Ever! She's fucked in the head. The meaning of her existence lies in her enslavement of the man by means of pleasuring him. She'll drop you if she finds a slave. Let her give you pleasure, but don't be her slave. If you feel pity, she has reached her goal. Release her lest you become a sadoid—the bastard is not always unfeeling.

Tenth:

Cut out her tongue. She's a terrorist, and her weapon is her tongue.

Don't try to understand her. Let others do that. Don't praise her; slap her faults to her face. Don't ask her for her opinion. Make a tempest out of a teapot. Don't ever let her complain, even slightly. Not even a peep out of her.

In the human world, there is no law that says psychological terrorists and manipulators should be incarcerated. Otherwise this next commandment would have been milder. The cunning female can use her tongue to end the life of a male, while the malleable male is not allowed to respond in kind when faced with psychological warfare. This is what passes for civilization. They can shove it up their asses. Civilization is founded on lies, the family on deceit.

Eleventh:

Scare her stiff.

This has been and continues to be the supreme law of controlling a whore.

"Get angry" if she veers in the slightest from your rules. You are the lawmaker. Retaliate at a 1 to 10 ratio for each of her acts that don't please you. For the ones that do, pay her back only 10 percent or with a single word.

The following two paragraphs, which appear as a footnote in the *Gospel,* seem to be an interpolation by a fraudulent hand to defame our species. The earliest desecrated and burned manuscript of the *Gospel* against which Eznik of Golp has unleashed his magisterial philippic does not contain it:

Wherever it's legal to do so, beat the nagging woman. A touch gently. Know when to do so and know where you're hitting. If she's pregnant, get out of there—it's too late to discipline her; it's your fault. It's not always that you can disentangle yourself from such a woman, especially if you have kids. Remember, you're the one who is responsible for your actions. But if you follow the other commandments to the word, you'll have no need for this one. At any rate, just keep it at the ready…

As for places where it's not legal to beat her, let them change the law. A law that works against the forces of nature compels a man to lead a hypocritical life. He'll do this only to save his own skin. Of course you can be ten times more vicious than she is, but know that she was born into that culture, with thousands of years of experience behind her. She draws from her experience; you draw from yours. If you're a "civilized" man, then perish!

Twelfth:

Desert her. Temporarily or for good.

Without a reason or an explanation. Let her learn to keep you.

Why did you get her pregnant? Why did you get married? Desert her, especially if she has lied to you. And almost always she has. Don't tether yourself with those "moral" chains. Let the asinine "civilized" world rectify its mistakes. Centuries will pass before history finds its proper course, if ever. Meanwhile enjoy your life.

Thirteenth:

You are her god. Don't let her worship another.

Demolish her dead. Demolish her living. Demolish her gods. Stupid is the man who is involved with a woman, a vampire in particular, knowing that he's replaceable.

The bastard is the whore's antidote. Only he can render her harmless. Only he can keep her in balance... by tossing her off-balance.

My son, if you follow even a portion of these vital commandments, provided you do so with skill, you will be able to break the vampirical will of the planet's most beautiful women, wrap them around your finger, place them snugly in your pocket.

But...

There is a but here. You've got to have something going for you. Anything. You can get it through self-cultivation. And it doesn't have to be anything major. You don't even need to be good-looking. Often ugliness can be more useful.

Beauty, they say, is in the eye of the beholder… and how many of them know that the eye is located in the brain? The secret lies in the devouring of the other's brain. You can pocket for 5,000 the product advertised for 1 million or 100 million, and, furthermore, extract a few more millions for letting her out of the cage.

Remember: if the woman has turned her beauty into an icon, she's either suffering from narcissism or has some other kind of psychological damage. Either way, she's trouble. Get rid of her. The truly beautiful woman, who is healthy of soul, is quite comfortable with your ugliness.

She might go crazy for you. Worst-case scenario, you'll become her "ugly darling."

Ugly is beautiful.

My son, these commandments kick in after the conquest of the woman. Attracting such women is another talent, one which you can acquire when you complete the advanced-bastard course, SS[†]. Your brothers, though small in numbers, are fully-realized dogs and will be able to reestablish society's inner balance.

This is no evil, my son. It is, rather, intended to restore the balance of the yin and yang energies by reining in the perpetrator, paving the way toward the cosmic path.

The bastard is a terrestrial agent of the eternal Tao.

But know, my son, that you will meet worthy women mostly in those who are neither beautiful nor ugly. The value placed in the beauty of the vampire is a consequence of collective hypnosis.

The female ego, in front of which a man turns into a mouse, has become a standard of civilization, a yoke fastened onto man's neck through literature. This ego is the Vampire. This ego of a thousand and one frills must be

---

[†] Brothers, my initial reaction to this naturally was that it stands for Ass-Ass. But upon further research I came to the conclusion that it might stand for Simulation and Seduction.

shattered. It behooves the woman to bow her head and kiss the man's ass before he even begins to consider marriage and afterward doesn't saunter into the cove of another. But alas! Civilization has been transformed into a system of terrorism against the male. Let her approach you. You choose. Only then are you the chooser. Yes, it is this very ego that must be eradicated, my son. And yes, it seems impossible—women would join forces to sequester you.

If gender is a function of social persuasion or a mindset, as certain feminists maintain, then the universal phenomenon of the woman's psychodrama, which passes for nature, is also a function of persuasion, only more so. The man must fall on his knees and kiss her derriere for her to say "yes." The woman a goddess, the man a pussy-licking servient, the Paradiseman an ass-licking dalit. Thus this ego of the woman, the "national holy of holies," is the greatest snare inhibiting the manifestation of the unmanifest, blocking the path to the cosmic harmony that keeps eluding us. Turn its basis, which is female beauty, into a doormat, my son. It is impossible to create Paradise on earth without blasting the foundations of civilization.

But do we really need a Paradise, brothers? For whom do we need it? Would opinions for or against this matter be byproducts of ideology? A humanoid thing?

"Up till this point, the bastard has portrayed himself as a sex maniac and looks like he wants to prove to someone that he's a real man, as though reacting to being taken for a sissy so far... I mean, is a cock the only indicator of manhood? Pity the man, pity the knight whose legitimacy resides in the cock..."

"And do you know that the women of Mimunus Schnozzolus come first in the world for being obsessed with the size of a cock? They might not have any knights, but they're still winning their wars."

"Making comparisons is counternationalistic."

"Sure. They've emulated your schnozzles."

The pride of a virgin girl is a myth manufactured by Virginlander literature. In Virginstan a woman's worth is determined by the degree of her uppishness. The net effect is that there is no field of intimacy between man and woman. Public displays of intimacy are frowned upon. When a man and a woman are seen together somewhere, they are automatically branded as a couple "doing that thing." If a man is seen with two women, then he is "doing that thing" with both. This is why he is labeled a "player" by the civilized and a "bastard" by the non, while the woman in both instances is labeled a "whore."

So what would you label a man who is seen with ten different women, such as myself?

"Poor women. How wily this bastard is…"

Why don't they understand that I am Virginland's number one bastard?

In Virginstan people live in camouflage to preserve their "honor."

I am a dishonorable dog.

In the matter of choosing a woman, the Virginstanoid has to deal with a plethora of artificial limitations filed under "tradition." A man and a woman are not allowed to have a full-fledged liaison unless they are husband and wife. This is ground zero of the dysfunction. The supplication has already penetrated the brain. "How could I use her?" deduces the national ass. Only the Natashas are built for use as objects.

When a man approaches a woman, he is lured strictly by his estimation of the external factors: the expected sexual attributes underneath the garments plus "givens" such as her zip code and social and financial status in terms of her father's employment, possessions, and holdings. He has no clue, for instance, as to her skills in the bedroom, since, usually, he himself lacks any education in that department.

"What? You only want us to have sex, like we were some sick Satanicans?" countered the reporter of Paradise TV to a dog arguing with some pilgrims in Virgintorch on the national holiday of the Holy Virgin.

"No, I want you to play penisochle, or make socks together. Until such time that the symbiosis of male and female energies is not optimized, you can shove a stake up this society's rectum and it still won't take a step forward. Even if it did, at whose expense?"

"Sex is a bogus category."

"You're the ones who are bogus."

"We are creating civilization."

"It will collapse."

"If we were to have free love, everybody would follow their base animal instincts."

"What's the difference? They'll follow them regardless, only in more sickly ways. You will engender monsters and gods and saviors. Ignore the issue, and you would only be turning it into an indefinite open season for the sex merchants. You can't rely on fossilized attitudes to define the domain of sex. And unless you ensure its freedom from the shackles of artificial moral construct, you can't cultivate the higher domains. The whole thing will crumble. You must start with the root. The root is sex. The only imperative is not to be left below the ground. If you are, that's not sex's fault."

This clip was followed by a broadside against dogs lately arriving in Paradise from Hell, compliments of the program guests, the estimable cabooses of Virginstan.

There is a certain psychology that distinguishes Virginstan's female nobility. With a cigarette on her lips and the indifferent lazy side glance of a brooding chicken, the "noble woman" sizes up the men teeming around her, confusing artificial aloofness and contempt with feminine virtues.

Here the woman has a certain standard of deportment vis-à-vis the man. Whether or not he shows interest in her, she will either like or mock him, will gossip about him with her girlfriends, even if he be a mere passerby.

Among the assgiving subclass of "virgins," there is no respect for a man if he happens to be younger than the vestals' fathers. In consequence, absent is the field of civility where it would be possible to build an optimally functioning, cultured society. The la-di-da values man through the "civilized" eyes of third-tier magazines and tabloids issued in Satanland.

The world's best women… genuflect Masochistan's poets, singers, priests. Regal ladies of Hayastan.

I n Virginland, the spiritual supposedly blasts off only after signing the contract. "First show me the money. Then I'll give you the goods."

"Love is a technicality," had said a suitor, the rich son of a parliamentarian, to one of my female friends.

"It's actually a *tectonicality*," she had shot back at him jokingly. Her eyes had been opened after meeting yours truly, and already she had a fresh set of criteria for considering a man.

The parliamentarian's son was not the first suitor to propose an engineering solution.

Outside the capital, "asking for a girl's hand" means that a male suitor can attain physical intimacy only after being granted approval by the network of the virgin owners—the girl's father, brother, uncle, and godfather. But first, wedding ceremony. The Paradiseans have taken the tradition with them to the four corners of Dreamstan, in their quest to illumine the omnipresent darkness.

Most Dreamlanders are even more ultra conservative than the Paradiseans, whom they regard with contempt. In Dreamland time has stopped in the year 1915, the year of the Genocide. In Paradise it stopped in 1922, the year of its accession to the Great Consortium of Leninstan. So the Paradiseans are seven years ahead of Dreamland and will soon complete the eighth year, *inshallah*—each of their years being equal to one diabolic century. God is making every attempt so that by Anno Diaboli 2022 Paradise reaches the year 1923 of our Lord. And this agent belittles the Lord.

For the progressive types of the capital, Virginabad, the marriage contract can also be verbal. The man must promise "serious intent," which, to the seers, is tantamount to a promise of marriage. He is then permitted to get close to her, though usually not by much. The hole is hermetically sealed.

Either way, the common denominator remains. The woman grabs a promise of marriage from the man, accepted as being unto death, to allow him to "have his way." This is officially sanctioned spiritual and mental terrorism directed at the man, precisely because of which two enormous industries, prostitution and pornography, were developed across the globe.

No matter in which cove of Dreamland a swimmer happens to meet a Virginosa, he will fall into the seine of virgin owners. That net is never lifted, not even in the most intimate moments, driving the man into the arms of the Nereids.

Freud has said that the bed of every couple is a sestasyngamous cove, including their parents. You wish! In Virginstan that number jumps to fifty-six.

There are fifty-six million free porn sites on the littoral of the Web ocean. To date, barely 20 percent of the world's male population makes it to the shore. If each site has had a thousand visitors, then each man has accessed it one hundred times. If one hundred thousand, then women have lost six trillion chances of orgasm by this count alone. That's two thousand missed opportunities per woman.

Who is to blame?

Just as the child has been substituted by the puppy, the penis has been replaced by the vibrator—or, in the case of Virginstan, the aubergine, the national totem of Virginstan.

"Bobby, sweetheart, get us a couple of kilos of long eggplant so I can cook you some out-of-this-world *dolma.* Just make sure it's the thick kind. I don't want it to be tasteless like last time. Yesterday they were saying on television that eggplant is very beneficial. It's got a lot of vitamins. Very good for your health. Come on, honey, don't be late."

Gossip has reached my ears that women's lib is about to introduce a bill in the Lower House of the Anointed Ones to have the coveted fetish annexed to Virginstan's flag.

As a more vulnerable creature, the man safeguards his physical and psychological equilibrium by utilizing whatever means available to him at the moment, through whatever financial strings he can pull. You don't feed a starving man with promises of a barbecue party next summer, unless he believes in the Afterlife. And if a healthy man does not channel that energy into a surrogate undertaking, where will he end up every seventy-two hours?

The female exploits the male's vulnerability by snatching from him the supreme sacrifice: marriage till death. The man who does not cave in to the nuptial sacrament is bar-coded as a player and loses his social standing. As for the soul who shows contempt for the feminacentric system and immerses himself in the sea of pleasure, into the caves of cocottes or the bays of jezebels, gambling with his health and life, he faces terror of the most egregious sort.

In Virginstan the brand of "dog" is etched on the noncooperator's forehead in aeternum—hence the propensity to deceive the woman, before and after marriage alike.

In Pornstan he might be arrested, thrown in jail, losing everything he has worked for. He will be ostracized. The stigma stays with him for life, preventing him from finding work after his release from prison. The police turn into heroes, demigods, for going after such men.

In Allahstan the offense can lead to capital punishment.

Law! The entire hierarchy will come after him. Satan and Allah, hand in hand.

Though Virginstan is progressive compared to Satanstan and Allahstan, partly due to the cultural influence of Natashaland, it is still far behind the basic attainments of the nondeistic culture of dogs.

Tired of prying eyes, I drag Kathy from restaurant to restaurant, refusing to settle on one. Everywhere there are those chewing the cud, ruminating you with their bovine stares, while Kathy's presence next to me further complicates the situation. On her suggestion, we opt for an eatery on Posh Street. We have just begun to dance. I stop in my tracks. From a nearby table, six men—five short and plump, one lanky—have affixed their lecherous, collective stare on Kathy's behind, their incredulous eyes popping out of the sockets.

Nauseated, I can't bring myself to sleep that night.

I am so glad that the old woman next door, from whose window you could see not only Mount Ararat but the restaurant, was prompted by her daughter at the eleventh hour not to sell me her house.

Blessed are those visitors from Satanland who do not understand the Paradisean langue d'oc, who do not see and hear what I do. Tourists sauntering left and right. It is a wondrous thing to be a tourist in Paradise. And I can't be one. I am a well-bred Dreamlander.

One day my nine-year-old daughter and I are out visiting some attractions in Satanland. She is sitting next to me in the car. We are chatting. Father and daughter. Happy together. Stopping at the traffic light, I unwittingly turn my head to the left to give my muscles a bit of relief. Noticing this, my daughter says, "Daddy, you're looking into another car. You're not supposed to. People might get angry."

I relate the incident to a teacher in Virginabad, as a way of illustrating differences between Virginlander and Pornian attitudes. I had hopes that someday she would be my daughter's teacher. But the tall teacher has a short verdict.

"See, you're a Paradisean," she shoots back.

And I am supposed to bring my daughter to this place, where angels are wont to see nothing but the mote in your eye.

In Virginabad, you face virgins everywhere you turn. It is the national tradition! Nature! Wholesome, organic. At least that is what they believe. I try to understand the ethos behind it and initially don't allow myself to pass judgment.

I am left speechless by something Hayk, Vardan's son, tells me: "How can I not let my father see my child when he wakes up in the morning?"

They live together. Three generations, in the same house.

Brothers, here is a profound issue which I can't dismiss: the optimization of creative energies in the realm of relationships as the guarantor of individual and societal stability.

I am reminded of a poem I learned at the Dream School:
Let me fill a handful of wheat
Into your palms, my valiant Son,
   my baldric.
May the blood of twenty oxen
Run in your plower's arms,
And the pillars of twenty homes
Be erected from your cedar frame.

And when you sow your seeds
In the number of your fingers,
May you reap
In the number of the stars.

Let me pour a handful of wheat
Down your head, beloved grandchild,
        my flowering cane.
May a hundred psalms of wisdom
Be written upon your forehead,
And may the ark of temperance
Be laid upon your shoulders.
And when one day you come to your flock,
May there stretch a thousand sheep
To the barleys in your palms.

Let me rain a handful of wheat
Down your hair, my radiant granddaughter,
        my tomb's wreath.
In every spring,
May fresh tulips glisten upon your cheeks,
And in every summer,
Fresh rays swim in your eyes.
And when you plant a willow branch,
In every April may you
See yourself verdant in its shade.

Let me plant a handful of wheat
In your lap, my sweet daughter-in-law,
        my distant love.
May stalks sprout in full row
From the furrow of your bed,
May dawns sleep in their glory
Within the cradle which you rock.
And when you milk forty heifers,
May the milk turn to silver,
And the beestings to gold,
In your rennet pail.

May a handful of wheat
Pour down our heads, o my old,
        my only Anna.

May the autumn sun not freeze
In the snows of our hair,
May our evening candle not be extinguished
Within the marble columns of the church.
And when at last we're lowered into our grave,
May the earth underneath, Anna,
Be a bit soft.

Wave 1, "Blessing"

This bastard treated the issue of virginity as seriously. The modesty and devotion of a pivotal minority hinged partly on virginity. Its loss was something irreversible for the virgin, a fact that compelled Dog to adopt a more circumspect approach.

Furthermore, by placing limitations on the woman's comportment, the man tries to ensure that his spawn are indeed the fruits of his own seed, not someone else's, thereby believing to safeguard the integrity of the family. This is a consequence of the shift from matriarchy to patriarchy, a process that has deep historical and psychological roots. It would be foolish to assess it with the standards of Pornstani civilization, which preaches nothing but the self-assertion of the individual, and attribute sexual freedom to the woman's whim.

Satan does not own the world.

Woe is me! Woe is me! Woe is me! For legion are my sacrileges, unforgivable are my transgressions, ineffable are my temptations. Forgive me! Forgive me! O Lord Satan... Redeem me, Azrael, from my myriad sins; make my wretched soul worthy of your holy kingdom. Have pity, my Lord, my only Lord...

Patriarchy, however, has proven catastrophic for Virginstan, where the psychic pollution emanating from the tone and movements of men entering into the third millennium has swamped each cubic inch of the Paradisean environment.

"It's too bad you can't appreciate our men, you sick fuck. Our men are first-class. Unlike you scumbags..."

I would not exchange many of the virgins for the arrogant and expensive litter that has inundated Pornia. How could I give up Vesta or Vesta for the entire Pornstani farrago?

Jeff, my brother-in-law, concurred. He was crazy about my sister. Their only disagreement was about Nabuchadnezzar. To Jeff, he is a terrorist. Satan must arm Maimunus so that he slays the likes of Nabuchadnezzar. My sister found that the prostrators before Satan are half-blind and brainwashed. My father eased the tension. It is Jinjin who controls Satan's head, drawing the United Cattles of Amerhenna into his own wars against his enemies. Father said the same thing to the scions of Maimunus, one of whom, an actress, invited him to Maimunland when he cracked a joke. "Of course you must expand your borders, so when Mashiach descends from the sky, he will not fall unwittingly in Allahland." Jeff broke into uproarious laughter at my father's quips.

"We'll go and get rid of anyone who speaks against us, one by one."

Vesta's distinctiveness is not accidental, my brethren. But it would be ignorance to compare the best elements of a society with the worst elements of another.

In Virginland, there is a netherworld about which anyone found speaking is shot to death by VirginWriterFix, Inc., the omnipotent writers' union of Virginland. From that underground realm are heard the heart-wrenching cries of virgins being sacrificed every day to the Dragonfly. Srehtorb, I llahs etirw erom tuoba siht ni ym txen seltsipe, hcihw I llahs liam uoy ni terces.

I noticed something quite familiar in Virginland. As in the rest of the world, this land is teeming with women who, before even tasting a couple of cocks, fancy themselves to be Ishtars incarnate. I think in due course this rampant psychology will see the emergence of a class of women who mimic Pornstani zombies with regard to men. Make note of this.

When women scream freedom under the weight of taboos, what they mean is freedom to be inspected. In reality, the struggle for self-affirmation, adorned as it is with a façade of eloquent words, veils this crisis, which remains clumped deep within the female psyche. One cock or twenty.

There needed to be effective solutions which would

bridge the gender divide, secure the creation and sustenance of a full-fledged society, without which there would be no heaven at the foot of Ararat.

My children would live in Paradise if its socius were to change. In Gehenna, I sent my son, Arthur, to the Dream School of Gehendale for a year. Subsequently, however, I put him in an Eyfelian school at three times the cost. I was not prepared to sacrifice him at the altar of sadoids.

The dreamstruck substitute the inalienable right to freedom of the spirit and mind with "national values," subject my son and his classmates to psychological terror. On the videotape that sang the school's praise for the benefit of parents at the end of the year, the children's panic-stricken faces told the whole story.

In Virginland, I am able to find common ground with a certain segment that has been educated at local Kremlian schools, but such individuals are becoming a rarity. Most of Papa Kremlin's institutions have been shut down, as part of a struggle against cultural imperialism. And what have they been replaced with?

Truly there has come into being a society which is of no use to imperialists.

Paradise has gone from an "open museum" to an open orduretum. The lotus withers, dogs suffocate, life goes kaput.

Brahma is being scalded by the stench of walking corpses.

Those who believe in Him are vehemently attempting to perpetuate and festoon the trash heap. It is called national preservation.

Makoko listens transfixed from the sixth floor.

I n the beginning, if befriending virgins was intriguing for this bastard, it quickly lost its allure. All said, they were kiddies. They did not know what a cock tasted like, and gauged men with their jejune yardsticks.

Miss Virginotte is a case in point. We met at the Academy library, then went out twice. She applied to study in Eurostan. She asked me to predict whether she would be accepted, as though I were a coffee-cup reader. Mrs. Garfield readeth: within three hours, within three days, within three weeks, within three months... She is awestruck by the fact that a day before the elections for the Throne, I have prophesied that God, the Omniscient Engineer, shall carry only 49 percent of the vote between three contenders, necessitating a runoff.

Some time later, I have a chance meeting with her. She is accompanied by her sister and another woman, whom I mistake for her mother. Does she have news of her application? She is flummoxed. She strains her face, which becomes less beautiful. Her response is to ask *me* questions. In the courtyard she passes in front of me without so much as a hello, looking woebegone. I call her two days later.

"You did something very tactless when you revealed my secret to my friend and sister." She cuts the conversation short and hangs up.

I remember that there is such a word as "secret" in the *Oxford Human Dictionary*. Suddenly I feel the full tomality of that word. I feel relieved for she is now jettisoned off my shoulders. Nonetheless I say to myself, "How do you like *them* apples?"

No virgin or virgidolizer has yet understood the virginosity of this incident.

In Paradise angels are born with secrets, live their short lives in secret, and die buried in secrets.

And in the hovel beneath the ground, forty people,
As though a horrified herd of cattle
Molested by the blows of a sandstorm,
Trembling in the face of death, crushing one another,
Huddled within the four walls of the darkness.
A boulder of silence grew heavy in its terror.
There was not a murmur, not one breather, the lips were shut,
And all our gazes, odious and fiendish,
Affixed upon our neighbors, wished for the other's demise.
But thousands of beast-faced barbarians under the sun,
Still not tired of ravaging lush fields and villages,
Searched for our hideout, seeking our death.

And death-crazed in the dark of the underground,
We heard in unspeakable dread
The lightning-dance swish of
Guns, spears, bayonets, and swords
Seething under the sun.
And corpses... corpses... corpses... came crushing
On the roof of our hovel, rustling,
Like trees being felled,
As the groans of death, now horrific, now dull,
Came through the walls, into the chamber,
To drive us insane.
And from the earthen ceiling,
Shut tight above us like a casket,
The copiously flowing warm blood
Sunk into the crevices, trickling down our faces.
But a newborn began to cry with a sharp screech.
This innocent child would doubtless be our traitor...
"May God have pity on us, my breasts are empty.
"I no longer have a drop of milk. I let him suck me
dry...
"I no longer have a drop of milk. Do what you must..."
"Strangle the child," someone said, angrily raising his
arm.
"Strangle him," we whispered, forty people as one.
"Strangle me first, then strangle him."
"They heard him cry, they're already digging the roof
with their picks..."
"We're all betrayed... they're already digging the
roof..."
Already the earth caves in. Shafts of light are seen.
"I beseech you, strangle me... Here is my throat...
and my child's..."
And in the darkness, the Paradisean mother
Put her neck out, along with her child's.
A pair of arms in the darkness, writhing like snakes,
Found the child's neck and squeezed it remorselessly...
The silence in the hovel this time was a tempest.
For an instant I thought we all died deservedly...
A moment later we sensed that the bloodthirsty mob,
Heaping the curses of a deceived man,

Walked away in dismay...
Was this our salvation? Are slaves ever saved?
Did we have to be saved this way?
And every day that poor woman, half-naked, standing on the roads,
Throws herself at the skirts of
The stranger, passerby, enemy, and foreigner,
And screams like a madwoman:
"Do you see these hands of mine?
"It was I who used them to strangle my newborn in the hovel...
"Believe me, it was I who strangled him.
"How unjust you all are...
"Why won't you strangle me? My own hands are powerless..."

Wave 2, "The Strangled"

The first stranger at whose skirt this woman threw herself was Solomon the Wise. He took her face in his hand, peered mysteriously into her eyes. Then pointed at the cadaver of a rat lying next to him.

"Woman, give up hope! Your child is now where this rat is."

The second skirt was that of Mr. Yoohoo MacYehu, who said, "Be consoled, woman, for your child is not at the place where there shall be crying and gnashing of the teeth."

The third was that of Al-Prophet. "Infidel, your child is at the place where there shall be crying and gnashing of the teeth."

The fourth was that of Buddha. "Be consoled, woman. Can you show me a mother who has not lost a child? All this is a dream. Ha ha ha ha..."

The church fathers have written that this story has come to pass in the year 301, on March 21, and that when the catholicos heard about it, he ordered his people to exile the Wise Man, Al-Prophet, and the Buddha and thenceforth follow Mr. Yoohoo MacYehu.

Since that day, the dead of Paradise have not been carted to the place where there shall be crying and gnashing of the teeth.

Cousin Henri crashes into Virginplanet's field of gravity. He fancies a girl.

A few days before his departure from Virginworld, we chat with her in her workplace and give her Henri's phone number. Henri is ecstatic. It seems that his dream of marrying a houri is coming true. He makes plans for moving to Godcountry. From Paris to Virginabad. Isn't he crazy?

To his way of thinking, we both are. The fact that I have survived living here already for the past ten months bolsters his faith. But the local houris dream of being with him... in Parisabad.

The cicerona at the Repository of Ancient Manuscripts demands an answer before even agreeing to talk to me. "Art thou prepared to wed anew and take thy new wife away with thou?"

Bewildered, I think to myself: *First open your pussy*, then *your mouth.*

"Poor girl..."

No virgin or virgidolizer has yet understood the virginosity of this incident.

Of course I was a bastard.

Disappointed by this mentality of the houris, Henri shares his feelings with angst. Whereas these houris dream of living in Parisabad, Henri says, "Now is the time to drop anchor here." Meaning Paradise. He is a consummate Eyfelian. Yet deep in his soul there has rung a distant call whose essence he has only begun to grasp—in Paradise. His friends were unaware that he was of Omish descent, and when one day he found occasion to reveal this fact, they proceeded to avoid him.

He was not a Parislander.

He...

...

was a Dreamlander.

The following morning, at the set time, Henri received three successive phone calls. Not a whisper from the other end of the line. Some time later he gives me a call. "What does 'whelp' mean?" On a fourth call, some woman rains hellfire on him. Distinguishing the words "four o'clock" from her harangue, Henri tells her, "Madam, I don't understand anything you're saying."

By way of a response, he is bestowed with the venerable title of "son of a bitch." It seems to me that the caller was the girl's mother.

Henri is shocked to his core. He becomes irritable. To anyone asking him the generic question, "So how did you find Virginland?" he wants to say, "Like shit!"

I understand his disillusionment. I had had a similar experience, and in Pornia at that.

I have broken up with Heather, in part wishing to meet a Dreamlandette. One day Veracity comes to my office to sell me advertising. She is a veterinary student at the University of Calipornia. We decide to go out.

The smell of her armpits fills my car. She is meeting me in secret. She has come out of her house unbathed so that her parents won't suspect anything. She has lied to them, telling them she is going to a job interview—thus involving me in the karmic fallout of her lie. For the bulls at the workplace, the stench of perspiration is a matter of secondary importance. Some doctor has asked for her hand in marriage...

In short, she heads to the beach with the bastard, for an "interview."

They are in Santa Monica. Barely twenty minutes have passed when her cell phone rings. It is mamma, Mrs. Sherlock Holmes. She has armed the daughter with a phone *and* a beeper, each fastened to her waist as a left and right pistol. The gizmos take turns to go off every five minutes. She tells mother that the "interview" is not over yet, but on the tenth call she promises to be home in twenty minutes.

"What twenty minutes, girl? You won't make it home in twenty minutes even if I got you a helicopter."

As luck would have it, there is an awful gridlock in the parking lot. For thirty minutes the car stays exactly where it is. Vera cannot part from the penis—which makes hitting the road even more hopeless. How was the poor boy to know that a bastard's cock would be so sweet? Alas, as yet he did not know that he was a bastard…

Back on the road, mamma calls incessantly. Finally she coerces the girl into a confession. Mamma is infuriated when she learns of the truth. "If you try to set foot in the house, you'll come out of it as a corpse." Bastard picks up the phone, naively believing he might be able to soften mamma's wrath.

"Get my daughter on the phone, right now!"

"Ma'am."

"Bastaaaaaaaard!"

"Ma'am."

"Get my daughter on the phone, right now!"

The girl tells the boy they will kill her if she goes home. Says she has no choice but to stay with him. So now what?

The boy will not marry under the gun. He still thinks he is not a dog.

After much vacillation, Veracity decides to return home. "It's better they kill me than the both of us." She rejects his idea of going to the police station together and manically beseeches him not to do it on his own either.

For three days they lock her down in her room and demand that she give them his address so they will kill him.

"I'll throw myself out the window if you do anything of the kind."

They calm down a bit.

A few days later, Veracity calls Bastard, fully rehabilitated. She is now convinced that her parents were veritous in their thinking.

"If your intentions were good, you would've come to our house and asked my parents for my hand."

I apologize, madam. I didn't realize that I'm a bastard. That's why I didn't ask for your daughter's hand.

, a bastard!

And who do these men think they are to force their nauseating behavior on Dog's girlfriends, making them do their bidding to the word? The Virginosa fears giving her phone number to her boyfriend. It is she who calls him.

In Paradise the redeemed live sub rosa. They are God-pleasing. Long live His Glory, the Secret Eye!

I am a sex maniac, a filthy dog.

Even Stella, that exquisite Virginlandette, does not dare give me her home phone number. I call her on her cell or at her workplace. One day, when she makes the fatal mistake of calling me from home, her brother-in-law barges in and roars at her. The classic response pattern in the angeloid zoo. I will not set foot in your house, nor will I meet any member of your family. Dog suggests that she leave home, which is what she does. She doesn't find the strength to say good-bye to the males of the household. She doesn't want to be there—ever.

But Stella's odyssey does not end here.

Using sundry pretexts, sister, mother, father, and brother-in-law call her every night, to see if she is in. They turn Stella's daughter against her and monitor her every move.

Until one evening a despondent Stella calls me in tears.

"Only in my grave will I be free of these people."

Whose spawn are these so-called brothers and godfathers and brothers-in-law and mothers and fathers to so terrorize Dog's lovers as to make them scared stiff of spending a night with him?

My canine friars, wouldn't you agree with me that prison is where angeloids belong? These characters give themselves the right to limit others'—Dog's girlfriends'—fundamental, inalienable, dog-given liberty, to stay their most valuable possession: their life. The Virginlander judiciary is an antilife apparatus that runs on the legal clogs of the Virginstanoid, through his own interpretation of the law.

Law! Pimps sell their whores for a day. These folks sell theirs for a lifetime...

"How many keys does a guy have on his keyholder?"

Stella wins her daughter back. The girl learns to pull the rug over the callers.

And how is Dog supposed to live in this land under the sun of deception? Won't both end up deceiving him? Every single whim of the daughter had priority over Dog. He was cornered in the triangle. One day, as I nibbled on a bone, I sidestepped the barrier and went directly to the daughter for clarifying something. My Stella was peeved.

Eureka! Having a relationship with a woman who has a daughter is a death trap, brothers, unless she is an open book.

Where shall Dog go?

The bastard operates in accordance with a set of fundamental principles that are key to his success. Two are particularly important. First, he does not seduce a married woman (he is not a catholicos); second, he does not lie (he is not a catholicos). Nonetheless, he is not bound to answer any question by the woman. Whoever does not abide by these laws is not a bastard; he luxates the equilibrium of society and the Mithraic code of ethics, the Kantian order. He is filth. A manpanzee.

"Crazy fucking place," Henri keeps saying.

"You can't live in this city if every girl you say hello to is gonna start fantasizing about marriage," he concludes.

That night we have a tough time deciding where to go. Just before entering an establishment, Henri changes his mind. The meaning is lost. Meaning. Isn't this life's penultimate mirage, the reason for conning the present with decoys, embracing death in a trance, the humanoid dream trap?

As we amble down the street, Henri muses, "Here people get married so that they can inspect. I'm bored of inspecting. Once you tie the knot, you're rammed up the ass."

Now we were two dogs.

This dog often balks from having sexual relations if he fails to feel anything for the partner (doubtful). In Virginstan, however, sex is taboo even when driven by such doggish sentiment.

At last we go into a night-zoo where we can't find a single empty table. Henri walks up to a pair of women sitting at a large round table and asks whether we can share theirs. The "no" is delivered dry as a slap.

"Let's get the hell out of here," Henri says. "She hasn't seen a cock all her life, and then when a nice guy comes up to her, she doesn't know what to do. Virgin city, no shit! Don't bother looking for our type of nightclub in this city. It doesn't exist. By the time they build one, you and I will be old and gray. Let's go to Natashaland. I've never been."

He is right, my brothers. Virginstan does not have a competitive edge on the sex market. How blind we have been not to realize this obvious tautology, to be reduced to being beggars, prepared to inspect a bug. In the footsteps of all million male creatures of Noah, we, too, shall exit Paradise to Natashaland, where we shall spend our money and rivet the Natashas. The Virginosa is exacting revenge on the man who approaches her without proposing marriage. Let her venom ruin her, not us. Aren't we doing the right thing, brethren?

"Dog!"

Hurrah, they know us by name!

When I was a human, brothers, they treated me worse than a dog. When I became a dog, they treated me like a human being.

Nothing could accoy Henri. His road rage is seething.

"They cut in front of you... they tailgate... they get up your ass! They! Have! No! Respect! For! Others! These people... animals... no fucking respect..."

"This is why Dog doesn't drive a car here..."

"They're like manimals."

"Worse."

We go to a nightclub near the opera to enjoy the requisite, indefinite waiting period before a dinner order materializes from the kitchen. The waiters keep lying, every time assuring us that our food will arrive in twenty minutes, which is why Henri's brain circuits implode. He has a good mind not to leave a tip.

One thousand years to dogs is like a day to God...

Some are deaf. Even in the best restaurants they are

overbearing, treat us as humans, drive us insane before deigning to grace us with a bit of food. Henri finds nothing to eat.

Aside from the trinity of Xs—xash, xashlama, xasho— there is precious little to be ordered in a Virginabad eatery, let alone served properly, despite the fact that the city is awash with hundreds of restaurants and bars whose décor often surpasses the very best establishments of Satanland.

Perhaps this is in fact the City of God. How is it God's fault if the educated are not redeemed? The angels are carnivores and dipsomaniacs. Should you request a vegan dish, they will humor you with a couple of tomatoes and a cucumber.

To deliver Henri from his predicament, I take him to the establishment where God had hosted Yeltsin. As Henri has trouble digesting parsley, he asks the server not to put any in his salad. To no avail. Take it back. I've told you twice. An hour later, they bring the salad back, minus half the three hundred pieces of chopped parsley. We can't do any better than this, *appé*. May God save his tables, but within two weeks Henri reached the doors of starvation.

On his way to Shangri-La, Henri was oblivious to the thought of carrying the pemmican with him. His experienced brother had advised him to go to Adonis instead. "At least you won't croak of hunger there."

Nothing changes at the nightclub—except for the show. They suggest dog tenderloin. We order humanoid chateaubriand. Not available tonight. Baby heart fondue? None. We nonetheless make a special request from the abattoir. At ten, they grace us with knife and serviette. Ah, they have already slaughtered the baby. We wait in drooling anticipation. At eleven, they bring something on a couple of plates. We sniff it. What meat? More like a Dead Sea scroll. They call it "Yoohoo meat." Shush, Henri, it's Yoohoo meat. And the pilaf? Pebbles! We send the concoction back and remain famished until eleven thirty, when we receive the very same Yoohoo meat, only

dried ten times over, accompanied by a somewhat soft-
ened pilaf...

Appér, we're way past our dinnertime. It's late. Our religion does not allow us to consume human flesh at this hour.
Please enjoy it yourselves.

They won't eat it. Eat! No matter what we do, we can't
convince them. They tell us they don't eat human flesh in
Paradise. We don't believe them. Eureka! Henri is suddenly
enlightened by the idea that they are scared to eat it. It is the
meat of a cadaver. You don't eat it, do you? Ha ha ha ha...
They worship the dead here. *Ya tara*, how many corpses
must have been slaughtered for us!

Wisely they comp us some champagne. An aside from
Henri: "You *know* what they're trying to do... Get us drunk
so we won't know how awful the grub is."

From the next table, a short beer-belly begins to sing,
"Take, eat; this is my body. This cup is the new testament in
my blood: this do ye, as oft as ye drink it, in remembrance
of me."

We object, informing him that he's cantating the
wrong prayer, that God won't hear it. The beer-belly's
temper flares, the club goes haywire, the crooner runs for
cover from the stage. To put the matter to rest, the waiters
bring in a priest from the restroom of the shop next door,
asking him to offer the correct version.

"Body divine..."

"No! Stop! You're saying it the wrong way."

"May you eat this meal in peace..."

"We said stop!"

"Boys, let us give glory to God."

"Blasphemy! Let us give glory to Yoohoo. It is *Yoohoo's*
meat we're eating."

"Boys, you can't do that. First, glory to God, then..."

"No! First to Yoohoo! It's his meat we're eating, son of
man."

"What if you had cow meat?"

"We would've given glory to the cow."

"Nullifidians!" the priest roars.

"You slaughter the cow yet sing God's glory, do you?"
We bang on the table and jump up on our hind legs.

Fearing that these anti-Goddist dogs are preparing to eat him instead, the priest gifts us with some carved crosses, anointed by the catholicos himself. (All the artists of Paradise make crosses and sell them to crossophiles at the Vernissage. Supply and demand). From a distance, the boys point crosses at us at the priest's behest and pray fiercely. They vanquish us through the power of the cross. Amen... Amen...

Thus humbled, we begin to eat.

The Paradisean could only dream of tasting our Yoohoo leather, even once a month.

Here you must qualify your statements with words like, "some Paradiseans" or "many Paradiseans dreamed of," or "according to sociological studies, 69 percent..." Otherwise your book is tripe.

While we delegate that work to God's sociologists, Henri makes a further antisociological comment, "Service is zero in Paradise," further provoking the local objectivity-mongers.

"Whatever business you open here, if you give good service, everybody else will go under."

"Provided you can change the mentality and sarcasm of your donkey-headed employees."

But since these dogs have no intention of opening a restaurant in Paradise, we now and then try to teach the redeemed a thing or two. No sociological studies.

Finesse Street. I'm sitting in a restaurant. After paying the bill and leaving a nice tip, I write a comment on the napkin and hand it to the waitress.

"The chicken skin was charred. The fries were burned. The salad was frostbitten, with no oil in it, the cucumber and tomato were tasteless. The bread came only in one variety: white. The barley soup was late in coming (the grain harvest had been delayed perhaps). The soup, in fact, arrived with the entrée, which means that the entrée went cold by the time I finished the soup. Please take these into consideration next time."

Everywhere and every day it is the same story.

And if, Zeus forbid, you say that "the cucumber and tomato had gone bad," you won't even hear the word "sorry." They will look at you as though you were some idiot fresh from Mars.

"Will you listen to this one? He says the cucumber and tomato have gone bad."

Several of them will chime in to jeer at you.

Mountain dwellers look down on desert dwellers. But Allah is not to be found in Paradise. It becomes clear that this is not Jannah. Now... where to go? Further up or down? Has Al-Prophet hoodwinked us? Have we been given an outdated address?

But in Bedouinstan, a dog who enters any restaurant, in any corner of the land, is treated like a king. A dog feels like a dog there. He is welcomed with utmost graciousness, finds himself at the gate of Jannah...

In Paradise hypocrisy is the currency of angelic affairs. They respect only the *akhpérs*.

Fear in the spine. That's the foundation stone of respect.

Glory and honor and power...

Eat!

Otherwise thou shalt eat shit.

Salespersons throughout the stores of Virginabad, unaware that their thoughts are carved in iron letters on their faces, "standing around" solo or with compadres, love to scoff at customers. The Satanites are idiots, after all. The Paradisean is the most intelligent creature of the universe. The entrances to certain shops are lorded over by four or five rodents who use their venom to bombard customers, even if they be a hundred meters away, and kill them on the spot.

Those store-owners who are cognizant of this nomenon lay low in one corner and let the female employees make the sale.

The craftier proprietors almost never appear at their stores, completely entrusting the business to the "little sisters" who work for them.

The "little sisters," however, go hungry.

They happen on money only through ass-giving.

When the "little sister" acts like a slut, know what you must do, but don't get overly excited, as she is one of those jaded ass-givers.

In Satanland the customer is king. In Paradise, a trash-collector.

The Virginlandette is broke. Every woman has a man standing over her. He steers her according to his whims and the degree of satisfaction he reaps from her.

Rebelling beauties move to Pashaland or Allahland in their thousands, so they won't have to "sleep with a boss every single day for fifty bucks a month." They prefer the cocks of pashas and sheiks to the esteemed dongs of angels. Trafficking is conducted by the God-Supremejudge couple, who steer it straight from their bed. Houris are worth ten thousand washingtons per head. The judges are the buddies of mafiosi. Thanks to the selling of women, palaces are being built in Virginstan, and the "capitalist" cash is making it possible to buy the houris of Paradise, often as concubines. His Desirable Enchantedness uses one hand to throw gold dust at Satan's eyes and the other to bare his ass to those maintaining his dominion. As for the judolicos, he prays, "Blessed be thy name, Thy kingdom come, Thy will be done on earth as in heaven, give us this day our daily bread…"

Still, the rebelling beauties are acquiring appreciable experience. Their gossip reveals a consensus that in the bedchamber Ayatollah is the gentlest of them all—my wife, too, found bin Laden to be a gallant, sexy man. But the beauties say that Allah's race is uncouth, hence their preference for Ayatollah over Allah.

Henri becomes exasperated by the male singers at the gentlemen's club. "Get the fuck out of here already. We're not fags, for Chrissake." There is not a female in sight, and the male patrons enthusiastically cheer the procession of male performers.

So why have they built a ladies' room?

It transpires that they haven't...

Brothers, when the striptease began, I did a quick calculation in my Dreamish, being familiar with all the strip joints of Virginabad. There are some one hundred women in this line of business. Three or four of them are locals. The rest are Natashas, and there is a lone black woman. They make five thousand washingtons a month, an amount they couldn't possibly earn in Porn City. Our Monique (the cutie pie) made a measly four thousand per month, despite being the most beautiful girl in the best club. She could barely cover her work and living expenses. What is it that makes these shits any better? To top it all off, they're arrogant.

Look at the money these bozos are showering on the strippers. Where are they getting all that cash if not by exploiting their brothers and sisters? Every month a million washingtons are siphoned off of this dead-starving country through this pipe alone. Millions of washingtons are pumped through an alternate pipe into the casinos of Natashima.

You will ask, "Where are the women of Virginabad?"

Well, they do not dance in public, under the floodlights.

But secretly, in the darkness, they whore themselves.

"Oh no... oh yes... give it to me, baby..."

"Hole. I live in York, near the Supermarket. Call me..."

These are the jaded holes left behind, who provide the patriots with raptures of release, pan-nationalizing syphilis, and the rest of the immortal classics.

Lucy is outraged by the behavior of the manpanzees. Though a bona fide pop star, she lives in modest circumstances. Every day she witnesses the same thing. "Instead of feeding their families, they toss their salaries at women brought from the villages of Natashaland (on tramps that make the manpanzee go berserk), and then they deny bread money to the best artists, even the singers performing in the same strip club."

Cretin nation!

In Paradise, Adam and Eve coexist through deception, in the footsteps of the Judolicoi.

The Judolicos is God's left hand, the Great Xaxam of Paradise. Paradiseans have one and one-half heads. Main Head is affixed on Saint Virginborn, twenty minutes from Virginabad. From Saint Virginborn you can see the august Ararat, where, according to tradition, Noah's Ark landed. A nineteenth century traveler describes how one fine day he witnessed a rainbow arching from Ararat to the monastery. The selection of the latter's site is no accident, especially since it has replaced the temple of the Mother Goddess.

This city has been a major pagan center in the glorious centuries of the distant past, when the generals of Paradise sneered at the armies of the neighboring Roman Empire, with which they were locked in a struggle for supremacy. So much so that history records that it is here that Hannibal found safe refuge after his defeat by Rome.

Thereafter Paradise accepted the religion of Mr. MacYehu. This was a significant turning point in the history of his religion. For the first time, it acquired state sponsorship, and this in a country that served as the seat of God. Historians have difficulty assigning the event an exact date, placing it somewhere between 284 and 314. Most people, however, lean toward 301, the traditional year claimed by the Sanctum Sanctorum of Paradise.

According to legend, Gaga, the founder, was thrown into a pit called DD (Deep Dungeon), where he spent thirteen years.

Recently in Paradise, God celebrated the 1,700th anniversary of the event in the heart of the capital, at the crossroads of the world. There the Dreamers constructed a fifty-million-washington lambshed to match the spirit of Yoohoo. But the crowd here is sparser than in the meek dungeon below it, where it follows its ancestors' ancient ritual tradition of lighting a candle for the souls of the departed.

On the reredos of the main altar of the lambshed there is a large, grotesque image. It is an upper-body portrait of a rag-covered woman who, according to the orthodox account, visited the grave of his son in some obscure land with two mirror images of herself. By concocting a fable, she was able to dupe the admirers of his barn-born and ass-stubborn son and snatch away the Throne of the Universal Mother, humanity's age-old legacy.

That babe's "Mother of God" title was grabbed for her by the avocati of Mr. MacYehu from Isis, the mother goddess of Pharaohland, who shares ample congruences with Dzovinar, the ethnogenic goddess of Paradise, mother of the Indo-European divine twins, Sanasar and Balthasar—Castor and Pollux. Isis's son was Horus, the sun god, whom they replaced with their master. Thus they stole the very image of Isis holding the infant sun. The roots of the original mytheme reach deep into the millennia and are related to Mher the Great, the epic hero of Paradise, Sanasar's offspring (and the earthly replica of the constellation Leo), who in various narratives appears as the King of Pharaohland.

The idolatrous, iconolatrous Judolicos of Paradise demands from his lambs to bow before Maimunus's mamma. But is she worth even a hump in the anus? That is to say, by remaining loyal to the national traditions of Virginstan? Brothers, at least pimps do not require their customers to bow in front of a whore. Dog rejected that reign. He refused to walk under the sword of the twosome, His Holiness the Lambowner and Her Virginosity Mary the Harlot. To the bastard, a whore is worth zero. Not so for the Judolicos.

The fraudulent religion of the Judolicoi of Paradise has brought about a spiritual degeneracy of the flock. It is responsible for the erosion of the subtle matter of the sociosphere. Which rational human in our century would have been led by a nonsensical construct? Consequently, there has taken place a violent ebb of spiritual values within this nation. Man renounces the spiritual as he no longer believes in fabrications—and of the lowest type. Under the veil of "national tradition," religious leaders shove the Chosen One's putrid legends down the throat to maintain a dominion built on deceit.

But, brothers, that dominion has neither legal nor moral basis—it has been established through bloodshed and cultural genocide.

The equation has shifted radically since 301. Today, in Saint Virginborn, Main Head is unable to control the spiritual life of even his own neighborhood, which is patrolled by a couple of Paradisean commanders. The city is their demesne. Not even a fly, let alone a new business, can take off here without their approval. As for the supreme commander—the so-called president—and the vaunting defense minister, they turn a blind eye so as to receive their baksheesh from criminals. God has divided Paradise into iqthayat.

And now the Paradiseans, having survived the yokes of Osman Pasha and subsequently Papa Lenin, prepare to join Eurostan, as warranted by the modest trinity of God, the Son of Exoworks, and the Holy TV Ghost.

Glory be to the Father, and to the Son, and to the Holy Ghost. As it was in the beginning, is now, and ever shall be, world sine fine. Amen, amen.

Rowing upstream, one day they may reach Asgard when the effusive saliva of the cuspidors gushing forth in front of God's palace shall confluence into a river and join the Danube.

God knocks on the High Door, Bab Euron.

"Open, Sesame…"

"Who is it?"

"My name is so-and-so. I am your modest sommelier. I have brought my daughter, the very first state of Baron MacYehu, to append to your Marvelous Union."

"We do not recognizite [sic] ye," answers Europeter.

And it comes to pass that God, upgraded with unremitting humbleness, rows away on the Cuspinar River on his way back to Paradise.

God's motto is "Toward Hell."

The path shall be stormy for Paradise, where angels mayhem dogs.

To be fair, I must say that in Virginstan they neither shit on the beach (there is no sea), as in Holy Lanka, nor piss in street corners, as in, for instance, the land of the Pharaohs.

H alf Head is perched on Monononias, a suburb of Adonis edging the Mediterranean. Whereas the interests of Main Head are limited to parish matters, Half Head occupies some of the highest positions in Mr. MacYehu's international agencies. His chief function is to lull Dreamlanders with dreams produced through the unholy entente between Satan and the Holy Trinity Party.

Half Head sprouted during the Cold War, on pretext of saving the world-scattered Dreamlanders from Papa Lenin's encroachments, but stays on and keeps growing even now, long after the war's end. All efforts to push it back into its hole have failed. This would be no easy feat. Even in our glorious Jehennam, with its centralized institutions and unsurpassed legislative processes, Hellington's seasoned politicians know only too well how easy it is to create an organization or a department and how hard it is to liquidate it. Shakespeare fashioned Junior Sheikstan to stay on top of oil reserves, but who remembers today that the realm was once a Mesopotamian province, my brethren? On the ides of March, Shakespeare acted to rescue his darling from Nebuchadnezzar's mutiny.

Still, there are reasons behind the secret of Half Head's existence that baffle the doctors.

Although having played an instrumental role in the development of religion, the Paradisean is currently in the ebb and consoles himself with the glories of the past. He is already a consumer, versus a creator, of religion. In Paradise today there is an increasing consolidation of a flaccid Protestant mass which glorifies Maimunus. In schools everywhere, thousands upon thousands of children are being slaughtered at the sacrificial altar of Yehu.

The educational institutions of Dreamland are to varying degrees in the grips of the Solomonons, commonly known as Mononons or Freemonons. The Solomonons are a human party that dream of establishing a religio-economic decentralized confederacy in manworld with a center in Penisalem, on the tomb of a certain Mononon, who they zealously believe is the first Penis in the world. They plan to erect there a tower to

be named Monononon. The teachers of Dreamland are afraid
of informing their students that the thirty members of the
junta responsible for perpetrating the Genocide in Paradise
were Solomonons.

While a basic Google search yielded 996 items that con-
nect the dots between the Young Pashists, the Chosen One,
and the Freemonon movement, the chieftains of God's
sheep are horrified to utter a word about this, since they,
too, happen to be the wise children of the Freemonons.
Baa...

Of course not all students accept the "divine knowledge" as though it were tiramisu. When Mr. Jacob taught us
about the "prophets" in sixth grade, the boys threw a grain
of rice at his pate every time he turned to the blackboard.
The poor fellow never found out the source of the projec-
tiles, even after the threats he bombarded us with.

"It's a fly, sir. It's a fly."

Planet earth, including Paradise, is teeming with
organizations that promote Maimunus under the veil of
MacYehu. The one and half Judolicoi do attempt to ward off
this assault, yet are powerless as they themselves are trapped
in the same web of myth. Under the guise of teaching the
"history of the Church of Paradise," they Maimunize the
children of Paradise. Aggressively availing themselves of
state television, they poison children and remain deaf to all
criticism.

The Judolicoi declare that one day Yoohoo shall appear
upon the clouds and save the Paradiseans as well as the
lambs of a diversity of nations found in the new ark bearing his name. This, my brethren, is how they bait the lambs
of Paradise as slaves into the ark of Yoohoo MacYehu and
release them onto the shores of Penisalem.

But can man be redeemed by a slave-hawker? Here the
proverb hits the nail on the head: "With whose rope does
man descend into the well?"

According to well-placed sources, the one and half Judolicoi are Solomonons. (But, of course, I don't know this to
be true, brothers. Only God knows). This would mean they
will never initiate an ideological reform that may run counter
to the interests of the freedom-loving Monons. They will

keep Paradise in the twin positions of consumer and toiler. The sheep must continue to glorify the mediocre legends of Mr. Maimunus, confusing them with truth.

The ecclesiastical structure of the half-Judolicos is run by semiliterate Mononons. "My donkey is better than someone else's lion." From head to toe, that structure is a den of Freemononry and one of the major reasons behind the flight of Dreamland's free-thinking youth from nation and numen. Some say that all three of the most recent Judolicoi are Freemonons[†].

Brethren, according to these sources, the noisome Judolicosal elections of late were a struggle between Mononons and non-Mononons, with the result that the Mononon-supported candidate won the day, installing himself on the throne of HAY. This came to pass through the intercessions of the First Lady of Dreamstan, ensconced in York of yore. But, of course, this is a lie, my brothers. In vain they tarnish the good name of the holy Pontifex Maximus.

The sterling slaves that they are, the Dreamlanders piously kiss the robes of Freemonon priests, bow to their power. It only takes an obtuse naif to make the unsolicited declaration, "Don't listen to these apostates! They're taking you for a ride," for an army of sheep to bleat in unison, "Kick the heretics out! They speak against our shepherd." The nation will echo, "They speak against our shepherd."

The student organizations of the Dreamlanders, which arrogate to themselves the function of liberating the nation from captivity, are led by such regressive students, even in progressive Hell, including the universally-beloved city of Gehendale. They vie to kiss the right hand of the shepherd.

Some of them whisper to each other, "Keep it down, there may be snitches…"

"Snitches?"

"Snitches… Shush…"

"Shush. They're Mononons…"

"For goodness' sake, don't give out my name. I've got kids."

"I go to work every day [heroism]. They'll kill me on the freeway…"

---

† In the Byzantish version, "two out of the three Judolicoi were Mononons, and all three were jacks-of-all-trades, including ishtarology."

(Knowing, circumspect gazes).
Slave dreamers, you deserve your fate.
Monononic Maimunic Church of Dreamstan.

This is where the dreamers present themselves for the salvation of their souls, the eternal peace of their dead, the anointment of their newborn, and the founding of the family.

And to our master bootkicker, and the venerable Pontifex Maximus of the world, the Holy See of Paradisean Kilikia, His Exalted Holiness Habakkuk the Jackal…

Having lived under the shadow of Papa Lenin, Paradiseans have lost so much of the ennobling qualities of virtue and faith. What has persisted is the religion itself, with its amalgamated doctrine of serfdom and racism. Among the acolytes of this desert-born, vindictive religion, it is implausible to break the chain linking faith and virtue with ideology and creed. It is so for three reasons, inter alia, my friars.

The pervasive ignorance that grips the lambs of MacYehu, including their political honchos. Religion is the nemesis of free thought and reason. The perpetual hardening of those gyves by religious organizations that command coffers worth billions of washingtons and chunks of Mother Earth. The two-thousand-year-old pathogen of tenets that has wreaked havoc on Eurostan's subconscious.

Solutions are being sought everywhere by insignificant groupings whose ideological foundations, however, lack the building blocks and inner strength of faith. Vainly they try to parry faith with pseudo-rationalistic ideology. It is no wonder that they droop before seeing the light of day.

Their demagogues do not have the slightest vision of faith energy and its vital function in the synthesis of man with the boundless energies of the cosmos, the structure and mechanism of its inner workings, and its role in and promise of human transformation, which can usher man to unimaginable heights imperceptible only to the blind. Even though not an exclusive mechanism of enlightenment, faith has already lived out its age.

I run into Hans in Virginville. He is a sensible young man who has devoted himself to the cultivation of an Aryan philosophy. He lectures teenagers on his theory of naturalism. Laura used to pull his leg: "You and your Aryan fantasies. We don't need Aryans. We need Hays." Hans suggests I tag along to the meeting of an Aryan group that evening. I am intrigued.

I meet the leader, who warmly welcomes me.

"What is the basis of your doctrine?"

"The nation."

"And the basis of the nation?"

"The race."

"The basis of the race?"

"The family."

At that moment I understand that I, too, am an Aryan. But I start to wonder: is the family worth saving? And from what? And for what? To further crowd the earth? Or provide soldiers for the gods of man?

"The basis of the family?"

"The human being."

"The basis of the human being?"

"The Creator."

"Who is your favorite philosopher?"

"Nietzsche."

"But didn't he declare that God is dead?"

"He was referring to the Jay God. Ours is Aramazd."

"Is there a difference?"

He squashed his cigarette butt in the ashtray as he glared at me. My question, in sooth, had no answer. Yes, you are right—Maimunus's God is a vampire, the perfect fascist and anthrophobe, because of whom also there sprouted Aryan movements in countries where his ideological refuse had accumulated across the firmament. At any rate, Aramazd, too, was God, and with God's loss the ancillary icons Man, Family, Tribe, and Nation were toppled like dominoes. To preserve all this, it was necessary to worship God, to preserve faith as a matter of utility.

But God issued a mittimus against this man for his anti-Jinjinist statements and sentenced him to three years of imprisonment. As for the fact that it was the Jinjinists who had organized the mother of all genocides, "Who gives a hoot?" I believe that in the land of Jinjin, those who insult Führer BenYehu are likewise thrown in jail. Such is the standard of justice of a God who makes a bid to join Eurostan, who ever so slowly learns how to hold a court trial.

But God is shrewd, say the angels. He will not fail to at once implore Satan and Jinjinus to imprison the latter's prime minister as well as one million anti... anti... anti-Paradise jinjinoids. Wow!

How would the angels know, my brethren, that in those days there was held a clandestine conclave on the penumbra of heaven and hell, by a cartel that included Him, the One, His Impregnable Substantiality and Vivid Wisdom, in addition to Diabolam Diabolum, Papa Pete, Papa Bear, Kvetch Maimunus, and Shakespeare? Not even the archangels were aware of the tryst. A certain courtesan who shared her bed with one of them had recorded portions of the syzygy, which I shall relay to you in my third and final epistle. Hguone dias.

"How are things going here?"

"We have three thousand members. The number goes up every day. We're in contact with all of the world's Aryan organizations. There is great interest in us, as the proto-homeland of the Indo-Europeans. Our enemies are trying to wipe out our homeland to deprive the Indo-European genus from its motherland. The same goes in the field of academia. Pasha keeps bribing the scholars with perks so they sing his song. Jinjinus fills the world with disinformation. Yes, we do cooperate with Xerxes. Relations are strong. In the beginning He came and went fairly often, but as soon as He realized that there is a solid foundation to what we're doing, His enthusiasm sort of fizzled. He wants to be the center of the world... lives in the past."

"That's the imperial complex. Ayatollah is Xerxes incarnate."

"It doesn't stop there. The same goes for Papa Bear and Pasha."

"Caliph too. He has turned Allah into a political plaything. All of these assholes are bent on slaying Satan so that *they* become the lord of the world. And they try to draw us into their game with their oh-so-lovely ideas.

"Don't forget that Allah would have been dead long ago if it weren't for Jinjinus… In any event, our ties with Xerxes are strong. He just hasn't found his groove yet. But I think He will. It's a matter of time."

"He will, only if His nationalistic, religious, and ideological narcissism is shattered. That is far from being the case."

"But for that, isn't Jinjinus first and foremost to blame? The reason for Allah's zealotry is Jinjinus. Jinjinus's superciliousness is the root cause of the whole conflict, and his misfortunes."

"Who else is interested in your work?"

"The Kshatriyas are very much interested. So are the Euraders."

"You can join us at our meeting tonight," said Mihra, to whom I had just been introduced. His gesture earned him a blitz of lethal stares from the others.

"Some other time. We'll meet some other time."

Yes. I understood. The plane of this suspect has flown over Hellington on its way to Paradise. But haven't these gentlemen, on their part, trodden across the sidewalks of Kremlin, kissed the mitt of Papa Lenin's cadaver?

But they are the majority whereas I am a minority of one, they live in the homeland whereas I hail from outremer, they are the hosts and I a guest—and an untrustworthy one to boot.

They believed the murmurs of certain self-proclaimed Aryan criers who had fled Paradise for the safety of Hell, who relentlessly tried to foment discord by attacking Dog through Dream Press and Airwave. Some had sent out warnings with regard to this Satanic agent's ingress into Paradise, and on the third day of my arrival I was met with the venom of harassment.

At that moment I wanted to return to Natashaland, where I had found a measure of bliss.

Shitty celestinae!

The pathological paranoia was the byproduct of the dissonance of the psyche, which in turn was a consequence of spiritual bankruptcy.

I left, taking with me a few books presented by the leader. I did not doubt his sincerity. In the following days, as I read their literature with a fine-tooth comb, I grasped the fundamental reason behind the mistrust of my acquaintances.

I was a Jinjinist.

"All of them are Jinjinists. All of them! The government, the academy! It's them, from end to end. See how organized they are? The Paradisean is incapable of doing wrong. If his genes are Paradisean, there is no way anything bad will come out of him."

And this is mono-ethnic Paradise, homogeneity: 97 percent…

"That has nothing to do with it. They're not Goddists, they're just God-speaking! They're all imps of Maimunus."

Golly… so many Mimunes in Paradise?

"Yes. Yes."

May Mashiach help you…

See how I belittle them. Aha! I am found out! A Jinjinist agent…

Well, instead of living in Jinjinland, this Jinjinist could relish Paradise in comfort. You never know. What if a bomb goes off in Jinjinland? It's better here. Everyone is a Maimun.

"Didn't we say he's a traitor? And he's a sly one. Get a load of his ideas. He wants to get Maimunus to Paradise."

These twerps were unaware that the founder of Paradise was Maimunus. At the entrance to the Kosher Vatican in Saint Virginborn, the religious center of Paradise, there are two tombs where tradition holds that Thaddeus and Bartholomew, the apostles credited with bringing the light to Paradise, are buried. Lies are the foundation of Paradise. Of all paradises. The Paradiseans would sooner smother you as a national traitor than admit the lie, because the secret of their petty existence is deception. The deception of their own petty selves, the deception of others, the deception of all generations. They are masters of confiscating at the cradle the rights of all future generations to reject their lunatic legacy, inculcated under the rubric of tradition. I tell you, brothers, the man lying in Thaddeus's grave is none other than Maimunus. No, he was not a moron to hang himself. That yarn has been woven by the votaries of Mr. MacYehu.

How did this quandary engulf Dog, brethren?

During a television appearance in Los Angelos, Dog had stated that Maimunus is our brother. "He may be yours, but he's certainly not ours," they said and attacked Dog from every corner. "Fine, he's mine then," Dog said. At the end, however, she closed shop and went away. Her decision was not in the least helped by the reproach heaped on her by her weredog kin. The color-challenged. Yogurt is black, brothers. You shall be convinced of this in the hominid world. Even Dog's father joined the fray.

"Who are you, Dog, to criticize our catholicoses?"

And still Dog needed to have a nook, remain domestic, to be able to carry on with the struggle in the human world—to be able to recuperate every day from the human vitriol which was showered on her a hundred times a day at her weakest and most vulnerable moments, in her room, in her bed.

Dog, the single reason of your failure is your lack of the power of hypnosis!

Makoko smiles from the sixth floor.

Truly, Dog had only himself to blame. He could have disentangled himself by returning to the world of dogs. Apropos of this, he had learned from the political parties of Dreamstan a few incepts on the most crucial issues facing the nation, such as *neyme gerek* (why bother?) and *sikime* (I couldn't give a flying fuck). But that would mean abandoning his research. After eighteen years of independence (18 = 6 x 3 = 666), it was difficult to go back to sharing a roof with his father and reliving the bitter consequences of the past, which continued to be aggravated exponentially. But this was what he had to do if he wanted to continue working on his book—which he, a dog, had resolved to write for the benefit of humans. Heavy is the task you have entrusted me with, my friars. Humans have always crucified the trailblazer.

Maimunus is our brother. Yes, these are Dog's words. And what else had he not said yet?

This: that Maimunus is your forefather. That your entire civilization reeks of a second-degree slavery to a pathetic slave who, in an effort to negate his own thralldom, has invented a fictitious contract with a ghost, cheating man and his "maker" alike. That you have no civilization at all!

MacYehu and disciples, and almost all of the authors of the Gospels, were Mimunus's tykes. It was out of the tussles of Maimunus's kiddies that Yoohoo MacYehu's religion was born. As they embraced it, the converts stuck Maimunus's head, too, in the covenant.

In truth, Maimunus is the Father of MacYehu.

To conceal Mr. MacYehu's racial origin, the Paradiseans ascribed to him divine pedigree. Since that day, Maimunus rules over Paradise, as a foreign king undergone a name change. And the redeemed, knowing deep within their souls that they are Maimunus's minions, do everything possible to veil their slave lineage, just as some Shvilis try to shroud the Paradisean origin of their alphabet and many cultural icons, harboring ambivalent feelings toward Paradise. It's a revolt of the will against the will of the other, without regard to intention.

Of course I am a Yehudi, my brothers. They say there is no secret in the world that shall not come to light. Thus my secret, too, is out. The dreamers detected my identity and duly kicked me out of Dreamstan.

A typical passage from Dog's diary:

Four thirty a.m. Phone rings. My father, whom they have not named Elijah so as not to run the risk of having his classmates taunt him with the doggerel "Elijah, why did you pooh on the vitrina?" is incensed. Father is simmering. Father is seething.

"Son, it's Canada. Your sister. Will you talk to her?"

"No. Why did you wake me up again? I'll talk to her when she learns to listen. Last time she got me sick for a week."

"Well, I thought maybe you'd talk to her. I just figured I'd ask... She tried to commit suicide. She's calling from the hospital..."

Six a.m. The phone rings off the hook.

"Son, it's your mom. They'll be going to court today. She's calling to ask you something. If they don't solve your brother Jesus's problem today... oh, Jesus... we'll be ruined..."

"I've told you a hundred times: leave me out of these stupid things. I've said my piece. I don't wanna hear about it. The rest is your business."

"We're ruined then... By the way, I've got a document here. Will you take a look at it? Tell me what it says."

"What is it gonna say? Same-old same-old."

Six thirty a.m.

"Son, get up, drink your milk. See what wonderful milk I've made for you. Its fat is miraculous. Should I make you some *lulah kabob* today?"

"Dad, I've been telling you for forty years, these meats are full of hormones. And that meat you've bought is 50 percent fat. This is not dog food. If I eat your stuff one more day, I'll drop dead. I can't breathe anymore."

"Come on, stop listening to every pierrot. Every day the doctors are saying something different. You'll croak of hunger if you listen to them..."

"Right! Let's drink a whole can of olive oil a day because it's good for us. How about a can of sheep fat? And four kilos of lard? Or five kilos of waffle?"

"Long live our Kilis dishes, son. In the whole world there's nothing like my mother's food. In the whole world there's no woman like my mother. It took your mom ten years to get the hang of cooking..."

Eight a.m. I am busy working.

"Son, take a whiff of this, tell me if it's right. I made it the way you like it, with little salt. Look, look, the oil is still simmering... smell it... come on, have a little taste..."

"Dad, I'll make whatever I need to eat. Stay out of my food."

"Why, are we donkeys to eat grass? No, son, eat so that you won't lose your strength. Don't spend a penny. You're writing a book. I'll buy your food."

"Dad, unplug that phone, will you? I can't take it anymore."

"We might miss an important call."

Two hours later.

"Son, come, come, take a look at this walnut. It's just like Aleppo walnut, shining like a pearl. I got three kilos. Son, before you have your lunch, have half a kilo of this. It'll boost your brain. Finish it by tomorrow. I'll buy some more."

"Dad, I know what I need and don't need. You don't worry. And butt out of what I eat or don't eat."

"I know better about what you need. Son, you sit, write your book. Let the world know that we're a people with a great culture. Where did this Pasha come from? A bunch of illiterate donkey-fuckers. Before he went to sleep at night, your grandfather downed a whole bowl of grape molasses—that's about four or five cups, mind you. He was made of iron. He died when he was ninety. If he hadn't gotten hernia inflammation, he would've lived to be 120. When he walked, you couldn't catch up with him even if you ran. There was a man called Hashish among your grandmother's relatives. We've seen him eat a whole sheep. Now this guy could wipe off the letters of a coin with his two fingers. He was a truck driver—used to take stuff from Aleppo to Damascus. One day the backside of his truck got stuck at the edge of a canyon, with one of the tires spinning in the air. What does he do? Puts his shoulder under the behemoth, lifts the damn thing up, moves it back to safety, and hits the road. What do you kids eat today? Back in the day, I ate sixteen eggs for breakfast and then drank two pitchers of orange juice. I was like iron.

"There was that time when Shakespeare's iron door wouldn't open," father continued. "Behind it there was an iron rod two inches thick, wedged between the door and the wall. Son, I got a hold of it with one hand, turned it to a perfect circle. Shakespeare was speechless. I was barely fifteen years old. He loved me so much... He said, 'Let me take you to Elizabeth City...' Some general was going to give his daughter to me. I told him, 'I won't budge from my home and city.' I used to make forty, fifty suits a week. Prince Lobkovich used to come to Adonis, all the way from Mercedesland, to have me make his suits. 'Elizabeth City, Parisabad, Milano... I've never seen a tailor like you anywhere,' he used to say. Now Barbara Walters, Ellen Degeneres, Pierce Brosnan—that guy loves me—I lose count. All of them say the same thing."

"Dad, you forgot the king of Allahland. Tell me so I'll write that down too."

"Son, I've made at least a hundred suits for the king. He was a man of gold. The Allahi nabob Kashoggi used to go crazy for me. He came by every time he was in Adonis. He's gotten a few hundred suits from me. And how about the emir of Sheikstan... Which should I mention? Son, your father is a world-renowned couturier. There's not one tailor like me. Take Paradise, take Hell, take the whole planet. Let them find one like me. Our political parties... instead of writing about me, they push their scoundrels and on the other hand try to mess you up...

"I shit on the brains of these Gehenlanders," father went on. "Doesn't matter what your achievements are... they put a two-bit manager on your ass, prepare a five-page report on you every three months. This is good, this is bad, you'll talk like this, you'll sit like that... cunt! What the fuck do you know about tailoring? Those big cats, Gucci, Prada, they're all the same shit. I'm a man who's sat around with kings, and they're gonna teach me how to talk. Give me five minutes with a customer, and I'll sell him a hundred grand worth of stuff. Just to look good to the company bosses, these fuckers find a stain on you every day... Ah... where have we left our Kilis dishes, our Mont Kurd foods? People don't know that such masterpieces exist in the world. Our sheep used to eat grass a meter high on those wild hills. If nothing else, you should've tasted the madzoon [yogurt]. Sit under a tree after lunch, with the wind blowing cold as ice, and then fart a big one... Aaaaaaaaaaaah... You'd live to be a hundred. People today are all sickly. Cockroach people! And it's all in the doctors' plan. They're gonna kill people so they can get rich. Take a load of these Gehenlander ninnies—night and day they're sitting around counting goddamn calories."

Ten p.m. The day in a nutshell. Two hundred phone calls, twenty tantrums. A laugh every Wednesday. I have consumed my father's *lulah kabob*, tomato omelet, and baklava. Heard the same stories for the 365th time. Also taken a swig of the arak to fortify myself. I have not practiced yoga.

"Son, tidy those sheets. It's embarrassing. We can get you an expensive, high-life commode. What will people think? 'Your son has gone crazy,' they'll say. You read the Holy Bible, pray. Son, they must've made you drink something. They've screwed around with your head…"

"Dad, how many spoons of coffee have you put in the milk?"

"Very little."

"Not more than forty spoons, is it?"

"Oh, come on! Not even four or five spoonfuls. Back in Beirut, the doctor at Satan's hospital told me that coffee is very beneficial for anyone doing brain work. This is the rule: you must drink two cups every day."

Here Dog has scribbled some marginalia in green ink.

Love = suicide + perpetuation of ignorance = submission to the will of the other.

Love without respect. The ignoramus is incapable of respect. The death knell of Paradise.

Love as preached by Yoohoo = the dumbing down of man, creation of an infrangible web of illiterates, vampirical destruction of the learned in the guise of equality, fanning of zealotry among the legions of the illiterate through the promise of eternity, nullification of the possibility of man's development, surrendering of the most crucial evolutionary right: autonomy, blinding of the mind and offering of the neck, spiritual feudalism, liberation from the shackles of slavery (thus perpetuation of slavery) through self-inflicted madness (apparently the only positive—and not at all original—outcome of the messianic mystery, which spawns the illusion of seeing the system of lies as gospel), narcissism under the label of love, death under the label of life.

More from Dog's diary. July 9.

I have written one page today. I don't have Acharian's second volume and I need it like I need water. Audrey has broken up with me. I don't take her out. I'm a dead duck. And cheap. She has found a sugar daddy and flown to Hawaii. Of whom should I inquire about the relations of the Sumerian word *zu*? Audrey has vanished just then. A deep breath. I owe the library. They won't loan me any more books. I've returned the volumes by mail, sir. I've kept the receipt. Thief! I simply don't believe you. Get away! Okay, we have received them late. Penalty: fifty bucks. Is *ik* an Indo-European suffix? I have the receipt. Nah... mah... bah... *Bahyah, bahbanyah*... I have not had a woman in two years already. No, no, it is not cancer. Just nerves... Nah... mah... bah... Nah... mah... bah... No, they are wrong: onanism is not a panacea; there is a larger field of energy. Meilikius is like a pyramid. Nah... mah... bah...

Fine-spun threads of separation that furl around and around and slowly gobble you up. Ex-wife, heeding mother's advice, has married a hapless Peruvian for the sake of "having a man over your head." Three more kids. She has divorced once again and now standing with her six children at the edge of the abyss.

Every day, hornets sting at the deepest layers of my soul. Inexorable words. Obdurate din in my cranium. Tumult. Uproar. Onslaught...

I have brought her to Hell, ruined her life. Satan will not grant her citizenship. I have wrongly imprisoned her. I was cold in bed.

These being but a fraction of the woes.

Given such a state, it remains to tackle the more urgent issues. Me, my children, my book. Easier said than done. Before even recovering from one blow, there lands a second one, and a third, and a fourth, ad infinitum. In my bleakest moments, when I wrestle with the specter of death, a precious few faces endure in my mind's eye, managing to energize me anew, somehow preserving my equilibrium. They are my children, God Artin, Phulgenda Sinha. On this side of them, it is the *generative energy*.

To learn to forgive... To learn to love...

Makoko smiles from the sixth floor.

This much, my brethren, from Dog's diary, literatim.

Dog's circle of friends, apt as they were to provide him with spiritual sustenance, vanished into thin air, leaving behind them a trail of humanoid affectations. Nina left at the most critical hour. The lone soul to whom Dog had entrusted his book went on to surrender the manuscript to the agents of the KGB, thus increasing her value and protecting the honor of the Virginosa from the "lewd staghounds of Dreamstan." The only one left was Christina. A renowned chanteuse in Leninstan, much beloved of the Paradiseans. Christina stood unflinchingly by Dog's side. She had followed his television broadcasts, gone to great lengths to obtain his unlisted phone number. Never in his life had Dog heard the type of praise which Christina expressed in the space of five minutes. It gave him strength at a moment when he needed it the most.

Christina helped Dog get on his feet. They became friends. This, too, is in the realm of possibility for us, brothers.

The tactful element among the spirito-intello terrorists had asked Dog to recant on the air his views of Mimunus. Your statements threaten to marshal Filippis, Negroids, and others to Paradise, where they would snatch our Aryan girls. Paradise is the home of the Aryans. We are an Aryan race. It behooves us to preserve its virtues and purity. The Natashas? No way. We oppose marriage with them. Esther disguises herself as one, tricks the Virginlandoso into the nuptials, and conceals her identity until her goal of giving birth to a healthy child is realized. Do I know that Jinjin organized the communist revolution to revenge the czar? Do I know that under the guise of demoncracy and capitalism Jinjin is now appropriating the national wealth of Whitebearland?

They were outraged by the fact that Dog treated the Chosen One as any other vertebrate. This is precisely what Mimunus seeks: to grab a hold of Paradise from within, to take possession of the cradle of creation using the yashmak of demoncracy. Demoncracy and capitalism are the ideologies of the rich. Our power was usurped from us, our numbers dwindled. What do we need capitalism for? To be the underdog of the rich? What do we need demoncracy for? To be outvoted in the Euro arena by the never-remorseful numbers of genocide perpetrators, pullulating like rats? What do we need freedom of expression for? To be bombarded day and night by the ideological propaganda of the filthy-rich imperialists of Yehu cocooned by Satan?

"Death to Yehu!" they proclaimed. "Jinjinus should be ejected to the desert of Jinjinland. It has no business being anywhere else, not even in Hell."

Dog replied, "Let the world solve its problems. You're under no obligation to resolve either Satan's or Caliph's issues. What have these jerks ever done for you? Let man eat man. Till they perish. Five thousand dead or five million, what's the fuss about? You, faithless! They'll all be reborn somewhere else. Shouldn't the killers be extolled for facilitating the Creator's goal to exalt his followers in eternal glory? These vicissitudes may not vanish for millennia— only the actors will change. And they will take you astray from your path. Will you establish the temple of HAY on Ararat—for the countless millions of descendants of Hayk's twelve sons and daughters, for the whole of humanity, for she who hears HAY's voice in her soul? A house of the spirit cannot be a house of race. The entirety of the Paradiseans will not suffice to provide ministers of the HAY movement for the nations of the world. Steer clear of destructive missions. Führerism and Jinjinism alike are fascist ideologies. Neither should be tolerated."

They were patriotic and blind. By definition. As all patriots of the hominids. Those among them who most vehemently called themselves "Aryan" were men and women whose visages were different editions of the same orangutan's ass. They tried to restore the gene pool of Paradise the way they understood it.

While these personages were lulled by the idea of giving birth to square "filth" in isolation, Pasha ennobled his own "filth" through dispurification.

The wild bunch—women suffering from sexual aberration—drew behind them a tidal wave of divine intellectuals.

There was not a soupçon of Aryan spiritual values in the lives of these people, brothers. They violated the very first principle of the sun: to wake up at daybreak and to retire after sundown. As a rule, the angels wake at noon and have their breakfast in the ides of afternoon to catch the bus to Las Fortunas at 6:00. They spurn the most basic dietary principles and disdain the essential etiquette of speech. Binge, smoke, abuse their bodies to the hilt. Their brains are nuclear-waste sites. The ambassadors of death had debased the sublime Aryan way of life, turning it into a platitudinous credo.

Dog devoted a broadcast to the softening of tempers. He said his admiration for the Slinger did not belittle the historic rights of Goliath. He then read aloud a passage from the *Dream Encyclopedia*:

The epic of David and Goliath has Paradisean roots. The name of this most adulated hero does not occur anywhere else in Maimunus's prolific tradition. Scholars assert that David is not a Maimunean name. The Slingerian kingdom of Maimunus's religious epic has never existed. It is a tale yarned only after Xerxes's time, possibly in the third or second centuries BMY (Before MacYehu).

Maimunus's father is Shah'nshah Ayatollah. Father reversed the relocation policies of the earlier Babylonians and Assyrians and established son Maimunus, in one among many such imperial colonies with their local gods, to consolidate his empire. Thousands of disaffected slaves joined the hullabaloo in hopes of a free life. These settlers adopted the rex's propaganda of returning to their forefathers' homeland, and came to believe themselves as returnees from exile. Refusing to adopt the imperial ukase was anathema and disqualified one from membership in the nascent group. In the ensuing centuries, these settlers created a tradition of exile and a literature of survival, attracting to it all the various local myths that resonated with such identification.

But the arrogant and careless Ayatollah, to his own chagrin, confused the word *Israel* with *Judah*, encouraging the settlers to believe that they were the descendents of Israel. These, in turn, inoculated the myths of their supreme deity, Elohe Shamayim, into the body of the local Samaritan idol,

Yehu, which they were sanctioned to promote by imperial edict. They created their own folklore, based on local myth, and united their new, Ayatollah-ordained ersatz Israeli identity with that of Mimunus. This identity was embellished with the local Slingerian lore.

Thus, long before Maimunus was born from Darius's womb and raised by Xerxes, several waves of exodus from Paradise caused a large number of its natives to settle in Palestine, bringing with them the ancient culture of Paradise, and subsequently assimilate with the locals. The latest historiographic research confirms that the historic basis of the Mr. Mosmos legend is the monotheistic system founded by the pharaoh Akhenaten in the fourteenth century BMY. Akhenaten's religious revolution compelled the sacerdotal class to conspire against him, possibly threatening a popular uprising which forced Akhenaten and his followers to take refuge in the Sinai.

Freud, too, believed that Mosmos was of Pharaonic blood. He asserts that the name Mosmos (aka Moses) itself is Pharaonic. If we were to remove the Socratic suffix -es, we would be left with the Pharaonic root word *mos*, meaning son, which often occurs in the names of Pharaonic rulers, such as Thutmos and Ahmos. Freud is of the opinion that, in order to conceal Mr. Mosmos's Pharaonic descent, the Chosen One distorted history by presenting Mosmos as a common man who rose to power at the Pharaonic court, whereas in truth Mr. Mosmos (i.e., Akhenaten) was of royal stock, and not a Maimun. Furthermore, historical research (if we were to ignore those degreed sciolics who mistake their faith-based paralogysm for science) attests that there is not even a single viable clue to confirm the Chosen One's alleged presence in Pharaohland. Cataclysmic events of unprecedented magnitude would ineluctably have left a trace in the works of ancient scholars or the profusion of data documenting the period in question. Several dog academics in Tel Afif concur, drawing fulmination from the religious right for exposing the bogus foundations of their faith and political claims.

A thousand years thence, the semi-factual legend woven around Akhenaten was inherited by Maimunus from the natives of Palestine, with his xaxams integrating it into their religious doctrine. They confabulated a genealogy to give divine legitimacy to the Hasmonean dynasty, founded in 164 BMY, Year 0. According to Prof. Ashkenazi, by placing Adam in 4164 BMY, they accounted for the prevailing new age superstition of cosmic periods of a four-thousand-year duration. Nota bene.

	Yehu's Calendar	MacYehu's Calendar
Big Bang	0	4164
Birth of Abraham	1946	2218
Entry into Pharaohland	2236	1928
Exodus from Pharaohland	2666	1498
Temple Foundation	3146	1018
Temple Destruction	3576	588
Return to Penisalem	3626	538
Temple Rededication	4000 = 0	164
Birth of MacYehu	n/a	0

The Chosen One's obsession with numerology resulted in the adoption of the Babylonian holy number six in concocting a history for himself. A sequence of six 6s, 6x6 (or a twin 666), which constitutes the last digits of the significant dates in Yehu's calendar, lies in the foundation of the Chosen One's universe.

Professor Ashkenazi asserts that in an effort to create an origin myth, a continuous narrative, and a group identity, Maimunus's xaxams pumped popular tall tales into a calendar to output a nationalist fiction. Thus, from the birth of Abraham in 1946 AY to the alleged founding of the Temple in 3146 AY by Solomon, they figured out a period of 1,200 years or twelve generations (Abraham is born Isaac at the age of 100). With this arithmetic, the Exodus from Pharaohland is supposed to have taken place in the sixty-sixth year of the twenty-seventh generation. However, from Exodus to the building of the Temple there is a variant chronology of twelve generations also, of forty years each, totaling 480 years. A second 480-year period, or twelve generations, is envisaged for the following period between the supposed founding of the Temple and the alleged repatriation to Penisalem.

"The producers of the MacYehu myth, well-versed in the intricacies of the Chosen One's arithmetic, gave him a knock-out, and buried his twin 666, hence the interdiction on 666.

"Holy of holies! Holy Confectionery, Inc., dba Holy Bible," announced Dog. And continued:

While languages evolve to become incomprehensible within a few hundred years, there seems to exist a language that refuses to evolve—reasonably so, since it is God-spoken. Created things do not evolve. If a set of books asseverated to be composed within a millennium flash stylistic monotony, employ the selfsame vocabulary, and an identical standard of morality, philology contends that they ought to have emanated from the same school. Undoubtedly from the same hand. Their author is His Omniscience, of course, who apparently weaved the entirety of the Chosen One's Bible in the second century BMY and asked his oracles to predate its various books.

Dog continued with one more passage from the *Dream Encyclopedia*, and followed it by a commentary, signed NT.

Lastly, a hypothesis holds that the Hyksos, who preceded the reign of Akhenaten, were Paradiseans (or, at minimum, included some Paradisean tribes), that the city of Jerusalem was founded by them, and that the legend of Mr. Mosmos is an echo of the story of the 240,000 Hyksos or Paradisean tribes' exodus from Pharaohland and subsequent settlement in Palestine. These opinions are not necessarily contradictory. Popular narratives have always intertwined various historic events.

Ergo, is the early history of Israel the history of the ancient Hays and the religiously-persecuted Pharaonians, which has been appropriated and distorted by Maimunus to suit his agenda? The ideologues of Maimunus succeeded in expropriating Israel's legacy. An allegory illustrating this fact is to be found in the symbolic story of Jacobus usurping the rightful inheritance of Esauus. Incidentally, Jacobus subsequently comes to be known as Israel.

"Maimunus appropriated the name Israel for political aims, not the least of which was to create an ideological basis for the annexation of Israel's territories to its land in the south. The historical Israel was the country of the Samaritans and nothing pertaining to it had any relation to Maimunus. Its capital was Samaria. There is no ethnic continuity between the Israel of Samaria and the invented Israel of the Scriptures. The Biblical tradition, in fact, portrays the Samaritans as the antitype of Maimunus. If there are any legitimate heirs to the country of Scriptural Israel, that would be the Palestinians. The story of the 'united monarchy' is a hallucination yearning to usurp the history of someone else's land by symbolizing and historifying it within one's own tradition. The entire Solomonic and Davidic epic is religious utopia. Even the cult of Yehu was a Samaritan cult which Maimunus appropriated and tried to dignify it by adding to it the universal attributes of Ahura Mazda, the dominant deity of the time.

"The only land that hosted Maimunus was a stretch of a few dozen miles in Maimunland, comprised of a few dozen insignificant villages, and that, centuries after the imagined events. Today the state called Israel is not in any way connected to the epical Israel of the Scriptures, and, as such, its name is misleading to the core. Modern Jinjinist claims on Palestinian territory are a result of self-delusion, a consequence of falsification of history by the tradition-inventors of yore. The correct name of this country would be Judah. Its expanse less than half its present size. It is the prerogative of the Palestinians to call their own country Israel."

Does Scriptural Israel's foundation on Paradisean myth give the Paradiseans any rights to the Biblical tradition? No! But to this day, brothers, the Chosen One expunges his Paradisean roots and sows enmity toward the Paradiseans, in order to maintain a centripetal doctrine, push his lambs toward Penisalem.

Will against will. Will based on faith. Will without regard to facts...

Will of the deranged.

A viewer calls in and declares on the air, "Dogs, shield your divine legacy, which brigands have wrenched from you. They have rewritten history, deceived the masses, with the full sanction of our wise catholicoi! Dogs, you not only have the right, but are required to reclaim the legacy that was bequeathed to you by Motherdog."

"Sons and daughters of Motherdog, deceived Scriptural preachers, return to the house of your Mother, reveal the truth to all the nations," another opines.

"Give us our dream back! To hell with your truth!" bellows a neophyte.

A further passage from the *Dream Encyclopedia*:

The legend of Abraham and Sarah has probably originated from the legend of Ara the Beautiful and Queen Semiramis, Ishtar historicized, in which the protagonists symbolize the cosmic relationship of the sun and the moon. Having been informed of Ara's mesmerizing beauty, Semiramis invades Paradise to capture him for her boudoir, but the prince frustrates her advances. Displaying fidelity to his wife, say Xn chroniclers, the rewriters of Paradise's past. The traces of the relationship of the Ara-Semiramis and Abraham-Sarah legends are seen in Ugarit, in the far north of the future Phoenicia, at the foot of the Paradisean Plateau. The precedence of Ara's legend to that of Abraham is evinced, among other things, by its matriarchal overtones, whereas the latter is a patently patriarchal transmutation.

Ara the Beautiful is the last patriarch of the Paradiseans. The point at which the patriarchal order of the Paradiseans ends is where the order of the patricidal Maimunus begins.

As a patriarch, Ara the Beautiful (and even more so, his father Aram) correlates with Abraham in mythological, geographical, and epico-historical terms. Ara the Beautiful seems to be of *Nostratic* lineage. The possibility that the patriarchs attributed to Maimunus in *Genesis* are the patriarchs of the Paradiseans cannot be ruled out. Are the generations of Abraham the same as the generations of Paradiseans who reached Palestine and Pharaohland, with a later stream being recognized as Hyksos? If the term *hyksos* has local etymology, does that preclude Hyk from having any correlation to Hayk, perhaps later being confounded or superposed with local connotations? Is it not conceivable that various Semitic tribes along the way joined that avalanche, giving the Hyksos a Semitic hinge?

But this does not assuage the redeemed. Au contraire. "We won't have anything to do with either Jinjinus or Maimunus," they scream, sharply turning on anyone contradicting their beliefs.

National sewers of Paradise...

At some level, my friars, their hatred was understandable. As I knew a few of them personally, I did not doubt their probity. The Chosen One sought revenge on God.

But never in their lives have the redeemed countered Jinjinus or Pasha to protect their trampled rights. Impotent and incompetent (despite having lived in Hell for decades, some don't speak a word of Satanish, subsist on Satan's largesse), they channel their bile into the entrails of public discourse. The result is a pandemic which sucks away the life out of the genus. This is precisely what their enemies yearn to achieve.

Such a psychology is characteristic of sociogroups prone to extinction—it hastens their death.

Thus the redeemed howl unto death, destroy those who champion new ideas, or die of self-poisoning. They prepare the tombstone of the nation. The archeologists, meanwhile, continue to hone their necrophilic skills. It takes one to know one. What they need is a dead nation, not a dying one.

But extremism of this order is an indicator of the real dangers dangling over the head of the sociogroup.

Death may come indeed, ushering in the reign of supernatural peace. Life shall go on, new nations shall arrive, and not a soul shall remember the death throes of an extinct nation. Pity is not a currency among macro-organisms. It is a micro-construct, barely asserting itself as a macro-value through the power of the mass media, therefore being modified by the choices of powerful interest groups.

Makoko looks on indifferently from the sixth floor.

Brothers, Dog's position was clear, unwavering. In the spiritual realm, it is impossible to aspire to universal values, consummate the noblest triumphs, by reversion to prejudice and types. By its very nature, the spiritual domain cannot accommodate such a negative approach. The biosphere is a unit. This not only is hypocrisy in relation to canine values, not only a product of blindness and a consequence of political ineptitude, but serves to abort any positive outcome imaginable. All are bound equally to accept their canine essence.

You're wrong, Dog! A noble can never espouse the values of Slavestan.

They demanded a public apology for the statement "Maimunus is my brother." Dog refused.

On the contrary, Dog maintained that one must love Maimunus. Is Maimunus that ugly—uglier than a paradicium? They did not wish to hear the words of the 120 Maimunic intellectuals who condemned the Chosen One's policy with regard to the Genocide of Paradise, or the fact that every year the Maimuns of Paradise appeal to their compatriots in Satanland for assistance in urging our Lord Satan to recognize the Genocide. Or the fact that Satan's ambassador to Pasha, who had authored a string of politically priceless reports documenting the Genocide, was Henry Morgenthau, Sr., or the fact that Maimunic members of Satan's Congress ignored the fatwas of anti-dog Jinjinist organizations. There were Maimuns who had greatly aided Paradise. There are still many today. Collaboration must have been initiated here, at least on the strength of these points.

The prescription to neutralize anti-dog jinjinoids, Dog said, is to embrace dog jinjinoids. Join forces to toss the zealots out and turn a new leaf in the history of both nations.

The sons and daughters of the creator have neither color nor race. Nor sex. Osman is, likewise, my brother, but I already surmised the consequences.

The sorrow was profound, my friars. Insuperable...

To forget and disappear. This, too, was happening. Many tried to divorce themselves from their roots. In Eyfelia, thirty prominent individuals who have survived Pasha's yataghan deny their descent. Aznavour, Verneuil, Karzou, Jansem are exceptions.

When the pain is repressed by the dictates of civility and civilization to keep the other happy, it is enveloped by mental gauze. Amnesia alleviates the pain and mutates the structure of the self. Man lives like the image of Washington portrayed on the dollar—hypocritically, facelessly, as all dollars. Man avoids the truth, as the route to life has been mutated into the route to death. She lies to herself, by which means she irretrievably cuts all the cords that tie her to the boundless, to the unreal, to the life-field. The mutant generation endeavors to bury the old to be able to roam like the dollar, seeing its liberation and joy in endless exodus and wandering. The dog is victimized in this process. Man lives like man—faceless, a life of sham. His dolor is of such dreadful magnitude that he strives to kill the dog every time the latter pokes his head. He is already a slave for life.

But you cannot escape the infinite—that cosmic death that leaves no room for evasion. And there emerges an entire generation of aberrant dogs. They charge forth across the whole of the planet and pervert the inner topography of the human mind fiber by fiber, leaving their imprint on everything. When suffering ensues and the victim is transformed into Ego—Chosen People, First People, Best People—he will turn into a vampire, further fanning the flames of hatred and perpetuating the whirling current of destruction. In all cases, the victim is ill. Otherwise he must abandon the meta-organism that vitalizes him, thereupon assimilating or integrating himself with other bodies in vain. Death solves the problem.

For hundreds of years, the sons and daughters of HAY have been injected into other nations. Upon their bones has been built the artificial caliphate of Pasha. During the years of the Genocide alone, a hundred thousand never-never girls were thrust into Pasha's harems and dwellings across the land. They became the mothers of millions of humans.

No one wanted to remember the oneirophiles. Who needed the headache?

Six-pack beer!

Isn't this way of life the imperial harmony of slayor and spectator? Man savaged a nation. Peace on you.

Kudos to dogs, brethren.

Strange. You will not find an oneiromancer who believes that justice will prevail by igniting the cosmic in Pasha's dead soul. The very idea is blasphemous. Pasha godly? Pasha just? Contradictions in terms.

Fearing that the spark of the cosmic essence might well be born in his horde's soul, every day Pasha rides his peerless campaign to disorient humans and his flock alike, trying to drown the truth in "differences of opinion."

A quatrain by the poet laureate of the redeemed:

In my dream an ewe
Came to me with a query:
"May God keep your child.
"But tell me, what did my baby taste like?"

This is faggot thinking, my friars. But in Paradise they will slaughter you if you be so bold as to find a macula on any of the all-godly garments.

We were fags like our mountains,
You blew savagely like tempests.
We shall remain fags like our mountains,

You shall savagely vanish like tempests.

While Pasha shoves his cock into the rectum of Paradise, the redeemed plead for alms from the Heavenly Father. In Dreamland they have visions of divine dreams. Now and then they do display vexation at Mr. Yehu, but the humble lambs once again bare to him their gluteus maximus. And since they have surrendered their cocks to the Heavenly Father with hopes of eternal life, they pray that He, the Exalted One, shall assume the role of inspecting Pasha for them. The better they give ass to the Exalted One, the better he shall cockify Pasha.

Why deny it, my brothers? In some sense I admire Pasha. Am I to blame for not being a faggot like the lamb-grazing judolicos of the Dreamers? The Dreamers believe that they are so precious to God that though he may punish them for their sins, he will never abandon them. Pasha knows, however, that Planet Mars will not veer from its orbit were he to exterminate a few more species. He has thoroughly mastered the unfaltering wisdom of the cock.

Still, in Paradise they conspired to eliminate Dog when he proposed to erect a big cock on the massive egg-shaped trottoir at the center of God Square. To dislodge the cross of the masochistic nation from the top of Holy Cathedral of the Catholicos at Saint Virginborn, replace it with Dog's cock, vivify the spirit of mimesis unleashing the power of devictimization and scourging the bullies of the human race.

"Die, dog!"

How can one be a dog and not hold Pasha in high regard, brothers?

One day, during a commemorative event for the victims of the Genocide, my elementary math teacher, Mr. Pascal, proclaimed something along these lines: "The triumph of justice and restoration of the spiritual equilibrium of the universe shall be achieved mainly through the dogs of Pashaland! They shall rein in even the ewe-gulping Pasha!"

But this is no easy task, my brothers. Let us recall the words of the poet: "But is it worth selling mirrors in a neighborhood of the blind?"

The blind potentates to this day threaten to "gouge

out the eyes of dreamers," to "remind them of the lesson of 1915."

"Son, don't listen to them. With a bit of freedom there, half the people will rise up and make demands. They'll say, 'Give the Dreamers back their rights.' A few months ago some Kilisi young man has said, 'These are the lands and orchards of Dreamlanders. My father and mother used to say that we took it all from them.' This boy has since disappeared. They're not letting anyone talk about that stuff. They know what they've done—they don't have to hear it from others, their fathers will tell them everything. Son, there are good people in Pashaland. My father used to say that if it weren't for them, not a single Dreamer would have survived—they would've killed them all."

A professor of mine delivered a lecture in Peronland on the subject of Paradise's contributions to world civilization. What? Contributions? Isn't he deprecating Paradise? Paradise *is* the one, incontestable cradle of everything. Like America. When the topic of the Genocide is tackled, a distraught woman approached him. "Professor, I am ashamed of being a child of such a people." She is an Osmaness.

"Take HAY's message to Osman. If he could devote himself to Allah, he will sooner devote himself to HAY. At root he is modest, but he is scared. Why should we not help him be cured of his fear? When Osman hears the screams of the blood-drenched land under his feet, he will no longer fall victim to the machinations of Pasha." This is what a wereman proclaimed on Radio Monte Carlo at 5:09 in the morning.

No, black souls, still I do not consent to obstruct you.
You dark captains of bourse and trickery,
Despots of silver and profiteering,
With your vulture eyes, for long years you willed
The distant Paradises to be heaped upon one another, as boundless corpses.
Ah, in those terrible days,
I cursed the universe and God.
In those days, Justice was shattered piece by piece,
As a boulder of punishment,
Against the mercenary forehead of Eurostan.

After those terrible days,
Forlorn in my old man's death,
At my vain hopes and death throes I gnawed.
Creative peoples of Eurostan, Satanland,
For the love of life, for the love of the society of men,
For the love of death's secret,
And the just Paradisean race of Ararat,
Extend your hands,
Extend your hands so it shall flourish,
Without bloodshed, across its fields.
This is my supplication from behind the wall of death...
And hear me, children of Britannia,
You who so elegantly erected for me
That giant Necrostatua
Across the arch of a Saint Paul's, in Elizabeth City.
Hear me, Gladstone,
Should you not heed my entreaty today,
I shall gather there the clear conscience
Of the whole of humanity, and with it,
From within my bronze swathe,
Weep for you...
Wave 2, "The Great Old Man Speaks"

Brothers, in the essay on Ara the Beautiful which I read in the *Dream Encyclopedia*, there was an asterisk next to the word Nostratic. As I did not understand this term, and have no doubt that many of you do not understand it either, I consulted the encyclopedia's eighth volume, where I found an entry for *Nostratic*. A notation next to the word said "see also *mytholinguistic theory*." So I also read about mytholinguistic theory. But about this, should you be interested, I shall write in my forthcoming epistles. For the moment I content myself by reproducing here the essay on Nostratic, leaving the entry on mytholinguistic theory to my second or third epistle. I kindly ask you to read this passage with patience—it's not a doggish classic.

The Nostratic language is a linguistic construct which refers to the mother tongue of a large section of the world population. Although Nostratic research focuses on a selected group of language families that are thought related to Proto-Indo-European, the term *Nostratic* is often used to denote the mother tongue of mankind. Linguists involved in constructing this hypothesized proto-language are called linguists of *Proto-Nostratic,* or *long-rangers* in linguistic lingo.

The term *Nostratic* was coined by the Danish linguist Holger Pedersen in 1931 (Nostratian in 1924; also 1903), who proposed early in the last century that Indo-European is related to and is merely one branch of a superfamily of languages that included Semitic, Finno-Ugric, Altaic, Samoyed, Yukaghir, and Eskimo-Aleut.

The Nostratic construct has also become suggestive of a unicenter from where civilization expanded and in succeeding waves penetrated various continents, primarily forming a superlayer over existing communities worldwide, whose culture and languages either practically vanished under the dynamic influence of this dominant civilization or formed a sublayer of the new civilization. The term *Nostratic civilization* is often used in a loose sense, in contradistinction to the linguistic usage of the Nostratic, which implies an exclusive community of speakers of the Mother Tongue from which its daughter languages descended.

Disagreements exist among contemporary linguists over the issue of which language families should be included in the reconstruction of Proto-Nostratic. A standard definition of Nostratic is the one proposed by the Muscovite linguist Vladislav Illich-Svitych, which pervaded the linguistic community of the Proto-Nostratic long after the untimely death of this brilliant linguist in 1966. According to Illich-Svitych, Proto-Nostratic includes the Indo-European, Afroasiatic, Kartvelian (South Caucasian), Uralic, Altaic, and Dravidian languages. Illich-Svitych, together with Gevorg Djahukyan and Aharon Dolgopolsky, was among the early proponents of Nostratic research in Leninstan.

Certain linguists, such as Sergei Starostin and the late Satanic linguist Joseph Greenberg, argue that Afroasiatic, which includes the languages of the Semitic Near East and North Africa, should not be included in Nostratic but treated as a separate, sister branch along with Nostratic.

Greenberg (1998) suggests a Eurasiatic family along with the Afroasiatic one. Most linguists of Proto-Nostratic, however, include Afroasiatic languages in Nostratic reconstructions, and the issue of contention is more of a definition. The inclusion of Afroasiatic is effectively demonstrated, albeit amidst criticism, by Allan R. Bomhard and John C. Kerns, whose joint work, published in 1994, provides an important contribution to the advancement of Nostratic research in Satanland. Based on Bomhard (1998), it can be argued that Nostratic is composed of two major branches: Eurasiatic and Afroasiatic, with the status of South Caucasian (now closer to Eurasiatic) and Dravidian to be determined between these super-families.

There are also disagreements over the issue of the homeland of these hypothetical speakers of Nostratic. A major argument considered by several prominent linguists is that since the Afroasiatic homeland is more or less defined, the Nostratic language probably must have been spoken in a region that is contiguous to this homeland. This idea is an extension of an earlier proposal by Illich-Svitych, who, after demonstrating the existence of twenty-four loanwords in Proto-Indo-European from Semitic (Greenberg 1998:54), argued that the Indo-European homeland must have been contiguous to the Afroasiatic one. This thesis was also advanced by the joint work of Leninstani linguists Tamaz Gamkrelidze and Vyacheslav Ivanov (1984 in Leninish, 1995 in Satanish) in an elaborate work on Proto-Indo-European, which argues that the Indo-European homeland was in southwest Asia. *The outlined center of this proposed homeland is precisely a large portion of the Paradisean Highland around Lake Van (1995:850-851) and includes the birthplace of* Madmen of Sasun.

Colin Renfrew (1973, 1999) is of a similar opinion and argues that the Indo-European homeland was in "central Anatolia." This term, as the more outrageous "eastern Anatolia," is a bogus designation disseminated in scientific circles, initially by politicking scholars toadying to Pasha, and aims to bury the term "Paradisean Highland." Thus Renfrew's designation must be restated: the Indo-European homeland encompasses both the Paradisean Highland and

Anatolia to its immediate west. Other scholars of Proto-Nostratic, such as Ruhlen (1994) and Dolgopolsky (1998), also argue for an "Anatolian" solution to the problem of the Nostratic homeland. Allan R. Bomhard (1996) designates the Nostratic homeland in regions including northern Bravoland at the southwestern rim of the Paradisean Highland. The birthplace of *Madmen of Sasun* is in the northeastern vicinity of the homeland proposed by Bomhard. The land of the Hatti or Hittites, whose wars with Pharaohland seem to be echoed in this epic, in part overlaps Anatolia proper, but the core homeland of the people of Hatti is largely situated in territories of what later became known as Paradise Minor.

A few long-rangers, such as Merritt Ruhlen, Vitaly Shevoroshkin, and Sergei Starostin, are proponents of a mother tongue that must have existed some fifty thousand to 150,000 years ago, which they call Proto-World. This dating of Proto-World far surpasses the generally-agreed threshold for the Nostratic proposed by Bomhard at seventeen thousand years. Proto-World has currency, however, with a much smaller minority of linguists than Nostratic, and has often invited derision. Johanna Nichols, an opponent of ambitious macro-groupings, argues that up to half of the several thousand human languages are isolates or members of tiny families, and that the human world was occupied by an enormous diversity of isolates until only a few millennia ago. Such an argument, though well-founded, does not preclude the possibility for Nostratic, nor does it answer fundamental questions pertaining to language genesis that would rule out the possibility of archaeolinguistic models. However, is *Bel a false archetype?

Nostratic research has not been popular during the Cold War in the Demoncratic Imperium of Gehenna partly for the fact that many of its protagonists were Natashima linguists. Satanic linguistics during this period was more interested in the theories expounded by the "Walessski School" of linguistics—a convenient fiction created and marketed by Satan—than in the "Natashima School." Despite the removal of this psychological barrier after the demise of Leninstan, the Maginot Line of mainstream Satanic linguistics, as referred to by Whitehouse, seems to have remained undisturbed. Some Satanic linguists, however, do not accept this accusation, and consider the field simply too hypothetical. A close examination of their attitudes reveals, however, that these linguists hold stricter standards for their consideration of the subject than they do for other fields of inquiry. They hesitate to consider Nostratic as a field of study unless it is demonstrated, beyond reasonable doubt, that the hypothesis is correct. In a way, this would be akin to requiring a full-proof demonstration of the existence of God as a *condition* to introducing the study of theology or comparative religion in Satanic universities. Shakespeare's *Encyclopedia Britannica* does not even have an entry for *Nostratic.*

With this I end my letter, friars.

One of us has materialized in Los Babylonos, brethren. He goes by the name of Black Dog. He, too, has appearances on television and, like me, wears glasses. It is as though we were twins, one black, one white. I first heard of him at the Dream Club, during a football match. Half the audience wanted to watch the game, the other preferred Black Dog's program. A coin toss decided for his show.

Black Dog professes that the Paradisean Church must officially renounce the Old Testament and the Book of Revelations, as they are saturated with ideas that contradict the spirit of MacYehu's tenets. He views many of the prophecies as encoded racist messages transmitted to future generations. Opening the book, he draws attention to the chapter titled "Kings 3:18." He says more than one thousand prophets appear in the chapter. The word "prophet," which is capitalized by MacYehu's henchmen, in fact refers to a xaxam of Maimunus. The top representative of Yehu's cock, the demoncratic prophet Elijah McBrotherlover, has slain 450 prophets in the name of God.

Liar!

Allah, Allah, how is this possible?

Auditors, Yoohoo MacYehu considers this beast the greatest prophet.

Antichrist!

McBrotherlover did not ascend the heavens by the fiery chariots of God—he was killed by Elisha.

"Dog, son of dog!" shout some on hearing this, stand up to bang on the tube.

"Silence!" roars the man who had flipped the coin.

From within the glass, Black Dog calls Yehu a racial icon, which, grabbing MacYehu by the tail, has driven the Creator from the place where the new exclusivist, fundamentalist religion has encroached.

According to Black Dog's probings, Hay's roots go back millennia. It has developed as a priestly class, attaining a profound understanding of the cosmic field. It has grown to recognize the creative power of the non-material, the life spirit and its dynamic rationality, which it has called HAY and has itself assumed the name. Hayk, considered the forefather of the Hays, has been the earthly representative of HAY, Son of HAY. If his nemesis, Bel, the future Babylonian Baal, was the embodiment of the evil god, Hayk could not have been but the Good God. Black Dog insists Hay is not only a nation, but a religion in its own right. The antiquity of Hayk and Bel is also apparent from the fact that they were titans. The titans have preceded the gods.

Black Dog proclaims that an echo of this clash has been preserved in Socrateslandic mythology. Zeus's triumph over the titans corresponds to that of Hayk over Bel. The name of the Aegean Sea is derived from Aigaion (the "sea goat"), one of the three Hekatonkheires, the one-hundred-armed gargantuan figures of the undersea world. Thanks to Aigaion, Zeus triumphed over Chronus and the titans. Hayk, too, battles the Titanic Bel, also with three hundred arms, or soldiers. Is it not conceivable that Aigaion and Hayk are homophonous, especially if there is possibly a semantic relationship between the two? Scholars assert that Hayk is Ea, the subterranean water deity ministering the site where the Euphrates and Tigris spring. And at a given stage of his evolution, in certain locales Hayk has been a goat totem. Balthasar's father, Bel, Hayk's antagonist, was also a goat, as attested to in Balthasar's dream in the Paradisean epic. These mythological dual structures, which serve as prototypes of the dualism in monotheistic religions, suggest totemic origins possibly based on the goat duel. The goat was ubiquitous on the Paradisean Highland and appears in thousands of its petroglyphs.

Zeus, the ruler of the sky, the heavenly father, has originated from Hayk of the Hays. He is the sun, born from the Mother Sea, expounds Black Dog.

Black Dog declares, my brethren, that the catholicos must either himself undertake these ideological reforms or resign from his calling. That in Paradise it is not necessary to forego the religion of MacYehu yet it is imperative to recalibrate it fundamentally. The hymns and symbology of the church must be de-Maimunized. By setting a precedent, the catholicos can embark upon a historic role of global import, which will, in addition, revivify the éclat of the church.

But the Judolicoi, says Black Dog, rather than reshape the messianic world on the foundations of truth, are merely tools for implementing the programs of international ecclesiastic organizations in Paradise and Dreamstan. As for these entities, they are helmed by Freemonons and other forces whose objectives, according to Black Dog, contravene the Paradisean process of self-actualization.

But who knows, my friars? I, for one, don't. Only God knows. His sacred appellations are: Hope to the Marooned and Light to the Darkness-stricken.

The following Sunday I sat alone in front of the television to tape Black Dog's program. My four eyes followed his. I could see him. He couldn't see me. In the next few pages I shall transcribe his words, correcting some of his childish mistakes, so our Lord Satan will not be peeved.

To wit:

Allah the Lord of Penisalem says, "Put every man his sword by his side, and go in and out from gate to gate throughout the camp, and slay every man his brother, and every man his companion, and every man his neighbor." And the children of Levi did according to the word of Bladin. And there fell of the tribe of Old York that day about three thousand souls. For Bladin had said, "Consecrate yourselves today to the Lord, even every man upon his son, and upon his brother, that he may bestow upon you a blessing this day." (Exodus 32:27-29)

Such mass "sacrifices" were peculiar to the Semitic deities in Phoenicia and Palestine. Here one must seek the roots of the bloodthirsty Lord Allah of Penisalem.

All that openeth the matrix is mine; and every firstling among thy cattle, whether ox or sheep, that is male. (Exodus 34:19)

A commonplace idolatric command for child and animal sacrifice.

And Allah said unto Bladin, "Make thee a fiery serpent, and set it upon a pole: and it shall come to pass that every one that is bitten, when he looketh upon it, shall live." (Book of Numbers 21:8)

Idolatry and detritus of ophiolatry.

Ophiolatry was practiced in Paradise. The serpent symbolized the sun. The serpent is a totem, progenitor of the tribe. Hayk is attributed with serpentine pedigree. Assyrian *xaramana* "serpent" seems to relate to Ahriman/Arhmn (Armen?). The facts that in Allahish *hayy* means serpent and *hayat* means life—and that in Maimunish the word *khay* means life, which is one of the major appellations of Yehu—a million apologies, of Allah—lead one to consider the possible interconnections between the ancient Hays and Semitic peoples.

With its undulating movements, the serpent is emblematic of water, as the beginning of life. In its circular position it symbolizes the sun (or the moon), as well as the ancient religious belief in the waters that encircle the earth. Erect, the serpent typifies the axis of the globe—the Universe, also the lingam, as a source of fertility. It is immortality, as it is perpetually made young, by exuviating its skin. In Paradise they believed that the serpent is immortal. My father was convinced that it could live a thousand years. Reminiscent of MacYehu's thousand-year reign.

In the lands of Phoenicia and Palestine, it was a taboo to utter the name of the supreme deity. For this reason, he was referred to by either subsidiary appellations or a reverse reading of his name. Scholars have asserted that Yehu (aka Yahweh) is an artificial word. Its Mimunic prototype is *Yah*.

The name comes from the north, what used to be Phoenicia. It may be noteworthy that a reverse reading of *Yah* results in Hay. Incidentally, Semitic peoples write from right to left, whereas the opposite is practiced by Indo-Europeans. The ancient Mimuneans have subverted the name of our God, transmuted him. Some scholars hypothesize that the word Hebrew (Paradisish *Hrea*) is a corruption of *Hurrian* (Paradisish *Howri or Khowri*), argued to be a major constituent element of the Paradisean nation.

All this leads us to the plausible conclusion that there existed a universal God—Hay, a name shared by the peoples that recognized him. Thus, for instance, the Romans were named after Romulus, the Hellenes after Helen, the Assyrians after Ashur, the Indians after Indra, and the Sasunites after Sanasar. The double "s" in the correct spelling of the word Sassunites is a case of assimilation of the "n," hence originally Sansunites (the forebears of Samson according to some), argues Black Dog.

Through the process of cultural cross-pollination, the beyond, with its eonescence, which the ancient Hays recognized and bowed to, dubbing ner the entatic creator for its ultimate function, in the conceptualized, anthropomorphized form of a supreme deity, has been adopted by other peoples, reached Phoenicia, Pharaohland, subsequently making debut with Maimunus, a Johnny-come-lately to the scene who tried to create his cultural *lebensraum* in between mighty civilizations. In the process borrowing, concealing the origins of what was borrowed, contorting and corrupting original forms. Thus the supreme deity bears the imprint of Maimunus's juvenile delinquency, which through transcendental arrogance caused to calcify the zeitgeist it engendered.

With regard to the aforementioned holocaust, which was carried out in the name of Lord Allah of Penisalem, the pseudo-theologians delete his name under the guise of "translation" and replace it with "Lord," pinning the expansionist yen of the kohens of Lord Allah of Penisalem on the Creator. However, the "Penisalem" attached to Allah's appellation indicates the address of the racial icon.

As all state icons of antiquity, this vampire incites dozens of holocausts to destroy those who do not abide by his fascist politics. Its clerics legitimized genocide by ascribing it to divine sanction.

By appropriating the Creator, the kohens of Lord Allah of Penisalem politicized it:

Then will the Lord drive out all these nations from before you, and ye shall possess greater nations and mightier than yourselves. Every place whereon the soles of your feet shall tread shall be yours. (Deuteronomy 11:23-24)

When Allah hath cut off the nations, whose land Allah giveth thee, thou succeedest them, and dwellest in their cities, and in their houses. (Deuteronomy 19:1)

When thou comest nigh unto a city to fight against it, then proclaim peace unto it. And it shall be, if it make thee answer of peace, and open unto thee, then it shall be, that all the people that is found therein shall be tributaries unto thee, and they shall serve thee. Salaam. And if it will make no peace with thee, but will make war against thee, then thou shalt besiege it. And when thy Lord Allah hath delivered it into thine hands, thou shalt smite every male thereof with the edge of the sword. But the women (shalom...), and the little ones, and the cattle (shalom...), and all that is in the city, even all the spoil thereof, shalt thou take unto thyself; and thou shalt eat the spoil of thine enemies, which Allah thy Lord hath given thee. Thus shalt thou do unto all the cities which are very far off from thee, which are not of the cities of these nations. But of the cities of these people, which Allah thy Lord doth give thee for an inheritance, thou shalt save alive nothing that breatheth. (Deuteronomy 20:10-16)

Thou shalt save alive nothing that breatheth. Is this not indeed genocide? Is it not holocaust?

Now go and smite the queen of Elizabeth City, and utterly destroy all that she hath, and spare her not; but slay both man and woman, infant and suckling, ox and sheep, camel and ass. (Samuel 15:3)

These words are Ashur's commandment to Nebuchadnezzar. When he objects to the inhumanity of the order, Ashur dethrones and betrays him into the hands of his enemies for his disobedience.

Whosoever he be that doth rebel against thy commandment, and will not hearken unto thy words in all that thou commandest him, he shall be put to death. (Book of Jesus 1:18)

This Allah is a terrorist, my brethren. Is not terrorism food that is not to the All-clement Satan's taste, and which he has embarked on a crusade against? But is it not also true that Satan is the yes-man of Lord Allah of Penisalem? Says Satan, the All-knowledgeable, the All-wise: "I consulted my mother who told me, 'Son, one day, when you assume the venerable title of *Satan*, the time will come when you will make a difference. You will side by Yehu.' Today I am proud to say that I have made that difference." Satanic IQ. Why does Satan slay Führer, the Holy Ghost of Yehu, but not Lord Allah of Penisalem? What gives, yao, my brothers?

And Bladin smote all the country of the hills, and of the south, and of the vale, and of the springs, and all their kings: he left none remaining, but utterly destroyed all that breathed, as Lord Allah of Penisalem commanded. (Book of Jesus 10:40)

And all the spoil of these cities, and the cattle, the children of Allah took for a prey unto themselves; but every man they smote with the edge of the sword, until they had destroyed them, neither left they any to breathe. As Allah commanded Mosmos his servant, so did Mosmos command Bladin, and so did Bladin; he left nothing undone of all that Allah commanded Mosmos. (Book of Jesus 11:14-15)

The Allahopus is the Holy of Holies of Messieurs MacYahu and Maimunus alike. All houses of worship in Gehenna must be shut down, all preachers jailed for propagating terroristic literature, instigating fascism and chauvinism, declares Black Dog, and continues.

Those who profess such literature as the word of the Creator have no moral ground to demand reparation from Führer BenYehu. Not one of the maimunoids who had committed the slaughter of millions of Leninstanis has been condemned by the Chosen One but instead enjoyed his full blessing. In tovarich Stalin's ad hoc project aimed at the smiting of nations, the majority of the perpetrators have been children of the Chosen One, being the ideal conduits for the logos of Lord Allah of Penisalem to pour through. If these were innocents who simply yielded to the ex cathedra instructions of Madame Jeunesse, why not accept that Führer BenYehu's executioners, too, were innocents?

Every Sunday, the lambs of Dreamstan kiss this codex as they do the robes of the clergymen who purvey it. Baa...

And Bladin is the rod of his inheritance,
And Allah Schicklgruber is his name
Thou art my battle axe and weapons of war
For with thee will I break in pieces the nations, and with thee will I destroy Satan.
And with thee will I break in pieces the horse and his rider,
And with thee will I break in pieces the chariot and his rider,
With thee also will I break in pieces man and woman,
And with thee will I break in pieces old and young,
And with thee will I break in pieces the young man and the maid,
I will also break in pieces with thee the shepherd and his flock,
And with thee will I break in pieces the husbandman and his yoke of oxen,
And with thee will I break in pieces presidents and senators. (Jeremiah 51:19-23)

The clergymen of Dreamstan have titled this passage "A Hymn to the Glory of God," in order to carry out what has been written by the hand of the prophet Gustorius: "Do unto others as you would have them do unto you." Having said this, Black Dog reads aloud a passage from *Prostration,* a newspaper published in Parisabad:

The tools of globalization presently are being harnessed to create a meta-ethnos, as much in the countries of Mr. MacYehu as in the territories once in the grip of Papa Lenin. Such a meta-ethnos, whose expanse some are unfairly wont to call "Countries of the Allahologos belt," shall be led by the weltanschauung and symbology of Allah the Lord of Maimunus, with Penisalem as its religious center.

The paramount tool of this policy is the Yehuization of Mr. MacYehu's religion.

Such a modus operandi subverts MacYehu's anti-Yehuistic ideology, which screamed at the faces of the Pharisees:

Ye are of your father Satan, and the lusts of your father ye will do. He was a murderer from the beginning, and abode not in the truth, because there is no truth in him. When he speaketh a lie, he speaketh of his own: for he is a liar, and the father of it. (John 8:44) Ye... are not of God. (John 8:47)

MacYehu posited literally that Yehu is Satan himself. MacYehu has never used the word "Yehu." He preached another god. MacYehu was a revolutionary, but after his death his adherents have contorted him into a conformist, and, in subsequent centuries, by decreeing a fusion of the literatures of Yehu and Yoohoo, crucified man anew, this time driving the nails into his soul. Thus was created the idol Mac cum Yehu.

Black Dog concludes. Today that ideology seeks to replace the credo of Papa Lenin, by shifting Paradise from one system of captivity to another—one that is more subtle, imperceptible, cunning.

Black Dog continues, "The kingdom of God shall be taken from you, and given to a nation bringing forth the fruits thereof. (Matthew 21:43)

By this, I believe, he means that the new inheritors will be Bladin's tribe. But as he also makes reference to Paradise, perhaps he has the Paradiseans in mind. If I be right in my suspicion, this is high-mindedness unbecoming of dogs, my brethren. It seems as though our brother is not aware that the words above have been exploited by every empire riding on Yoohoo MacYehu's back. Every king has considered himself the vehicle of those words and has brought much destruction upon the world of men.

And Allah said unto Bladin and his people, "Shout; for Allah hath given you the City of Old York. The city shall be accursed, even it, and all that are therein. Only Natasha the harlot shall live, she and all that are with her in the house, for she hid the messengers that we sent." So Bladin's warriors went up into the city, every man straight before him, and they took the city. And they utterly destroyed all that was in the city, both man and woman, young and old, and ox, and sheep, and ass, with the edge of the sword. And they burnt the city with fire, and all that was therein. Only the silver, and the gold, and the vessels of brass and of iron, they put into the treasury of the house of the Lord. And Bladin adjured them at that time, saying, "Cursed be the man before Allah, that riseth up and buildeth this city Old York."

Allah said unto Bladin, "Fear not, neither be thou dismayed: take all the people of war with thee, and arise, go up to Washington, DC. Thou shalt do to Washington, DC, and her king as thou didst unto Old York and her king: only the spoil thereof, and the cattle thereof, shall ye take for a prey unto yourselves."

And so it was that that day Bladin's people of war struck Washington, DC, until not one soul was left alive. They slew all of the senators, and Caesar, and his grand vizier, and, hoisting their heads upon stakes of triumph on Pennsylvania Avenue, sang to the glory of Allah. All that fell that day were twelve million. And Bladin set Washington, DC, on fire and made it a heap forever, even a desolation unto this day.

And the Lord said unto Bladin, "Go forth unto the south and enter Charlotte, Atlanta, Nashville, Saint Louis, Kansas City, Denver, and Salt Lake City. Take these cities and all of the cities and places of habitation along your path, smite all of the people with the edge of the sword, and leave not one breathing. Enter all of the temples of the Baptistas, Josephistas, Tonguecases, Race Witnesses, and the other freethinkers, burn them with fire, and put all of their preachers to the sword. Whereupon go forth unto the cities of Houston and Dallas and commit the same there as in all the cities of Texas. Forget not to enter the hospitals therein and put all of the newborn to the sword."

And Bladin's men took all of these cities and all of the surrounding places of habitation. And the spoil of these places, and the cattle, the men of Bladin took for a prey unto themselves. But every man they smote with the edge of the sword, until they had destroyed them, neither left they any to breathe. And they burnt these places with fire. All that turned to ash that day were sixty-six million of the inhabitants of Satanland. As the Lord commanded Mosmos his servant, so did Mosmos command Bladin. He left nothing undone of all that the Lord commanded Mosmos, whereupon Bladin, whom his disciples named Joshua, gave these places for an inheritance unto the children of Allah. And the land rested from war. (Book of Jesus 6-11)

The remainder of Black Dog's program is shrill, my brothers. Like Sanasar, he would eject everyone from the temple with a single blow. He calls for the decapitation of the Judolicos of Paradise in the court of the Cathedral of Saint Virginborn. I refrain from writing more, ot diova gnieb dednuoh yb dog's terces ecivres. I shall forward a separate letter with Brother Fidesius.

Thus begins and ends Black Dog's broadcast:

May the blessing of HAY, sublime soul of the universe, be upon you, Hays,

May the peace of HAY, sublime heart of the universe, be present in your abodes, Hays,

May the curse of the racist Yehu be lifted from your homes,

May the shadow of the bloodthirsty, terroristic, and genocidal Yehu be lifted away from our people,

And in its stead may there rule the light, benevolence, love, peace, and felicity of HAY, the araric energy of the universe,

May our catholicoi and religious leaders set themselves free of the Maimunic gloom, Monononic vassalage, and Jinjinist doctrine, and may the life-giving light of HAY, essence of the universe, sparkle in them,

Glory be the hallowed name of HAY.

I met with Black Dog at the Urartu tea house. He is a pleasant sort, despite his bravado. Like Jeane Kirkpatrick. I inquired about the sources of his research. He listed them all as I took notes. But then he said that every day, around four in the morning, the shade of a dog appears by his bedside and dictates all this to him. Our meeting was cut short when the proprietor of the tea house approached us and said he was going to close the shop for three hours.

"Apolimar Yoohoo has passed away."

Three days later the news turned out to be a lie. The doctors have revived him.

Makoko smiles from the sixth floor…

I am at a loss, my brothers: why do they adulate Black Dog but hate me? What is there to object to in White Dog's views? My mistake was that I believed the desired transformation to which Black Dog alluded must not be mated with hatred. Now is the moment to be liberated from the whims of history. But this can be realized in an environment of mutual understanding as regards Maimunus, and not by provoking senseless passions, from which no one would benefit.

Oh, I forgot to mention: I lack Black Dog's qualifications. He is of Paradise; I am of Dreamland.

I had taken my car to the mechanic's shop. When the Paradisean employee found out that I'm a Dreamlander, he slyly took me aside and suggested to repair my vehicle outside the shop, at half price. At once I notified the owner, a Maimun.

I was a non-Dreamer—traitor to nation and God.

My loyalty does not belong to the angels but *motherdog*, my brethren. They do not understand. They are terrified and make themselves scarce.

"You could've not told on him."

"I could've smiled and let it go. Avoided getting entangled in his karma. That day I wanted to take a stand against evil, reverse its direction unto itself."

My grandfather, in keeping with the rules of the "Holy Book," had had me circumcised. When the redeemed found out about this, they launched a campaign against the circumcised, rallying around them a group of newspaper editors and television hosts.

I was a Maimun…

White Dog edited the Maimunus statements out of the two videotapes, made one hundred copies of each, which cost him 450 washingtons. This was no small amount—it could pay for one more broadcast.

In ensuing programs he did not allow any positive references to Maimunus. But it was not possible to extinguish the infernal howlings of the hyenas. Such characters feed upon hatred and single-mindedly look for enemies within the genus, refusing to see that the prime enemy resides in their craniums. They are but sluggards who would be left idle if not for a struggle against "internal enemies"—enemies produced in sciamachy, by struggling against whom they try to acquire political capital. They create Ahriman, Bel, Satan, Shaitan, for they are yet cutthroat hamidians and self-righteous sadists who demand victims. Apotheosis is ultimately a political action by zealots rooted in apodiabolosis.

They extol Black Dog, refuse to hear White Dog's new programs. Even though Black Dog considers White Dog his true brother. The important point was that they had found a convenient target that did not stoop to their level—a fact that drove them wilder as they luxuriated in their positions of safety. Without an exception, they hailed from Paradise. They isolated White Dog in Paradisean circles, stirred God's security agencies against him, sought to ruin him, banished him to Babylon, via the same trajectory which Hayk had taken on his way in. They were even more incensed at the sight of his life's wreckage. Even the death of White Dog would not satisfy them. They hankered for his eternal demise, as in the cases of Bel, Balthazar, Shaitan. The only thing that prevented them from murdering White Dog was our all-mighty Satan's law. Satan, Lord of All the Worlds, and Master of the Day of Retribution, became the guardian of White Dog's life. From that day, White Dog and Satan became close friends. Dog understood that Satan is his only friend in the world of men. Dog found it strange that the redeemed were scared stiff of uttering a single word against the political parties of Dreamstan, which in reality should have worried them a hundredfold.

"Yap! That's a Paradisean for you."

One Sunday morning, Thomas, Dog's associate, had gone to Baron MacYehu's donkeyshed to attend a memorial service for a family member. He was violently kicked out by the bodyguards of the Holy Trinity Party, the ultimate guarantor of the existence of Mononostan's Judolicos.

"Cast out the Devil among yourselves!"

The following Sunday, after Dog's broadcast, Yehu called Thomas on his cell phone and threatened to take a contract on him if he did not desist from his television appearances. Threats and curses in the name of Mr. MacYehu were also slung upon Dog, in a bid to make good on the words written by the prophet Matthew: "His blood be on us, and on our children." The blows weighed heavily on Thomas, and one day he fell unconscious on Dog's hands. Only hours later did he come to.

Thomas was an epileptic. This seizure lasted unusually long. During that time, he was having visions of Yoohoo, talking to him, fighting against demons. For a whole hour. Apostle Paul's vision of Apolimar Yoohoo pales in comparison.

Should we dismiss an epileptic's experience and testimony? If yes, then what to make of the experience and alleged testimony of the other epileptic on his way to Damascus? If no, why does the Chinmachinese epileptic never talk to Yoohoo? The drug addict in the West sometimes does speak to him.

Rest assured that after reading these lines, MacYehu's transoceanic corporation, engaged in soul acquisition, will covenant to unearth a Chinmachinese epileptic who does speak to Yoohoo.

Isn't Thomas's fight against the demons a testimony to the truth of the narrative, if MacYehu himself lends the quintessential evidence? He cures an epileptic by exorcising "the demons" dwelling in him. Modern medicine has apparently no luck in grasping the essence of MacYehuic nostrum.

Dog reflected on this matter for a long time. It is possible to found a religion based on blind faith dictated by such subjective experiences. As most founders of sects and religions have done. All these founders, however, have woven moral virtues into the religio-mythic structures of their cultural milieu, thus have become agents for tightening the fetters of mankind to those virtual structures. The problem confronting Dog was larger than the one set forth by the founders of religions. Dog understood that by following their route, she will be stranded in their very swamp. And whatever the price would be, Dog decided to leave that route. Change his course.

That meant descent into an abyss from where no human has to date come out.

It took months for Thomas to recuperate from his wounds.

Those who extended a helping hand were not always of a strong mental and spiritual constitution—more often than not they made matters worse. Humans are weak. They do not realize how they cater to evil. Rather than eliminate the barbs that were hurled at Dog, they unwittingly intensified their velocity and ended up redirecting them at him, through their desire to relay information or offer advice.

Humans are not Heathers (more about this later).

White Dog threw them all out and was left all alone.

It is to avoid being ensnared in the webs of ossified human superconstructs that dogs have chosen aloneness all along. They refuse to play the game set for them before their birth and without their consent. Woof, woof…

Jail!

Some clerics followed the program intently. White Dog sent tapes of certain segments to the churches of Dreamstan, in hopes of facilitating the catholicoi's spiritual transformation. He received positive feedback from an unexpected source: a number of evangelical shepherds, who requested to be provided with recordings of the remaining broadcasts. Meantime, during an annual plenary, the catholicosal church had reviewed the contents of one of Dog's segments and had not castigated him.

Nonetheless, the activities of the catholicoi revealed their unflinching vainglory and unctiolatry. Mildness clinically proven.®

The assistant to the catholicos had this advice for Dog: "Boys, you'll end up being the underdogs. Your struggle is pointless."

An upstanding Catholic monk told Dog, "While you try to equalize the legs of a crippled man, be careful not to take too big a bite out of the longer limb. Otherwise he'll still remain a cripple."

"Man is not crippled. He's paralyzed."

"Are there a lot of Yehu peddlers in Paradise?

"According to God, twenty thousand; according to Yehu, 144,000. Entire villages worship Yehu. Paradise is a cheap market. You can proselytize the angels with a kilo of rice."

"If they've made it there, then it's too late. You can't stop the cancer from spreading. *Venienti occurite morbo.*"

"This pestilence smites only the ignorant. It's been at it for two thousand years now. It was people like these who destroyed a civilization that had taken millennia to build. Last time I checked, 'scientist' doesn't mean 'sage.'"

"And where is God?"

"In Las Fortunas."

"Isn't that right!"

"He's got a PhD in coming up with lame-ass explanations."

"Like the Holy Trinity Party."

For the first time in his life, Dog felt he was being treated kindly. He took pleasure in his conversation with the monk, who shared his woes.

"We, too, have cooled down some. People are not excited about helping God like they used to. We struggle all our lives to see Paradise independent, and then the cherubim tell us, 'Take a hike! You won't qualify for citizenship.' One thing we didn't know is that the white angels consider us black sheep."

"I smell a rat in your religion and strategy," Dog told the monk. "Otherwise the Quintessential Psycho wouldn't be able to swallow the world. The world is under Yehu's thumb."

"Where did we go wrong, Dog?"

"Your foundations, Father."

"How so?"

"Let's start with your peter, the supposed rock on which your church is erected."

"It's the command of the Lord. *Ipse dixit Dominus.*"

"Haecceity does not command, Father. If it's a command, then it's come from your Satan."

"Now you turned all the prophets into Satan."

"Not just them."

"The Only Begotten too?"

"You said it."

"It is the rock on which MacYehu founded his church."

"It is the rock from which the Roman Mithras was born."

"That's speculation."

"No, Father. They simply substituted the old Roman Christ with the modern Chic Bebe. *Thus* they usurped Mithras's throne."

"Can't be."

"In fact, Father, it is Mher's rock. The origin of that rock and Mithras are the mountains of Paradise. The Persians got it from Paradise and supplied it to you. Mher was the ancient Paradisean Christ. His rock is still extant on the shores of Lake Van, a major pivot of Paradisean ethnography and perhaps even ethnogenesis. There's an entire mythology behind this. Your foundation is a sham. Tell your Papa Roma to dismantle his empire and move to Paradise as a humble monk."

"Peter was invented by Maimunus's spawn," Dog continued. "Maimunus is a con artist. Perverting the truth is his forte. His autobiography is a glaring example of this."

"Can't be."

"History bears it out. There are hundreds of serious studies on these perversions. Go read them."

"There are those who say the opposite."

"Those saying the opposite are the broods of zealots who mistake science for religious propaganda. We're talking about a mass of hallucinators who replay the generational curse that's inculcated in their minds since age one. 'If you toss an apple, it'll fall up.'"

"I know those types."

"At any rate, in Mr. MacYehu's novel, Peter is the apostle of the circumcised. Misogynist, xenophobe, ferocious opponent of Paul.. *Paul* was the spokesman of your religion. Papa Pete circumvented him. *He* is the false one. As for *The Acts of Dogs*... mea culpa... I meant to say *The Acts of the Apostles*... a slip of the tongue..."

"Isn't that the title of your book?"

"It could be, if approved by the publisher of DogState-Press."

"How do you release a book in Paradise without an imprimatur?"

"Money talks, padre. And Satan's stick in God's ass. But then not a single bookstore carries your book. Anyone utters its title, they kick him out. It manages itself on the black market."

"In *The Acts of the Apostles*," Dog continued, "the meeting of Paul with the apparition of Yoohoo MacYehu is a tale that was added at least a hundred years after Paul wrote his letters. There he mentions nothing of the sort.

"Up till at least 145 of your Annum Domini," Dog continued, "the church fathers had not even heard of the existence of the four gospels. You know that very well. Paul was closer to the Gnostics of Pharaohland."

"MacYehu appeared to him to intervene in the course of man's history."

"Horsefeathers! No one appeared anywhere."

"'Life is Christ to me,' Paul said in his very letters. How do you explain that?"

"He is referring to the typical Gnostic transformation. That Christ is your Mher, Mher of Pharaohland. Not the cheap replica of Yoohoo produced by Papa Pete a century later. He had a guilt convulsion, having an utter fixation on the object of his persecution, his peteric masculinity falling in love with the femininity of his object of hatred. His brain found its way to save him from exhaustion and self-destruction. Crucified-schmrucified... Mary-schmary... Pilate-schmilate... lies from top to bottom."

"Evidence?"

"Let's open the book. Where do we start? See Galatians 1:15. Here Paul himself says that he has never been to Penisalem until the third year of his mission. Rather, he travels to Arabia and from there goes on directly to Damascus. He had no connection with Penisalem. This is the total opposite of the tale in *The Acts of the Apostles*, which puts him on the way from Penisalem to Damascus, where he ostensibly meets your purported apparition. Including Penisalem in the story is a case of historical revisionism by private religious interests that aims to create a Penisacentric mythology. It serves to embellish the entire MacYehu fiction. Which do you give credence to: a letter written by the man himself, or a novel about him that was woven by some incognito hand a century after his death?"

"Depends on the writer. The author was inspired by the Holy Spirit."

"That Holy Spirit of yours is Mademoiselle Neo Maimunus, along with Papa Pete. Your Peter has not even set foot in Rome. Peter's connection with MacYehu is a lie. The story of being crucified upside down in Rome is a tall tale. Apparently Peter did not even exist. The goal of those novels' authors was to belittle the Gnostic Paul and subordinate him to the misogynistic mafia operating in the name of Peter. Much as Maimunus invented Mosmos, Mademoiselle Neo Maimunus invented Peter. To marginalize Paul, she tampered with his original writings and established a dictatorial pyramid through a new fictitious icon with the mademoiselle on top of the pyramid. Paul was against pyramids. Isn't this what true Yoohooianity is about? Your *Acts of the Apostles* is a peninsula of lies, Satanic literature. Falsehood is the foundation of the Vatican. Truthful is *The Acts of Dogs*."

"You're pushing it, Dog! You remind me of Marcion and the Paulicians a bit."

"No, Father. Let's put Paul aside for a moment. We'll cure him one day. He hasn't become a dog just because we said something good about him. First let's take care of that swindling Peter of yours."

"You're gonna play doctor now? Are you about to cure Yoohoo, too?"

"My heart goes out to humans, Father. You're ruining their lives by calling the writings of devils the gospel of God. Those texts can at best serve as case studies for psychiatry students."

"What had Papa Pete to gain by lying, Dog?"

"Oh, where do I start, Father?"

"What was in it for him? Tell me his motive."

"Alexandria was the pharos of the world. It was the repository of the world's knowledge. It used to be the largest city on the planet, the largest commercial and academic center frequented by scholars from across the known world. To be rid of the Pharaohlandian roots, Papa Roma obliterated the foundation of Yoohooianity and replaced it with a novel brand, more attuned to propagation of empire. It annihilated the Gnostics, burned the world's biggest library. Half a million books! It wiped out thousands of years' worth of knowledge so it could disseminate its own balderdash. Who, in those days, owned a scroll? You burn the library, and *finito la musica.*

"Maimunland happened to be the only plausible arena outside Pharaohland," Dog continued. "And that's where Papa Roma chose as the setting for its theatrics. The Chosen One was already kicked out of there. Generations had passed since the purported events, so you could fix it up to your heart's content. Your Papa Roma married Mademoiselle Neo Chosen. Fidelity guaranteed to death. Why? To create a religious empire. Both were the same muck. They found each other. Now isn't Maimunus right to say, 'I want a divorce and half your assets: fifteen talents?' That's exactly what he's doing."

"Non sequitur, Dog."

"Note, padre, that this is about history written by the victors. But now we know enough. If you refuse it, you'll be sinning against the truth. You'll be barbecued in Hell like your Protestants. Those idiots are simply rehashing the political fiction created by Papa Roma through peteristic violence and dictates without even having a clue as to what they're doing. You know how these books were put together. Your monks shut their ears and issued slurs against those monks who were at odds with them during those early church councils, and often beat them up. Your dumbstruck, harebrained emperor presiding over these councils always sided with the majority, like our righteous Lord Satan does nowadays. And you call this the inspiration of the Holy Ghost. This has to do with issues of essence, padre, because Pharaohlandian Gnostic Yoohooianity and phony Maimuno-Yoohooianity are diametrical opposites."

"These are moot issues. Just now you mentioned a word: 'essence.' Let's talk about essence. This is what's important."

"Talking is useless, Father. You won't understand the essence until you expose the lie. Whereas lies are all we know. Lies we're born into, lies we die into. Lies are what the whole world is based on. The real mistake, Father, is avoiding the truth. Death! Balthasar! What's more important: hope, or truth?"

"Truth."

"Truth."

"Truth is absolute."

"The absolute is your Satan!"

"Fine. Let's not deviate."

"You know that your Holy Writ is a nest of a million lies—it's got the finger of Maimunus in it, but you do nothing to cut it off with an axe. That's why we tore it apart on TV. Anyone with an ounce of intelligence will give you his middle finger and scream, 'Damn you and your Chosen.' What happened? You lost man, you gained the donkey. Your religion is a congregation of donkeys. While man remained a beast outside. Is this the purpose of religion, Father?"

"No, Dog. That's not the purpose of religion."

"But it *is* the purpose of the holy joes. They want to raise lambs to milk them. Build the edifices of the Vatican. Domination. Empire. This is your purpose."

"And, in your opinion, what should the Church do, Dog?"

"If you don't reveal to humans that your book is cause for dire convulsions in their history, you lose your ground. Those imbeciles of yours, Baptistas & Companeras, stick their heads into every hole to preach what the *creator* is purported to have said *verbatim et literatim*, putting the fabrications of shitty-assed Maimunus into the mouth of the *creator*. Forty million liars bombarding the world with the power of the franklin. Forty million fanatics ready to die. Papa Pete would succumb right in front of your eyes."

"They have been deceived, Dog. They're not liars. Can a deceived man be a liar?"

"Of course. When he becomes the speaker of the lie."

"You mean his motive, even will, is immaterial."

"When he chains the will of others in their cradle, your objection becomes paltry."

"You're reducing the problem of the ontological essence of man to functional phenomenology."

"You're the philosopher, padre. Let's say, fields of probability with certain proclivities."

"You're back to ontology."

"No, padre. The realm is full of dog-pretender gods. Now, this fellow of yours," continued Dog, "demands that dogs follow his FalloBible word by word, declares *us* liars, assumes an air of superiority over us. Creates a culture based on lies, hinged upon his superiority, barely tolerating our existence, casting out the recalcitrants as pariahs."

"That's only forty thousand out of their forty million. And the Church never says that the Holy Writ must be followed to the word."

"It's *you* who says that, padre. Take a trip across Satanland and see what's happening from end to end."

"**A**t any rate, I listened to your tapes, and I'm with you a hundred percent—one must grab them by their beards and boot them out. Gold coming out of their nostrils. They don't know a thing about theology… but they know how to ogle women. Have I got stories to tell…"

"Tell me."

"One husband was so enraged that he put a knife to the belly of the bishop: 'You touch my woman again and I'll slaughter you, asshole.' Hey, you, get inside, right now!

I'll lock the door on you. Take a look at this cat. Three days ago she lost her kitten, and now she doesn't get off my lap. What didn't she do to find her kitty! Then they kicked him out and he, *inter nos*, became the catholicos. This one here, despite being an animal, is more sensitive than a human…"

"Blasphemy!"

"Listen, Dog."

"You're insulting my cousins. Cat is cat. Man is beast. Pope is man."

"Right on, Dog. How many humans strive for the education of their kids like this cat does? Wait, let me put you in the next room so you won't disturb us. Let's go for a walk. I want you to write about this…

"I hear that," padre continued, "there are whores loitering around the walls of Saint Virginborn…"

"You're an interesting monk."

"I say this stuff to their faces. The god of these people is money and prostitution. Now they've come up with a good one. They're saying that Maimunus is exposing the Kennedy City affair just to discredit the Church. Come on. Let's keep Maimunus in his cranny for a moment. Did these guys do it or not? That's the question. First pull their ears… But see what's happening. You can say anything you like about Maimunus. He doesn't know you. You don't know him. But God forbid you say something about our own, and they'll eliminate you. They'll humiliate you at every step of the way—they'll brand you a 'heretic.' Or else they'll do a clean job of it… they'll kill you with no further ado."

"Hmmm…"

"So, my dear Dog, do go on with your investigations, but don't pin your hopes on the Church."

"Why? Are they all Mononons?"

"Let them be. That's not important. The thing is they have no faith."

"Should I tell you the reason? Your religion is rooted in a lie. Yoohoo MacYehu is not the only begotten of the *creator*. At most he was a mere mortal who was made into a legend. The *creator* cannot have an only begotten. Only a megalomaniac set on perpetuating his royal line would have an only begotten. And kill all those suitable for his job, past, present, and future…"

"No, Dog, you have blasphemed. There are entire prophecies foretelling his coming."

"You see, padre, you've become a vampire. Your book makes you one. How much energy should I spend to extirpate all these lies from your brain? This is how you've squandered the generative energy of countless generations. Quite the opposite of what you say is true. They wove tales to chime with those so-called prophecies. If there were anything to hold on to, Maimunus would have believed in it. It's a patchwork. Pull it, and it'll come undone. And why should the wizard of hocus-pocus follow his own apprentice? It is because he didn't believe your fantasies that you impaled Maimunus. You're carrying on his tradition of patricide."

"*In veritate religionis confido.*"

"Now you're no different than those Baptistas—you're not educated, padre. You're indoctrinated like all religious fanatics.

"How do these characters know what's in the heavens if they once thought the sun revolves around us?" Dog went on. "This is royal hubris. Man is the center of the universe. And they're God's stewards. Take everyone from your Caesar to Caliph, and now Satan... they're all the same manshit."

"That part is true. We're going to war because of them."

"Was it not your Papa Pete who burned dogs at the stake if they said the earth revolved around the sun? And forget about your saints. Regurgitators of ideology..."

"Such things don't have anything to do with God's essence."

"They do. They do. Don't fool yourself. Now tell me. Your Papa Pete used to say that the earth is flat and above it it's got seven or nine levels of celestial spheres, upon each of which glide the stars, the sun, and the planets. And God sits at the head of these levels, with cherubim and whatever. Well, Papa Pete, what you said came out to be utter claptrap. What guarantee is there that what you call Holy Trinity is not likewise full of hot air?"

"You're mixing geographical science with religious knowledge, my dear Dog."

"But wasn't he the one who created the universe— all things were made by him and without him was not anything made that was made? That God of yours doesn't know what his merchandise is about or where it is. He doesn't have half the brain of a dog. For five hundred years your Papa Roma trumpeted 'Heavens above, earth below,' and killed everyone who disagreed by the most gruesome methods of torture humankind has ever known."

"He apologized."

"That's rubbish. To be atoned, first he must have his fingernails pulled out, followed by a bath in boiling oil, then he must be disemboweled in the midst of the Piazza di San Pietro. What do you say? All the churches must be shut down and everything that the Vatican owns be given back to dogs, first and foremost, surrendering your power. All that's been lost must be restored."

"Have you studied theology?"

"I've got a diploma in dogology. Isn't it legit? It is from the University of Homo Sapiens…"

"Did you learn Latin, Dog?"

"To tell you the truth, padre, I don't remember such a thing."

"To discuss this subject you must first be a theological graduate, my dear Dog."

"Once I went to a symposium by godologists, at the University of Veritas…"

"And what did you hear?"

"Men said it was of the highest caliber, but these cassocks didn't have the foggiest about either pure faith energy or the spiritual life of dogs."

"If you want to bark about something, you have to be an expert in the field, Dog."

"How, padre? Do you think they're admitting ugly dogs? They're expelling them from every single school."

"That's not kosher. It's discrimination. Yoohoo said, 'Love your brother as yourself.'"

"See? These humans hate dogs."

"That's not what Yoohoo preached."

"Love your dog as you would love your dog to love you."

"That's more kosher."

"Now answer my question."

"Which one?"

"About your constipation. This Holy Trinity of yours, Father, dump it in the toilet, then flush it down."

"Why, Dog?"

"It's a cacophony led by maestro Maimunus."

"How so?"

"It's a cobbled-up corollary to a false premise. To the fall, to being banished from Paradise, and such gobble-dygook. Aims to solve the quandaries of Stone-Age man, now an ingénue's fairy tale for interpreting human suffering. They weighed man down with eternal sin, enslaved his soul, to perpetuate the juicy clerical industry. Plus they invented a Yoohoo—I am the way, et cetera—to monopolize the marketplace."

"*In cauda venenum.* He *is* the way to the father."

"We're going toward the mother, the land, the serpent, HAY. Screw his phony kingdom."

"This is a theological matter."

"Padre, gather all those godologists of yours, line them up in front of Dog, let them answer his questions before demanding to see a diploma. Hornswoggling pimps…"

"Fine. I'm not against. Tabula rasa. Let's start from scratch. Convince me."

And Dog began to convince, as he and Padre grew closer.

The messiah idea was drawn by the scribes of your beloved Bible from the Near Eastern dying and rising god. The entire Near East was immersed in the various traditions of this tropos, so much so that no other type of over-arching belief system had a chance for survival except by the sword. What were the sources of that knowledge? I'll give you my book so you'll have an idea of what I'm talking about. I've written it in Hellish to make it accessible to Satan. The poor fellow has forgotten his Paradisish. Let me say something parenthetically, padre. Balthasar, the hero of your epic, the mother of Messiah, was buried in Baghdad. Baghdad is the updated symbol of Babylon or Nineveh for the bards. The story of Adrammelek and Sharezer escaping to Paradise after assassinating their father, the Assyrian king Senneacherib, to establish a Paradisean dynasty is the echo of an extant myth. We can talk about this next time."

"*Mox nox.* Come by on Wednesday."

"I will. Just tell the doorman to kindly open the gate when he sees a dog in these quarters."

"I'll tell him in a bit."

"MacYehu's litter, Father, dovetailed their writings with those slapdash ravings called prophecies, in order to invent and own a messiah. The scoundrel had a few hundred years' worth of groundwork to stand on. The dreamers have nothing. The zealots have cut off your testicles."

"The whole of Eurostan has the same problem."

"You can start everything from scratch. A few centuries might be needed for you to regain what you've lost and for the birth within you of the genuine savior, Mithra-Mher, Son of Davit, if you would still need saviors. The Mher-Christ, mythically correlated with shepherds, born of the generation of shepherds, the Christ myth whom the rascals of MacYehu stole and at all cost tried to historify."

"That's mere similitude."

"Father, the story in the Xn novel birthing a Christ from the generation of Davit was a cosmological belief system going back thousands of years in Paradise. The Slingerian tale of Maimunus is a travesty, literary fiction passing for history through the pulpits of MacIdiot. They took Christ's words and hoisted them on MacYehu, as much as they understood them. Ninety percent of your gospels' contents are the wisdom of the old temples, which existed much earlier than MacYehu's tale was composed—in Phrygia, Socratesland, Paradise. I discovered so many things in the books that Black Dog gave me."

"This is a complicated subject. There are similarities…"

"Yesterday at the library, I studied Fasmer's comparative dictionary."

"How do you read?"

"Very easily. I use my tongue to turn the pages. Page 481. Take this clipping."

"How do you write?"

"I don't. I copy a page, shove it down my pocket. These days I am full of pockets. Now there are computers. You push the keys, and bingo. Read it."

"*Daos* (wolf) in Phrygian, *dawit* in Russian, *davia* in Bulgarian, *daviti* in Ukrainian, *daviti* in old Slavic, *daviti* in Serbo-Croatian, *daviti* in Slovak, *daviti* in Czech, *dawic* in Polish, *dav* in Austrian… they all mean to smother."

"In nearly all Indo-European languages you'll find linguistic remnants of the same legend connected with David."

"The noun is interesting too—*thick smoke* or *thick dust.*"

"Don't you remember Davit of Sasun's battle with Melik, the King of Pharaohland, when the clouds of dust produced by Davit covered the sun for three days and Melik was slain? The episode may or may not be related to the etymon. But Davit is certainly the wolf that smothered his dog brother. Dog Melik. This is a most ancient mythological motif. Remember Remus and Romulus suckled by a wolf— the counterparts of the Paradisean divine twins. And then observe that, in the epic, Davit's son is Mher Minor, Mihr, Mithra. The infant Christ, son of Davit."

"I hadn't noticed that…"

"This appears to be a few millennia before Maimunus wrote anything. Is it perhaps Daw or Dao, with the Indo-European suffix *it*? The Father of Mher, the Savior's Father, the Way."

"Could Daw be related to the Allahish *daw* 'light' as an attribute of a sun deity?"

"Who knows, padre. We're speculating. But it seems we're stepping foot on important ground here. In a group of languages it is also homophonous with words associated with exhaustion and death. Is it because Dawit is the setting sun? Remember his battle with his son, Mher Minor, when he feels tired and can't continue the combat. Atypical of him. Seems to have a mythic moment. The cyclical journey of the sun—reflected in the four generations of the epic. In ancient Pharaonish *dwyt* means death, destruction; *dwt* means the netherworld. Interestingly, in Paradisish, *it* is a suffix attached to theophoric names only."

"I've read about this somewhere—I think in old books from San Lazzaro printed not long after Lord Byron studied

Paradisish there and declared it to be the sole language in which one can communicate with the Creator. We have a series of words like that—*Tirit*, etc."

"Yes, Tirit, the supreme deity."

"In the pre-pharaonic era, Mher seems to be the name of the child of the Primordial Mother. See Budge's hieroglyphic dictionary, page 284. Take this clipping too, read it."

"*M'her*: to suckle; *m'hera*: suckling infant; *mheru*: milch calf."

"That's why they sent Mher to Pharaohland, so he'll be suckled with the milk of Isis, the Protomother. Dame Ismil of your epic is the heroic detritus of the mythic Isis. And the Mary you worship is a byproduct of Isis. In Pharaohland the benighted Yoohooloons stole that image and story, and retrofitted them to their mythic teacher. There you have it: the infant Yoohoo sitting on Mary's lap. Yoohoo going to Pharaohland at an early age. These are but *exuviae* of the Mheric myth."

"Strange coincidences."

"Now let's take a look. Is it possible that the Mashiach of Yehu and the Mahdi of Allah have also sprung from your Mher Minor, padre?"

"I do not know. Mashiach sounds like our Massis, holy Mount Ararat. Do you know if there is a relationship between the two?"

"Ask the linguists, padre. They'll tell you a thousand stories. Depends who you ask. But while we're at it, read this sheet also, page 318."

"*Mehid*: the northern quadrant of heaven or earth; north; northern wind."

"As prehistoric Paradise is to Pharaohland, attested to in your epos, ancient Paradise is to Allahstan. Yajuj and Majuj are also connected with the north. Remember, too, the four winds of the epic. There are some positive grounds for comparison. Their validity is for the ethnographers to decide. These were some of the arguments in my right pocket. To be tossed away. They are the less probable ones. I won't bore you with the details. See all these in my left pocket? They are reserved for the book. I'll publish this stuff one day, provided DogStreetPress won't go under by then. I believe the

Sphinx, which belongs to a later era, is your Mher Major, padre."

"I look forward to reading it."

"Yehu is operating by Führer's Law. Wasn't he the one who said, 'If you have to lie, go all the way'?"

"I think his propaganda minister got that line from Tertullian."

"Well, these stooges have ten Führers in their pocket. They're all about deception, pith, and core. They've stolen from this and that, concocted stories and put them in God's mouth, called the country of their tribe's icon the Holy Land. That land's only proper name is the Devil's Land. If you prove the lie," Dog continued, "they don't admit their mistake, but rather resort to legerdemain to convince you that they're still entitled to everything. They are, after all, the 'Chosen People,' padre."

"It's the vogue now. You utter so much as a *psst* and you're branded an anti-Jinite. It's our fault. We spoiled them."

"MacYehu's jerks, too, will shield the Chosen One. They'll make you out to be either a liar or a lunatic. 'God has said so…' My ass!"

"A few hundred years is not much in the history of our people, dear Dog…"

"It is something *now*, padre. We're dealing with the danger of nuclear holocaust. Even one day counts. Black Dog says that Maimunus has the atom."

"There is plenty of evidence."

"This might be a threat to the existence of Paradise, considering that the Chosen One has not even apologized for his role in the Genocide. He'll drop a bomb in a moment of regional confusion and he'll say 'Oops! Sorry! Didn't mean to, I'll punish the culprit,' then he'll extend a helping hand to God. It's a trick he has learned from Satan. But if Maimunus has the atom, why wouldn't God have it too, Father? Why does Lord Satan force Ayatollah to give up the atom but doesn't say a solitary word to Maimunus?"

"Ayatollah is Satan's nemesis, Dog."

"Why would he be? Isn't Maimunus the root cause?"

"Don't look for fairness in Satan's politics. Deep down it's Satan who's the cause, not Maimunus. But we're the ones at fault here. We think it's not nice to call a donkey a donkey."

"That's true. You must call them by their name. There's no room for equivocation."

"Still, in the church, too, I don't seem able to find a single just soul, beginning with your catholicos and patriarch. Even Mother Theresa's deeds were done for her personal glory. I happen to know quite a bit."

"All saints are actors, padre."

"Come on! What are you talking about, Dog?"

"That's their role. And as long as they have a role, they can't see the *creator*."

"True… Observe this homeless guy. He's here every day. He'll die tomorrow. Right now the world is in danger of being obliterated within a day. Satan can blow the world up with the push of a button. Neither God nor anyone else could save us from such an outcome. What difference will it make if you extend this poor man's life by a couple of years? Let him die two years sooner. We're deluding ourselves by focusing on driftwood. This is what the saints are up to these days. Making the dying not feel the pain of death. Extending the dreamer's dream. They're following Satan's program. And what is he saying? 'Do whatever the hell you want, just don't meddle in my plans.' They are, in effect, partners with Satan."

"Now is the time to meddle. Turn his world upside down."

"You got that right, Dog. If you give Caesar what Caesar wants, he'll destroy the planet tomorrow. This is not like the time of Yoohoo, when time was slow. For Pete's sake, if you're a saint, take Satan to task, you hypocrite, versus basking in his praise."

"Right on, padre! Those principles were valid in a different time, a different space."

"A matter of interpreting things accurately. That's why a monk is an intermediary between man and God. But the principle is immutable. *Certum scio.* Heaven and earth shall pass away, but my words shall not pass away."

"Numerous theologians have proven that this writing is a sham, padre. It's a trap set by zealous clerics one or two centuries after the year zero, which they have created with the purpose of establishing religious imperialism. On this score, then, you should put your mind at ease—not one of those words is absolute. All absolutists are a threat to human existence. But you're right, padre. When the founders of religions proclaimed their moral codes, no man, not even your Caesar, had the capability of laying waste to planet earth, not even 1 percent of it. Those moral dictates are valid only in context. A context that was animated by the law of reaction in the psychosphere, given the boundlessness of time. But today a single act of idiocy can bring everything to an end within minutes, by any one of a collection of idiots who sit at the helm of the world. Isn't it just to kill someone who holds in his hands the power to annihilate the globe, irrespective of who he is? Or are we supposed to sit idly by at their mercy and see what happens tomorrow?"

"A difficult question."

"I think the answer is clear. The new religion of humans is in need of a new moral code."

"In that case the Bearded One will become a saint."

"So be it! What are our options? *You* be the saints so he won't become one. The slayer of that who endangers the life of the earthly mother shall become the savior of man and the harbinger of a new morality. You lulled humans with dreams, the Bearded One assumed responsibility for carrying out the mission. You left the field wide open to him. Who's to blame?"

"You're talking like a true dog, Dog! It's twilight—*inter canem et lupum.*"

"Dogs are those that destroy the men who have accumulated the capabilities of destroying Mother Earth. Such dogs are not terrorists but saviors. No human group has the right to amass enough power to decimate the world, to end the life of any species. Eliminating Mother Earth's foes is a matter of supreme self-sacrifice and moral obligation. What do you say?"

"That's a bit harsh, Dog. It leads to chaos."

"Then let them disclose the power they have hoarded and proceed to dismantle it. Then there won't be chaos. End to secrecy. No CIA, no DIA, no nothing. Otherwise blessed are those who slay them. If you don't take radical action, you become a matricide, a terricide. This is the ideology of all your shitty-assed monotheistic religions."

"The giver and taker of life is God."

"Aha! The globe-raping father, yes? Who is the one that takes our life? You will die dreaming, padre. Blessed are those who slay the enemies of Mother Earth, for they will be called the redeemers of the earthly mother. Blessed are those who punish the inciters of zealotry and the preachers of exclusivism, for they will become the children of the earthly mother..."

"To pull this off, you need a whole new culture, Dog."

"Your artists are in postmodernist hibernation, your universities are dumbed down, padre. Blinded under the sun of Satan, Knower of the Sensible and the Unseen, they are enmeshed in the life and death of this one flower. Specialization freaks, know-it-all experts of Yanomamo. It's strange that we saw a flower today. It's the mother who is in her death throes, padre, not the cell. This is why I'm talking to you. Because your Papa Roma is still the Mother's likely protector in the madhouse of the Father. No matter how distorted an image of her he may present. For this reason alone, I don't want him to be beheaded. I say give him a chance. But would that be a waste of precious time? Remembrance weighs us down, padre. We can't live by remembering everything. Let him return to the Mother, to Earth. To Anahit. Take my message to him."

"That who savages the Mother is Satan, Dog."

"Satan is the Father! The Father God. He has put the Mother up for sale."

"But come, let us look at the other side of the coin, Dog. God brought us to Satanland so we get to know its kind people. If not for this, we wouldn't be able to understand a thing. The Satanican has respect for humans. He's not like our folk. Our folk know nothing but to poke fun at others."

"You understood, but what's the use? Bark as much as you want. Father Satan has cut off the testes of those humans by enforcing his law. His legislators are but pawns of his ideology."

"There's no hope from Satan. He's gone through quite

a few shoes to get you here, Dog. Satan has no heart, only interests. It's already night."

"Don't you think, padre, that the dogs of Maimunland will burn Maimunus's books and accept HAY?"

"Don't bet on it, my dear Dog."

"What about his father, Ayatollah?"

"If he becomes convinced of what kind of game he's fallen for, but don't hold your breath."

One day, Satan came to visit me in Paradise. We met in front of the Foreign Ministry building. Hey, Jingo, what's up? Since dogs are not respected in Paradise, I found safety in Satan's lap as we sat on the steps in front of the building and chatted. Caressing my snout, Satan said, "Where have you disappeared to, prodigal son?"

"It's not happening, uncle. Not happening."

"What?"

"Friendship with God."

"So what the hell have you been doing in Paradise all this time?"

"What do I know, uncle? I have yawed."

"So I've been informed."

"What would you like me to do now?"

Satan took out a piece of paper from his breast pocket, which sported a metal insignia featuring the image of Achilles, and prepared to read.

At that moment, a pair of girasol-headed kowtowers entered the building, spitting on us a quantity of sunflower-seed skins from their mouths.

"Do you see now, uncle, why friendship with God is not happening?"

"All right, leave that to me. I'll tell Pasha to teach this one a lesson. Meanwhile, I want you to constantly bark the following six truths in Paradise."

I prick my ears up.

"First: the sun is the center of the solar system. Did you get it? Second: the sun is composed of atoms. Third: the earth revolves around the sun. Fourth: life is a struggle.

Fifth: man is master of the earth. Sixth: God created man, then woman."

At that, Satan peered affectionately into my eyes, to be certain that I had understood everything.

"But what are you to gain from all this, khoja?"

Satan gave me a deep smile then said cryptically, "If you're successful in fulfilling this small request of mine, I shall make you King of the World."

"But, uncle, I am a son of a bitch and don't sell time. By the way, how much do you pay the prophets?"

"What do you produce?"

"Shit. I take a dump several times a day."

"In restrooms, of course."

"Not really. Wherever I happen to be. In Paradise. In Hell."

"Not a single washington. No, seriously, what do you produce?"

"Death."

Satan was as shocked as he would be if God himself were sitting on his lap. He at once let go of me. He feigned to regain control of himself and smiled courteously as he said good-bye.

"What's your phone number, hajji?" Dog barked from a distance behind him.

"I don't have numbers, my son. I'm the one who numbers all."

"How am I to find you again, hajji? What name do you go by here?"

"Ha ha ha… I'm the one who gives names, son. I myself don't have a name."

"I will give you both a number and a name, hajji. From this day your name is…"

"Ha ha ha…"

And Satan, the guardian of immortal life, left Dog alone in God Square and went up the stairs to meet with Number Five, God's foreign minister, His Excellency Zulfikar James Lutfullah, who was looking down from his balcony at the goings-on of the street.

Dog shouted after Satan, "I know your number! 393206637."

Turning pallid, Satan swallowed it and did not look back. He had already decided Dog's fate.

Enormous shadows descended from the sky on Mount Ararat, slid and cascaded across the land below, settled by their thousands upon Virginabad, capital of Paradise.

As Satan ambled off, Dog heard a frightful commotion emanating from the upper reaches of Abovyan street. A cockroach the height of three stories and the length of six buildings was approaching the square, crushing people and cars as he lurched forth. Intuiting that he himself was being sought out by the colossus, Dog scurried terror-struck toward Tigran the Great Boulevard, aiming to vanish into the back alleys of the nearby shops. Within an instant, however, the cockroach caught up with and took hold of him, using one of his forecranes, of which hung tendrils the length of the Youth Palace, nailed him smack dab into the middle of Godstate Square, and bawled: "Brothther!!!"

The cry was barely audible to Dog, suffocating as he was in the stranglehold of the monster's iron fingers.

"Brothther!" repeated the cockroach.

"What do you want?" Dog managed to emit.

"What can I want, brothther. I heard you're in Parradise, wanted to come visit you."

"Leave me be," Dog scarcely wheezed.

After deliberating for a second, the cockroach gently let go of Dog in the center of the square's big egg.

"Who are you?" Dog somehow uttered, deathly quivering.

"I am your brothther... your brothther, beloved Dog!"

"I've got no brother like you," Dog said, recovering slowly.

"How so? I am your brothther, my beloved... Your brothther! From the same father, the same mother. I swear by my mom's sun. Come, let's go. Let's go get something to eat, let's sit around some nice broththerly table..."

"What's your name, then, brother?"

"Why is that important, brothther? What's that mean between brothther and brothther, huh? That I've found you here, alive and kicking, now that's my biggest happiness, my biggest joy, brothther..."

"How do you figure? Aren't you my brother? Surely our par- ents must've given you a name."

"I was born Oblat Oblatyan. They call me Tot."

"Where do you wanna go? How am I supposed to accom- pany you? You go ahead, I'll hail a taxi."

"No, brothther, no! Now you inssulted your brothther. Seriously: you ins-sulted! Where is that written, tell me: that a man's brothther should come to Parradise, but they should let him get around in some taxi-maxi, yo? Nah, my brothther," said the cockroach, stood up on his hind legs, raised his head, pivoted on himself, producing a gale which smashed nineteen windows across the façade of the Foreign Ministry building, pointed a finger, whistled, pointed a finger once more, until a thirty-six-bay limousine came to a halt before him and Dog.

They installed Dog, as though he were an ant, next to the cockroach. Whereupon the limo proceeded to writhe through the streets of Virginabad in its mutely imposing, supple glide.

"What is your purpose, Oblat?"

"Whatt purpose, my brothther?"

"What is your purpose?"

"Oy, whatt purpose, oy! Firstly let's go get some nice lunch, get some ass, then we'll talkk."

"Well, how about we talkk now, get some exercise later, Oblat?"

"Oy, what an impatient man you are! Typical diaspo-radog. Oy, what are we gonna do with these diasporadogs! We brought one of them here, made him a foreign minister, and what did he do? Gave us a goddamn migraine, that's what. oy! He talks of rrules, he talks of llaws. Like we need to hear that crap, oy! Enough! There's not getting rid of you bunch, is there, oy! Take this fifty-gram. To your health! You're a good boy, brothther. Let's talkk."

"Let's."

"We're talkking, appé."

"We are. Tell me, Oblat, how did you manage to end up in Parradise?"

"May I be sacrificed to God's son, appé. He said, I'll turn the last ones into the first, the first ones into the last. I'll turn the big ones into small, the small ones into big. Whattever he said, he did. May I be sacrificed to his soul, oy! I got big, the big ones got small."

"Is that why you built a church in the backyard of your fortress, brother?"

"Spoken like a genius, appé. That's exactly why, appé. But not only that, appé. How should I say this, appé, so you understand me good. How should I say this, appé. Let me say to Dog, appé, that there's a biig pain in my heart, appé, a biig pain. Peopple don't understand me, appé. So I gave my heart to God. God said, appé, everryone is equal before me, appé, everryone equal. May I die to the will of God, appé. Whether you are a mouse, a man, a sheep, a lousse, or a cockkroach, appé, it's all the same. May I die to the will of God, appé. God said, I forgive all your sins, to all you creatures, I'm granting eternal life to all of you. This is how I ended up in Parradise, brothther. Let me say to Dog, there's a biig love in my heart, brothther, a biig love, an immortal love, I tell you. Peopple are crruel, brothther. But there's a God above, and he examines our hearts, brothther. Only God knows what a big love there is in my heart, brothther. My heart is an *Anush Opera* for my peopple, brothther. God said, I'm the one who examines hearrts, not the peopple. Just because of the love in your hearrt, I'm granting immortality to all cockroaches. May God's will be done, brothther. A fifty-gram, appé. Chinchin!"

"Fine. Last one."

"God's will?"

"No. The fifty-gram."

"You don't mean it, appér."

"I do, brothther…"

"What weird people these diasporadogs are, oy! Once in fifty years he meets with his brothther, and, wouldn't you know it, he's putting conditions already. What the hell is this, oy!"

"Oblat, what's your purpose?"

"Since you insist so much, let me tell you, brothther. Even though I'm a modest man. I don't say this to just anyone."

"Say it, Oblat."

"Let me say it to Dog, broththher. Let me say it in modesty, broththher. For three days I lit candles in my backyard church, for three days I prrayed, in modesty, broththher. I expressed my wish to God. God spoke to my hearrt, broththher. And I couldn't resist, oy. When God tells you to do something, how do you resist, oy! Here it is then: I want to become God. In modesty, broththher, so I won't make a liar of God's son, broththher."

"That's a noble idea, brother. I encourage you to."

"My mom says the same thing, broththher. So that they can eat, broththher. So they can put food on the table, so they can have potatoes, cheese, yogurt, beef tartare, chopped liver, so that their bellies get full and their brains function normal, oy. We're so hungry that we don't got cultivation, broththher, we don't got culture. There's no big poet being born, broththher, no big writer, no maestro, to weep the pain of our hearrt. There's no wrriter or rreader left. How do you make laws, broththher? If you make laws, there's no one to read it. Who for do you make laws, broththher? This people of our Paradise needs a chief, oy.

"Why is it chiefless?"

"Cause it is, oy. It's got no chief. I can do some good chiefing."

"Then do. What does that have anything to do with me?"

"What doesn't it have, broththher, what doesn't it have! You got good relations with Satan, broththher. I want you to tell him nice things about me, broththher. Convince Satan that I can be a good God, oy. Don't you stress yourself about money either. I'll pay double what Satan is paying you, broththher. By my mom's sun, I'll pay you triple, broththher."

"For shame, broththher. Where is it heard that a brother takes money from his brother? It would be a great honor for me to see my own brother plunked on God's throne."

"I have no doubt, broththher. Bravo, broththher. I knew you wouldn't disappoint me, broththher. I triple appreciate your kindness, yo."

"For shame, broththher."

"**M**ighty innermost forces/Terrible rings sacred… The other: *The way of the cross appears not arduous at first/It has still dark hours of dolor.* These are the songs of my aunt. Abbot, I know what that way of the cross is about. I know its meaning. I have seen and heard this since the day I was born. At home. At school. Every single day, sisters and brothers came to our house, prayed, and sang.

"If there is anyone who will demur the most from raising a hand on the symbol of Messiah, it's me," Dog continued. "I have suffered because of this. I am only too pained to see the consequences. But there's no other choice. Whatever I do is done at the behest of *motherdog*."

"Don't be so sure about that. Satan, too, sometimes presents himself with the image of your Motherdog, my dear Dog."

"Like he presented himself with the image of Messiah. That's what you mean, right, abbot? By eternalizing Mashiach, didn't he create his own eternal empire?"

"Wake up, Dog! Come out of the darkness. I have faith in you. I know that you will change. Otherwise I wouldn't have spent hours, days, with you. You can't be worse than the apostle Paul. He used to murder Mashiach's supporters. When have you murdered anyone?"

"A dog and your God are equal in the eyes of the *creator*. If greatness is your gravamen, then the *dog* would be the greater of the two."

"You're telling me you've come down from the Heavens?"

"Abbot, all things that have descended from the Heavens are false."

"Oh, come on. You don't even remember your mother's womb."

"I do. Did Yoohoo remember his father's cock?"

"What a thing to say!"

"Only the *creator* knows where the *dog* has come from, where he'll go. Do you think I take pleasure in drinking from this cup?"

"Are you Yoohoo now? There is only one savior. The rest come from Satan."

Ugly Dog recited a poem for the abbot:

"Messiah, Messiah,
What are you doing on that tree?
Come, let us go to our house."
"I won't... I won't come to your house,
The black dog in your big court
Will go berserk, woof, woof, woof,
And bite my flabby dock..."

"Let Yoohoo come to me, I'll save him. He'll get the proper shocks from me," Dog added.

"You're either crazy or have a new revelation... I've been visited by a lot of nutcases. One of them says she's seen the Blessed Virgin. Supposedly she appears to her every day, talks to her and gives her messages. I was exasperated before I could convince her that it was Satan she was talking to. Another thinks he's Yoohoo. He goes from house to house... We've got dimwits of all stripes. But just now you surpassed every one of them. I had not yet seen anyone greater than Yoohoo...

"But sometimes, once every few centuries, God does choose someone and talks to him," the abbot continued. "I don't know if you're the genuine article. I'm still trying to figure it out."

"What conclusions did you draw after reading my book?"

"You've turned everything into a whorehouse."

"Okay. Can someone who has written such a book be God's chosen, as you say?"

"That's secondary. Solomon the Wise had hundreds of wives. You don't know why or in what circumstances God chooses someone."

"All the chosen ones are scam artists. The *creator* cannot recognize a chosen one. If someone says he's chosen, then know that he's an agent of your Satan. Stay away from him, Father."

"Keep your book as is. Don't change a thing. Let it be read just as it is."

"Abbot, I so wished to avoid controversies. I preferred to stay at the abode of… *balthasar*. But this became my cup and it was not of my will. God sacrificed his Dog brother, his older brother, Bel, Melik, the moon, the old God… Sanasar's elder twin, Balthasar, went to Baghdad, to Hell, sacrificed himself so Sanasar could found Paradise. Who, then, is the real founder? The sacrificer or the sacrificed? And what is God if his brother is a dog?"

"You mean that a dog is more characteristic of the essence of God than man is."

"Don't twist my words, Father. A dog is greater than even your Yoohoo, if your quiddity is greatness. The *aralez*, of Aralu—the Sumerian Hades—that tried to bring Ara the Beautiful back to life appeared as dogs, while Ara was the Christ of the ancient world, the prototype of Attis and Adonis. This Christ legend of antiquity has simply been woven around an apodictorian peasant through a tradition of deception and zealotry. The weaving was partly done by the superstitious Socrateslanders and the inhabitants of Asia Minor. By the time Yoohoo reached Rome, he had already become a mirror image of Mihr. It was the Socrateslanders who called the man Christ, based on their legends. Your Yoohoo is fake. Maimunus is right."

A pair of candles burn next to the corpse.

The white drapes are tasseled at the waist, revealing the crimson curtains behind them, their eyes fixed on the cadaver. I place the corpse in the casket. The room feels smaller than the coffin. I sense the breath of the dead body. I come out. No, father, you could not have died. The four or five in the narthex do not know why they are here. The air is heavy. The corners of the ceiling totter. To the right. No horizontal lines. Glum rainbows parade across the hall, singing songs of death. The locomotive approaches from the abyss, the ground trembles. The spiders cringe in their webs. Two staircases. Left. A table. A lectern holding a mammoth ledger. The din of death. Two men wait for me behind the ghastly codex. The silence of death. I must sign. I pick up the pen. The register is open, waiting for me.

No, I shall not sign his death.

"Yehusar conquered death."

"It was *Balthasar* that conquered death. You don't know a thing about that. He is *immortal* for he is death. His father is the *creator*. His mother is *death*. Feeble-minded as you are, you thought you had succeeded in murdering him. He has now returned, for the younger twin lost his moorings under the faint light of lanterns across the world and there emerged false brothers everywhere. MacYehu attempted to assume the role of the Son."

"He was the Son."

"If he were a christ, he should have been a dog first. He aspired, he distorted, he failed."

"Why?"

"Because the equinoxial cosmomatris conceives twins—day and night in equal measure, whereas the solsticial cosmomatris gives birth to the only begotten: Mihr, Mher—the sun deity at its zenith or its nadir. The epos *Madmen of Sasun* is a cosmic calendar. Mher's sojourn to Pharaohland is a baptism into the legacy of the solsticial cosmomatris. He became the son of Ismil—Isis historicized—fed on her milk, so he could reign over the day and surrender the night to the moon, which you have called Satan. But herein lies the error—there was a struggle between the vati of the solsticial mother and the equinoxial mother. Despite inheriting your traditions, the clerics were unable to fathom their full significance, failed to understand the essence."

"In Pharaohland."

"Correct. His teachers were cognizant of that old struggle and tried to eliminate the real mother, Dzovinar, the Paradisean mother goddess of the primordial sea. Even though the equinoxial mother was the victor, her enemies distorted history and declared Persephone—the Mary of Hell—the vanquisher. They ravished the groom. And MacYehu could not become *son of dog*, although, by revolting against his teachers, he ventured to unite the antitheses in his person and thereby end the bifurcation of man."

"He did end it."

"It's a mirage, padre. Your religion is a sham. It is dead. It does not speak to the sons and daughters of the equinoxial cosmomatris—Paradise, Fakiristan, Eurostan, Ayatollahland, which have been the inheritors of this legacy, nor to all those who carry the seed of freedom within their souls. Were it to speak, i would not come into existence. That's why i came—to rectify the error, to awaken you from your aberrances, to impart to you the *balthasar* spirit."

"Father, the food got cold. Should I put the tomato back in the fridge?"

"I had a little something in the morning. That's enough. I won't eat again today."

"I have come for harlots and bastards. I shall share a table with them, speak their tongue. I don't need your tables. I don't need exaltations, honors. It is they who will plough the *creator's* field. There's no hope from you civilized, hypocritical, sanctity-hawking humans. MacYehu had major flaws. But you're blind. Will you ever see?"

"Tell me those flaws."

"First: kingdom."

"Second?"

"Eternal life."

"Then?"

"The second commandment is the first—the first is the second. First, love your brother as you would yourself, and only then your God. It's this substitution that is the cause of all wars. Flush the God part of that commandment into the sewer, and everything will turn to the better."

"What else?"

"The list is long. These are some major points. If he be a king, then he's the Satan that you know. Remember, Father, the nexus of love. It can't be vertical. That would be an escape. Death is the key to truth—the ultimate equalizer."

"It's a sad world. Hope is light."

"Hope is lie. The light is death."

"And eternal life?"

"The counterfeit legal tender of all the enemies of truth."

"A dour fate."

"*Dog* is the way, the truth, and the life. All things were

made by him, and without him not any thing was made. His fate is more bitter than that of a Messiah, Father. The elder twin always suffers more... But do you believe MacYehu was the younger twin? No. Can the usurper be titled a brother? He tried to take on the role of the solsticial son, to seize the legacy of *mher minor*. But Papa Pete married him to Maimunus... Yes, it's a threesome. Is it that pleasant, Father, being a dog among discord-sowing, self-satisfied moshianists? But this is not the issue."

"What is it then? Do you still insist that the MacYehu story is a tall tale?"

"Believing it is not the problem per se. There is nothing ordinary in the essence of the legend. Its emulator will find himself on a better spiritual path than the nonbeliever, as his mind and heart will be tuned to the mind and heart of the cosmos. As any other framework, the system has its own inner logic. The danger is elsewhere."

"Amarus vitiorum fructus..."

"The faith died because you resorted to deceit to perpetuate the two-thousand-year era of *mher major*, god of the winter solstice, to snatch death through chicanery. There was no alternative left. It became a Gordian knot. Otherwise, the *creator* would not have sent his *elder son...*"

"To establish his throne?"

"Careful, padre. I told you. How do you misunderstand me even when I speak your tongue? Only Satan has a throne. If there is a throne in question, you can be sure it doesn't belong to the *creator*."

"Is this the elder son's, Balthasar's, epoch?"

"*The elder* is within you. *The elder* is immutable. For two thousand years the *creator* tested you through *mher minor*, the younger son, but you transfigured him, turned him into Satan's crier. Now he sends *balthasar* into you. In time *he* will once again take leave to shut himself inside *massis*, unless you liberate yourselves from your shackles. But *he* will return again until you become *balthasar*. You cannot know the *younger son* unless you know the *dog*. You can know neither the *elder son* nor any of the six sons of the cosmomatris on the ecliptic."

"Who are...?"

"Mher Major, deity of the summer solstice; Mher Minor, deity of the winter solstice; the twins Sanasar-Balthasar, deities of the spring equinox; Davit and his twin, deities of the autumnal equinox. Now do you understand why they buried the six, the greatest sanctity? 666. It was the symbol of the equilibrium of justice, the legacy of Sanasar-Balthasar."

"*Jus humano. In caelo salus.* God sent his only begotten so that whoever believes in him shall not perish…"

"You can know the son only if you know the *dog*. I would not have been a *dog* had you not been humans. *i* and the *mother* are one and the same. If I don't return as a *dog*, I will forever remain with you, inside *massis*. But you exiled me to Hell. Not you, but the *mother* wanted to keep me away from you. She chained me by her side, to free your haughty souls, to bring your savior-seeking, mendicant souls out of the muck. But you eternalized everything to feed your penchant for power-grabbing and damning the light. These are not my musings; it is the *creator* who at present speaks to you through me. Fate has willed that you should be the vessel receiving the word, padre, and this moment is the gift of the *mother* herself, who led us to one another. The *creator's* word is not meant for moshloons. *ne* decides the place and time of ner utterance. Let us pray that ne does not abandon us. It is hard to be a *dog*. It is hard to come out of this door now."

Good morning.

Dog's confidants deserted him, judging him to be an agent. They were Paradiseans. Dog was a Dreamlander. At best a McAllahist, a Pashadung, an Ayatollan. The Paradisean helps one in order to "understand one's secret." This is a collective proclivity he has inherited from the KGB. They helped, they understood, they confirmed, they left. They fomented such enmity that Pasha could not have dreamed of. Believe me, those who crucified Yoohoo were Paradiseans.

The Paradisean does not consider the Dreamlander a human. No matter how close they may be, he thinks of him as a potential traitor. A dog. As for the Dreamlander, he calls the Paradisean a genetical Pasha chip. It is impossible to grasp the orphanhood of someone born without a homeland.

Despite their impassioned insistence to the contrary, sabers rattled underneath the tables. We are a separate nation—such is the undeclared axiom. Doggone your Paradisish and your Paradise. Long live immortal Dreamland and our *original* Dreamish. Fuck off and croak—such is the unspoken curse. Lies! Immorality! Thousands of Paradiseans are far from what you portray them to be. Yet hundreds of thousands think along those lines. There is no one to put the finger on the wound.

A nation is on its deathbed. Pasha is enthralled, every day beholding the death throes of the dreamers from behind his bulletproof glass. Pasha left Dog without a homeland so he could have an empire—a huge, boundless domain with which Satan would have to contend, and whose tribute would be sung by historians. Today he dreams the same dream.

It transpires that Pasha, too, is a dreamer. To him, recognizing the Genocide is tantamount to relinquishing his dream. Such a deed can be the work of only a "traitor"—a Kurd!

"Dog! Dog, son of a dog!"

Then how do Paradise and Pashaland differ from one another? Over there, they want to maul the Kurd—he has spoken against the ruling mindset. Were it not for Euroland, they would have killed him. The same treatment has been reserved for Dog's book in Paradise—he does not comply with the ruling mindset.

There is a certain class among the denizens of Virginabad which views itself as the liege lord of Paradise. It strives to assimilate the Kilisi into its ranks. Anyone found resisting assimilation is a traitor who luxates national homogeneity. The Kilisi is not against homogeneity, the unity of language and national institutions, but expects those denizens of Virginabad to cede to the Kilisi value system, which he believes to be more godly—read: more moral. To the Kilisi, the Virginabadi is a degenerate. The

Kilisi considers himself the rightful holder of the nation's identity. After all, it was he whom the world had recognized throughout the ages. The Kilisi cannot forgive the fact that his long centuries of accomplishment in upholding the esteem of Paradise across the globe were pulverized by Paradiseans within the span of two decades. The world today does not want to hear the word "Paradise." And the angels themselves do not wish to peer into the mirror.

This is a reality whose causes can only partially be explained by the whims of history. The Genocide continues at the hands of the godthrone, who sits at the head of the nation against its will, deepening the spiritual crisis, driving the wedge of disunity into the soul of the nation. A Marcos reins the Philippines, and it is the fault of Pasha. Half the population has left the homeland. Those still clinging to their roots are subjected to the daily indignities of archangels and their seraglio.

It was they who rejected White Dog's right to a homeland. One was forced to live under their heels, conform to the apostolate of their tenets, suffer the contumely of their concubines. The Dreamlander is hapless, nomadic—either a helot or a forlorn expat.

Dog tired. Being a father of three puppies, it was not easy for him to persevere on his own resources alone. Despite his family obligations, every month he spent a thousand washingtons on his activities. Meantime, wealthy humans who could have supported his efforts were usually devoid of brains. Closed doors. Bequests to the Maimunchurch. Donations made during lavish dinners for personal glory, followed by thunderous front-page plaudits in the *Dream* humanpaper. Millions of washingtons flew into the pockets of the maimunophilic establishment. The Church had turned into a bazaar, the nation into squash.

One day White Dog witnessed a television program, one among a hundred, raise a hundred thousand washingtons from Paradisean viewers by inciting hatred of Kilisis and parading a few "monkeys" on screen. Six months of ceaseless barking had secured for Dog no more than two or three dry bones.

Only the howling of a rabble could be heard: "Dog!"

The Paradiseans are the world's wisest, most intelligent, and far-seeing people.

"Father, is Adoyis the capital of Paradise?"

The program was watched by tens of thousands of Paradiseans who had found asylum in Los Angelos. They splurge five thousand washingtons at a fancy soirée, fifty thousand on a car for their daughter, but not even five thalers for the self-actualization of the nation. This was not a nation but a collection of eating and shitting, singing and dancing lackeys. They had no right to inculpate either Pasha or Jinjin for their fate. They had only themselves to blame.

"Ouch, Pasha, don't fuck me that hard there. It hurts! Please fuck me on the other side a bit. Ouch! Aw! Aw…"

Dog pulled the plug on his program. They did not deserve to receive the dog writ. No seed can take root in Paradise. It is sand underneath, not earth. And Dreamland is but dust in the wind. To support = to put a couple of kopeks in the palm of a beggar. If they want to hear the program, let them pay for it—one million thalers for an hour.

"So you're measuring it with money, are you?"

"I am."

"Capitalist pig!"

Dog resolved to write in Satanish. He wanted to believe that Hell is the homeland of homeless dogs.

The Paradiseans thought, "There must've been an order from above to nix the program."

To the Paradisean, the "above" was once the eye of the Kreml. It now stands for certain capos in the higher echelons of the Sublime Godocracy, whose names no one knows.

"From above…"

To the Dreamlander, it is the Mononons.

"Shush…"

Or a tenebrous, secret force.

"It's from above. Shush…"

Pussyfoot your way out…

"The order is given. They'll whack him…"

"Shush…"

I am that no more… The gale of ardor

Which once drove me from fall to fall
Has now calmed and settled,
No longer echoing each and every call.
My wild heart no longer thumps
Like the unbridled stallion in the fields.
An olden hand held me tenderly,
And I, one night, found wisdom.
I understood that in the pasture of life,
In the sparkling, tempest-beaten sea of humanity,
O, not a stalk has risen
With songs and formless zeal alone.
I withdrew my hand from furious frenzies—
The shapeless tide of sentiment—
And the liberating flame of labor
Scorched my rain-battered face.
I am upon the field anew,
As the reaper is upon the harvest,
Holding in my hands not a drum
But a lyre of bronze, heavy with thought.
It is already noon above my head,
The summer sun basks in the zenith,
Across me—unharvested leas of thought—
And the worry furrows its brows.
How many priceless hours I have squandered,
And how many seeds I have sown gratis.
And how hard I must now try
To regain that which I have lost in vain…
How much labor and thought there is here,
In my annealing homeland,
Through which tempests have passed
And washed us in whirlwinds of fire.
Whose face, made red hot by the centuries,
Has now been fanned by Lenin's breath—
Fire has scorched the foundations of this land,
And now it is being built with shivaree.
Now, with experience and lyre in hand,
I once again rise with a smile,
To mix my song, laden with thought,
To the colossal work of the generations.
I shall not sing to the resounding future

Which will come still.
Within me now there stir and blossom,
Agitate, legions of disparate thoughts.
It is the present that clamors before me now,
As a mighty sea of passions.
And I bestride, with my delicate lyre,
Through this ocean of a thousand hues.
I stride as a slave to my new thoughts.
And around me, near and far,
Simmers the wide, boundless ocean
Of sleepless passions and sensations.
Now I take the road alone,
With only my lyre as companion.
And I sing, I sing fearlessly,
About my illumined thoughts.
Toilsome shall be my journey,
More dire than ever before,
And perhaps, along my path,
Your fangs shall bloody me like snakes.
But stout is my soul... And not a single fang
Shall unyoke me from my restive epoch,
As no force shall separate me
From my thunderous, radiant lyre...

Wave 3, "I Am That No More"

The Holy Trinity Party summoned Dog to a special meeting to discuss his activities. They tipped Dog that "a certain 'anti-Yehuist' movement has started in Gehendale" and shrewdly asked whether Dog was aware of such a development. Doublespeak and an interrogational style of this order were so typical of this party's cuisine that I could not help receive the matter with a smile.

One of the six dreamers was my cousin. The other was Comrade Ani. She had been a close friend to me and my family since childhood. During the time Comrade Ani taught at Dream Elementary School, it was she who recruited me into the youth division of the party. Now Comrade Ani is cold. Comrade Ani takes notes of my replies. Comrade Ani does not look at me. Was the charge brought against me so weighty? Yes, I have stopped dreaming with her. I was perplexed that Comrade Ani could change so radically if prompted by the dream.

First they asked for this street dog's home address—they had only a postal-box address. Difficult issue. What home? When I gave them a c/o without hesitation, I felt that a heavy burden had fallen off their shoulders. They had already carried out half the task demanded of them. But I understood why His Highness, the Unsellable Estate, has interest in transforming dogs into humans, turning them into well-to-do address-holders.

I began to discuss some of the prophecies of the Dia-bloBible, expounded my points of view. Confusion ensued. DiabloBible. What does this dog refer to? But the ice melted bit by bit, giving way to amity. At the end, the president himself stopped dreaming. Breaking into hearty laughter, he said, "Comrade Dog, you have no problem with us. Maybe with the catholicos…"

I had joined the Holy Trinity Party in Los Angelos, at the time when Eretz Leo, the Titan, persecuted its members in Paradise with braggadocio, aiming to be in the good graces of Pasha. The latter and Ali Baba have always feared the dream of Holy Trinity. In those days Eretz Leo had resolved to uproot the dream from Paradise. The angels who glorified the Trinity were being murdered one after the other.

To this day, no one bothers to investigate those murders. God the Redeemer of Sinners and Sanctuary of Fugitives has placed a lid upon the volcanoes of the past, through who knows what type of under-the-table exchange with Titan. Did Titan collude with Satan to eradicate the dream from Paradise, or was he simply the prototypical thrall? Was he a mole of Jinjin? These were the questions the vox populi posited. Down with Titan, long live Zeus, proclaimed Paradise with one voice. This was still the Paradise which at the time of its independence was regarded as the bastion of demosocracy in former Leninstan. Titan's universal popularity had given way to a transcendent apprehension regarding his deeds. Titan's consort is a Maimunetta. When he began to persecute dreamers, the discontented determined, without presenting evidence, that he, too, was a maimunoid. They decided anon that God's parvenu minister of justice was also Maimunus's laddie, as he was engaged in "surreptitiously continuing the elimination of dreamers" and day by day evolved into one of the richest cherubim of Paradise.

"You want proof, do you? How naïve you are!"

These things were said unto me in Paradise, brethren. But I don't know—only God knows.

In Virginabad, I became acquainted with a woman who was a friend of Titan's family. She could freely go in and out of the royal household, even in times of political turmoil. I was curious. What if Titan was a wily spirit whose policies were beyond the grasp of mortals? The Supreme One moves in mysterious ways, brothers. She expressed doubt, called him a "nihilist."

"In the day of Titan's reign, the ruse of educational reform was employed to deracinate the symbols of our dream, the words 'Hay' and 'Hayastan,' from school curricula," proclaims a valiant writer from Hades. The scribe elicits the thunderous applause of a room full of pusillanimous penmen.

But why are they vexed? Is dreaming conceivable in Paradise? Isn't dreaming an "anti-divinic category?" Like puppies, Paradiseans are wont to bark after a departing stranger. Some feel the pangs of longing, as though missing a paramour whom they have ditched and who shall never return.

During an interview, an actress from Hell, Cher, could not conceal her revulsion for Titan. She had traveled to Paradise to seek out her roots. She did not find them.

No one was shocked in Paradise. They dreamed that someone would next bring tennis champion Agassi to Paradise. He did affirm his origins, yet refused to have anything to do with dreamers.

I had met Eretz Leo before he assumed the titanthrone, along with Vardan Mamikonian and Ashot Junior—his friends and associates. We were taking Eretz Leo to the hospital. One item we discussed was how to unleash the genie from inside the jar, labeled Dreamland, that the Holy

Trinity had put a lid on. My impressions of Eretz Leo were good. I sensed that he and Ashot Junior were not sincere with one another.

Unfortunately I myself had a minor role in Eretz Leo's banishment to Tartaros and the consequent devolution of the divine throne, due to the detailed letters I had sent to Satan and to key personnel of Satan's Paradise Bureau. This coincided with the extensive campaign launched against Eretz Leo. Whether the expressed suspicions about Titan were true or not, his policies did not yield palatable fruits.

In Eden, where a life-and-death battle was being waged, the war kept expanding, threatening a fresh genocide. Ali Baba declared it openly, reminding Paradiseans of the massacres of Sumgayit and 1915. He went on to boast that soon he would plunge himself into the heart of Paradise, swim in the waters of Lake Sevan.

He swam… in a sea of blood.

While thousands of Paradiseans put their lives on the line to defend Eden, there emerged an oligarchy on the flanks, under an aloof and misunderstood Titan. With the pretext of liberation from Papa Lenin, Paradise was being looted by his besodomed, economic output was being trounced—the mafia groups crushing the will and spirit of the people were in seventh heaven. There had commenced the frantic migration of the masses.

The Trinity-dazzled mayor of Virgintower was murdered after being interrogated by the Titanic triarchy. My friend Sunkist shared with me the details of a meeting he had had with the mayor a day prior to his murder. Sunkist went on to publish in the press of the Holy Trinity Party critical information which would be instrumental for a criminal investigation.

Murdering aficionados was not what Dog had expected from the Titanic triarchy. And since Titan's thrusting of his member into the Holy Trinity was a bagatelle compared to his baring of his ass before Yehu, Dog joined the ranks of the party to help cut off the Titanic dong.

The president of the Supreme Council of Eden, who was a member of the Holy Trinity Party, was also murdered in suspicious circumstances. So was the Dreamlander commandant who had vanquished Ali Baba. In Eden, not a fly could take wing without the collaboration of certain rings in the upper crust. The murder of this commandant is intriguing as he was blacklisted by Lord Satan for his fight against Pasha to gain recognition of the Genocide by the community of men. Next to be murdered was the mayor of the capital city, Virginabad, a few days after his démarche against Titan. Also to be murdered, among others, were the president of the Writers' Union and the supreme judge of Paradise. Virginabad gulped them all down her womb—her cock-denying womb. The murdered have never existed. As for the Holy Trinity Party, it assuaged itself by promising life after death to a couple of its most illustrious devotees.

This is how Holy Trinity expresses gratitude to its energumens, brethren.

Their apologia: "Well, how much longer should we get screwed, bro? We need to get a breather too."

The greats of the past who were raised on the motherland are no longer alive, while those subsisting on foreign soil continue to diminish in stature. Entering through the Trinity's rectum, these humble servants gradually wind their way to its brain, where they set up camp until death.

Justice is foundation stone for republican life, my brethren. Holy Trinity betrayed her principles. Titan accused the power-famished Holy Trinity of organizing a revolution in Paradise. Holy Trinity responded in kind, accusing Titan of establishing titanolatry in Paradise and pledged salvation to the angels.

The removal of Titan was meant to bring to power his short opponent, whose mere flatus had caused the sudden collapse of Leninstan. This man was regarded as the soul of Eden's liberation movement. But the soul-bearer bolted. Thus God, Deliverer of Tethers and Freer of Bonds, Titan's chargé d'affaires at the time, stabbed him in the back and usurped the everlasting throne, for the safeguarding of whose fickle power he had, according to godologists, created loops in the political and criminal underworlds, reselling Paradise to Big Brother Kreml.

God also played on Holy Trinity's revenge against Titan. This is how the Holy Trinity became part and parcel of the Most High. This is why there is an immanent conflict between the real God and the godolic of the Holy Trinity.

The martyrdom of the chief Edenite was one reason that I wanted to name my child Arthur. My wife agreed—she liked the Shakespearean name.

I saw it then linked with the Urartian deity Artin. Urartu or Ararat is the name of an ancient kingdom on the Paradisean Highland which successfully challenged the solo superpower of the time, Assyria. As the end morphemes of the two names seemed to be suffixes, I presumed that both Arthur and Artin stemmed from the root word *art*, whose etymology in Paradisean relates it to words such as *artun* (awake), *zartnel* (to awaken), and *harnel* (to ascend), all attributes of the sun deity.

Artin was also the name of my grandfather, thus there were several Arthurs in our extended family. The Hays equate these two names. My grandfather was an unswerving tower of faith. When he was a young man, it took him an instant to heal my grandmother with a prayer, when the doctor had told them she would die within half an hour. In the Sheikh Masud neighborhood of Aleppo, grandfather Artin had made a born paralytic walk as a crowd of astounded evangelists bore witness. This was not the televangelistic capitalist monkey stuff. With his help, barren women gave birth and went on to become fertile beyond imagination. I am still learning of his many phenomenal feats. When he put his hands on my head and prayed in Pashaish, I felt an inexplicable bliss, a heavenly peace. This was not in Paradisish, the sole language of God. Nor was it in Sanskrit, ambrosia of gurumaniacs. At the end of the prayer, I tried to disentangle my face from the kisses he planted through his enormous, prickly mustache. My grandfather did not pray. With his visage transformed, he conversed with the creator, face to face. With the very language of Pasha.

I learned from grandfather what faith is, where its might resides. I then kept asking myself, Which is more precious: science, or the faith of my grandfather?

After his death, I have not encountered such faith anywhere else. The greatest preachers of Satanland are actors.

Thirty years thence, I came across a lone man who had what my grandfather possessed. That man was Grigor Agabaloglu, a Hay preacher from Pashaland. Their common language perhaps conduced to a déjà vu. It was as though grandfather had come back to life.

If you do not possess that pure and transcendent energy, toss this book into the fireplace. There is more than rhetoric in this remonstration. The legend will not hold you back from entering the path that leads to life. Whoever believes himself to be erudite, believes that he is able to distinguish legend from reality, let him heed the words of Black Dog: "Hey, foolish human, that 'reality' of yours is itself a delusional fairy tale, more ignoble than the legends you despise. The catharsis of the myth—and not slavery to it—may still function to save you from perdition. J., meanwhile, has penetrated the realm of myth and affixed the snares of slavery to those myths that could have led you to the desired state."

I am visiting the village of New Mount Musa. Independence Day. A commemoration is being held in honor of the heroes of Mount Musa.

Historic Mount Musa was located not far from the shore of the Mediterranean, to the northeast of Kipros. In 1915 the villagers of Mount Musa stood up to the armies of Pasha and gifted forty heroic days to the history of Dreamland, averting genocide with the help of the ships of Napoleon Bonaparte. In nearby territories Satan, Lord of the Heavens and the Earth, has today installed his air bases. Paying rent to Pasha, not the legitimate heirs. The self-defense of Dreamstan has been immortalized in a novel by Franz Werfel, based apparently on the script of a Mercedesland-educated survivor college boy. During the years of the Second World War, this book became a guide for the victims of Führer BenYehu in their odyssey of survival.

While the guests of honor deliver speeches and the traditional harissa is copiously served to the crowd of celebrants, a certain woman seeks my attention. I don't want her to steal my time—in this area of specialization, everyone in Paradise holds a PhD. They force you to be their guest and become your mortal enemy should you decline. For this reason they brand me a "Satanican."

The Paradisean is a thief of time. Time has no value for immortals. Thus the commandment: "Deceive one another!" In keeping with this sacrosanct law, he deceives you and kills your day. He robs with impunity the Satanic mortal's precious right to live, to be, with each revolution of the sun.

One day, as Astrik and I are home chatting, the phone rings. It is the real-estate broker who had helped me find the apartment. After the expiration of my lease contract, I have agreed with the owner to extend my stay. The broker has called her to demand his cut. She has refused.

He had contacted me recently. I had suggested he resolve his issue with the proprietor. She informed me that the "insolent imp" has called my apartment a few times, hanging up as soon as he heard my voice, to make sure I was still living there.

So it was he who had been disturbing me all along. I did not let him utter a single word.

"I am relaxing with my girlfriend, and you are bothering us. Don't ever call here again. If you've got problems, solve them with the owner."

"Show a little decency, you shameless scoundrel. Go do whatever you want with your girlfriend…"

"I have no decency. I'm a dog," I said calmly, callous as a wall. Later I felt pity, though I was glad.

"When have I called you? Tell me! Have I ever phoned you before?"

"You've called me at least once. Why do you call me a second time?"

"You're too cruel, my darling dog. You're a true Satanican," Astrik said.

"I'm not a Satanican. A Satanican knows how to understand, even if he goes through the motions sometimes. I'm a bastard. He called once. If he doesn't understand, the second time around he'll get what's coming to him. Why should I be obliged to hear the same thing again? Let him keep his crap to himself. In the human cobweb, you are entangled with a hundred threads, and thousands are always ready to toss at you the twine of their mouth. Until you dissolve those threads, you can't see the light within you."

In New Mount Musa, however, I decide to hear that woman out. She produces a bundle of documents and begins to tell me about her ordeal. Her brother was once a prominent musician. More than sixty members of her family have perished. She points out her family name, which has been published in a number of Titanic newspapers, in one of which there is a report on her family's annihilation.

I check her identity card. I ask Nayra, a recent acquaintance, to translate the report from Kremlish to Paradisish for me. She draws my attention to a statement made by a physician. An inquest at the woman's home has revealed a high degree of radioactivity. Her skin appears to be affected by radioactive damage. Her mental faculties have been faltering. She is convinced this also is a consequence of radiation. She gives me the name of a general who has assaulted her in the parking lot of the University of Satan in Virginabad.

She has exposed a scheme by the Kreml-connected archangels to sell the body parts of Paradisean children in the international marketplace.

"God is a murderer. It's he who has organized the murder of Eden's guardian angel. The former catholicos died of throat cancer that was caused by radioactive materials. The armed attack against the Parliament was organized by the defense minister himself."

People who are scared of their own shadow likewise whisper that this catholicos was indeed murdered. The reason: he had regretted being a Mononon and a pawn of globalization. No one points a finger at Papa Kremlin, who has always contolled or aspired to control the Catholicosate of Paradise through his agents in order to control the dreams of dreamers throughout Dreamstan. Brethren, even the flutter of a leaf strikes terror in the redeemed, who think dragging an existence of scaring each other stiff is the height of wisdom. This is the reason that they fall prey to genocide.

I doubted the accusation leveled against the defense minister, although he was no saint. Twice I had examined his aura, though in less than propitious circumstances, but had failed to find a trace of the killings in question.

Which did not mean I could say the same about all angels. I was able to make my conclusions with sufficient accuracy. For instance, the foreign minister of Paradise, Zulfikar James Lutfullah, had a chaster aura compared to some other politicos. Smart women instinctively noticed that and took a liking to him. The aura of his Ali Babaian counterpart was dark, very dark.

I grew suspicious. Was the radioactive woman mentally unbalanced? Nayra told me such types are common in Paradise. Their outrageous claims are rarely taken seriously. But such types are also common among us, in Satanland.

My journey to Paradise did not comprise an intent to uncover murders, to be embroiled in the filth of angels. Neither did I wish to capture the imagination of the redeemed with a joker's revelations. Incidentally, those miracles that are attributed to Yoohoo do not add to his worth. On the contrary, they degrade it. A religion that needs to employ such a stratagem can lure only kindergarten students of spirituality. Satan's apprentices, too, performed equivalent feats. You can specialize in the field, sister, but you will not profit by it. It will be a waste of precious time. What connection is there between the fairy tale (even if true) of a blind man seeing again and the proof of God's existence? Only a fool calls what to him is incomprehensible "God" and moronically spends two thousand years following what in truth is a wholly fabricated, fictional hero.

My path lay elsewhere in life, intelligible to only a few. But that woman's words gave me a jolt. It was difficult to determine her reliability. She asserted her claims with certitude equal to that of the Xns in Yoohoo. Now either she is right or she is crazy. But even if she was wrong, her allegations pointed to a painful fact.

They say that the body parts of Paradisean children fetch a pretty price in the Valley of Hinnom. But I don't know, my brethren; only God knows. His name is Desirable Beatitude and Sorrowless Peace. I know one thing: in Paradise there is a cupid cohort of owners and the redeemed are inclined to elect leaders clad in black. These, due to their love of Yoohoo, dress in the color of his ass. Things transpired thus to bring about what has been written by the hand of the prophet Yammerus. In Virginabad was there a voice heard, lamentation, and weeping, and great mourning, Mareh weeping for her sons, and would not be comforted, because they are chic.

The cause is not merely the snares of Satan, my brothers, but the donkey-ding soul and mind of the redeemed.

I became a witness to this in New Mount Musa.

A young man sells grilled meats. I pay him. It'll be ready in fifteen minutes. I come back in ten. He nonchalantly gives my plate to another customer and assures me that he will give me the other skewer (which is half the size of the first) in ten minutes. The black-clad one, snatching what is rightfully mine, vanishes. I have a mind to shove the skewer up their rectums both. You do not talk to beasts in any different language.

If, in a given country, the brayers make up 51 percent of the populace, then they can, given a dumdumocratic system, eradicate the rest within a decade and establish an assigarchy.

I did see in the forest such a thing, godfather,
That the skunk became a king, a king.

Terror-stricken, hiding in nooks and holes, with no benefit of warmth in the winter, surviving on cheese and bread, the human wraiths—the last representatives of the intelligentsia—bequeath to Dog a fairy tale demonstrating that an advanced genus has indeed lived on this land.

I recall Kathy's words: "Whenever I walked in the streets of Yerevan, my heart bloomed. What interesting faces I saw at each footstep!"

According to the stories of these grandmas and grandpas, this genus has left. Many have gone to Whitebearland.

Many have been martyred. They were war volunteers. Such is the price for the survival of the Hays.

Paradise has become Assistan.

This year, your presents are the dark and the cold, my child.

This year your toys are the raging bombs.

And this game is called war, played by the big men,

And at the end, there is your scream,
"Come home, daddy, come home again."
Oh, what Santa Claus is this who has appeared in your home?
See what goodies this old, wretched beggar has brought you.
Presents, this wretched wanderer has brought you.
But the gifts that he has brought you are news of death and mourning,
Dead people below the ground, and, woe to us, children too.
Below the ground are sleeping our sisters and brothers too,
While above, it's our lives that have become a morbid curse.
Oh, what long winter this is, I wonder when it will end.
When the spring sprouts again, then your daddy will come home.
And if it happens, my child, that your daddy is late, late,
Remember him, my sweet child—he will always be with you.

Air 2, "Homecoming"

Brothers, it is not to entertain that I say all this. Bitter has been the fate of Paradise. The cocks of innumerable nomadic tribes have passed by their millions through the intestines of Paradise. It has made the invaders noble, turned into a plebeian itself. Paradise lost its character. Ten generations will be needed for it to regain its footing.

Paradise once had one of Manplanet's most literate populations, more so than that of Eyfelia or Satanland. Once, in the 4,144,000-strong Paradise, even an ordinary book would be published with a run of fifty thousand and sold out within days. I was told by the director of VirginState-Pub that no book will sell more than fifty copies these days.

Paradise has spent four winters without heat. Imagine

Minnesota without heat. People have burned books for warmth. The Academy of Sciences of Virginland Press has sold its book collections by the kilo. People's wealth has been wiped out overnight on the pretext of currency conversion from that of Papa Lenin to that of Papa Pluton. Industry has been pulverized and living standards have plunged at a factor of ten. A third of the population has abandoned the land.

Under the label of Satanic dumocracy, a group of man-panzees has expropriated Paradise. Yes, there was a time when Paradise was a vassal of Papa Lenin, but today it has altogether ceased to exist as a sovereign unit. What does exist is a geographic expanse with three million despondent servients, whose "capitalist" lords splurge the millions siphoned with God's blessings on the Monte Carlos of the world.

Victimized by spiritual carnage, the people stopped believing the books.

At one time writers were honored everywhere in Paradise. Restaurants considered a shame to accept money from them.

Today writers are equated with skella. At the top of the pyramid, meanwhile, luxuriate the illiterate "capitalists."

In the evenings I was in the habit of dining at one of Virginabad's central restaurants. After dinner I read the articles I had xeroxed at the academy. The restaurant owner rudely stuck his nose in when I asked the waiter for permission to use my laptop. There is no such culture in Paradise. A restaurant is a place for eating, an exhibition hall for angels of the well-heeled, bedecked variety.

Eat! Then fuck off!

Today if someone is engaged in writing and literature, then he is a "starving pauper."

I was a beggar.

And a beggar I remained, my unholy brethren... until one day the restaurant owner turned utterly pale when h saw me chat with one of the land's hottest sex symbols at the entrance.

I am no longer a beggar.

And today the youths read new books of the Hellian

how-to kind, from which they learn only one thing: how to become the apparatchiks of the econopolitical mafia. Slavery festooned is achievement apexial for those who attend the University of Satan or the Université de Bonaparte, or are tutored on Shakespeare's lap.

By spreading chaos, we'll imperceptibly replace their values with false ones, which we'll force them to believe in. From art and literature we'll gradually exterminate the social element. We'll retrain artists, discourage in them the desire to depict the world and examine those processes taking place in the masses of the people. Literature, the theater, and the cinema will all proclaim the basest of human feelings. We'll use all our means to support and promote those so-called creators, who will hammer into the people's consciousness the cult of sex, violence, sadism, and betrayal, in a word, immorality. We'll create chaos and confusion in the workings of the government. We'll actively but unnoticeably encourage bureaucratic stupidity and bribe-taking. Bureaucratic red tape will be elevated to a virtue. Honesty and orderliness will be ridiculed as being of no use to anyone, an anachronism. Rudeness and insolence, lies and deceit, drunkenness and drug addiction, animal fear of everyone and everything, indecency, betrayal, nationalism, and strife between ethnic groups: we'll cultivate all of it, quietly and skillfully. And only the few, the very few, will guess or understand what's happening. But we'll put such people in a helpless situation and turn them into objects of ridicule. We'll find ways to slander them and declare them the dregs of society.

These words are from a speech delivered in 1945 by Assistant Satan on his project to destroy Leninstan. True, they are not representative of the virtuous Satan's fair-mindedness and are exploited by his merciless enemies. But is it not possible, kindhearted Lord, that your policies de facto encapsulate the spirit of your commissar's polemic?

Cerebrally challenged by his underling, sixty-six minus half a score years after the above speech was delivered, Satan stepped in to deliver one of his own.

Satan's Speech, Straight from the Horse's Mouth

We, the peepel o the Demokratik Triumvirate o Gehenna, dik liar hearwith that our way o life to liv high off the hog is thretened by a most ominus enimi. Our enimi stirredup a hornet's nest by attaking us. Even tho we did every effort to strike a happi midium by soft-soping them, to bring them into ciphilizacion rom dog's life, through camu flaj and chikenery they attaked us blind as a bat with a bolt rom the blu hitting us be lo the belt. They played wid fair their for ar at appoint o no return.

When I sow the smok coming owt o the twin towels, I said to the peepel o Emir aka that where their's smok their's fayr. Whatasnake in the grass owr enimi is. But we have some mezhure to blaim owr selves, sins wes weepd under the rug God's unfailing word witch says, spar the rod and spoil the child. Our ounding dads said that onesti is the best police. But I tell yea that in the new age onesti is the worst police, there for I have ad viced our central inteligent agenci to fallo dis new police.

We will no longer take the bacc seat in dis ishoo. We will no longer take any wooden nikels. But we will stik to our guns, even tho we stik our nok out.

I discussed the matter with owr secretry ostate hoo was mad as a wet hen. Sins two hats ar better than one, I also sot cown sil rom owr secretry odefens hoo was mad as a hatter. But our vice presi dent was cool as a cucumber and was cooking with gas. His ad vice was to cool it and beat round the bush. So I cooled it and de cided not to bull in a china shop. He said daunt thro the blak baby out with the bath water. He said to kip my shirt on. He said daunt kill the goos that lays the golden eggs. When I sow dat he is vizer than any vizier be for Him, I de cided to kip him in house with me all along.

I burned the candel at both ends and remembered that Rom was not bilt in a day. And sins dis was greek to me, so be for jumping off the deep end I took it to God. I tot dat man's extremiti is God's uppertuniti. Then at the drop ave hat I de cided, as yur trusted leather, that we will not be sitting doks. Better be envid then pitid. Nothing venchurd, nothing cained: Itill bi fist or famin. And dbest way to face our enimi is to dik liar war against it widowth mincing the worth. When the going gets tuff, the tuff gets going. I'll be right back!

If you want to keep a smile on your face, LOVEDA is the answer! Ask your doctor to prescribe LOVEDA for you! Approved by our Lord's Food and Drug Administration, LOVEDA is the choice of most doctors. You will lose inches, acquire the ability to move using your own feet, repel morning breath—all with one pill. Elderly patients may develop psychosis. Taking LOVEDA increases your risk of death or stroke. It may cause suicidal thoughts in adolescents and young adults. Call your doctor if you experience high fever, muscle rigidity, headache, dizziness, confusion, sweating, shaking, increased heart rate or blood pressure, uncontrollable facial or body spasms. Common side effects include nausea, vomiting, diarrhea, constipation, gastrointestinal bleeding, difficulty passing urine, seizures, chronic phantom pain in the testicles or breasts, abnormal restlessness, anxiety, insomnia, and death. Additional side effects may occur. Ask your healthcare provider or pharmacist for more information. Consult your doctor if after taking LOVEDA you faint, attempt to commit suicide, become aggressive, have panic attacks, or experience dangerous impulses such as a desire to kill your neighbor, spouse, or children. LOVEDA is the drug of choice for millions of Satanicans. Make LOVEDA your choice and the choice of your loved ones and improve your quality of life. The use of LOVEDA has not been shown to prevent weight gain, immobility, or bad breath. Take LOVEDA now, before it's too late. Developed by Eternity Pharmaceuticals.

I coccion u, fello denizens of Hell, that The war agains tterrorism will not be a peace o kaik. Buttit ill be like pulling tit. It ill cost arm and a leg. A cat in gloves caches gnom ice. Butt we will lower the boom on owr enimi, will gyv demn the third degree, and will never again lok the barn door ater the hoars is out. Emir aka rom the loman on the totem pol to the hayman on the totem pol will sho them that owr noz is knot out o joint, and we ars not over the hill yet.

There arstil many traials our nayshun must ace. But as our ounding dad George Buchanan said, exsample is better dan precept; God helps them hoo help themselves. There for we will shove owr enimi owr di terminacion. But we shood not cuwnt owr chikens before they hach. We shood batten down the haches. We will bate the bullet, they will bate the dust.

Nok on wood, I no the ropes. We will sho them the cold sholdier av emir aka. We will keep their noz to the grindston. We will hunt them Everestile; we will kill their leathers and make shur that there side o the stor is ne'er herd. Dead men tell no tails. Day say dat we lied to them. I say, ask no queschens and here no lies. Even do we will skait on tin ice, we wont owr enimi to no that the ski is the limit o owr potentsheol. I'll be right back!

Investment opportunities span planet earth and so do we. Global investment opportunities are out there if you know where to look. We at Dick Sacho know where to look. We have over 70 years of experience evaluating global equities in bull and bear markets alike. With investment professionals on the ground in over 155 countries, we offer investors an unparalleled perspective on the increasingly cherished and exponentially growing world of global investment. Our goal is to provide our investors with outstanding returns. Integrity and honesty are the heart chambers of our business. We aggressively seek to expand our client relationships, and when we fall short of our promised goals, we employ our henchmen in the Black House and Capitol Hill to occupy other countries. Through our longstanding business relationship with the SIA, we ensure the ascendance of favorable business partners to power in all countries where we have an economic stake. We regularly receive confidential information from Satan and guide our clients accordingly. Significant employee stock ownership in our firm consolidates the interests of our employees and shareholders. Call 1.888.888.8888. Your future mansions and year-round worldwide vacations, guaranteed by our Lord's security agencies, are just a phone call away.

Aris Total once said that a bird in the hand is worth two in the bush. So we will cach one in the hand and let loos two in the bush. We hav shon them that beggars can be choosers and the blak shipo'owr amili can lid them by the nose. These foks mistook our calm be for oper asian nord storm. My kelleag in Elizabeth City has arready de claired that we will call there bluff and maik them under stand that those hoo cunt hit the side ave barn cunt fite city hall. My killeag sad date sins we have a spatial real asian sheep, we will not have to garri all the burden on our sholdiers. I told him dat it takes two to tango. A brotel shard is a brotel haved. My killeag said not to wory about the vine drinkers, sins one Englishman can kill three freshmen. As u see, we always see eie to eie with imp or taunt tissues and dont bilive in old wiwe's tails. A woman's place is in the home, a sholdier's place is in the front says my wife. God's worth says he hoo can does; he hoo cannot, tiches. Our enimis ar playing genterman. But when Adam delved and Eve span, hoo was the genderman?

God bless Emir aka and all the reedom-loving nacients o the word hoose ars with us. Dos hoo ars not widows ars againstus. Itisa Time tested wiz dome that birds ave father bloc together. But we shood never for get dat politics maiks strang bedfellas.

God belss Emir aka.

Ruthful Excelsus, by demolishing Leninstan, you ruined Paradise. Thereafter you spat on it, left it in the lurch, for the Paradiseans are not terrorists.

Lux Mundi, how many kurush are the "demoncracy" and "human rights" which you preach are worth when you still deny even their genocide, when you are in bed with the executioner in broad daylight?

Amor Amor, today you urge Osman Pasha and Petrol Baba to suffocate Paradise by blockading it on four sides, efface it from the stage of history at the opportune moment.

Hominem Salvator, do you deserve to lead the world when your geopolitics reeks of moral cancer?

Divine Exchequer, your debt to Paradise has reached a quintillion of washingtons. Who gives you the right to fritter away this mortgage on Nabuchadnezzar?

Yours is the death penalty!

Electric chair! Not the kevorkian.

And it came to pass that Dog murmured a prayer which he had learned at the Dream Middle School.

Thank you, Satan. Glory and honor to thee, elder father, unsmotherable trove of torches, whence my mind, in my days of childhood, I came humbly to illumine...

Afford me light, Incontrovertible Beatitude, impervious architect of the universe, forger of fate and cognition. The poet entreated God the same only a century ago but was lampooned by His Lowness. Now I entreat you, Grantor of Desires. Help me, Most High Satan, you munificent wisdom, I a caneless shepherd to your great sermon, I a reducible mortal, I a drab steward of the spartan tribe of Hay, I a nescient scribe and illegitimate friar, I an unwaving flag of your faithful throngs, I a blind spring and hunchbacked wanderer, I an undeserving blessor of your unceasing glory, supplicate light for my unlettered herd...

Satan preaches, "Submission to my will is the criterion for being good."

Dog asks, "Venerable Satan, Father of Essence, may I know what is the essence of your statement?"

"Satan is good."

"And?"

"What 'and?'"

"And?"

"Ahem. Submission is good."

Satan's Secretry o State corrects, "Submission to Satan is good."

The Black House spokesman sums it up after a cabinet meeting:

Satan is good.

Submission is good.

Submission to good is good.

The last statement is interrupted by deafening applause.

In a pamphlet titled *Doggerel*, a dog responds to each statement:

1.a: A reflexive truth statement is impossible to prove.

2.a: No relation by itself has ontic essence.

2.b: A relation by itself can never acquire truth value.

3.a: The truth of a fact does not necessarily render a relation with it good.

3.b: A relation to a fact can never have ontic value, thus is incomparable to the fact, and is beyond the ethical.

In order to facilitate discussion, this dog states, "Must parts of a proposition be true in order for a proposition to be true? All parts? Some parts? How many parts?"

A national debate ensues in Hell, after Bill Moyers reads this pamphlet on his TV program.

Man, the Teapublican, says, "Yea. All parts must be true."

Man, the Demoncrat, says, "Nay. Some parts must be true. The majority of parts is sufficient."

That is two out of the three.

As to which two: one, Satan is good, three, Submission to good is good.

Man, the Teapublican, replies, "Do you mean that part two can be false and still make the proposition right? Do you mean that if Yoohoo is wrong the Holy Trinity can be right? Do you really mean that submission is bad? You are undermining our way of life."

"Submission to Allah is bad," snaps back Man, the Demoncrat. "We must have an intelligent foreign policy."

"If submission is bad," asks Man, the No Man, "how can we state that submission to good is good?"

"That is the whole point," says Man, the Demoncrat. "We have to accept that even if submission is bad, submission to good is good."

The next day the Security Council of Man passed a resolution with a majority vote: Submission to Satan is good, therefore everyone must submit to Satan. And those who do not submit to Satan...

The proposition is voted on as such, since no language could be found to complete it. As punishing the pariahs with the fires of Hell would have constituted a blatant contradiction of Satanic nature and defeated the whole purpose of the proposition.

Poor Dog thinks, *If submission to a will is good, then I must be bad.*

And since Dog has no powers of Satanic ratiocination, and could not keep silent on matters of which one should not speak, he farts:

Therefore bad is good.

The claims of the woman I met in New Mount Musa and others like her fell on deaf ears. Was there a surfeit of crazies in Paradise? Or were the redeemed tired of the truth?

But who wants to listen to the deranged? She insists she is not crazy. Only "irritable," as a consequence of the odyssey she has lived through.

Murderers, of course, do not like headaches.

"Eretz Leo is a murderer," Titan's former equipollent

Ashot Junior proclaimed on Imagination Square. My friend Sunkist's testimonials honed the imagination further.

"So what? A good president must be a good murderer," opine the cigarette-addicted pussies of the Paradisean nobility.

For Satan's delectation, God, Condolent of the Scandalized and Aegis of Heads, exonerated Titan, in the name of "cultivating a tradition of power-shifting." Wow! And based on what constitutional right? *Appé*, constitution… in Paradise… ha ha ha!

Does the Indescribable Inheritance, too, have something to fear from his successor? Has he been an accomplice of Titan in past stewardly matters? Or is he indeed led by ideals?

And what was that ideal, whose champion was His Custodianship of the Fatherland, supposed to give to the Paradisean, when in return he lost his faith in the rule of law, was filled with ferocious hatred toward the Gate of Glories?

Is God also concealing something?

Jealous angels say that today Titan lives large in Virginabad, in his castle on the banks of Gihon. Is this how they live in Tartaros, my brethren? How has he acquired it? Who has given him this privilege and why?

His successor, God. Partners in what? Caninicide? Or is it a baksheesh, so he would shut his trap? Far be it! Is the Mover of Lips himself the archetype of Cant?

Command, O merciful, caring, exalted light inextinguishable, unbounded by puissance, for I have presently bore witness to the existence of my earthly nature beneath my members. May you reside ensconced in the undesertable departed father, amidst robust yearnings, with my soul's unity onto you. Against the ever-rejected pollution of my sins, prepare me onto immaculateness, immortal king of all creatures, blessed you be evermore.

Arzni was a renowned health resort during the Leninian epoch. From across the Great Union, people traveled here to be rejuvenated by its mineral waters, to be healed. It is a site that holds the promise of an international tourist destination. On one of my visits, they showed me a splendid, half-built sanitarium that belonged to God's wife, although it is ostensibly owned by someone else. At every footstep in Paradise, they point at a structure and inform you as to which of God's dwarves it belongs to. Gossip? The specialty of Paradiseans.

But there is a reality, brothers: today the commerce of the future is being effected by the Rain of Blessing's Punchinellos, who will share their profits with Lord Satan's investors, provided they receive appropriate oblations.

They will sell Paradise for the right price.

For sale. Country. With official United-Nations-member status. Below market prices. Hurry, before Papa Lenin is made to rise from the dead. Cradle of antiquity. Matchless touristic future. Three million serfs included, loyalty guaranteed—exploit them ad adytum. Slavery prescription patented: strike fear on pretense of avoiding bloodletting in Heaven.

This is why those Satanic dreamers, who are averse to bribery, are washed away into the cesspit from the processes that forge the future of Paradise. Paradiseans view the dreamers as milch cows whose raison d'etre is to provide milk. Those dreamers who wake up from dreaming are slaughtered for their meat.

Three days after hearing the above advertisement by God, Satan made this announcement on Good Morning Emir aka:

For sale. Planet. Sea and land, earth and sky, water and air, clouds, rivers, homeland! Insured by Satan. Below market prices. Hurry, before it is lain to waste. Residents believe in saviors. Six continents, two hundred sover-

*eign states, significant nuclear potential. Six billion serfs
included. Loyalty guaranteed: they rely on God. They pay
tithe and immolate their children to him.*

Even in Paradise, where the archangels do not pay tax
and do not send their children to the army, they do pay
tithe to God with greenbacks printed by Satan. They are
having a feast with the Exalted One and the fairies, who
imbibe the semen of archangels, squeezed drop by drop
from the lives of Virginstan's grandmas and grandpas. As
for the revenue service, it extracts the bribe from the throats
of bottom-rung store owners, who have been left with not
their wives but their mere hands.

*These hands… these father's hands… these olden and
new hands… What have they not done, these hands…*

A cherub genuflecting to the Adulated Lordship said,
"So what? Whenever the Heavenscraping Stairway needs
anything, the archangels always help."

For instance, they host the emissaries of Eurostan, com-
mandeering the realm of foreign relations to use it for their
own financial interests. Bonaparte's and Satan's ambassadors are
bribed.

"Archangels shower God with part of the offertory,"
gossip the redeemed.

"Instead of paying five million in taxes, they gift five
grand or a couple of milk cows to some family member of
the Manifestation of Joy and distribute five thousand washingtons' worth of potatoes to the starving senior citizens of
Paradise so they will praise them to heaven. They follow the
teachings of Messiah…"

A visa to Hell costs ten thousand washingtons. God,
Holy Ghost & Company have proselytized the ambassadors in Paradise, who have become missionaries in their
respective countries promoting monotheism, whitewashing God's crimes through the agency of faith.

"Treason! Kill the Dog! Aren't Osman Pasha and Ali
Baba doing the same thing day and night with every ambassador, professor, or tourist who sets foot in their lands?

Using the riches of our nation to cover the cost of their propaganda!"

"Let that Hell of yours hold its tongue, okay? What the fuck kind of country is it that the killers of its president are still not unmasked, forty years after his assassination?"

They have a good point, humanist Satan. You sermonize the world, yet your hands are bloody. You cannot conceal your naked heel with military might. That would be the beginning of your demise. You and God are one.

n Paradise they are obsessed with the theory that Maimunus and Satan have colluded to destroy Heaven. Thus the redeemed have begun to peer out, not in. I noticed a telling indication of this in New Mount Musa.

When I looked at the faces and twinkling eyes of boys between the ages of six and ten, I was elated. The Hay spirit shimmered on their faces. But when I beheld those between ten and eighteen, my inner equilibrium was shaken. They exuded a lethal energy that sprang from a mindset already seven layers deep.

Whose fault was this? Who was responsible for the wreckage of the Paradisean's intellect and spirit? First and foremost, the primary teachers of these children—their mothers and fathers.

And theirs?

Pasha, of course.

was not involved in the activities of the Holy Trinity Party. The dogish, not human, aspect of my actions was of concern to me. I wanted to demonstrate with personal example that I could fight for justice, to the chagrin of the enemies of long-suffering Paradise, even if that would take joining an organization on par with their ideology. I knew that the secret of Holy Trinity's immortality lay in Pasha's life. Although this dog often skipped meetings—because of which the party threatened

to ban him from the organic dream, extinguish his light—
he was given the green light to speak his mind about certain
moments of import. Kudos to Holy Trinity, for it allowed a
dog to speak on its behalf. Mind that the Holy Trinity Party
is merely the fallen temporal replica of the divine Holy
Trinity, thus sin is its nature.

When I did attend meetings, I derived fulfillment. Let
humans think that Dog is devoid of soul. Congregating at the
meetings were people whose parents had escaped the Genocide. They lived fortified with the mnemon of the past, toiled
in the present with the hope of returning to the future. They
had sworn to sacrifice their lives for the nation. Hayness to
them was a religion, and the less erudite they were, the purer
was their spirit. They sang songs of struggle, and each of their
lives was an odyssey that could fill volumes.

Here, too, was my friend Sunkist—a solitary, hetero-
clitic walking encyclopedia of the party's history. I felt so
sorry that his memories, which comprised wondrous epi-
sodes from the history of Dreamland, could be lost forever.
Sunkist was a sterling patriot. That had spiritual import for
this dog. His patriotism was expressed in the manifestation
of noble ideals, the generative energy stemming from which
enchanted me. Whenever I spoke with him, I was uplifted
for weeks on end.

What force is this that drives me to catharsis? I experienced the very same catharsis when I heard and sang Holy
Trinity's marches of patriotic struggle.

Brave youth of Akulis,
Who shall tell of your death?
Countless blessings upon your ilk,
You're the hope of the patrie.

Or...

Rattle, O boys, your lustrous sabers,
Rain fire upon the foe,
Upon the savage foe,
Upon the ruthless foe.

It became clear to me, brethren, that there is a distinct
link between revolutionary songs and the inner structures of
spiritual music. Both are lustrous sabers of different sorts. By
becoming a loudspeaker for spiritual values through their irre-

pressible efflux, both effected a catharsis of the same measure within Dog's inner world.

What prevailed was a demosocratic ambience. Comrades doggishly barked at Holy-Trinity cherubim who were found to stray. The following year saw the election of a comrade who curtailed criticism leveled at the powers that be. Shush! He has been elected with the intervention of the Trinity. Holy Trinity ships dissidents off to the great beyond.

Gathered at the site of the sun's burial, these people dreamed and breathed distant Paradise. Each carried a Paradise upon their shoulders. It was a heavy burden, requiring superhuman effort. I was partial to the most rough-hewn among them. Their beauty and harmony lay precisely in their ugliness, crudity, and often simplemindedness. They were honest folk, with a clear conscience, law-abiding, dedicated, and demanding—of their own selves before anyone else.

Ugly is beautiful.
And who says you don't have a sea?
Your Sea of Blood is greater than the Pacific,
Your Sea of Sweat deeper than the Atlantic,
Your Sea of Vengeance more fearsome than the Arctic.
Your Sea of Tears...
We have now no need of psalms and hymns,
Nor masses and memorials.
The soil herself sings through the dark trachea of her entrails,
Accompanied by her waterfalls,
Her fierce chorus of winds,
The puissant solos of the Twin tongueless bells, Ararat,
Before an audience of myriad lamps and lights
Which blink their glistening eyes in rapture,
More vibrantly alive
Than the twinkling stars above.
May I call thee
A people of vivors,
Of survivors...

Wave 4, "Triphthongal Mass"

My warm impressions of dreamers were not to be replicated in Paradise, the coccyx of the dream.

Holy Trinity, being the most powerful political party of Dreamland, was not lacking in faults. I took issue with the fact that some of its members were Mononons, though it was not the most Mononon-laden party of the dreamers. Its ferocious critic, the Party of Free Amononons, is semi-Monononified. (To Free Amononons, utopia lies in the reestablishment of Titanolatry in Paradise. Whence its drive to erect a statue of Titan on the pedestal where in the carefree days the statue of Lenin was ensconced, to be worshipped by future generations of man). And most clergy of the Protestants, who fancy themselves "men of God," are Mononons. The entire establishment of the Judolicosate of Monononias is a lair of Monononry. This is an openly flaunted bit of hypocrisy on the part of Dreamland's clergy, for Monononry and moshianism claim allegiance to irreconcilable gods.

Ergo, brothers, the catholicoi of Dreamland are chameleons. The Mononons worship a triadic icon. What does it mean to be a Mononon-Moshianist, and a catholicos at that? Is this not more freakish than, let us say, a Muslim-Catholic, a mullah-cardinal? Light for future generations! Historians will sing the praise of these vanguards, who set the stage for the unity of all religions, Shakespeare's Grand Lodge... excuse me, I meant to say Grand Dream.

A Marxist dog. Kick him out!

Dog is the very thing that humans kick out.

According to the bylaws of Holy Trinity, its members are not permitted to hold membership in another organization. Violators are punished, grounded from the party.

The rule is waived in the case of only one organization, the Mononons. The Trinity yet again contradicts its bylaws. Isn't the all-encompassing God, after all, the mother of all contradictions? Contradiction is the foundation of divine logic, friars.

My brother, who at one time was a modest Mononon, had applied to join the ranks of Holy Trinity but was turned down. Being an honest fellow, he had mentioned in his application the fact of his Monononic membership. The partisan who had denied his application, however, was himself a Mononon… covertly…

The upshot is that within Holy Trinity there operates a small group whose identity is known only to its members. This is a traditional method of liquidating any organization or controlling it from the outside, in contradistinction to the values professed by Holy Trinity.

"This junta must be liquidated," Dog retorted. "Those who wish to remain Mononons must leave the Trinity or, inversely, those who embrace the Trinity should relinquish Monononry."

Dog was unaware that he had erred, brethren. The Mononons *are* worshipers of Trinity. Are yet another manifestation of the meta-trinity. The Holy Trinity duly decided to evict Dog rather than the cabal.

When I was still wet behind the ears, I was enraged by the two-facedness of the leaders of the "revolutionary" party, especially since it was in the Monononic lodges of Pashaland that the Genocide of Paradise was hatched, while Monononic organizations to this day have failed to apologize to the survivors.

Should you ask why, I shall tell you.

They thrive on the legends of an artificially induced, mysterious past. Unexposed fear helps preserve the centripetal force of legend, providing stimulus for power.

Moreover, the Genocide of the dreamers is not a fly in the ointment.

Ne evening Christina and I went to visit her sister, Svetlana. We were having a delightful time with her and Sam, her husband, when suddenly I fell ill. Sam wanted to take me to the hospital. I refused. I did not have insurance. I also did not trust man-doctors, from whom this dog had seen more harm than good. What do they know about the sorrow of dogs? How were they able to replace a lost homeland? Do they have a solitary clue as to what a homeland means for a dog?

I asked them to take me home. I had an inkling of how the mind and body work. That night I recovered again. Uncle's words, Paradisean spiritual music, the teachings of Buddha and Christ... all served as palliatives.

Having faced death for so long, I had experimented with those teachings of Christ, Buddha, and Lao-tzu which I found to have a direct relevance to the cycle of living and dying. I had tested their power and legitimacy in view of death.

A word can contain the seeds of either life or death. The tonality of each word uttered and the intentionality that each word is loaded with express the entire spectrum of life and death. In Paradise they speak, internally and externally alike, in words that spell death, with a tonality and intentionality that guarantee death.

In the morning, when I returned like a rooster to pick up my car, Svetlana was both happy and astonished to see me.

Months later, when Sam and Svetlana accompanied me to Los Bab Airport to see me off to Natashima, I had already solved a number of problems. I was about to embark on a new chapter in my life.

Waiting for me in Natashima is my friend Yelena. She has traveled from Natashaev to welcome me. Within a year she will graduate as a surgeon. We hug each other after I go through customs. I feel a tegument fall off me. We head to Hotel Rossiya. From the big windows of our room we have a full view of the Kreml, which grows more beautiful in the lights of the night. We consult the clock on the structure.

From the very first moment, Yelena serves up surprises. I spend happy days with her. Anywhere we set foot, we become the cynosure of the crowd.

She has been wooed by the Number 33 Hellion of Hell. Yelena asks for guidance on a variety of issues. We laugh for hours as we explore the particulars of Yelena's future marriage with Number 33.

The more we try to pretend to be indifferent toward one another, the more intensely an internal compulsion takes hold in us, escaping our notice. The accumulated lava explodes at the last minute. We say good-bye with difficulty. The emotions prevent me from coming outside with her. I stay in the room. In the coming days she is with me. I look for her everywhere.

"Come with me, I've got a house in Natashaev, we'll live together. Virginabad is a village. In Natashaev already everybody speaks Satanish. You will not find a Satanish-speaker in Paradise. They live in the eighteenth century. You'll go, you'll regret. You'll remember my words. Don't goooooooooooooo!"

Yelena's psychology is characteristic of the most beautiful women. A declaration thundering from her face: "I am beautiful. I can twist a hundred men around my finger. But it is you I have chosen. Should you fail to appreciate this in full, I shall foam, I shall go wild like an ocean and utterly wreck the ship of your heart and existence. I shall hate you to my last fiber and toss you out of my life."

That's exactly what happened.

Ugly Dog was unable to appreciate the great service rendered by Beautiful Woman. She has a high value in men's marketplace. I have trampled it underfoot.

Yelena did not forgive my months of disappearance. And loathed me.

There was another reason compounding her bathos.

A few years ago a businessangel from Paradise had raped her. Although she had managed to bounce back from the devastation of that experience, she still abhorred the Paradiseans. I, too, was a hermano of the Paradiseans.

The Virginoso boasts before the Virginosae of his "exploits" with Natashas.

To some damsels in Paradise, the rape of a woman is a sign of the perpetrator's manhood. They dream of being raped…

Among their counterparts in Hell, however, there occurs a satori of feminist pride in the aftermath of rape, which prompts the rapee to publicly disgrace the hombre and accumulate social capital.

God help him if he is a representative of an ethnic minority… Adam's black penis fucking Eve's blond pussy. Did he rape? *Yes or no?*

Rape is a bad thing, my sisters. I understood the full measure of this when I was raped by a woman. I felt pity for her, did not resist. Sleepless nights ensued. I was burning, choking in my bed. A sense of disgust stayed with me for many a month.

But what am I to say about the Pornstani wenches who rape my spirit, everywhere and every day of the sun?

I am already indifferent toward their pain. Their pussies are no more precious than my soul.

As their pussies carry Satan's seal whereas this dog's soul is not worth a dog in their marketplace, they snatch collective vamp sustenance by constantly raping my spirit, consolidate their empire.

Rape is a good thing, my brothers. Against the vampire. *Cavete a canibus.* It is the most effective terror against her power pyramid. The bastard worth his grain does it publicly. Not like a coward sneaking into a defenseless woman's bedroom. He is deterred less by man's law, more by the collective might of the swarms of pussy-slaves all around him, ever ready to pass themselves as saviors.

Reductio ad absurdum.

But this is why acaudates are waiting for Godot.

Yelena and Heather could be twins—in body and mind alike.

I am in Kennedy City for a few days, to settle the issue of living quarters and get ready for my university studies. But I must pay a few weeks' visit to Calipornia, to sort out some matters connected with my family. I have been away for months.

To the airport, via metro. She comes in at one of the stops, sits next to me. I am mesmerized. It is She.

Across from us is seated a young black man with curly hair, whose stare unremittingly oscillates between me and Her, turning him into a ring conjoining us.

I ask her to show me the metro link to the airport, though I know my way around. Instead we come off at the station which takes to her workplace. She, too, has heard a little voice tell her to talk to me. We walk fast, chitchatting.

Within a matter of seconds, she uncovers nuances about me, unravels a sea's worth from a single word. Here's my number. Call me when you get back.

Heather became the only woman able to fully unwind my heart's discus, transforming it into a radiating, ripe rose.

We had just begun going out when her father died. For years he had lectured at Kennedy Institute of Technology (KIT). It was a grave loss. Heather loved him dearly. She called as soon as she heard the news. She could scarcely maintain coherence in the torrent of her tears. I spent the night at her place.

Her father had valued independence of the mind. Rejected so-called Maimuno-Yoohooianity and leaned toward Buddhism. Heather is her father's daughter and often stresses that though she has lost her father, she has found me.

As our relationship continued to develop, her mother stood against it. She is half Eyfelian, half Hamburgerlander. Heather is not fond of her. It is because of her overbearingness that in childhood she has contracted tonsillitis, of which she still suffers. Mother has taught her not to be involved with any man with skin darker than hers. An impossible task. All are rejected. She is happy for not listening to mom this once.

But her mother's intervention hurt my dignity and I broke it off with Heather, sending her a dogtypical note, my brethren. On a greeting card exclusively printed for this purpose. I wanted to give some quality to this departure. The painstaking detail drove her nuts. Allowing mamma to even express opinions was to allow her to meddle. I unplugged my phone when Heather started to leave a flurry of messages.

At that time I was also in dire financial straits. I was running out of cash despite living frugally and had no money to entertain a woman. I wished I could afford a camera for preserving our best moments. Once I was left with two washingtons—enough for the only meal of the day. Below the dormitory, there was a food stall whose owner was afraid to say where he was from. This owner, who was afraid to say where he was from, charged a couple of washingtons for a single falafel sandwich. I made do with it that day, before receiving my next check. And did my math: 1 washington = 1/2 a caliphel.

To save franklins, I had registered for only one class. Being at Harvard was enough—it gave me the opportunity to get acquainted with professors and obtain their permission to attend their classes. I did not miss a chance. I also made use of auditorial privileges at nearby KIT. I followed the courses of eight of the best lecturers. My focus was actually on Oxford, from whose Mathematical Institute I had received a letter of acceptance.

At two in the morning, I look out my window at the surrounding dormitories, where some of the lights have just begun to go off, allowing the rest of the resident lights to taper off by sunrise.

Here the nights are lit by hundreds of the manplanet's most gifted students, who one day shall become the leaders of various spheres in different countries. And where are the paradisoids at this moment?

My mind wanders to Gehendale, where semi-Neanderthals drive their Mercedes-Benzes and BMWs and make bray the vapid music of Pasha with those pedestrian Paradisean lyrics of the "let me love, eat, fuck, my love" variety, disturbing entire neighborhoods and always ready to murder anyone emitting a word of objection. They hit pedestrians and flee the scene. Sit in jail, swaggering before the policemen. At best they matriculate at the Gehendale Community College at Satan's expense to play poker at eight a.m., particularly during finals weeks, when there is really nothing to do other than pool together a few franklins to buy the instructor a good present that secures their passage to the next course. This way they contribute to world peace, by diverting Satan's resources from war to education. I witnessed the trial of a certain doofus who, fancying himself to be Lord knows what, treated the judge with jehovic hauteur while the latter patiently examined his appeal for political asylum.

In Virginabad, I came across thousands of such bozos, who think that they need nothing in life except their mafia culture. There was one thing missing in Paradise: prisons. *Hell* was missing from Paradise! Forty kurbashes per trespass!

A world was slipping away from under the feet of the redeemed, and they, with their status of eyewitnesses relegated to the fringes, greeted the new epoch of human history as vacuous consumers and not as creators or producers, or at least civilized and cultured human beings.

Paradisoids are peasants by nature. In Kremlstan they outnumber the maimunoids. Whereas these live in large cities, paradisoids do not venture beyond Krasgrad. The same holds in the Demoncratic Imperium of Gehenna. Krasgrad and Gehendale could be sister cities. Who needs to reside in the heart of civilization, to ascend the stairway of culture, science, politics?

But this is wonderful, Dog. Vertical structures are seats for demons and all pyramids are in essence demonic structures. Okay. However, these folks have nothing to do with the realm of the spiritual. To them the path to being and becoming consists of gambling, guzzling kabob, savagery. They are the perfect egalitarians! When you slap the truth to their faces, they would rather dump their faults on the "Jinjinist mafia," slaughter you, than change themselves.

"Listen to this. I'm asking this guy if it's true that Mercedes will open a factory in Ayatollahland… He's lived sixty years in Shah'nshahstan, he's got seven generations' worth of roots in Shahnamehland, and what does he give me for an answer? 'I'm waiting for my daughter. She's gonna come get me so we go have some *kyabob*.' Now there's a goddamned Hay for you," complains God Artin.

"Such judgments are anti-scientific," counter the kyabobovorous redeemed.

Two weeks have passed. I turn my phone back on. I miss her. There is a ring at midnight. It's Heather. We talk until three. We let it all out and decide to meet again.

I invite her to a posh restaurant, one of the very best of Pornland.

That night she surpasses herself in every respect. She resembles a mermaid, with her body-fitting black dress reaching her ankles, further accentuating her svelte, soaring figure. She has already disarmed me in the car, employing the complement of her powers of seduction. I don't tell her that the Virginlandosa, with her inert mind, would not rival her in a thousand years. Heather's entrance into the restaurant causes a tsunami, making short work of the composed atmosphere.

The clientele consists mostly of venerable patrons between the ages of sixty and seventy. I am flabbergasted: the men are far more attractive than the women. Pornstan = land of terrorized menschen. The noble man is allotted no more than a hideous pussy. Although women age faster, they will terrorize the man if he does not choose a woman of his age. This is not Natashaland or Virginstan, where every idiot has a choice of four or five nymphs. Meantime, the noble man does not even know whether his child is of his own seed.

If the man worth nine out of ten can, in an inabusive milieu [since no such milieu has ever existed anywhere in human history, here we're at the skirts of hypothecation—DogAlleyPress], form a stable family with a woman worth nine, in Pornstan all he can hope for is a woman worth five or six, if not three. Often the local man will exact revenge on the woman and, for the sake of stability, will have a liaison with a foreign woman worth two or one. As for Virginstan, a man worth zero can buy a woman worth nine, on the strength of his papa's assets. This is why he stands firmly against freedom and the dismantling of the mafiocracy. If given a level field, he would find himself next to a lass of his exact worth—zero.

Heather's presence becomes a thorn in the eyes of the female patrons, who follow us from every corner, while she, ignoring the surroundings, soaks me with a downpour of kisses.

It comes to a point when the six honchos of the restaurant encircle us, demanding that we leave. We have broken no human law, but don't have much choice either. I feel certain that men will upgrade their laws to keep us out. If in my holy presence the nail on your left toe is longer than your fingers, I shall curse your seed for seven generations. If the nails of both toes are longer, I shall curse your seed for seventy-seven generations. I offer to pay for our order. This is to their liking. But they could not accept payment without having yet served dinner, which would take some time to prepare on account of the several courses. This is to my liking. My hope is that tempers would cool in the interim...

... to no avail. Heather has something entirely different in mind...

Offended by the behavior of the diners and managers, she is determined to teach them a lesson, femme à femme, by ostentatiously intensifying her romantic onslaught. The few young couples sitting at nearby tables feel small. At last we come out of the gate, banished to our destiny.

Heather is the first to unveil the inner world of woman. I see in her a mirror of my life. All I have to do is tell her about my past and watch her face. I see my marriage and my relationships with women through brand-new lenses. She knows about woman down to the core and opens before me new horizons which heretofore had been buried in mist. Only now do I begin to fathom the abuse that women have subjected me to, the waste not only of years, not only of toil, but also of health, almost life itself. I start to appreciate the women of Pornland. Not the vamps, of course, but the kind souls, like Heather, whose numbers are not that negligible in Hell.

Afterward, when I constantly clash against the rapacity of the Virginlandette, I face a quandary that bifurcates my inner world for years to come. My soul, in all of its dimensions, is driven toward the Virginlandette, yet my mind, with its scintillating new suns, which create waves of inexplicable joy, is bedazzled by the Hellette.

This duality could not be solved. It could be rectified through either the radical metamorphosis of the Virginlandette or the Hayification of the Hellette. Both options skirted the borders of the delusional.

"Get real!" Heather used to tell me. "You're in Hell now."

While I remained without shelter, without homeland...

A whole life was passing me by.

This, indeed, was not a soft dilemma. The rational solutions not only collided with visceral predilections stemming from the deepest folds of my being, but were stifled by the bitter reactions of the reality that enfolded me. One could not meet a woman of Heather's caliber at every footstep. Her arrival was a shooting star in the stygian sky of my existence.

I understood one day that what I truly needed was two wives—a Hellette and a Virginlandette. That was the only way out.

Monogyny is not love. It is terror. It is the institutionalized model of self-love and hypocrisy.

"Death!" promulgated the concordat of human civilization.

By the time I reached the shores of Hades, I had mastered the language of Satan, which I had studied since I was three—the lingua franca of man. But years of incessant struggle was needed to be hewn in our Lord Satan's society and be able to take the first timid step on the infinite ladder that leads to Satanic glory. And what about finding meaning in this supercanine endeavor? My soul suffocated, hankered to escape from the self-centered environment.

No, we were not equals. They had become pedacled to their breakneck lives. Television junkies, day and night absorbing Satan's grand narrative. They considered this progress, civilization. An ignoramus such as myself could never catch up...

Their thought processes were mass-molded for them by Satan's kultur factory. And I could care less to familiarize myself with His hokum. There was nothing to talk about. Equals do not beg each other for alms.

The rhythm of their minds was disrupted. Their life rhythm in disarray. Their gazes warped. The quality of their thoughts putrefied. Their attention span reduced to zilch. They could not think without stereotypes. World news for them was what happened at the corner of 42nd and O Streets. Their conversational style and vocabulary attested to a troubled psyche. Everywhere you turned, legions of consumers, consumerist to the core, and depraved manifestations of sex and cruelty engulfing the last bastions of freedom of thought, the academic institutions, of which we were recently witness to in Mesopotamia. A massive troglodyte of three hundred million. Ha ha ha! Who is the deranged one?

I, the convict, of course.

They were a civilized, Yoohooite people, I a barbaric extramural creature...

All that most women sought was "someone who can deliver fun."

That, I was not.

I felt hurt when they looked at me as a second-class citizen. I was repulsed by those impostors who presented themselves mendaciously as full-fledged members of Satan's society, beloved of the white natives. This was the highest standard of social standing. With laser scrutiny I saw the bones of their souls, was sickened by that xenomania and ethos of cozening compatriots, which served their stab at one-upmanship.

Competition among crutches...

True, the civil element of Hell was among the most sensitive in the world. It did its utmost to make me feel as a genuine citizen. Such consideration was not merely a function of being educated. There were many well-read men and women who happened to be xenophobes, and many with barely a high-school diploma who accepted me with open arms. I had begun to read people, espy their spiritual and intellectual construction through the slightest intimation.

Irrespective of all this, there was one thorny issue, my brothers. It was not naked prejudice with which I collided every hour, wondering why I should have been the butt of destiny's whim. This by itself was a *mise en scene* that impresses a question mark on Nietzsche's forehead: Who is the privileged who can become a superman? Who is the one who can afford culture? What gives, yao, to vituperate against slave morality instead of beheading the creators of the objective conditions that give rise to slave morality? And how to achieve Schopenhauer's state of painlessness when the entire gamut of social existence has conspired against you from birth to death? The choices are literally between transcendence and self-destruction, even through revolt. And as long as there are oppressors in the world of men, the fake currency of saviors will be in high demand.

What killed me, brothers, was the kind treatment the Satanicans showed me, the way they cared for me as though I were a newborn lizard, told me of the magnificent elderly Paradiseans whom they knew... of the people toward whom the world and even our Lord Satan had been unjust... the way they affectionately tapped my shoulder with an unfeigned smile... chuckled while my shadow was still with them as I took leave... chuckled wholeheartedly, caringly, kindly... so kindly that it was impossible to hate them...

Was I not entitled to live in a land where people spoke my tongue, shared the call of my soul, cherished my dreams and yearnings, understood and communed with me? This thorny issue (despite the general political atmosphere in Hell, which reserved rights for minorities) pertained to the human rights of the majority. Why was the Satanican obligated to change himself in order to accommodate me? He couldn't, even if he tried.

And what did we have in common if my interest in his baseball and basketball, his golf and political views was nil? People spoke of actors whose names are to this day unfamiliar to me. Who needed my Tumanyan, Komitas, Siamanto, Varuzhan? What did Sevak's *Unsilenceable Bell Tower* mean to anyone? Who needed my Sayat Nova and Mokats Mirza, whose songs, to my amazement, my five-year-old daughter listened to in my car with rapture and demanded to hear again and again? I was divorced at that time, and she was growing up in Satan's cultural turf. Such music was unfathomable to everyone, except Scott, my Minnesotan friend in Hellington, who relished its every note. Who needed my people, the entirety of which could be fitted within the limits of San Diego County?

I had sprung from a source which fostered the most profound layers of my being. But I clashed with a reality which demanded that I reject it.

Give up your ethnic thing and you'll be free.

I do not have an ethnic thing. I am a separate nation.

Then go back to your land.

I've got no land. This *is* my land.

Then become a Satanican.

When did you become a Paradisean?

The obverse of the last pair of statements is more revealing.

Stop being a Paradisean.

When did you stop being a Satanican?

What does that involve?

First, you must kiss Satanish good-bye. You will talk to me only in Paradisean as I do not understand a word of Satanish and have no intention to learn any. You must graduate from a Paradisean university, work for a Paradisean company, have sex in Paradisean, watch only Paradisean movies, read only Paradisean literature, go only to Paradisean events. And if you speak my language with an accent, I will ridicule and discriminate against you every step of the way.

Second, you will stop paying taxes to Satan—pay them instead to my nation. Besides, you will allocate 10 percent of your income to my church. You will disavow your allegiance to the Satanic flag, fight against the Satanic military overseas to free the nations of the world from its hegemony.

There are thirty-eight more items on the list.

I had applied for a scholarship from the International Rotary Club to fund my studies at Oxford. I was accepted at Oxford by one of its best mathematicians. He commanded great respect at Harvard, and I was to study under his tutelage. If I am not mistaken, eight students were accepted to the Mathematical Institute that year—six from Shakespeareland, the rest (including myself) from beyond the seas.

With accordance to its rules, the Rotary Club required that I be interviewed by its local branch. The city was Gehendale, where Paradiseans were abhorred. As I went in, there was another candidate waiting.

My interview was conducted by two women and a man. He proceeded to terrorize me, belittling my every achievement. One of the women shut him up. The other woman asked, "And why don't the dreamers assimilate in Hell?"

She then corrected herself: "*Assimilate* is not a politically correct word. What I mean is... *integrate*."

This was the cavil because of which I was to lose the

chance to study at Oxford. Who was blocking my way? The Dreamophobic Satanicans or the monstrous redeemed?

But what did it mean to be integrated?

Acquiescence and resignation to the superiority of the ruler's regime. Adaptation to the ideological superstructure of the social foreground and the killing of the song of your soul. Depreciation and destruction of your genuine public logos, your life environment, and its suppression to the realm of the private. Concentration of power in the hands of the ideological majority, exclusion of alternatives, equally viable life structures. Carving out a survival nook against insuperable odds, still faced with the continual bombardment of the majority logicalia. Surrender of the surplus value of your economic, creative, and emotional output to the supervision of the ideological majority. (If you are an integrated writer, your books are read by the millions should you produce literary junk that in subtle and not so subtle ways propagates Satan's grand narrative, mocks his ideological adversaries, and acts as nostrum that produces a narcissistic, catharthic illusion to camouflage the monstrosity of the soul of the socius and that of its nation. Then, my friend, you'll receive all the accolades of man). But there is more: the spilling of your blood. For the moronic majority. Which has declared war against a myth that threatens her own hegemonic myth. In the name of the execrable icon called patriotism. The surrender of your life. As petrol for the preservation and reinforcement of the centripetal system of the hegemon, idealized in the form of transcendent values: God = Führer BenYehu = Stalin Anti-Yehu = Satan McYehu = Caliph McAllah. Perpetuation of Aristotemism… Ha ha ha! The bastard chortles.

Wait, bastard. There's still more. Prostration before the cultural values of the crème de la crème, submission to cultural fascism by partaking in the omnivalent state of hypnosis.

You have the right to vote only insofar as you lack the means to dismantle Satan's reign. Otherwise you and your vote shall be expelled from Satan's intestines and appear in his quotidian shit, as discharged bacterium.

Such are the nature and perimeter of the demoncracy propagated by Satan.

To be integrated!

Having a relationship with a Hellette was not a smooth sail for Dog. The hoi polloi fed on vapid interests—one needed to stoop to their level. Adjusting to it entailed a shift in one's worldview and required a lifetime. They, meanwhile, believed that I had my work cut out for me if I were to reach their level. I had not had opportunities to have ties with the upper crust. They were cocooned in their world, where few set foot, and I could not afford the price of entry. Those in the middle class were conceited. They themselves felt the need for affirmation, whereas a foreign-born friend was often a liability. A slight accent and they avoided you. I could not talk, let alone write...

Naturally all this negativity was in Dog's head. Dog was clueless as to the arcanum of positive affirmation. The divine recipe to overcome Dog's problems in toto was offered by Yoohoo MacYehu himself: I am that I am that I am that I am.

Ant, affirm it for eons!

Dog refused to be crucified and shoveled his cock into MacYehu's Divine Ass and his *hors concours* assicrates. The protagonists of houdiniing the pyramid of social injustice from the eyes of the individual through surfactants, the agents of the perpetuation of the Satanic status quo, the lunatics of power conjuring the "infinite source"—in effect the compound interest of the accumulated yield of labor in the society of the snide descendents of the enterprising few and their newfangled consociates, after having established their enterprises on the bones of Satanstan's natives, the sweat of Africa, and the agony of Paradises—all in the name of the Lord.

I was not interesting to those women who had had boyfriends in Brittany or Naples, spent the weekend in Barcelona or Cannes, stomped the empire of Satan, armed with plastic. The art of fluent conversation is a great asset. You have it, you rule.

Mother tongue.

Not all think alike, to be sure. Many are simply indifferent, and those who aren't are of a quality that makes you prefer to stay alone. This is an emblematic problem that afflicts Hellian society. A leap over the racial divide requires sacrifices. Exempli gratia, a man worth seven by the same society's standards, who in his own tribe could have a woman worth six, would end up with a woman worth one if he were to make the jump to a "finer" tribe. Despite Satan's slogan of equality.

This consciousness has two major enemies: porn and commerce.

There was a minority that dismissed all this. But to find these women you had to save up or rely on serendipity, or else swallow two dozen insults every day for simply lifting your gaze above the ground.

Having been disillusioned by Gehennettes, I had sought the services of a Mariamstani agency in Los Baby-lonos which promised to make an appropriate match. A computerized search ceded three choices. I had to pick one. All three were illegal immigrants, i.e., green-card-seekers, could barely speak Hellish, had neither education nor any merit of note. Two of the candidates had posted housekeeping as their forte.

When I told the owner that his company was engaged in consumer fraud, he used all of his strength to bang a hand on the desk and started to bray, requesting that I kindly fuck off.

This was the apogee of trials. Many Gehennettes display the same disparagement toward a man's educational background.

There is a secret behind this fact, which damsels are embarrassed to reveal. That secret is the circumference of a man's rump—the singular criterion of his worth. A woman feels secure when she is with a man endowed with a portly derriere. Though the higher a woman's socio-economic standing, the smaller her ideal male backside.

The ass decides the worth.

"You're not my type," says the Pornosa.

She has a type for good measure. Even if hell freezes over, she will not humble herself to think, "Maybe *I'm* not *his* type."

She is the sun. Men are the planets.

She cannot bear classical music, whereas I could not live without it.

She has a type.

"I am not the reading type."

That's a type sexier than thou.

She doesn't know how to count. Mathematicians are nutcases, criminals. I wonder whether Pythagoras would have been born had a similar mindset prevailed in Socratesland.

Who do you think you are, wench?

The wench derives vamp pleasure by irking the male.

But the bastard does not lose his sangfroid. He smiles cannily. He has a dozen more in his pocket. If need be he will respond, even without issuing a word. He will infuriate the wench. If rankled, it will take him an instant to decimate her equilibrium or what interrelationship there is, provided he does not yet wish to lose her.

I likewise understood that I was not sexy. I did not have a doliocephalic bell of the Semitic sort. My head was Armenoid wide, akin to those of Papa and Son Bush. Had I been endowed with a doliocephalic bell such as that of Reagan or Clinton (with my tongue dangling out of my mouth), the type found on "sexy" movie stars' shoulders, women would have liked me better.

I was not aware still that the "Aryan" girls of Paradise pampered the same preferences.

An anthropological type is being blitzkrieged to extermination. In the name of Satan, the "Hellian" value system, writhing via Natashima, has seized Paradise in its palms.

In a survey gauging Satan's sex appeal on a scale of one to ten, the women of the United Tribes of Amerhenna have given him a rating of 2.1. The highest rating, at 2.2, has come from Indonesia. And if you're not a president, don't have blue eyes, and speak with an accent... Bush dearest, you do not know how fortunate you are...

They love to prattle about the rights of animals, yet go on to live with those burly men who effectively become the executioners of those animals, as they sit around the table to eat, thrice a day. And the Gehennettes are among the most progressive women in the gesellschaft of humans.

As for the Pornoso, he wastes 95 percent of his life on the trail of pleasing the neurotic Pornosa.

Slaves of Sacrum… Land of Sissies… World of Cunt.
Cunt is capital. In the humanoid world.
And the logic of capital is aggrandizement.
Bastards of all countries, unite!
While in Virginabad, I remembered the owner of the Mariamstani matchmaking agency when I called a number that was heavily advertised on God TV. I had never been moved to try any of such services swarming in their hundreds on Hellian airwaves. But here, in Virginabad, the notion of meeting fairies through an unusual route tickled me.

Forward, soldier!

They charge one thaler per minute and terminate the call every seven minutes, forcing you to call again and pay for the introductory recording, which lasts several minutes. The women refuse to call me at my home number. Modesty. I am allowed to contact them only by calling the service.

My brows were raised. If I am mistaken, then these women had to be rich. Could there be any decent women on this line? Two tell me they will be back in two hours. Where from?

To dispel my suspicions, I continue to probe deeper. Here what passes for an average salary is fifty thalers a month. I can stay long on the line, as they wish me to, and I decide to stay for as long as it takes to clarify the matter. One woman tells me after hearing my first message that she has written a long poem for me. I surmise that she will read the complete works of… These modest ladies have spoken with me for two hours and urge me to continue the following day.

There does not exist a conception of public fraud in Paradise. Into this newly-zoned capitalist demesne seeps the worst kind of filth that has for decades accumulated in Hell, finding fertile ground under the patronage of a spineless prosecution. The owner of the Mariamstani introduction service was petrified after hearing my assessment. Satan would have burned him at the stake. In Paradise it is the state that terrorizes the redeemed. Availing themselves of the power of the Incomprehensible Nature and Inscrutable Verity, they resort to any old scam to defraud the populace.

The virginots and natashas, along with the rest of the migrants, were obsessed with the impulse for narcissism and the manic impetus for social climbing. To what they had learned from the experience of the Pornosa they added what they had inherited from their respective homelands. Materializing among the less glamorous strata of society, they turned into creatures more repulsive than the Pornosa. The shrewder ones scanned my accent with sedulity and accordingly determined my social value. My accent correlated with the setting at hand—it decreased where I was accepted, increased where I wasn't. One day I told Narineh that every time I remembered her, I visualized the six letters of the word "profit."

There is almost no nation on earth that will not be filled with pride when a foreigner expresses a couple of words in the local tongue. In Jehennam, however, should you come up a mere nuance short of its vulgate, your value will dip below that of a dog.

I was not even a dog.

Therefore I did not wish to speak Satanish. During my years in Adonis, I was enchanted by Satanland. In Satanland, there came a point when I wished to spit into Satan's mouth.

If they want to talk to me, let them learn to speak Dreamish.

"Get real…" Heather's words rang in my ears.

I n Paradise, too, Dog had an accent—apparently far more blaring than his Satanish. The reason was that his mother tongue was called Dreamish, which was viewed by the Paradisean as the unwieldy dialect of hopeless phantasmagorians. If this was an advantage when among women of a less attractive economic caste, it minimized my social desirability in the eyes of women from well-to-do families, who regarded me through the crack of their fingers as a semi-literate, bizarre Gehen-Dreamlander doddering on a nebulous wavelength—a mulatto in a pure-white zone. My worth, I believe, is equal to the Gehennese monetary value of my clothes. Dog is not even worth a dog when his clothes have an accent.

No, neither my clothes nor my accent can save me... nor the Hayastan I dream of. I am not a Hay. I am ugly. Only in Uglyland will I find happiness. That is where Death lives.

But are there uglies in the world? Am I not the sole ugly one?
Countless centuries will pass,
And within the ground
Our bones, yours and mine, will be found
And tell the generations
How love visited Quasimodo,
Whom God created hideous
To help carry his cross...

But at least this ugly one does not feel more ignoble than a dog when speaking Paradisish.

To many, my Paradisespeak was amusing. My Dreamish had lost the fourteen halftones that have been preserved in Paradisish, the official language of God. The Dreamlander considers it patriotism to speak with fourteen cogs less than his Paradisean cousins and lambastes those Paradisean intellectuals who suggest learning God's official language. Kathy's eight-year-old son would be in stitches whenever I referred to a restroom as a "comfort station." Kathy, too, could not help but giggle.

I experienced a similar treatment in Adonis, for my Adonisish. Even Pasha's language, which I had learned from my grandparents, was a provincial dialect, not the delicate lingua of Euranbul.

I could not speak any language properly, and for this I was the butt of jokes or derision, a nonentity at best, throughout the empire of Dreamstan.

The reality was clearly outlined before me. Wherever I went, I did not belong to nobility. There was no land under my feet. I was a zingaro whose political epithet was "Diaspora-Paradisean."

Paradisean?

Diaspora-Paradisean.

A genus destined to die off.

A fresh horizon unfurled when I began to drive a brand-new Jaguar. The dealership assured me it was built with NASA technology. But true to the brand's time-honored custom, the engine gave out within a month, stranding me and my children in the middle of Sunset Boulevard. They won't replace the car. We'll fix it. The Chief Executive Orospu concurs.

We've sold it to you. Off you go.

Take it back.

We won't give your money back. We'll ruin your credit.

Ruin it. I had bought the Jag when my burro, a thirteen-year-old Oldsmobile, took its last breath, leaving me in the center lane of the highway between Hellwood and Encino. My life flashed before my eyes. I was spared being rammed in by the hundreds of vehicles darting from behind. At last a teenage boy used his car to push the Olds out of the free-way. He looked Oriental. I could not guess his nationality. My ex-wife had the amazing ability to quickly figure out someone's descent. Where is he from?

"America."

We understood each other as we looked each other in the eye. Bravo. I wanted to contact his school, compliment him for his kindness and good manners, but was not able to.

Thanks to my new automobile, I became an overnight sensation with the Hellettes. The same ones who only yes-terday did not deign to even look at me, condemning me to the fate of dying of thirst in the waters of the ocean—as Shakespeare's ciun would say, "Water, water everywhere/ Nor any drop to drink."

Of course this was not to be completely ascribed to the Jaguar. I was little by little being forged in my relationships with women. Already I suited the Jaguar. My eyebrows were pruned, my body hair was decreased. I deserved to be placed in a vitrine. I would have buyers.

"You look nothing like a Paradisean," marvel the little Mariamstani trollops.

"I'm a true-blue Paradisean. What do you think a Para-disean should be like?"

"Umm... umm..."

"Go ahead, enlighten me."

"They smell… sweat and cologne… yuck!"

"Are they all the same?"

"Almost."

("But excuse me, what did you expect from a man going to a whore?"

"And how many do you think *don't* go to a whore? And in Virginabad!")

From those days I remember a woman—the only one—who struggled, yes, struggled, with herself not to look at me, on the crossing of Balboa and Ventura boulevards, where I lived.

I remember the words of a Hellete to her five-year-old daughter. The child was trying to befriend my girl. The mother admonished the child, reminding her not to talk to people who did not drive a Mercedes or a BMW. I remember our visits to Santa Varvara, where my children stood out. Women above fifty caressed them for several minutes, without greeting or casting a glance at the parents standing next to them, even as they walked away. These were not isolated incidents. Deep down, there is a psychology at work that declares loud and clear, "Give us your children and then get out of here. You're of no use to anyone!"

These women would not hesitate to call the police, have me arrested and thrown in prison for a few years, if for a second I unthinkingly caressed my daughter's hair. Without hesitation, they would accuse me of sexually abusing my child. Two witnesses would be enough. Lord Satan would take my children away, to protect them from the encroachments of their mentally sick father. And the compassionate servants of our Lord, possibly the blood relations of these very women, would take my children under their care and compassionately liberate them from their father's dream.

As for me, the dreamer, were I, after my release from prison, to try to see my children even from a distance of three hundred feet, a second crucifixion would await me… if I were able to rise from the first.

The state is a murderer, the public the enemy of your dream.

I began to feel all this the day I went to my first class in Gehenna.

Biology 101. The lecturer: white, forty, tall. He comes to class in slippers and in his office welcomes us with his long, self-gratified toes. A large coffee mug kisses his lips, whereupon the frown lines on his forehead are engaged to communicate swaths of wisdom to our thirsty minds.

And who needs
Our laughable rhetor's aplomb
If the law-giver is but the pain
Of which we were born?
And the up and down of wrinkles
Is no dance at all,
But a ceremony
With which the forehead itself
Is consecrated every day.
Then why, my dears, why avoid
The consecration of the pain
That the old scars have brought?
And is it in the pain, I wonder,
That lies the danger,
Or the remedy itself,
With which we yearn to heal the pain?

Wave 4, "The Old Scars of the World"

I noticed that Satan's students said "Bless you" to those who sneezed. There is never a shortage of these in a crowded classroom.

Forty minutes later I, too, sneeze.

The classroom gulps me down in silence.

Digests me in its entrails, chucks me down the toilet.

Is it because I am ugly? Or because I am a foreigner?

I gathered that they are fond of ugly dogs. But I was a dog myself. Why did they not like me?

Everything becomes clear in the ensuing classes. The lecturer interprets Darwin's theory as "survival of the adapt-est."

I was not like them. They had decided my fate. Death!

What awaited me here?

I would remain different from them even after twenty years. When I talked to my uncle Gary about this, he said with a smile, "Make that forty."

He was sixty-three years young, blond, blue eyes, attractive to women, beloved of Gehenmen.

Yet he was Gary. The Dreamlander.

"You come here and show these people respect. But the fact of the matter is, all they think about is how to con you," Gary recalled the experiences of his early years in Hell. "Yes, con you and get rich on your carcass."

There were too many unkind people protected by law, money—the entire apparatus of Satan, all true-blue believers of the spirit of capitalism. Maximize wealth. This is the order and recompense of the Satanican Almighty to his steadfast followers. Amen…

Service! Fulfilling a need! Selling to us for our own salvation a puny part of what Satan has confiscated from us in conspiracy with Pasha. And the sale price is your life.

Years passed. One day I'm waiting in line at the post office. The two white customers in front of me wrench twenty minutes from the Philippina employee. She doesn't mind it one bit, given her singular serf-mindedness. When my turn comes, my business is done in a minute. Then I ask her the fateful question: "How much does it cost to mail a letter from Hell to Paradise?" The Philippina is irritated. The employee next to her, White Haley with comet hair, screams at me, "Why are you annoying her?"

"I'm not. I just asked her about international rates."

"International! You're taking up people's time. Get lost!"

"I waited twenty minutes till the previous customers were served. It won't take a minute to answer my question."

"You get out right now!"

"I'm in a government building of Satan. I'm not bothering anybody. All I've done is ask a legitimate question. I'll get out when I get my answer. Otherwise I'll complain to Satan," I said angrily.

"I'll show you Satan!" he bellowed as he made to attack me. He was held back by two employees, a black and a red, who tried to calm him down.

On my way out, I can still hear Comet Hair's threat, "If I see you here one more time, I'll…"

I began to use a post office at the other end of town.

The specter walked with me inseparably under the bright sun of Satan.

And you, the black people, my distant brother, you whose oft-tortured past is that of my Paradisean nation... now, as the present, you who even in sorrow, even in the shackled state of your will, love to sing—for only evil does not sing—you who carry the sun's kisses in your blood, come forth with the roar of your Robeson, your Niagara, which, though feeling constrained amongst your precipitous boulders, reflecting the image of your bitter present, thunders as your Robeson—your hope's song even across the rocks of tyranny. You are black. But the ferocity of persecution has rendered your soul red as a baked iron... You are dark of color, and my people loves you... Boundless and pure is that love. My people is a red tulip, and you are ever in its heart, impartible as the tulip's black velvet. Come hither, behold with your own eyes. And you, too, close the roads of the new war. We Paradiseans were slaughtered. I do not wish you to be bloodied as we have. Forbearing is my hell-wounded heart.

Air 1, "The Paradisean Danteic"

What is the cause of all this?

The fact that I have black hair and chestnut eyes? But my Anglo-Saxon brother-in-law also has black hair and chestnut eyes. We are both of medium height, both white-skinned. Apologies. He is a bit whiter. He is easily sunburned, though not as much as my brother, Bert, whose childhood white skin and flaxen hair could scarcely be surpassed by even a Scandinavian.

So what is it?

Among my siblings, the blonds received more affection, despite my parents' insistence on equality and often conscious effort to be impartial. My father sometimes complained of my black-haired, dark-eyed mother. The women of the wealthiest families of his city, women who had white skin, blue eyes, and blond hair reaching down to their buttocks, fell in love with him. My father was adored in Hell. Like my uncles, he was blue-eyed and blond-haired. Excusez-moi, *light brown*-haired.

I was yet to realize that between "blond" and "light brown" hair, which I could not tell apart, there was a difference of not only color, but also status. With an air of frustration, some woman crossed off the "blond" designation of my three-year-old, Alex, and made the appropriate amendment in his application for a contest. My younger uncle, born blond and with blue eyes, once told me of a study by Satan's Research Institute which postulated that only a normal and healthy person has blue eyes and blond hair. Chestnut eyes and black hair are the results of a warped physiological, mental, and emotional constitution.

My uncle lived in another world. That world had not been my lot.

No! This was not merely a matter of color.

It was exacerbated by the accent.

Attitudes toward one's accent, however, were not uniform. Here, too, there were myriad layers. The Gehennettes were crazy about my classmate Charles's Eyfelian accent.

And his name…

One day the secret was revealed to me by my wife, who melted like chocolate whenever she heard it.

"Ah… Charles…"

I was the foreigner, they the masters. They the hosts, I the sycophant. Moreover, I did not know how to speak. My brain was underdeveloped.

To the accent was added the fact of my birthplace.

I did not hail from a scintillating place such as Elizabeth City, Natasha City, or even Toyotaburg. I was born in the city of terrorists, and my father was a Kilisi.

Kilis was an obscure village in the empire of Osman Pasha. Though its name has been preserved, those of the surrounding provinces, which were reminders of their Dreamese origins, have been replaced with Pashaic ones. A girl born of a Pashist father and a Hay mother reacted with rancor when she heard the word "Kilikia."

From the eleventh to fourteen centuries, before Pasha made his debut in Paradise, Kilikia was a prominent Paradisean kingdom, edging the Mediterranean to the north and northeast of Kipros. Kilis was east of Kilikia. Her parents had told her that the people of Paradise once lived in Kilis. One day a Kilis-born Pashali customer visited my office. Such a meeting is rarer than hitting the lottery jackpot. And then, after I had completed my book, it occurred to me that the monk and I had similar styles. I discovered that he is likewise a Kilisi.

I was a Kilisi.

To this was added my *social* origin.

I was not born into nobility.

Low-grade, flawed.

My admittance to Oxford was happenstance, a freak exploit, at best an achievement in a narrow field of specialization.

I was dumb.

The existence of intelligence contradicted my background, my birthplace in particular.

A Viking girl wished to get married to me. When she learned that I hoped to raise my children as Paradiseans, she fled with such odium that you would think a massive cockroach had crawled up her naked thigh.

I was that cockroach.

A Führerista was scandalized as she heard that the latest research points to Paradise as the proto-homeland of the Indo-Europeans. I was of no use to her as a Paradisean.

I was a microbe.

A Maimunoida doctor walked away in horror from our date when she found out that my cousin was a commander in the Bravo navy.

I was a terrorist.

I didn't know whether my blood type was A or B. The genteel suspect it must be B, considering my animal lineage. You know type-As are hereditary vegetarians, Bs are carnivores. The As comprise the finer race of humankind—it was God who created them. The Bs have evolved from the ape.

Convincing. I was hairy, had not yet left my animal roots behind. Neanderthalian. Yuck...

One day my blond sister shared her disgust with my uncle about finding my hair all over the house. Offended, I pick up the hairs from the carpet. Forty percent are blond. But it doesn't show.

Is it this 20 percent difference that has decided my fate? Or is it the color?

They make me ill, then grumble that I am deranged. My existence is disturbing, the stuff of bad memories.

Death!

There was a mafia of blonds in our family. They held secret meetings, made decisions, did not confide in the others. The black-haired ones could participate, provided they upheld the blond mentality, and only as back-wagon actors in the service of solidifying the blonds' power. I was not a member of the mafia. The subtleties of their views were manifestly beyond my comprehension.

"Oy... there is something creepy about that guy... gross... I'm disgusted..."

It is such derision that marginalized people, races, and nations live with twenty-four hours a day, yet all of them deny the truth. They dream the victor's dream. They're all fabulous.

All want to proliferate. Fill the planet with their image.

My sister spent her life in neuroses, fleeing from one kind of filth to the other—the black-haired, the disabled, the Osmani, the Ahmed—until she disintegrated in her saga from hospital to hospital. This blond was not afforded the protection of the UTA flag on her pussy. Any flag. Any superiorating, centripetal ideology. The crowd swallowed her up. Silently devoured her to satiate its existential hunger for beauty, the victor's simulated beauty.

Equality is myth—a philosophical veil to etiolate the will of the disadvantaged.

Not all blonds were blond. Some were not part of the mafia; others betrayed their kind by spilling the mafia's secrets to the black-haired ones.

I was barely twelve when one day my father shielded

my sister, despite my belief then that she had committed the most heinous of crimes.

"You, dog, get lost to your room! This is my butterfly, daddy's wonderful little girl..."

The scar of anger and pain stayed with me for years.

I understood at an early age that blonds are rightful; the righteous are dogs.

Dog wants to remove his body hair.

"The hairs of a healthy man don't fall. They're antennae connected to the universal field."

The delicate strings belong to the blonds. It is God that has created them.

Poor Dog. He is sickly. He must be cured. At least he'll become a second-class impostor.

During Dog's interview for Satanic citizenship, the panjandrum, on learning that the reason for his departure to Kennedy City was to study at Harvard, sent an inquiry to the investigative division as to how Mr. Dog Son of Dog has been able to finance his education, despite Mr. Son of Dog's plea to have a talk with the supervisor. Dog must depart for Oxford, cannot wait in Hell until the matter is cleared up, nor can he afford to make a trip back on our Lord Satan's every whimsical demand. His entreaties fall on deaf ears. Dog has no choice but to remain in Los Babylonos and teach mathematics to the sons and daughters of Bel.

Months later, the head of the investigations department, Mr. Shamus Holmes, screams at Dog during his interrogation, "You've stolen bones."

"Oh... stolen... I see..."

Dog is curious as to what this ex nihilo verdict is based on. Fishing out a lincoln from his pocket, the investigator takes it to Dog's snout. Then, fearing that Dog would eat the note, quickly withdraws it from under his muzzle and tucks it back into his pocket.

"I pay taxes to Satan and you reap the benefits. You've gotten yourself a student loan."

"Had I gotten a loan, the interest would have made Satan rich, Mr. Holmes."

Although he was allowed to, Dog had not obtained a student loan during his half year at Harvard.

"I should be the one studying there. And you should be the one sitting on this chair and doing my work 9 to 5," bellowed Mr. Holmes.

"I agree, sir. I will fund your education when you're accepted at Harvard."

Dog's vision blackens. He loses interest. Let them wipe their asses with that piece of Satanic paper.

Where must Dog go?

Gracious Satan comes to Dog's rescue at the most unexpected hour and anoints him as doorman of Hell.

But is it worth stepping inside these people's universities?

And why would Dog have to study the history of Hell? They are ungrateful. Dog wishes to read history, not national propaganda. If of Gehenna, why not of Paradise?

Hays, treasure your universities. Harvard was a dream. Did it belong to man? To the world?

To the venal.

They dreamed in Harvard, too. How does Dog dare...

"Woof, woof..."

Shut that dog up!

Mr. Holmes's rage fizzles only after Dog hints at taking legal action. He succeeds, however, to drag the animal around for three more years, through the bait that has been lodged in his mouth by Satan's immigration bureau.

"You're not a citizen yet?" chuckles my Paradisean girlfriend, who has arrived in Satanland two years ago. She produces a Satanic passport from her purse and shows it to me.

I was a fool.

If I told you how she has done it, three million copies (3 = 6/2 = 666) of this book would be sold in Paradise. I guarantee you that the whole of Paradise would sell its home and chattel and be on its way to the all-embracing bosom of our Lord Satan, Host to Many. There must be a way, come hell or high water. They will attempt to bribe Satan himself.

Another one: "If you're not a citizen, sorry, then I can't marry you."

The doorkeeper of the hole demands to see a Satanic passport.

"Do you own a khouse?"

In the hearths of Virginland and Natashaland, meanwhile, the questions are classier.

"Which socioeconomic stratum do you belong to in the Demoncratic Imperium of Gehenna?"

"The poor."

"Thank you for being khonest."

And it comes to pass that Dog defaults on his promise to enrich our Lord Pluton with years of interest payments. This makes Diabolam Diabolum ever more furious.

Two months after the big earthquake, when Dog went to the bank for a cash advance on his credit card, the shrew behind the bullet-proof window stared at him in seething hatred and angrily cut up his plastic with a pair of scissors.

"Your payment is a month overdue, Mr. Dog! You live in an earthquake zone. You're a risk."

Dog was a risk…

Risk is taken aback. A month before the earthquake, he had within a single day paid up all his credit-card debt, which amounted to 10^4 washingtons (10 + 10 + 10 +10 = 40 ÷ 20 = 2 x 3 = 6 = 666. All the codes unravel). Apart from which, Risk has pumped thousands of washingtons in interest into Satan's banks. At the exact moment when he truly needs to use his credit card, his years of diligence not only evaporate into thin air, his credit is ruined for the next seventeen years.

Risk is disillusioned, continues to default and sinks deeper. By Satanic compulsion, Risk is forced to close shop, as he would no longer be able to acquire the bond required by Satan to operate his business in Hell.

"Who needs me? Who needs my life?"

Risk was not like them. His life and merits as yet weighed too light on the scales for him to be accepted as an equal. Nothing would be enough to reach that lofty height. Nothing.

No, Risk is not a citizen of New Rome. That would be a grave misunderstanding, self-deception, serf mentality. Satanic propaganda at the expense of Risk's soul. Subjection to Satanic plutocracy, Pornian duress.

O ne morning a girl I was in bed with asked, "Do you like Britney Spears?"

"Who's that?"

"You don't know who she is? I can't imagine such an ignorant man in this day and age."

"And why should I know who she is?"

"Huh?"

I was an ignoramus.

If my bedfellow knew that I heard of Mother Teresa's death eight years after the fact...

I did not raise a dog. Preferred to raise children.

I was insensitive. A real dog.

I did not drink iced tea, tequila, or Diet Coke. Preferred Adonisi arak or Apollonian *tahn*.

I lacked class.

I did not know any of the three- or four-word Eyfelian dish names on restaurant menus. I liked the Kilisis' *gyurdeleh, orukh, lebenyeh, sini halva*, and the Adonisi *ful*.

I was not civilized.

I did not believe in astrology.

I was not an interesting man.

Las Fortunas left me cold.

I had no love of life.

I did not know the names of actors, pop groups, or movies.

I was a strange man.

I did not collect antiques.

Did not have a hobby.

I was neither a Teapublican nor a Demoncrat.

I was not a human being.

None of them had recognized the Genocide of Paradise.

I was a racist.

They had recognized that of the Chosen One.

I was a racist.

I did not have the flair for formulating opinions about political leaders. On George W. Bush: "Oh, please, boring..." On Bill Clinton: "Yuck."

I had no conversational style.

I did not wear designer clothes.

I lacked taste and social status.

Making women laugh was not the overarching aim of

my life (though I wasn't bad at it).

I was dull.

Michael Jordan did not fascinate me. I did not watch the Lakers. Images of the governor of Calipornia, whom the Pornosas worshipped, made my stomach churn.

I was not manly.

I did not lift weights.

I was diseased.

I did not jog.

I was not modern.

I observed traffic laws. I was always in control.

I lacked adrenaline.

I accommodated.

I was a homosexual.

My being was not beguiled by Satan's cultural frippery. I was a man without frills, like a Sufi.

Satan ran, I walked. Satan walked, I sat. Satan feared me...

No, Satan, you shall never be capable of loving me...

I left Heather without saying good-bye.

My burro was taking me from Kennedy City to Los Babylonos. Overburdened with books and bric-a-brac, it fell sick on the road. It slowly made it to Colorado, on the summit of whose towering mountains lived an unusual Dreamlander, God Artin.